ORCHARD COVE

Thirst For Me

OTHER TITLES BY JAINE DIAMOND

CONTEMPORARY ROMANCE

Bayshore Billionaires Series

Charming Deception

Darling Obsession

Vancity Villains Series

Handsome Devil

Rebel Heir

Wicked Angel

Irresistible Rogue

Players Series

Hot Mess

Filthy Beautiful

Sweet Temptation

Lovely Madness

Flames and Flowers

Dirty Series

Dirty Like Me

Dirty Like Us

Dirty Like Brody

A Dirty Wedding Night

Dirty Like Seth

Dirty Like Dylan

Dirty Like Jude

Dirty Like Zane

EROTIC ROMANCE

DEEP Duet

DEEP

DEEPER

For the most up-to-date list of Jaine Diamond's published books and reading order please go to https://jainediamond.com/books/

Never miss a book—join Jaine's Diamond Club Newsletter to get new release info, insider updates, giveaways, and free bonus content at https://jainediamond.com.

ORCHARD COVE

Thirst For Me

JAINE DIAMOND

Montlake

This is a work of fiction. Names, characters, organizations, places, events, and incidents are either products of the author's imagination or used fictitiously. Otherwise, any resemblance to actual persons, living or dead, is purely coincidental.

Published by Montlake, Seattle

www.apub.com

EU Product Safety Contact:
Amazon Media EU S.à r.l.
38, avenue John F. Kennedy, L-1855 Luxembourg
amazonpublishing-gpsr@amazon.com

ISBN: 9781662540332
e-ISBN: 9781662540349

Cover design by The Brewster Project
Cover photography by Michelle Lancaster PTY LTD

Printed in the United States of America

PLAYLIST

Listen to the full playlist at https://jainediamond.com/thirst-for-me/

"Hot Blooded"—Foreigner

"Hold the Line"—Toto

"Da Ya Think I'm Sexy?"—Rod Stewart

"High Horse"—Kacey Musgraves

"Hotel California"—Eagles

"I'm Fine"—Ashe

"APT."—ROSÉ & Bruno Mars

"Cry"—Benson Boone

"Love To Hate Me"—BLACKPINK

"I Got You"—Jack Johnson

"Somebody That I Used to Know (feat. Kimbra)"—Gotye

"Ice Cream"—BLACKPINK & Selena Gomez

"Everybody's Got to Learn Sometime"—Beck

"Somethin' 'Bout A Woman (feat. Teddy Swims)"—
Thomas Rhett

"Flowers"—Miley Cyrus

"And Then the Quiet"—Margot Todd

"Sugar Sweet"—Benson Boone

"Lay It Down"—The Rubens

"Into You"—Ariana Grande

"enemies"—Artemas

"Go Your Own Way"—Fleetwood Mac

"Fine Line"—Harry Styles

"Magnetic"—ILLIT

"One of These Nights"—Eagles

"Harvest Moon"—Neil Young

"Try"—Blue Rodeo

"I'm On Fire for You Baby"—April Wine

"These Eyes"—The Guess Who

"Compare to You"—Lauren Jones

"Let Me Go"—Benson Boone

"Serial Monogamist"—Ashe

"SOS"—Margot Todd

"Sweet City Woman"—Stampeders

"The Edge of Heaven"—Wham!

"Fade into You"—Mazzy Star

CHAPTER 1

Sierra

I check my phone, where the most aggravating two words in the modern world continue to stare me in the face. *No Service.* I squint up at the impassive blue sky as sun-dappled waves lap the rocky shore below me. A fat seagull pinwheels overhead, and I would not be the least bit surprised if it shit on my face.

It's been that kind of week.

I've been standing next to this sea-battered, cedar-shingled building on the wooden pier, gazing out toward the other islands and the water that separates me from the city I can no longer see for way too long, when it occurs to me that maybe the woman who owns this charming waterfront building on Vancouver Island's scenic coastline isn't just late to meet me. That maybe she isn't actually coming.

I turn to face the picturesque two-way stop intersection that is downtown Orchard Cove, British Columbia. Population: very few. An SUV is approaching along the same winding, tree-smothered rural road I came in on. The town is quaint, with its two stop signs, small cluster of commercial buildings, and handful of visible houses glimpsed through the abundance of trees, but I'm definitely not seeing the "abundance of tourism" I was promised.

And right about now, I'm seriously rethinking my life choices.

The SUV pulls into a parking lot diagonally across the intersection from where I stand and parks in front of an old building painted a moody teal blue. The sign reads *Sea Haven Bar & Grill.* Eight very loud twentysomethings pile out of the vehicle, wrapped in sparkly red sashes, the kind worn for a bachelorette party. One of the girls trails a glittering veil as they rally into the bar, and classic rock briefly spills out through the open door.

Then I'm left alone with the seagulls again.

I check my phone one last time, swear under my breath, grab my handbag, keys, and other essentials from my van, and head over to the bar, sucked in by the music. It's the only business in the town center that seems to have a pulse on a Friday afternoon.

When I draw the wooden door open, the lusty strains of Foreigner's "Hot Blooded" pour out. As I step inside, the bachelorette party is getting settled, a waitress pulling together tables for them in the middle of the room, and a few other customers are scattered throughout the bar. The whole place is unironically retro, from the music and the glowing jukebox in the corner to the mirrored vintage liquor signs and the young man with the mullet and mustache wiping down tables.

As my eyes adjust to the interior lighting, another man walks out of a back room and strides behind the bar.

I stop in my tracks.

As he sets the liquor box he's carrying on the bar, his gaze sweeps to the loud table of women, then to me. The electric shock that crackles through my body when our eyes meet lands somewhere between the base of my spine and my ovaries.

His gaze holds mine for way, way longer than common decency requires.

I am in no way prepared for this.

I'm here to meet a grouchy seventysomething woman, not the Hottest Bartender in the Galaxy. I don't even have makeup on.

His gaze sweeps down my cropped *KPop Demon Hunters* T-shirt, Lululemons, and platform Adidas. I'm not even sure if he's checking out my legs or wondering why I'm still standing here, staring.

The term *ruggedly handsome* was obviously coined by the admirers of this man's genetically superior ancestors. He's tall and built as hell—his shoulders, chest, and rock-hard biceps straining his snug, dark-blue T-shirt. An alluring hint of black tattoos snakes up under both sleeves, his manly beard is just a day or two past "trim," and his brown hair is longish on top in a haphazardly sexy way.

Blinking, I approach the bar, my eyes still adjusting to the dim lighting. He can't be *that* hot.

But then I reach the bar. He's *more* hot.

"Um, excuse me. Could I possibly use your Wi-Fi?"

This is my polite-Canadian way of asking a fellow Canadian what the Wi-Fi password is, because of course I can use the Wi-Fi, right? But he frowns, giving me an almost comically blatant untrusting-of-outsiders look. It's gone as quickly as it appeared, replaced by an unwelcoming mask of indifference.

He says casually, "Why would we have Wi-Fi?" in the sexiest, manliest voice I've ever heard. Shivers actually run down my spine as he tears open the liquor box like he's ripping open my shirt, and his arm muscles flex all over.

I cough briefly as I almost swallow my tongue for the first time in my life. Where the hell am I? There should really be a warning on the front door of this place.

"Uh . . . why *wouldn't* you?" I glance around the room, but no one is paying attention to us. To *him*, incredibly. There's no one sitting along the bar. And I don't see a customer-facing sign with the Wi-Fi password anywhere.

"Well, most people show up in a place like Orchard Cove," he says, pulling bottles from the box and setting them on the bar between us, "to get a break from all that . . ." His sentence dies as his cool-blue eyes slide over me.

"Technology?" I venture, confused.

He completes his slow assessment, and seems to sum up my gel manicure, abundant jewelry, and the items I've dumped on his bar—structured pink tote, sparkling watermelon charm on a keychain loaded with keys, giant insulated coffee mug covered in stickers, and my phone in its bedazzled case—with his next two words: "City life." He tips his sexy beard toward the very loud group of young women behind me. "Your friends, for instance, seem to be doing just fine without internet."

Ha. He thinks I'm with that bachelorette party? While I'd *love* to be drinking my face off with a group of girlfriends right now, I'm easily five years older than those girls, which in my experience means five years more jaded—and right now, their lust for life is making me feel ancient. They're *giggling*, for fuck's sake.

"Look closer," I say, leaning on the bar. "They'll be uploading those selfies the moment they reconnect to the outside world."

He glances over my shoulder and frowns; I don't even have to look to know that those girls are in full-on selfie mode as the waitress collects their drink orders. I'm stunned they're not ordering off the Hottest Bartender in the Universe, but I guess they haven't noticed him yet. I need to get the Wi-Fi password before they trample me when they rush the bar.

I'm not even above begging for it. I think I lost my last shred of self-respect when I begged my boyfriend not to dump me four nights ago.

Spoiler alert: he dumped me anyway.

"Pretty please? I haven't been able to get cellular service since I left the highway."

The bartender's blue, bottomless eyes meet mine again, and my ovaries *squee!* at the eye contact; they don't seem to understand that this isn't foreplay and he's not buying us a drink. They must be confused by all the smolder and the liquor bottles.

"Depends what network you're on," he mansplains gruffly, which is zero percent helpful, and returns to unpacking his bottles.

"Look, I wouldn't press the issue, but I'm not trying to get on TikTok to check my Likes. This is important."

His brow furls grumpily, somehow ramping up the smolder. "Important, how?"

I hesitate, considering how to put it. He *is* a stranger, and I'm at a major disadvantage here. June Spencer, the seventysomething woman I met at a food and beverage industry conference last autumn, is the only person I know on Vancouver Island. And since she's supposed to provide my lodging tonight, I'm really not sure where this leaves me.

I texted her before I left Vancouver this morning by ferry to let her know I was on my way—long before I lost cellular service—but received no reply. Considering I've only met June once in person and spoken to her since by infrequent email, I'm not even sure she knows *how* to text.

For a moment, I entertain the grim thought that maybe the poor woman died and no one told me.

"I just need to make a couple of calls. I was supposed to meet a local woman named June Spencer like half an hour ago," I explain, and I don't miss the way the bartender's frown deepens. "Do you know her?"

He grunts, then returns to his task. "Good luck with that. If you can't find June, she doesn't want to be found."

Okay. That is not encouraging.

"Look, I'll pay for it." As I start digging for cash in my purse, he looks offended. "Come on, you must have Wi-Fi for your business."

"Of course he does," drawls an amused voice near my left ear.

I startle as I realize an entire adult male has somehow sat himself on the barstool directly beside me and has been blatantly eavesdropping on us. For how long, I don't know. He's got sexy-messy dark hair, a jawline that could cut glass, and even more tattoos than the Hottest Bartender in the Universe down his muscular arms. He's dressed like a carpenter who just came from a job site, sawdust and smears of dried paint on his otherwise white T-shirt and worn-in jeans, with work boots.

The bartender scowls at him, and the newcomer draws back, lifting his hands in the air; his brown eyes twinkle at me. "Sorry. Didn't mean to startle you." He flashes a charming smile and winks at me like some old-timey movie villain.

Well, shit. *There are two of them.*

I live in a bustling, well-populated city, and I've never just randomly stumbled upon two regular guys this hot.

So this is where they all live.

Hottest Bartender in the Universe pours a draft beer and places it in front of Hot Carpenter, grouching, "You're late," as I openly stare.

And they know each other?

"Yeah. And now *you're* late," Hot Carpenter says pleasantly. "Shouldn't you be working on the house by now?"

"I'm leaving in a minute," the bartender grumbles. "Got caught up."

"I see that." Hot Carpenter smiles—at me—his gaze dipping briefly to my yoga pants.

Hottest Bartender in the Universe scowls at the man, who is clearly his friend and is busting his balls right now. Over *me*.

Before this conversation completely derails, I ask the bartender, "Not trying to be that Karen, but could I please speak with the manager or owner?"

Hot Carpenter snorts. "You're speaking to him. And you really don't want to go above his head to his grandpa. Believe it or not, Tommy Grant is even grumpier than his grandson."

I glance at the chatty, tattooed hottie next to me, dubious about trusting that white-toothed smile and easy confidence, which has never worked out well for me in the past. But then he does me a solid and says, "Please, put your money away. Mason Grant, for fuck's sake, let the woman use your Wi-Fi."

Mason gives his friend a glare that could melt solid steel. When his blue eyes meet mine again, I try to give him my best "harmless, completely non-crazy stranger" face.

"Or, if it's really that much trouble," Hot Carpenter drawls, "I do have Wi-Fi back at my place . . ."

I really try to keep a straight face. I know he just said that to irritate Mason and force his hand, because it's clearly working.

I blink innocently at Mason. "And I could really use some privacy to make those calls," I say hopefully.

Mason glowers briefly at his friend. Then he makes a growly sound under his breath and stalks toward a door at the far end of the bar. I scramble to pick up my things, flash a thumbs-up at Hot Carpenter, and hurry after Mason as he pushes the door open and stalks inside.

"Network and password are on the router, there." He points a thick finger at the sleek white router, completely out of place on the ancient wooden desk piled high with papers and junk.

Then he leaves just as abruptly as he showed me in. "Thank you!" I call after him, but he just shuts the door like he didn't hear it.

I blow out a breath and dump my things on the chair behind his desk, because there's nowhere else to put anything. The shelves along one wall overflow with old bar equipment, tools, and more papers. Liquor boxes are stacked precariously along another wall. The small, vintage tufted sofa is buried under a landslide of more papers, file boxes, and bar towels.

Even the walls are covered with framed newspaper clippings, dusty certifications, and what look like old family photos, most of them in black and white.

I connect to the bar's Wi-Fi and try to focus, absolutely itching with the urge to straighten, declutter, and spruce. I'm already rearranging the whole place and giving it a fresh coat of paint in my head. I can't help it. I'm such a sucker for a fixer-upper.

Unfortunately, this weakness of mine also applies to men.

I enable Wi-Fi calling on my phone and call the number June Spencer gave me while trying not to stare at the framed photo on the wall in front of me. Mason and his carpenter friend hold up a couple of giant fish they presumably just caught. They're both shirtless, revealing mouthwatering abs and more tattoos.

I eyeball Mason greedily. A girl could really have a nice nap on that broad chest after all the sex. He wears a backwards ball cap, and he's clean-shaven. He looks younger. Deep dimples slice into both cheeks.

So, he *can* smile.

The call goes to voicemail, just an electronic message that informs me no one is available at the number I've called. I leave a message for June, then call Sophie in Vancouver.

"Dear fucking lord, Sierra Daniels, where the hell have you been?" My overtly loving, squishy-hug-giving, one-woman-funhouse of a best friend picks up the call, absolutely breathless. "I've been trying to reach you for *hours*."

"You have? Sorry, it's been a day. Cell service is spotty around here. I'm in Orchard Cove now, but I can't find June Spencer. You know, that cranky old lady who walked up to my booth at an industry con, took one sip and told me that my smoothies are 'perhaps too ambitious,' then invited me to her tiny-ass hometown in the same breath, and I said, 'Why, yes. How soon can I sign the lease?' Like a damn idiot. Why did I think this was a good idea?"

"Well," Sophie says carefully, "because you thought it would be fun to spend a few weeks on the island this summer, sipping wine and eating the local raspberries or whatever, with Kyle."

"Yeah. What a dumbass. *Please*, I fucking implore you, if I ever plan anything more than a week in advance with a man again, kick me right in the junk."

"How will that ever work? You'd be black and blue. You can't help romanticizing—"

"Nope. That was the old Sierra. New and improved Sierra does not fantasize about her future with any man. She's got enough on her plate, just trying to unfuck the here and now."

"Si, come on. You've got to stop blaming yourself—"

"As of next month, I am completely winging it," I insist. "I just need to fulfill this stupid lease agreement and get back to the city, so I can *fix* what's left of my life—"

"Sierra. *Sweetie.*" Sophie's unusually forceful tone makes me shut my mouth. "I've been trying to reach you for a reason. And maybe you should sit down for this."

"Oh." I shove my things over and squeeze onto the leather chair that Mason has very possibly had sex on. I mean, if I were a guy that hot and I owned a bar, I'd definitely be fucking someone in my office. "Tell me what?" I ask her, slightly distracted as my eyes drift back to that shirtless photo.

"Well . . ." Sophie groans, like she really doesn't want to say it. "If you thought things were bad before you left . . ."

"You mean, this morning?" I laugh humorlessly. "What could possibly have gone wrong since this morning?"

Sophie takes an audible breath before she forces it out. "There's a meme."

I don't quite know how to interpret this, or apply it to the conversation at hand.

"A meme of what?"

The words aren't even out of my mouth before it hits me.

Oh. *No.*

"Where? *Why?*"

"Don't watch it!" Sophie cries as I pull the phone away from my ear and tap my messages app, where the little icon tells me that twenty-three unread messages are waiting for me. The first few are from Soph. The rest seem to be from my family.

And Kyle. At this point, this is probably not good news.

"Sierra? Are you there? Please don't watch it. I can tell you what's in it. You don't have to—"

Too late. I've opened the texts from my stepsister, Kim, and I see the meme. It's a video clip. From a video call I was on four days ago, with my then-boyfriend's entire family.

But I'm the only one onscreen.

I tap it and the few-second-clip plays. Wherein I exclaim, wide-eyed, "*I can't believe how BIG it is!*" A quote that is taken completely out of context, but which any casual viewer would assume is referring to the large purple dildo that is plainly visible, sitting on my nightstand in the background, over my right shoulder.

Whoever made the meme has outlined the purple penis in bright yellow, so you can't possibly miss it.

It's not all that clever, as far as memes go. But it is funny.

I mean, to anyone who isn't me or someone who actually cares about me, I'm sure it's snicker-worthy.

Kim's text reads, *Are you okay? Call me.* And is accompanied by a screaming-in-horror emoji.

"Oh my god," I breathe as all the blood drains from my face. And I ask the question that no one can reasonably answer once something hits the internet. "Who's seen this?! Has this been uploaded anywhere?"

"Babe," Sophie laments softly, "tell me you didn't just watch it."

"And *who* would make a *meme* . . . about *me*?"

"An absolute asshat with nothing better to do—"

"Do you think it was his mom? I swear she never liked me . . ."

"Kyle's mom probably wouldn't have the first clue how to *make* a meme."

I know Kyle didn't make it. He wanted to get as far away from my embarrassing blunder as possible.

I scroll through my messages and tap on Kyle's name. The only text he's sent me since our stupid argument last night is unread, from about an hour ago. *Did you get the email from my parents?*

Dread seeps through me as I hurry to open my email and find it. The subject line reads *Update on Our Proposed Investment.* I click it open, my stomach sinking like I've swallowed a lead ball, and the words blur as my eyes grow hot.

"Sierra? Babe. Are you still there?"

I raise the phone back to my ear. "I'm here. *Fuck*, Soph. Kyle's parents . . . they've withdrawn the investment."

"What?!"

"They're dumping me, too."

"Oh, Si. Shit. This is *not* your fault," she says firmly. "And it's not right. You don't deserve this."

"But I—"

"You made one silly little mistake, and Kyle dropped you like a bad habit. He chose his family over you. Someone who truly loves you wouldn't make you second-choice, honey. He'd fight for you. He'd stand up for you, because you *are* his family."

Tears burn my eyes. She's right. I know that, logically. But the hurt and the humiliation are so fresh . . . my heart can't quite accept the fact yet: that I can't do anything to change or undo what's been done.

And I know, just like there was no fixing things with Kyle . . .

There's no fixing this.

The money's gone, and my business is dead in the water.

CHAPTER 2

SIERRA

"Maybe I'll just have to stay in this tiny little blip of a town," I tell Sophie as full-blown panic sets in, "where there's no cell service and no one will ever find me. Maybe I can change my name, and sling drinks at this bar, and—"

"You're in a bar right now?"

"Oh, yeah. Did I not mention that I just met the hottest bartender in the known universe? Maybe if I hadn't sworn off males for the rest of the year—you know, for mental health reasons—I'd take it as a good sign."

"Okay, listen to me, Si. I say this with so much love. Whatever you do, *do not* get distracted by that hot but probably narcissistic bartender who's already slept with every girl in town. You have not had the greatest luck with men this year."

I sigh. "True." Though "this year" is generous. Have I *ever* had any luck with men?

"Fuck Kyle, and fuck his parents, okay? You don't need them. Who's running your business?"

"Me."

"Fucking right. There's money to be made in Orchard Cove, so go make it. You've got this lease, and you've got smoothies to sell. So, keep your phone handy, and keep trying to reach June. If you can't, get a hotel room. And I'll see you tomorrow morning as planned. I'll be over on the first ferry. We'll talk more then."

I blink away the tears that are stinging my eyes. I refuse to let them fall. "Okay."

"Just go find some cute café to hang out in, and keep in touch with me. We're going to get past this, sweetie," my best friend reassures me. "You'll see."

"Yeah. You're right." I say the things I know she needs to hear, reassuring her that I'm okay, and say goodbye. When the call disconnects, I will myself not to check any more messages on my phone until I'm certain I won't burst into tears.

I haven't cried over Kyle or the breakup, I'm not going to cry over my entire fucking life falling apart.

Crying won't put dollars in my bank account.

Sophie's right. I'm fucking fine.

My eyes creep over to the photo of shirtless Mason.

I need to clear out of this man's office before it gets weird.

I collect myself and emerge from the room, hugging my bag to my chest and feeling like I just took a nosedive into a gaping, dignity-gobbling chasm.

It's a feeling I'm getting used to.

I feel so out of control. Maybe that's the worst part.

The fact that Kyle dumped me with such a vengeance was out of my control. The fact that I had to watch his suspiciously pretty "best friend" swoop in to console him afterwards was not a hell of my own making. He chose those things. He chose *her*.

And I chose . . . to come here.

Now he's in the city with her, I'm here alone, and I have no idea how I'm going to fix anything. I would laugh if I wasn't still halfway in shock.

Mason is behind the bar, and he looks over at me. For someone who said he was leaving "in a minute," he doesn't appear to be going anywhere. It's almost like . . . he's been waiting for me?

Probably just wanted to make sure I didn't rob the place.

He doesn't frown, just takes a long, long look at me, and his eyes seem to soften a bit. If I didn't feel like utter shit right now, it might be enjoyable, being looked at like that.

"Bad news?" he ventures.

"Not great news," I admit.

I move along the front of the bar. His friend is gone. The lone waitress is chatting with the bachelorette party, who now have drinks strewn across their tables.

The volume of the music has gone up a bit. I point at the ceiling, not really sure if I'm pointing at the speakers playing "Hold the Line" or the heavens. "Toto. My grandpa would love this."

Mason looks surprised that I know the name of the band, but then frowns a little. "Yeah, well, your grandpa has good taste."

Had. But I don't correct him. "Ah. So the classic rock is your doing, then. I wondered if it was you or that fancy jukebox in the corner." I smile a little. It almost hurts. I really haven't used those muscles all week.

"Guilty." He seems to realize that I'm actually *not* making fun of him or the music. I think I catch a subtle flash of dimples deep in that beard before he dips his head to open a bottle behind the bar. "You're welcome to change the song, if you want. Jukebox is free."

"My grandpa was the coolest human on the planet. Just so we're clear."

The dimples are unmistakable this time.

"Thank you for letting me use your Wi-Fi."

His eyes flash to mine, and I feel that electric zing right down to my ovaries again. "Anytime," he says gruffly.

I'm not sure how to take that, since getting his help was like pulling teeth, but I feel his attention lingering on me as I head for the door. I'm not even sure where I'm going, just that I need to fall apart a little bit and I don't want to do it in front of the most effortlessly sexy man I've ever met. Maybe I'll do it in my van.

"Hey," he says.

I pause and glance over. He's pouring something from a bottle into a tall glass: a golden, sparkling liquid that looks incredibly refreshing.

"You look like you could use a drink."

I'm not surprised. But I am curious about whatever inspired this change in his mood.

Pity, maybe.

"Is it that bad?" I say.

"Professional observation."

He slides the drink across the bar toward me.

I consider for maybe half a second; Sophie's advice is in my head. But so is this whole terrible week, and I'm drowning in it. "Well, you're the professional, so." I drop my things on a barstool and lean on the bar, eyeing the effervescent drink. "Beer?"

"Apple cider. From my family's orchard."

He leans on his elbows on the bar, watching me, all massive shoulders and muscle-corded forearms, and deep, endless blue eyes. His sleeve has ridden up, revealing more of the tattoo on his right bicep. Amid the flowers and leaves, the scripted letters clearly read *Samantha*. Which is a level of commitment that goes well beyond anything I've seen demonstrated by most of the men in my life, that's for sure.

Maybe he *hasn't* slept with half the town?

I try not to be too impressed by the muscles or the tattoo or the orchard thing, but this man just gets more interesting by the second.

Hopefully Samantha is his sweet grandmother, or his dog, or his beloved dead sister or something. And not, you know, the love of his life, who's sitting at home right now wondering where the hell he is, while he's right here, staring at me.

What are you doing, the Sophie in my head says, but I ignore her.

He seems to be waiting for me to taste the cider, so I lift the glass and take a sip. I close my eyes, savoring, and maybe trying to escape the intensity of his attention. The cider is cold and tart, then sweet. Refreshing and bubbly. I taste apples and honey and maybe a hint of citrus?

Holy Christ, it's delicious.

I open my eyes, careful to fix a serious expression on my face, just like his. "There's alcohol in this, right?"

"Yup."

"Great." I take several deep, unapologetic gulps of it.

Something like amusement, or maybe lust, sparks in his eyes. I have no idea which, and it doesn't matter.

No boys for the rest of the year.

Probably Samantha is his drop-dead-gorgeous wife, anyway.

"Thirsty?" he murmurs.

I set the cider down, trying like hell not to blush from the double entendre I *think* he intended. "Very."

His gaze drifts to my mouth. "Good?"

We stare at each other as I wonder if he's talking about the cider or this simmering, nonsensical heat that's growing between us.

Finally, I say, "You know it is," sounding weirdly breathless.

I'm talking about the cider, though. *Just* the cider.

It's the cider that's making me warm.

I totally look for it, but he's definitely not wearing a wedding ring. I lick my lip unintentionally, and his gaze tracks the movement.

I clear my throat. "I thought you had somewhere to be."

"I do."

"Something more important come up?"

He doesn't look away from my face, doesn't even blink, when he says, "Ask me tomorrow."

CHAPTER 3

Mason

The prettiest disaster of a woman who's ever walked up to my bar polishes off her glass of Citrus Zest spring cider, then fixes her haunting green eyes on me. "Will we be seeing each other tomorrow?" she says neutrally.

"Let's find out."

She holds my gaze for a moment, pink coloring her cheeks—maybe the effect of the alcohol, or whatever she's thinking right now. Then she slides her glass toward me. "Can I have another, please?"

She's so polite, it does something to me. I'm not even sure if I like it. I just can't stop staring at her.

It's not just that she's pretty. Or how hot she looks in that yoga-wear, her cropped T-shirt sliding off one creamy shoulder. Or the silky, slightly disheveled brunette ponytail I want to slide through my fingers and wrap around my fist.

Maybe it's the way she's still trying so hard to be polite despite whatever went so sour for her in my office.

She reminds me of a wilted flower that someone forgot to water.

For some reason, it kind of outrages me, the idea that maybe she's been mistreated somehow. It arouses every protective instinct I have.

Maybe I misjudged her when she first walked in, assumed she was like all the other city girls who strut in here, impatient for quick service and more interested in making Reels about their meal than actually tasting it.

Maybe she's different.

Either way, her day clearly went to shit on whatever phone calls she made. Turning that around for her is a bartender's job, right?

It's not a job I'm here to do right now; I usually only help out at the bar when we're slammed and I happen to be in. But there's no way I'm leaving her to Beckett, my daytime bartender, who's prepping the bar for the night shift right now. Let him cut limes and make drinks for the other customers.

This one is all mine.

I push off the bar and select a bottle from the glass shelf behind me. When I turn back, her eyes widen at the shot glass I place in front of her.

"Really?" she says. "*That* bad?"

"I'm afraid it'll take at least two shots to fix what ails you, ma'am. Bartender's orders."

"Well, alright," she says, with mock disappointment. "Bartender knows best, right?"

I pour the shot without a word. If Jace was still here, he'd probably wink at her and deliver some smooth line. But thank god he's living in the house I'm renting out next to the bar right now; I sent him over to load some tools into my truck that I don't even need. I'm not going to examine why. His smirk told me the reason, even if I wanted to lie to myself.

I'm looking at the reason right now.

She lifts her eyes to mine. They're light green, with faint circles beneath that suggest a lack of sleep. "You're not going to have one with me?"

I consider that for a second. Then I pour myself one, too. We pick up the shots, clink them together, and throw them back.

She licks her soft, plump lips and something stirs, low in my gut. Lower. "Wow."

"Wow good, or wow bad?"

"Good, obviously. What is it?"

"That," I tell her, "is award-winning blackberry gin from my family's distillery."

She rests her chin on her palm, gazing at me as the gin works its way through her system. "Orchard *and* a distillery, huh?"

"Among other things." Now it sounds like I'm trying to impress her with my family's assets, so I change the subject. "Just one shot for me, though. I'm working."

"I see that. What happened to that house you're supposed to be working on?"

"I am. I will." The truth is, it's getting harder to walk away the longer she gazes at me like that.

"Well, then. Before you go, can I get that second shot?" She slides her shot glass toward me. I refill it with violet gin, and she throws it back; gin didn't earn the label of "panty peeler" for nothing, and this is the smoothest gin I've ever drunk.

Dangerously smooth.

"So . . . classic rock, huh?" she says, and licks gin from her lip. "Is that your musical jam?"

"One of many."

"Interesting. I consider myself a melomaniac."

"Oh, yeah? You have an obsession with music? Me, too."

"Really." She narrows her eyes at me in disbelief. "There's obsession, and then there's *obsession*."

I lean toward her on the bar, close. “I’m sorry, is this a competition?”

Her cheeks flush as her mouth opens slowly. I think she’s flustered.

I think those are fucking butterflies I feel in my stomach as we stare at each other.

“I have been known to be disturbingly competitive about my musical knowledge,” she says.

Adorable.

“Well, I’ve been told I’m polyjamorous,” I tell her. “I seriously enjoy almost every genre.”

She raises an eyebrow. “I’m calling bullshit. You’re gonna tell me anything goes? Deathcore? Happy hardcore? Mumble rap? You’ve got the windows down and a jaunty polka cranked as you drive down the highway?”

I chuckle. “I said *almost* every genre.”

She smiles.

Forget butterflies. It feels like an entire flock of doves just lifted off from my ribcage because I made her smile.

She slides the shot glass toward me again. “Third one’s a charm?” Her eyes twinkle at me, and everything around her seems to blur out. There’s nothing but her, me, and some vague sense of an annoying world somewhere beyond.

I have to force myself to look away.

It would probably be best to slow her down, so I open a cold bottle of award-winning Sea Salt cider, romanticizing it for her as I pour her a glass. “How about a crisp apple cider, with fresh lime and a hint of sea salt? Like a margarita, but better. You’ll want to savor it. Maybe with some guacamole and flatbread. I’ll put an order into the kitchen for you.”

"Ah. He's trying *not* to get me drunk. How gallant." She closes one eye and tilts her head like she's trying to make sense of me. "Or, he's just trying to drive up my tab . . . ?"

"It's on the house."

"Pity food? No thank you!" She digs in her pink bag and extracts a credit card.

"Nope. Your money's no good on this."

"*Why?*" She glances around like there must be some hidden camera and she's getting punked.

"What, you don't have gentlemen in Vancouver?"

Her chin lifts. "And how do you know I'm from Vancouver?"

"It's obvious."

She frowns.

"Not in a bad way," I amend.

"I'll pretend to believe that."

"I like your coffee mug," I say, as seriously as I can.

It's sitting on the bar between us, and there's a big, sparkly sticker on the side facing me. It's a heart with an arrow through it, and one word on it: *BOYS*.

"Don't expect to get it refilled for a few miles, though," I tell her. "The nearest place to get a latte is like twenty minutes away, in Duncan, though that probably doesn't seem far to a city person."

"I'll try to survive," she says.

I move to the computer and start putting in her food order, asking casually, "Have you checked out any of the sights yet?"

"No. I just followed GPS straight to the town center—what there is of it."

"It's not Vancouver, I'll give you that. But don't go thinking there's nothing to see out here."

"Heavens, no."

"You should have a local show you around." Our eyes meet briefly, and there's that spark, low in my gut.

"Maybe June Spencer will," she says lightly.

I make no comment.

When I finish at the computer, she slides the credit card toward me. "Trust me, you may need all the room available on this thing to cover my tab. I may just be getting started."

"May?"

"I haven't decided yet." She raises an eyebrow and sips her cider. She's definitely getting more playful as the alcohol sinks in.

"How about this?" I pour her a tall glass of water and set it beside the cider. "You drink some water and I'll take the card. Just in case."

"Deal."

I take the card, mainly so I can check out her name. "Sierra. Like the pickup truck?"

She wrinkles her nose, which is all kinds of cute. "Like the mountains."

I'm about to ask more on that when a blonde woman wearing a sparkly red *MAID OF DISHONOR* sash leans across the bar between us. Actually, she's kind of on top of the bar, and in my face. "Hello. We need a round of shots," she informs me.

Then she slides back until her feet presumably reconnect with the floor, grinning at me.

"Need" is debatable.

I glance across the room at the bride. She looks fairly stable on her feet, maybe a little glass-eyed, and very happy. Her sash announces *SAME PENIS FOREVER*.

Beckett and Abby, the server on duty, have already served the group a few rounds of shots and opened four wine-sized bottles of Sea Haven Gold classic cider for them. The dinner menus Abby handed out seem to have been tossed aside.

I ask the blonde, "What can I get for you?"

Her eyes rip off my shirt so violently, I almost hear fabric tearing. "Flaming Orgasms all around, please." She gives Sierra a girl-to-girl eyebrow wiggle that maybe she thinks is subtle.

"Coming right up," I tell her.

She sings a "Thank you!" and wanders back to the group. Their laughter is loud and very possibly annoying to the older couple eating ribs by the front window, and I decide to turn up the music a bit more.

As I line up shot glasses on the bar, I feel Sierra watching me. She's still leaning in. I'm trying not to be cocky about it, but the only reason to linger here is *me*.

"So, where's your sash?" I ask her. "I'm dying to know what it says." I am, actually. She's the only one of them not wearing one.

She blinks at me like she's trying very hard to keep a straight face. "More importantly, what's in a Flaming Orgasm?"

"You know, I've been running this bar for most of my adult life, and I have no idea. For all I know, she just made that up."

Sierra full-on grins as I fill a cocktail shaker with ice. "Well, I'm pretty sure they'll drink whatever *you* make for them." Then she bites her lip, like she tried to catch the compliment before it slipped out, but missed.

"Let's hope so." I pour Baileys Irish Cream, Kahlúa, and Goldschläger into the cocktail shaker, give it a good shake, then strain the mixture into the little glasses. I slide one in front of her.

"For me?" She seems flattered but tries to cover it by flirting. "You tell me, since you're the expert . . . Is it advisable to accept a Flaming Orgasm from a virtual stranger?"

Our eyes connect and there it is again, that spark.

Followed by a rush of adrenaline, straight to my cock.

"Sometimes those are the best ones," Jace drawls, strolling up behind her—and startling her again.

I guess she didn't notice that he just walked in, took one look at the two of us, and sauntered over to the jukebox to put on Rod Stewart's "Da Ya Think I'm Sexy?"—to fuck with me. A song that I didn't know he knew existed. Usually, Jace is a hard-rock-only type of guy, with the occasional Bob Marley or classic rock banger thrown in.

Sierra blows out a breath. "Ugh. You, again." She sounds deeply unimpressed, and I kind of love that she's giving him grief. His timing is for shit. But Jace is Jace, so he's unfazed.

He responds with his trademark charming grin. "Me again." He sticks out his hand. "Jace Crofton. Nice to meet you."

She shakes his hand so reluctantly, I might have to grant her free drinks for life. "Sierra Daniels."

"Sierra," he says, "like the truck?"

She discreetly pulls a face at me, like: *Is anyone educated in this town?*

I fill him in. "Sierra means 'mountains' in Spanish."

He leans on the bar next to her. "Your family speaks Spanish?"

I wonder if he's actually interested, or just faking it to annoy me.

"Nope." She picks up the shooter and gives it a sniff. "My parents happened to be backpacking in Spain when I was conceived, and my father thought the word was pretty."

"Sounds romantic," he quips.

"Oh, yeah." She throws back the shooter. "Decidedly more romantic than when he ditched me and my mom three years later. Wow. That is good." She slams the shot glass down, then waves her thumb over her shoulder, toward the bride. "But hey, maybe she'll have better luck in that department."

"Or maybe not," Jace says. "Statistically."

Sierra frowns a little, that vaguely haunted look returning. Leave it to Jace to really run a conversation into the ground.

"Trust me," I tell her, "Jace knows even less about relationship statistics than he does about relationships."

He laughs.

But Sierra seems distracted now, her mood regressing to where it was when she stepped out of my office. She watches me load the shooters onto a tray, drumming her fingers lightly on the bar.

"You know what?" she says with forced brightness. "Put those on my tab, please. And hit me up with another one of these heavenly ciders when you get a chance?" She holds her glass up in cheers. "It's five o'clock somewhere, right?"

"Actually, it's almost five o'clock right now," Jace provides helpfully as she takes a swig.

"May I?" she asks me, holding the cider out as if to add it to the tray. "I won't even drop them. Probably."

"Go right ahead." I give her a small smirk, trying to steer us back to where we were before Jace interrupted. "They're on your tab, right?"

Doesn't work.

She just says, "Thank you," puts her cider on the tray, and whisks the whole thing away. I watch her walk over to the other girls, carefully, and put the tray down on one of their tables to a round of cheers. She pulls up a chair and sits down.

Jace watches her go, too, and says to me, "I'm sorry," not sorry at all. "Did I just ruin that for you?" Then he smiles, the fucker.

"Always."

Abby comes out of the kitchen with the guac and flatbread I ordered for Sierra, just as Oscar, my night bartender, shows up for his shift. I put in a few more orders of appetizers for the bachelorette, on the house, tell Abby to keep their water glasses full and, if they stick around, slow their service and try to get them to order dinner.

"Let's go," I tell Jace, rounding the bar.

"What, we're not even gonna have a beer?"

"You already had a beer. You're cut off until you square up on your never-ending tab." Same thing I tell him every time.

He just chuckles and follows me out to my truck.

"I can feel you grinning."

"You're in quite a mood," he notes as we climb in.

"I never took you for a Rod Stewart fan."

"I never took you for a fucking virgin. Did you need *help* back there? It's like you'd never asked a woman for her phone number before. Thought I was gonna have to ask for you."

When I say nothing, just start up the truck and pull out onto Water Street, then turn up Cherry Way, he prompts, "Well, you want intel or not?" He lights up a joint and I roll down the windows.

"Do I have a choice?"

"The bachelorette party checked into June Spencer's guesthouse today."

Makes sense. Explains why Sierra was looking for June.

"You know, right next door to your house," he says.

"Yeah. I got it."

"They're here until Sunday. That's two nights."

"Thanks. I can do math."

It is not surprising to me in the slightest that he knows all this. Orchard Cove is a *small* small town. And Jace Crofton has a talent for sniffing out attractive newcomers.

I'm assuming some of the other girls in that bachelorette were attractive. It's only occurring to me now that I didn't particularly notice. There was Sierra Daniels leaning on my bar, and the rest of them were just a general blur.

I'm pondering this, not loving it, when Jace presses, "Come on. You're gonna sit there with that frown on your face, pretending you're not interested?"

I didn't say that. I didn't think that.

Far from it.

What I'm interested in, apparently, is doing a whole lot of naked, sweaty things with a woman who just walked into my bar. And thinking about that electric charge I felt whenever she looked in my eyes.

And wondering how she might look beneath me, naked, as I taste every inch of her body . . .

"Or is this you pouting because she has to leave in two days?"

I clear my throat and try to stop thinking about going down on Sierra Daniels, because I'm getting hard and Jace is *right there*. "You know I don't think that far ahead." *Not where women are concerned.*

"Oh, I see. That's how you're gonna play it. So you're *not* interested in that total smokeshow who just stood at your bar for like half an hour, drooling all over you."

I don't respond. There's no need. He'll keep talking regardless.

"And here I thought you two looked good together. But maybe I was wrong. Maybe you *don't* like her pretty green eyes or that round, juicy—"

"Too high-maintenance," I cut him off, irritated as shit that he noticed her eye color. And her ass. "That manicure. That purse. And what the hell was that shirt? KPop whatnow? We'd have nothing in common. And the only thing she was 'drooling over' was the alcohol."

"You're right," he says, deadpan. "Nothing in common. She likes to drink . . . too bad you don't own a bar and an alcoholic beverage company."

I ignore the sarcasm. "City people vibrate at a different frequency. You know what Vancouver women are like. They flock to Orchard Cove every summer slathered in Lululemon and Sephora because they saw it on the 'gram, so they can make TikToks doing yoga on the beach to show their followers how down-to-earth they are. They're all the same. And they're all Type A. I'm not interested in competing with a woman or her social media following. The power struggle alone would be a major cockblock."

To my shock, Jace doesn't laugh or agree. Instead, he makes a downright judgmental sound as he smokes his joint.

"And what does *that* mean?"

"So, you're an expert on city people because you've screwed some tourists?" he says. "You grew up here. How many times have you actually been to a big city?"

I take the turn onto Honeymoon Lane, slowing the truck down in the middle of the road. "Should I just kick you out here, or . . . ?"

He snorts. "Always gotta be in control, huh?" He pinches the butt of his joint and flicks it out the window as we pass June Spencer's property, with the old *Twisted Tree Orchard* sign that needs fresh paint. "Well, I tell you what. Kinda sad that at thirty-four years old you still haven't figured out that you can't control who you fall for."

It's an oddly philosophical comment for Jace.

"Sure you can," I retort automatically. What the hell is he talking about anyway? *Fall for?* I'm not falling for anything. Least of all his bullshit.

He's just trying to get me to admit that I want her, so he can flirt with her to try to annoy me. It's one of his favorite pastimes.

Normally, I wouldn't care.

I don't know why it's bothering me this time.

"Unless you'd rather just keep pretending that you're dead inside—"

"Who's pretending?"

"—and just live alone forever," he says.

We've looped all the way around the block, so we're back at the waterfront but half a kilometer south of the bar. As we pull into the drive of my family's property overlooking the water, it strikes me how grouchy this will sound for a man who's temporarily living with his entire family, but I say it anyway. "I like living alone."

"Sure you do."

I toss him a *please shut up* look.

He holds up his hands in surrender. "Fine. Go to bed alone. Don't even bother heading back to the bar tonight to see if she's there. I'm sure someone else will show her a good time while she's in town . . ."

When I say nothing, just throw the truck violently into park, he chuckles.

Best friends know you annoyingly well, right?

Because he already knows, maybe before I do, that there is no fucking way I'm letting that happen.

CHAPTER 4

Mason

When I walk into the bar just before last call, the bachelorette party is still going strong. The music has completely changed, and Sierra Daniels is leading a very drunk group of women in a passionate singalong to "Survivor" by Destiny's Child.

At some point, she donned a *MISS BEHAVING* sash. Upside down and backwards.

The bar is decently busy, and the Friday-night crowd, a mix of locals and visitors, is fairly riveted on the spectacle of nine drunk out-of-towners going hard on the karaoke.

We don't have karaoke, so the girls are singing loudly to be heard over the late-night volume of the music—using empty cider bottles as microphones.

I grab an unoccupied table near the bar, followed closely by Jace and my brother's best friend, our orchard manager, Evan Garnett. It's been a long day—Evan and Jace helped me work on the house all evening, and I told them drinks are on me tonight. I'm not even sure if Jace told Evan the real reason we're here.

Once again, I'm looking at her.

I've kept in touch with my bar staff, and according to their updates, the bachelorette party enjoyed the free nachos and wings I sent them, eventually ate dinner, and took over the jukebox shortly after their eighth bottle of cider.

At least all the singing and dancing will help them sweat out some of the alcohol.

Jace puts in an order for us with Oscar at the bar, as Evan and I sit back and take in the show.

If I'd ever been under the impression that the purpose of a bachelorette party is to celebrate a woman's impending wedded bliss, this little performance would've proven otherwise. With a bunch of drunk women belting out such *fuck you* songs as "We Are Never Ever Getting Back Together," "No Scrubs," and "good 4 u" at the top of their lungs, anyone walking into the bar would sooner guess they'd stumbled into a divorce party.

I can only assume *SAME PENIS FOREVER* isn't in charge of the song selection.

I limit myself to a few shots with the boys and sip a couple of Traditional Dry ciders while I take it all in. The way Sierra keeps serenading the bride, and getting the crowd singing along, and generally enthralling the entire room.

Or maybe it's just me who's enthralled.

Sierra doesn't look my way once. She hasn't noticed I'm here, or doesn't care, or maybe she's just too drunk to notice anything beyond her immediate surroundings.

At last call, the ladies all throw back a round of Sea Haven violet gin, the bride's arm slung around Sierra's neck as they cackle at some shared joke.

The music mellows out a bit, and toward the finale of a passionate group singalong to Kacey Musgraves's "High Horse," the party finally starts to slide out of hand. *PARTY ANIMAL* climbs up on a table singing lead, followed closely by Sierra and

TROUBLEMAKER singing backup, and while Jace applauds along with the rest of the crowd, Evan and I exchange a look. We set down our drinks, get to our feet, and approach the party.

"Sorry, ladies," Evan announces, his booming ex-military voice carrying easily over the music, "but you'll need to come down from there. For your safety." He offers *PARTY ANIMAL* and *TROUBLEMAKER* a hand, and they appear eager to comply with his request.

Evan has that effect on women.

Sierra stops sing-shouting along to the song, looking affronted as Evan helps the others climb down. "Don't let men rain on your parade, ladies!" she shouts—into her microphone/cider bottle. "Don't give away your power! You are perfect just the way you are—!"

Then she notices me standing directly below her. She stares, open-mouthed, as I offer her my hand.

She takes it and jumps down, stumbles, and falls into my arms.

My pulse races at the unexpected full-body contact.

She blinks up at me, cheeks flushed, her green eyes bleary. "You came back," she gushes. She feels hot and damp, and I wonder if she realizes that she's smushed herself right up against me, her breasts flattened against my chest.

My cock has definitely noticed.

"I own the bar," I remind her.

"Oh. Right."

"That was quite the performance."

"Oh, I know *all* the songs," she says. As "High Horse" ends and "Hotel California" starts playing, she grows heavier as she sags against me, staring up into my eyes, and the room around us gets blurry again, like no one else exists except as some vague concept.

Maybe I'm just drunker than I thought.

"Water."

Her gaze drops to my mouth. "What?"

"Have you been drinking water?"

She blinks. "I think so. Maybe?"

"Let's get you some."

"Okay."

She makes no move to extract herself from my arms or support her own weight.

The tempo of "Hotel California" kicks up and she starts to sway a little, moving with the music. And singing along, though she clearly doesn't know all the words.

I resist as she tries to dance with me, my pulse thudding and my cock inconveniently hardening. "I should really help close up the bar . . ."

My staff don't need my help. But I am trying to be a gentleman here. She is *very* drunk.

"Please?" she pleads.

A shiver runs down my back and my nipples actually harden.

When my feet remain rooted to the floor, she pouts dramatically.

The second I let her go, Jace swoops in to dance with her. She smiles, delighted, as he whirls her away, and irritation climbs up my spine one vertebra at a time, finally lodging in my throat as I watch them dance.

Jealousy.

Humanity's most useless emotion.

I stalk behind the bar, raise the lights and turn the music down low, and tell the staff, "Closing up."

As they hurry to clear up tabs with other customers, I open Sierra's tab and comp most of it. I print out the bill, leaving a couple of rounds on it so she won't make a fuss. Something tells me if I comp the whole thing she'll make a big deal out of it, and at this point she probably has no idea what's actually supposed to be on it.

Abby charges Sierra's credit card and gives it back to her, along with a big glass of water, interrupting her dance with Jace.

By then, the bar has cleared out except for the bachelorette party. While the rest of the girls pay up, Sierra checks her phone.

I take a seat with Evan as he finishes his beer, keeping an eye on her—and pondering what I'm going to do about her.

See her again when she's sober, hopefully.

Jace is busy talking up *BAD INFLUENCE* and *RAGING DIVA* now, probably trying to figure out if they're into threesomes.

I can't believe I let him dance with her.

My pulse is beating in my dick, making it hard to think straight. And those shots I downed are making it so much easier to undress her with my eyes.

That loose shirt that keeps sliding off her shoulder . . . gone.

The stretchy yoga pants on that fantastic ass . . . also gone.

Panties . . . ripped off with my teeth.

That long, silken ponytail spilling down her naked back, bra ripped off and tossed to the floor as I slam my mouth down on hers . . .

She drifts over to our table, and I stare.

"Excuse me," she says politely, like we're meeting for the first time and she didn't just flatten her body against mine so tightly, I'm still fighting down the hard-on. "Do you know of anywhere in town I can get a room for tonight?"

This surprises me, and it takes me a moment to respond. "I thought you were staying at the Twisted Tree guesthouse."

She looks confused.

"June Spencer's guesthouse," I clarify. "Isn't the whole bachelorette party staying there?"

"Oh. Right." She glances over her shoulder at the other girls. "I'm not with them."

"You're not?"

"I just met them tonight. Fun girls, but no." She looks at me worriedly, twists her lip between her teeth. "I asked them where they're staying tonight, but they said they'd booked all the rooms. It's full."

I consider that. "June's guesthouse is the closest thing to a hotel around here. We have a couple of B&Bs, but those are full, too . . ." I look to Evan to verify this.

"They book out in advance from May to October," Evan tells her. "Including mine. Nearby towns, too. Every bed is full right now, leading up to Sunshine Fest. It's a pretty big thing around here."

Sierra frowns and sits down with us. "I know. That's why I'm here."

Okay, *that* is interesting. The festival is a few weeks away.

So she's not just here for two days?

"June Spencer said she'd provide lodging for me," she says, poking at her phone. "I've been trying to get a hold of her all day, but no luck." She peers up at us. "I guess I'm stranded?"

Jesus. Leave it to June.

"Where was she putting you up, if not the guesthouse?" Evan asks her.

"A private cottage. That's what she said. Why?"

Jace snorts as he overhears, sitting down with us. "Cottage?"

"Yeah. That's what June said." Sierra frowns. "A cozy cottage."

Evan and I exchange a glance. June's putting up Sierra in that old shack behind her house?

Nope. That seals it. Tomorrow, I'm finding her somewhere decent to stay. Even if it means evicting Jace and his roommate from my place next to the bar and making them sleep on my couch together.

"I guess I could just walk over there with the girls now . . ." Sierra glances over at the bachelorette party, who are gathering up their things to leave. "Maybe if I just show up at the guesthouse, someone can let June know I'm there, and she can direct me to my cottage . . . ?"

"It's midnight," Evan points out. "June's seventy-six. And if she's anything like Mason's grandpa, you wake her up now, she's more likely to shoot you."

Sierra's mouth opens, but nothing comes out, as maybe she considers the likelihood that June Spencer sleeps with a gun under her bed. "Well, shit. I mean . . . could I crash on the couch in your office, then?" She looks to me, gorgeous green eyes flooded with hope and drunken desperation. "I'll pay for it, of course."

The answer to that would be a resounding *no*.

If I let her sleep at the bar and anything happened to her, my grandpa would murder me, heir or not. Not only would it be an insurance issue, that is not the kind of hospitality Tommy Grant would expect me to show a "stranded" young lady. I'd never hear the end of it.

But more than that, I don't like the idea of leaving her here, or anywhere, in the state she's in.

As if he's reading my mind, Jace pipes up with "Well, there's a couch at my place."

Not this again.

"It's much bigger than the one in Mason's office," he adds, "and more comfortable." Somehow, he makes "bigger" and "comfortable" sound just wrong. "It's next door to the bar—"

"My family's property is right next to June's," I interject, before Jace can open his big mouth again. "We have space."

I ignore Evan's eyebrow-lift and Jace's victorious smirk.

"Oh, wow. Really?" Sierra blinks at me. "And it's not too much to ask?"

Just then, the music shuts off as my staff prepare to leave.

"I'll walk you there now." I give Jace and Evan a pointed look, one that says they're going to help me round up all these drunk ladies and escort them over to their lodging, stat. "We'll all head over together. And tomorrow morning, I'll walk you over to June's to get it sorted," I tell her.

"Good luck," Jace mutters. "June would shoot *you* any time of day."

Fortunately, Sierra doesn't seem to hear it. She gazes at me with something like awe bordering on hero worship glistening in her eyes. I try not to let it go to my head.

As we all get up from the table, she's so focused on me that she trips on the leg of her chair, and I catch her. She smushes against my chest, again, as I pull her close.

There was really no need to pull her right up against me.

Just instinct.

Her hands go to my waist, her fingers digging into me. I tell myself it's just the alcohol making her look at me like that; no need to get carried away with the adrenaline surge.

Once again, it goes straight to my cock.

"That's really nice of you to walk me home," she breathes.

"It's either that or let Jace do it," I can't believe I hear myself saying. Maybe I *am* drunker than I thought. "Disappointed?"

She laughs a little and glances at Jace, as he and Evan rally the bachelorette party over to the door. "No."

"Not interested?" I ask lightly.

Her eyes meet mine again, and my breath catches in my throat at the soft, boozy, truthful look she gives me. "In Jace? No."

"No? How about Evan?"

She stares up at me. "Who's Evan?"

"The other one."

She still hasn't broken eye contact when she says, "What other one?"

And I have to wonder if it's the same for her—this magnetic force drawing her to me as everything else fades into an inconsequential blur. I proceed to get lost in her eyes for so damn long, the next thing I know, the entire bachelorette, my friends, and my staff have left the building.

We're standing here alone.

"I think we're the last ones left," she whispers.

I let her go and clear my throat. "Let me just lock up."

"Okay."

She waits as I turn out the lights, then we walk out the front door together. I set the alarm and lock up behind us.

The parking lot is almost empty. Jace and Evan and I walked here earlier, knowing we'd be drinking. My friends are already making their way across the dark lot with the girls as my staff drive off into the night.

"This way," I tell Sierra, about to head after them. But she catches my arm, stopping me.

"Hey . . . Mason? Thank you. For helping me out. But . . ." She glances at the group who are now making their way up the road, loudly, leaving us behind. Then she meets my eyes. "I know I flirted before. But I should probably just make it clear that we probably shouldn't do anything tonight."

"Anything . . ." I murmur, the mere suggestion of *something* making my cock stir. "Like what?"

"Like kiss goodnight. Or . . . anything else." Her eyelids grow heavy as she looks at my mouth, and my gaze drifts down to her succulent lips. "I just want to say thank you now, so there's no awkwardness. Or . . . pressure."

I get that. It's sweet.

She's sweet, in a way I didn't expect when she first walked into my bar.

I shift closer to her, and she leans back against the door, so we're almost pressed together again. I place my hands on her hips, gently, and she makes no move to stop me.

"Well, as charming as it was being serenaded by your special rendition of 'Hotel California' while you stepped on my toes, you are drunk, Sierra Daniels. And I'd like to think I'm a gentleman."

I'm really, really glad my friends are out of earshot so no one laughs out loud at that one.

Sierra nods, biting her lip. "Yeah. I suppose that's a very reasonable reason not to kiss someone."

I smooth my thumb over her hip, slowly, back and forth. "One might even say gallant."

A smile twitches at the corner of her lush mouth. "Plus, we are strangers."

"Virtually."

"Plus . . ." The smile disappears. "Today was literally the third-worst day of my life." She dips her head, then peers up at me again. "So, you probably don't want to be lumped in with *that* in the memory bank."

"Probably not," I say. And I wonder what made this day so bad for her. I wonder if she'll tell me.

"Plus . . . I'm on a sexual hiatus."

"Lots of reasons, then," I agree as heat floods my body.

She looks away. Laughs.

I feel it, too. The total high of standing here with her in the dark, where anything could happen. There's an unexpected euphoria pressing up against my lungs like an inflating balloon. My heart is pounding and I feel like I can't quite catch my breath.

When she looks up into my eyes again, we stare at each other for so long, I'm not even sure what's happening, or what's about to happen. All I know is this woman is making my heart fucking race for the first time in *years*.

I don't even want it to stop. I could have a heart attack right now and it would be worth it, just to see her looking at me like that.

"Could we forget I said that last thing?" she says shyly. "It's personal."

"It's already forgotten," I lie.

"It's just that I'm on a *relationship* hiatus. That's what I meant to say."

I'm not sure that's what she meant to say, but I'll try to be a gentleman and not mention it.

The thing is, I'm really not *that* much of a gentleman.

"I promise," I tell her, my lips so close to hers, teasing, that I can practically taste the blackberry gin. "No goodnight kiss."

She takes a deep breath, shudders. "My last relationship ended pretty recently in disaster," she explains, "so 'no boys for the rest of the year' seemed like a really smart decision . . . earlier today . . ." She fades off as we stare into each other's eyes.

I lean in, closing the polite space between us, and everywhere our bodies touch there's heat, electricity.

Arousal courses through me.

I'm overcome by the total rush of being this close to her, the mere inconsequential bits of clothing between her skin and mine, how close we are to actual fucking. A zipper, a peel of fabric, a shift of hips and thighs . . .

I know she can feel my erection against her hip. Stiff, unapologetic, thrumming with need. Her eyes widen, pupils dilating as my cock throbs.

She lets out a soft sound of want and shifts her hips. And I *know* she's feeling what I'm feeling.

I have never in my life been so one hundred percent sure that sex with a woman would be *fucking amazing*, for both of us, *before* I even kiss her.

She whispers my name. Her hand slides up the back of my neck, into my hair, her nails scraping against my skin.

My lips graze her jaw, and she shivers. "No boys, huh?" I murmur in her ear: "How about a man?"

CHAPTER 5

Sierra

My head is *hammering*.

I peel my eyes open, squinting into the crisp daylight. It lasers through the edges of the curtains, closed over the window.

As I try to roll over, try to orient myself, my skull feels like it's in a vise and my mouth feels like it's been vacuum-sealed in parchment.

God, my throat hurts.

And my head throbs with music. I think it's Beyoncé.

Did I convince a bride to sing "Single Ladies (Put a Ring on It)" with me to a crowd of strangers last night?

And was the Hottest Bartender in the Universe in that crowd?

His name is Mason, my brain provides helpfully.

I blink, trying to remember how I got from *there* to *here*. Here being in a bed, snuggled under the covers, alone.

I know I'm alone, because it feels like something is missing.

Like *he's* missing.

I slide my hands along the mattress on either side of me, carefully, feeling for a warm body, just in case. But no one's there. I find the edges of the bed rather quickly, though. It's a very small bed.

And there it is again: the hammering. It's not just in my head. It's an actual hammer, banging away, somewhere above me and off to the right, through the walls.

I look up, squinting painfully into the light. On the wall above me, there's a bunch of sports pennants with team names I've never heard of, maybe from a school.

I push myself up on my hands, disoriented.

The bedsheets are dark blue with patterns of stars on them. Constellations. The kind of sheets you'd find on a kid's bed.

Where the hell am I?

Did Mason put me up in his little brother's bed last night? Or—shudder—his *son's* bed?

Does this man have a family *of his own*?

Shit . . . what if he's a single dad and his kids now know he brought a drunken floozy home from the bar last night, and *I'm* that floozy?

Or maybe they're used to him bringing drunken floozies home.

I toss the covers off me as I toss away that unpleasant thought, remembering in a sudden rush Mason's heat and hard muscles covered in silky skin, his strong hands all over me, tingles of warmth and pleasure spreading all over my body, even now. Delicious memories of last night.

Drunken memories.

I struggle to pull more *specific* memories from the murk, then immediately wish I hadn't. Because Mason is in every one of them, but so am I, and I'm a *mess.*

I remember Mason standing over this bed, speaking to me in a soothing voice.

Mason, trying to tuck me in like I was some overtired child.

Mason saying, *I'll sleep on the couch.*

And me, clinging to his arm like a leech and asking him to stay. To sleep with *me.*

And so he did.

He slept with me in this tiny bed. He also spooned me, because I asked him to.

Actually, I'm pretty sure I begged.

"Ughhh," I groan aloud.

Too. Much. Alcohol.

Alcohol should *not* taste that good when I'm in the middle of a life crisis. However, if I learned anything about alcohol in my twenties, it tastes *better* in a life crisis.

At least I'm not naked. I'm fully dressed. In yesterday's clothes, but still. I'll take it as a win that I didn't peel them off and climb all over a virtual stranger, begging him to fuck me.

Maybe I mercifully fell asleep before that could happen.

Or maybe that *did* happen . . . and he said no?

Wait. Did he refuse to kiss me?

Did I *ask* him not to kiss me?

I can't remember.

I promise, no goodnight kiss.

There's his husky voice, and a murky memory floating just beyond the edges of my sanity that has me and him pressed sweatily together saying *very* hot things to one another that I can't quite recall. The word *cock* was in there somewhere.

I'm pretty sure I was the one talking about it. And maybe trying to touch it?

I am so hard . . . I think that's what he said to me. I can still hear the pain in his voice in my head.

Was that at the bar or here? Or somewhere in between?

What did I say to him??

I fall back on the pillow with a groan, silently praying that he was as drunk as I was last night so maybe he doesn't remember, either. I do remember, hazily, walking home with him and his friends and that bachelorette party because I couldn't reach June

Spencer all day. And what had to be hours upon hours of singing and drinking at the bar before that.

And Mason looking all hot and smoldering in his tight blue T-shirt, pouring me drinks. And trying to get me *not* to drink. He kept giving me water.

And the phone call with Sophie, earlier.

Kyle.

The meme.

My fucking dumpster fire of a life.

"Fuck." I really would've thought it would be impossible to sink any farther into that chasm that gobbled up my dignity five days ago, but last night I think I managed to plummet a little lower.

I take a deep breath and force myself to sit up again as my brain cells gradually come back online. I blink at my surroundings. Real hardwood floors, walls painted blue, a small wooden desk and chair. I see no clock anywhere to tell me what time it is. But the room is definitely decorated like a teenage boy lives in it.

The glittering red *MISS BEHAVING* sash that dangles from the doorknob looks incredibly out of place. As does my pink Kate Spade handbag, sitting on the bedside table by the football-shaped lamp.

I look around for my phone but can't find it anywhere.

I wonder if I left it in the bar. Seems like something Very Drunk Sierra would do.

My suitcase sits on the floor, and there appears to be a note on top of it. And now I remember. I got the suitcase from my van after we left the bar, and Mason carried it here for me.

Where is he now?

I hear nothing else beyond this room but that distant hammering, on and off.

I slide out of bed, carefully, woozy as I get to my feet and blood thumps through my body. My organs are incredibly angry at me for drowning them in more delicious cider and gin than they could possibly process.

I pick up the scrap of paper, and my insides effervesce with way too many feels at the sight of a man's handwriting—because I know it's from Mason, and I already like him way beyond reason.

Sierra, it reads, *I didn't want to wake you. Please help yourself to anything in the kitchen and let me know if you still want my help with June.* He signed it *Mason Grant* and wrote his phone number carefully at the bottom.

I tuck it into my purse like Gollum stashing his precious ring of power, my pulse flying as I absolutely refuse to acknowledge what this man is doing to me when he's not even *here.*

It's too dangerous.

You don't even know if what happened last night was real, I scold myself as I lay my suitcase open. *You are rebounding. And you were very, very drunk.*

However, I wasn't very drunk when he poured me those first few drinks, and he seemed pretty fucking fantastic *then.* Which definitely confuses my survival instincts.

I choose some fresh clothes and manage to stumble my way into them. Unfortunately, while Very Drunk Sierra had enough forethought to bring the suitcase, she forgot that my toiletries and cosmetics are in a different bag, which is still in my van, which is still parked on the street across from Mason's bar, which is god only knows *where* from here.

I pack the suitcase back up and leave it on the rug, and make up the bed. Then I grab my handbag and bring it with me as I quietly ease the door open and peer out. A hallway greets me. A gleaming stretch of hardwood floor, several other doors, a staircase leading down at the far end of the hall. At the opposite end, plastic sheets hang over a stairway leading up, and that hammering sound drifts down.

I wonder if Mason is up there.

I tiptoe up the hall feeling like a felon, with no idea who I might run into or potentially terrify. When I find a bathroom, I dip inside and do my best to clear up the raccoon eyes. I finger-brush my loose hair; my hair elastic has mysteriously disappeared. Then I finger-brush my teeth with some toothpaste I find by the sink.

There is an odd mix of grooming products in here that suggest a child and a grown man are sharing this bathroom.

This is all too weird. I need to get out of here.

I creep down the stairs, past a wall of family photos I'm too uncomfortable to really look at. They seem like old ones, mostly black and white. I definitely hear and smell someone cooking, and fucking pray it's Mason in the kitchen I'm clearly about to enter at the bottom of the stairs.

I may have enjoyed some wild nights out and messy mornings after as a twentysomething, but thirty years old just feels *too* old to be wandering into someone's kitchen with yesterday's mascara on and no idea where I am.

And yet here I am, and that is definitely *not* the man I shared a bed with last night who's making breakfast. This man is scooping juicy slices of back bacon out of a pan, his back to me, and I stop dead, just inside the sunlit, modern-farmhouse-style kitchen.

The smoky-sweet smell of the meat fills the air and my nostrils, and while I might be half-starved right now, I actually retch.

The stranger glances over his shoulder, sees me, and does not look at all shocked or startled to find a random, bleary-eyed woman retching in his kitchen. Nope. He *smiles.*

"You okay?"

"Uh, yeah. I'm very okay," I lie. At least, I'm fairly sure I'm not about to actually throw up on the floor.

He smiles wider.

To my dismay, he's objectively hot. Loose work jeans and a tight white tank top on an underwear-model body, tan skin, white teeth.

Sexy scruff on his jaw glinting gold, blue eyes, shaggy blond hair. Sort of Jax Teller in *Sons of Anarchy* vibes but without the tattoos, leather, and angst. And with a tea towel draped over one shoulder.

What the hell is in the water around here?

Or is it the cider? What's responsible for this breed of men? David Attenborough really needs to make a documentary.

"Well, good morning—afternoon," he corrects himself. "I'm Mason's brother."

Of course you are.

"He told me to expect you," he adds, eyes sparkling.

I shuffle a little deeper into the room, unsure. Afternoon? Is he kidding? There's a lot of sunshine coming off this man, above and beyond the light pouring through the windows behind him, so it's hard to tell if he's fucking with me or just being friendly.

He's smiling *a lot*.

"Okay . . ." I clear the frog from my throat, side-eyeing his natural glow with suspicion. "Are we sure you're related to Mason?"

He laughs easily. "Pretty damn sure. I look like Mom, he looks like Dad, and I've been told by the ladies that we have identical asses."

My face flushes as red as the tomato he's now slicing as I do everything in my power not to look at his ass.

"I'm Layne," he introduces himself.

Fuck me. Even his name is sexy. I'd call all my single girlfriends and tell them to come here, stat, if I had any.

And if I had a phone.

"Cool. I'm Sierra. Uh, what time is it, Layne?"

"Just past noon," he says pleasantly. I watch as he constructs sandwiches—which I now realize are lunch and not breakfast—with the back bacon, plump basil leaves that look freshly plucked from a nearby garden, slices of that bright-red succulent tomato, and fresh, squishy-looking bakery bread, my stomach churning.

"If you're hungry, you're welcome to join us. I'm just making lunch for—"

"Hi." A young girl pops out of nowhere, startling the hell out of me.

"*Shit.*" I think she almost startled the puke right out of me. I press a hand to my mouth and swallow, hard.

She frowns. "Sorry." She appears to be in early tweendom, with wavy dark hair almost to her waist and wide, dark eyes.

Which explains the Hermione toothbrush I glimpsed in the bathroom.

"No worries." I take a breath. "I'm just a little . . . out of it. Hi."

She's holding a big glass bottle of what looks like apple juice. On second thought, I think she popped out of the pantry. She shakes up the bottle in both hands, vigorously, then goes over to the butcher-block island and pops off the top. Definitely apple juice. The label has a golden apple on it and says *Sea Haven Cidery*.

"This is my daughter, Kaylie," Layne says.

"I'm ten and a half," Kaylie informs me as her bottom lands on a barstool and she pours herself a glass of juice. She eyes my BLACKPINK T-shirt and adds, "I like your shirt," which I imagine is one of the highest forms of praise one can hope for from a ten-year-old girl.

She's wearing a kid-sized Nirvana T-shirt that I have to assume her dad or her uncle picked out for her. "I'm Sierra. I like your shirt, too."

Her eyes light up, and I'm pretty sure this means we're friends now.

"Do you have a son, too?" I ask Layne.

"No. Why?"

"The room I slept in. I just wondered . . ."

"That's Uncle Mason's room," Kaylie provides.

Mason's room . . . as in, the one he slept in when he was a teenage boy? The sobering dots gradually connect in my head. "Oh. Did he grow up here?"

"Yup. Are you staying for lunch?" she asks me.

Hell, no. This is awkward enough.

"I really can't. I'm not feeling so well." It's not just the mild nausea and dehydration and pounding headache that are bothering me. Sophie was supposed to arrive in Orchard Cove this morning. *Past noon.* Yikes. "Thank you for the invitation, but I should really get going . . ."

"You can have some juice." Kaylie slides the second glass she's just poured toward me. It looks refreshing as hell, and I *am* almost thirsty enough to drink toilet water right now.

So I thank her and down the whole thing in a few gulps. Before I'm finished, a gray-haired man has walked in the back door. He sees me, stops, and stares. He wears work jeans and a flannel shirt, and looks very much like a several-decades-older version of Layne.

"Hey Grandpa, this is Sierra," Layne says. "She's a friend of Mason's."

The man grunts a hello.

My cheeks must be bright pink. They're burning.

"This is my grandpa, Tommy," Layne tells me.

Tommy. The grandpa Mason's friends warned me about. *Even grumpier than his grandson*, Jace said.

"Hello," I say. "Sierra Daniels. Nice to meet you." I can't believe I'm meeting the entire extended family of my ridiculous one-night stand that wasn't even a one-night stand because we didn't have sex *but they don't know that.* "Uh, where is Mason?" I ask, edging toward the door. "I'd love to thank him for helping me out last night."

"Oh, he's gone," Layne says casually. "He may have gone down to the bar. Or to pick up supplies for the renos. He has a lot to do." He doesn't actually say *especially since he met you yesterday, then vanished.* But there's a teasing implication in his tone that I hope goes right over his daughter's head.

His grandfather follows the conversation like a hawk.

"Uncle Mason never misses breakfast with me," Kaylie informs me, and it's clear she's picking up on *something* the adults aren't saying. "We're not sleep-in people."

"I'm sorry if he missed breakfast this morning," I tell her, again trying to slink toward the door. "It's totally my fault. I kept him up late last night."

Mason's grandfather makes a grouchy *hmmm* sound. Even if Jace hadn't warned me, it's quite obvious he's the grumpy type, and when he frowns, I can totally see the family resemblance to Mason. "And how do you know my grandson?" he asks me.

I stop in my tracks. "Oh. I met him at his bar. I was kind of stranded last night, and he was nice enough to let me make some phone calls and then, uh, walk me . . . home." My face grows hotter as Kaylie stares at me, trying to connect all the dots in her ten-year-old brain. The dots that her father and great-grandfather have already connected.

Sex.

They definitely think I had sex with Mason last night. In his childhood bedroom, on that little bed.

"Stranded?" Tommy says gruffly. "Why?"

"Uh, just . . . new in town." While Layne and Kaylie gaze at me curiously, Tommy eyes me with suspicion. Much like his grandson did when I first walked into his bar. "I was trying to get a hold of June Spencer."

Tommy snorts. "What the hell would you want with *that* woman?"

Layne says, "Grandpa."

But the way they're looking at me, they all seem to be wondering the same thing. It's clear I'm not standing in the middle of a June Spencer Fan Club meeting.

Same vibe I got when I brought up June's name to Mason and his friends at the bar last night.

"I was supposed to stay at a cottage on her property. Actually, I should really go find her . . ." Since Mason told me that June's property is next door, and I have no idea how deep this neighborly feud or whatever it is goes, I should probably clear out of this family's kitchen and get on with the search.

"You sure you don't want to eat first?" Layne places a big platter of sandwiches on the island in front of Kaylie, and his grandfather immediately digs in.

"Thank you, but I couldn't possibly."

"Okay, then," Layne says. "We wish you good luck with tracking down June."

"Yeah," Kaylie says, selecting a sandwich. "Good luck with that old battle-axe."

"Kaylie. We don't call people names."

"Gramps called her that yesterday!"

"Then maybe Gramps needs to work on his patience." Layne shoots his grandpa a pointed look, which Tommy ignores. "I'll show you out, Sierra. Get you headed in the right direction."

"Oh, great. Thank you." Embarrassingly, I have no idea what the right direction is. Other than some wobbly memories of moonlit country roads, I have no idea how I got here.

I follow Mason's brother out the back door, with a quick "So nice to meet you both."

Kaylie waves, mouth full of sandwich.

Tommy watches me go, not hiding his suspicion. "You take care, Sara."

I pop my head back in the door. "It's Sierra."

"Hmm," he grumps, gray eyebrows twisting over shrewd blue eyes.

I follow Mason's brother across the back porch and down the steps to a wide gravel path that meanders through the lush backyard. "Well, that was embarrassing. Your grandfather thinks I'm a strumpet."

"My grandpa doesn't take easily to strangers, Ms. Daniels. Especially beautiful ones from the city who distract his grandson from his duties." He smiles disarmingly.

"It's Sierra, please." I smile back tentatively. "I slept with your brother last night, so I think we can skip the formalities." We're walking through trees now. They grow tall and lush, bending lazily over the path. "I take it your family and June Spencer aren't all that . . . amicable?"

"You could say that. Around here, you could also say the older generation likes to hold a grudge."

"I really didn't mean to cause trouble. Yesterday was . . . kind of a rough day."

He considers that. "Better now?"

"Other than the hangover, actually, yes. I think so."

He stops at a fork in the path, so I do, too. "My brother have anything to do with that?"

My cheeks heat traitorously. "He might."

I catch the small smile as he looks away. "As you can see, that's the orchard. You'll want to follow the path to your left. It'll take you around the cider house and out to the main drive."

"It's beautiful," I say politely. The orchard consists of row upon row of leafy trees, not much taller than I am, extending across the lush field ahead. I can't see what lies beyond, but it seems to go on forever. "And what's that?" I point to the quaint cottage that can be glimpsed at the end of the path to the far right, through some more trees.

"That's my place. Mine and Kaylie's. As soon as we finish fixing it up."

"Wow. It's adorable." It looks like a scene from a storybook. A stone and cedar A-frame with a green front door, the front porch dripping with flowers that cascade from plant boxes all along the rail. If I were a small-town type, it might be a dreamy place to live.

Since I'm not, it looks more like a nightmare. Living *that* close to my family? No fucking thanks.

I wonder if it has running water or if he and Kaylie always have to use the bathrooms in the big house.

"Once you get out to the road," he says, "you'll see it only goes in one direction, away from the water. Just follow the road to June's place next door."

"And how far is it to walk to the town center from here?"

"About ten minutes if you're slow." He eyes me. "Maybe fifteen, state you're in."

I groan involuntarily, and he smiles again.

"But if you're really hurting, it's even faster if you go along the beach."

"Why didn't you say so?"

"You'll find the beach walk at the bottom of our driveway. Just follow it along the beach northward."

"And north would be?"

He tips his head, eyeing me like maybe I'm just an ignorant city girl. "Well, we're in the northern hemisphere and it's midday, so that big fireball in the sky going east to west will be about due south right now, don't you think?"

I groan again. "Okay, I deserved that. But come on. I drank a lot of booze last night *made by your family*, so it's mostly your fault that I have no idea how to sort out what you just said."

Layne smirks and points me northward.

"Thank you." I slide my sunglasses on. "I'll come back for my suitcase as soon as I can," I add apologetically.

"No problem."

"If you see Mason around before I do, please tell him I said thank you. And that his brother is quite a smartass."

"Will do," he says, still smiling.

CHAPTER 6

Sierra

I follow the path Mason's brother indicated. It loops through trees and shrubs, around the family home, and past several buildings on the left: equipment sheds, and a couple of larger buildings that appear to be the cidery and distillery. To the right of the path, the orchard stretches ever on.

Up ahead, I find a cute building, all wood and climbing vines and flowerpots in the windows. The sign over the open door reads *Sea Haven Cider House*. It's midday Saturday, and the parking area in front is filled with cars.

A big old tree out front has several wood signs hammered onto it pointing in various directions. They mention a gift shop, cider tasting lounge, and patio. On the lawn near the tree, a young couple plays cornhole while sipping on glasses of golden cider.

Just past the cider house parking lot, I pause. The walking path connects to the long driveway that snakes off to my left. And directly ahead of me, through the gaps in a tall stand of trees, I glimpse the blue-gray waters of the Salish Sea.

Mason's family's property is right over the water.

It's like something from a postcard.

This place is *very* pretty.

But I wonder what it would be like to grow up here.

Shitty, because everyone knows you and your business, and you're potentially in an echo chamber? Stifling, maybe, for anyone who's creative and entrepreneurial? Or *different* in any way? And especially isolating when you're a teenager, trying to spread your wings and figure out who you are?

Too familiar.

But for someone like Mason who chooses to stay, maybe there's a good reason?

I can't imagine why anyone would stay in a small town. I couldn't leave the one I grew up in fast enough.

I follow the driveway to where it meets the road. There, a carved wood sign reads *Sea Haven Orchard, Est. 1905*. And beneath that, *Estate Cidery & Distillery*.

Has this property belonged to Mason's family all that time?

This level of commitment seriously boggles my mind. It's fascinating and completely mystifying to me, like that *Samantha* tattoo on Mason's arm.

The road here hits a dead end above the beach, and a street sign reads *Honeymoon Lane*. The rural road with its thick trees and overgrown ditches, lush and green everywhere, is impossibly picturesque. It's almost trying too hard to be perfect.

But perfect is bullshit, or an illusion. This town must be hiding several serial killers or something.

I feel like a fucking disaster standing here in my sweats and T-shirt, sweating out last night's alcohol and wondering if I'm going to puke. Yesterday morning, I couldn't wait to get Orchard Cove over with and get back to the city. Now, I'm dreading the responsibilities that await me in the outside world, everything I've broken and now need to fix.

I feel overwhelmed, with too much to do, all at once, and severely lacking the faculties to do it all. My day has barely started and I'm already behind.

I wish I could put on some music. I need to find my phone.

I need to find June Spencer.

I also need to find Sophie and get to work.

But what to deal with *first*?

When I picture my best friend stranded like I was last night, locked out of the building on the pier and trying to get a hold of me, her phone maybe not working, and worrying about *me*, about where the hell I ended up last night . . . the decision is easy. *Sophie.*

I cross the road to the path Layne mentioned—the beach walk. It runs just above the beach, at the base of a sloping cliff; above, backyards slope down from patios and decks, and impressive houses overlook the sea.

I follow the well-worn gravel path with the sea-salt-battered railing in the direction Layne indicated. Below the path, beyond some wind-matted shrubs, the pebbled beach stretches to the water. A couple of women walk a dog along the shore, but it's otherwise empty.

The beach stretches from one end of the sprawling cove to the other. Out in the water, the tree-spined ridge of Salt Spring Island seems to enclose the cove. The tide is out, leaving clots of seaweed and a scattering of seashells, and the faint stink of fish turns my tempestuous stomach.

I can already see the pier ahead. It's a simple boardwalk of wood, stretching out into the water. A few people dot the pier, walking along it or gazing over the edge into the lapping waves below.

As I make my way there, I prioritize my day. First order of business, apologize to Sophie for being so late. And hopefully get inside the building at the pier so we can start setting up. Then I can pop over to the bar to hopefully get my phone (and see if Mason is around). Later, I'll go pick up my suitcase from his house (and see if he's around).

Basically, I'm just hoping I get to see Mason today, to thank him for taking care of me last night.

And then . . . who knows? Maybe we hang out?

I seem to remember telling him about my "no boys for the rest of the year" thing, but I think it was clear to us both that that idea went out the window.

How about a man?

I remember his words in my ear, his lips brushing my skin, his body hot against mine.

Who am I kidding? I would love to spend time with him. Preferably sober and after I have a shower.

When I reach the end of the walk, I follow the wooden steps that lead from the path up to the pier as seagulls swoop lazily overhead. Where the pier meets the land, it widens into a large, unused patio area that surrounds the cedar-shingled building.

As I round the building, I find the town center not quite as empty as yesterday.

Kitty-corner from the pier, across the short main street that runs parallel to the water, creatively called Water Street, a few cars are parked in the lot in front of Sea Haven Bar & Grill, though I don't see any sign of Mason.

Yes, I look for him. First thing.

Directly across Water Street from the pier, customers are walking into the small grocery store. And on the final corner, across the path that leads from the street to the pier, a ramshackle-looking place called *Bev & Bill's General Store*, offering hardware, liquor sales, auto repair, and postal services on its various signs, is open.

There's not much else to see of the small town from this view but trees, and the start of the main road, Cherry Way, that winds from Water Street westbound out of Orchard Cove, eventually meeting others that lead to the highway.

But parked at the curb in front of the pier, behind my van, is my best friend's car. The door of the pier building, on the street side, is propped open, and I can already hear the music of ROSÉ and Bruno Mars playing inside—bouncy, flirty, and upbeat. Above the door, the building's name, *Pier Seven*, is carved into a raw slab of wood, and walking through that door is the most wonderful human being in the world.

My best friend is unmistakable, anywhere on earth. Forever in her rockabilly-pinup-girl era, Sophie has raspberry-streaked dark hair swept up in a pile of curls and wrapped in a bandana, and she wears an effortless denim jumpsuit with her multicolored skate shoes. Seeing her is such a relief for these puffy, bloodshot eyes.

"Soph!" I cry.

She turns, sipping on a reusable *Cutie Fruitie* smoothie cup. "Si!" She rushes over and gives me a big squeeze of a hug.

"Ergh." I recoil as the contents of my stomach complain.

She slides her sunglasses off to reveal winged black eyeliner as she eyeballs me carefully. "Are you okay?"

"Not really." I slip my sunglasses off, too, giving her the full visual.

"I see." To her credit, she doesn't recoil in horror. Now *that's* love.

"I drank a *lot* of gin last night. And alcoholic apple cider. Which, by the way, does not taste like alcohol. Or apples."

"Can't wait to try it. Let me guess. The bar?"

"Yeah. The one across the street."

"I wondered. When I didn't hear back from you—"

"If I got distracted by the hot bartender?"

Sophie sighs. "You really wouldn't be *you* if you didn't."

"Hey. You make it sound like I meet the Hottest Bartender in the Universe on a regular basis."

She raises an eyebrow, interest piqued. "That hot, huh? Don't tell me you're already in love . . ."

"Pfft. From here on in, you're the only one I love."

I mean it. Sophie Moore is my fucking soulmate. I'd marry her if I could. I mean, sure, neither of us is into women that way and she's already happily married to Pete, who may actually be the most wonderful male human ever and yada yada, but whatever. Pete knows he has to share his wife with me. She's the light of my life.

In typical Sophie fashion, she drives this point home while ratcheting up my love for her another impossible few notches by filling me in casually: "Well, most of the heavy lifting has already been done here. The smoothie bar is practically ready to open. Your van is unloaded, et cetera. I've had a very productive few hours."

"Wow. I'm so sorry I'm dragging my ass here so late. How did you get in? And into my van?"

She shrugs. "When I got here this morning, June Spencer was here, waiting."

I throw up my hands. "Of course she was."

"She was very nice. And you left your van unlocked."

"Shit. I did? And nothing was missing?" If I did that in Vancouver, it would've been cleaned right out.

"Nope. This town is so sweet! Imagine, a place where you can leave your car unlocked and no one takes a thing," she muses. "You really made the right choice in coming here."

"I'm not so sure. I'm halfway convinced June Spencer may in fact be the Antichrist."

"Hmm. Hiding out in an adorable small town, running a farm and this cute old building on the waterfront? Seems rather charming for the angel of darkness."

"That's the disguise. Look, I know you're doing everything in your power to distract me from the fact that my life is falling apart right now, and I love you for it, but the damage has already been done. Just hit me with it."

"With what?"

"I haven't looked at my phone today. What fresh new hell has cracked open beneath me since yesterday?"

"None, I swear. I called Kyle after we talked, and I told him he'd better erase that meme from existence and figure out who made it. Like, immediately. As far as we can tell, it got texted to, like, everyone in his contact list. Someone had to have accessed one of his devices to do that."

"Oh, god."

"So, whoever it was must be close to him or tech-savvy or both. But at least it didn't actually go viral or anything. You're not famous."

"I've never been more glad."

"And Kyle swears up and down he had nothing to do with it. Maybe someone just thought it was funny. Like cute-funny?"

"Right. Adorable." I might be able to laugh at it myself if the blunder immortalized in said meme wasn't responsible for ending my relationship, throwing my boyfriend dick-first into the awaiting comfort of his hot female bestie, and now, losing me my much-needed investors. "Well, the only people on that video call were Kyle's family. So, if it wasn't him . . ."

"Are you going to call him?"

"I really, really don't want to. Not right now."

"Then let me take care of it," she says. "You have enough to deal with. Your focus should be on the smoothie bar. Your business. Making sure it survives the loss of the investment. And taking care of yourself. After that, maybe you sit down with Kyle and get closure?"

"Yeah." Truth be told, until I fully sober up from last night's drunken singalong, I'm in no shape to deal with any drama. "I appreciate you looking out for me. You know I do. But I'll get closure with Kyle once I have my shit together. So, maybe never?"

Sophie frowns at my joke. "Well, in good news, everything is as promised here. Fridges and freezer are up and running. I picked up some things at the grocery store and a couple of farm stands along the way. I managed to load in the stock I brought, sanitize the counters, set up all the blenders, even made myself a slushy." She holds her cup out to me. "Taste?"

"New flavor?"

"I'm calling it Watermelon Sugar. Like the Harry Styles song."

I take a sip but say nothing, just let the cartoon hearts shooting out of my eyes say it for me.

Sophie grins. "All that's really left to do is a little cleaning and all the fun decorating. You and I can rock that out easily."

"Sophie, you're a goddamn angel. I'm buying you dinner tonight. For now, can I sit down?" I sit down on the curb before she can answer, rubbing my throbbing temples, and she joins me. The Watermelon Sugar really didn't land so well.

"Headache?"

"Oh, yeah. You know how music is my go-to when life sucks? But usually I have the decency to sing alone in the shower, like the good lord intended?"

"Oh, no."

"Oh, yes. I crashed a bachelorette party and screamed 'You Oughta Know' at strangers. You know how Very Drunk Sierra can get."

"I haven't seen her in so long," she says wistfully, and drapes an arm around me. "But that song should not be allowed at karaoke nights without proper supervision."

"I know. You should've been there to stop me. Or at least sing backup." I cover my face with my hand and peer out between my fingers. "And there was no karaoke. It was a jukebox. With no microphone."

"Oh, Si."

"Positive note: met some cool girls from Calgary. They're gonna swing by tomorrow to taste-test smoothies for me before they leave town."

"Cool."

I cringe and just spit it out. "And I slept with the hot bartender."

Sophie's jaw drops.

"I know. You warned me. And I know it sounds like some dumb rebound thing—"

"No, it sounds like a *fun* thing. I hope?"

I find myself trying not to smile, but it's impossible. "It was, actually. He walked me home and spooned me all night. And we kind of made out without really kissing. I was *really* drunk, and I think I asked him not to kiss me? So there was a lot of just rubbing against each other. And laughing." By now, my cheeks are hot with the memories. I'm not embarrassed to talk about sex with Sophie. But I'm still floored by how much I *like* this guy. "He made me laugh a lot. I think I made him laugh, too."

"Wow. I guess I was wrong. He sounds awesome."

I scrunch my nose. "I think he really might be."

"I'm sorry if I sounded cynical yesterday. I just don't want to see you hurt any more."

"I know."

"And we both know you have a real knack for attracting . . . well . . ."

"The utter douchebags of the world?" I fill in for her.

"I was going to say 'works in progress,'" she says diplomatically.

"Fixer-uppers who can't be fixed," I agree sadly.

"So, if you actually met a great guy, I should eat my words? And maybe this whole week from hell is turning around?"

"Yeah. Maybe." God, I would love that. I *need* that. "When I first met him, honestly, he acted like a giant grouch. If I wasn't stuck here, I probably would've just walked out of that bar and never given him a backwards glance." There's a warm knot in my chest as I speak. Hope and fear and this impossible thrill that maybe I met an amazing human when I least expected it. It's making me feel mushy. "But he really stepped up to help me out when I needed it."

"Then I like him already."

"I really think you will."

"So, what's he like? I want details." She slurps her slushy, hanging on my next words as I try to find the right ones to sum up Mason Grant.

"Hmm. You know those big, burly, but pretty guys who are half lumberjack and half *GQ* model?"

"Uh, do you?"

"No. Not until last night. But imagine such a guy, and then he turns out to be all sweet, warm teddy bear inside . . ." I fade out, because a truck is approaching along Water Street. A black pickup . . . with the golden apple *Sea Haven Cidery* logo on the side.

My insides cartwheel in excitement when I recognize Mason behind the wheel.

"Oh my god. That's him." A ridiculous grin spreads across my face as he pulls over in front of my van and parks at the curb.

I get to my feet as Mason climbs out. His eyes cut to mine, and at the grim look on his face, my stomach plummets. My smile fades.

He retrieves something from the back of the truck.

My suitcase.

He stalks over to me and drops it at my feet.

When his eyes lock on mine, they're heavy and dark. I almost stagger back.

Why is he looking at me like that?

Like I'm . . . the enemy?

"Mason. What happened?" My heart is pounding. Clearly, between leaving me that sweet note this morning and dumping my suitcase at my feet, something happened. Something shitty.

"What happened," he says gruffly, "is you didn't tell me that you leased Pier Seven from June."

This does not compute. Why does he look so . . . angry? "I don't understand."

His chest rises and falls as he takes a slow, deep breath. Like he's really trying to rein in the anger but barely succeeding. "When you showed up at my bar yesterday and said you were looking for June Spencer," he says slowly, "and you had no place to stay for the night, et cetera . . . you never once said that you were in town because you were leasing this building."

"Uh . . . why would I?"

"Because my family runs a pop-up restaurant in Pier Seven as of June first."

"But . . . I have it leased for a pop-up shop for all of June. We're setting up this weekend." I'm so utterly confused. "Do you have a lease? In writing?"

His jaw sets. "No," he grits out. "It's . . . more complicated than that."

Yeah. I'm getting that.

Family feud, maybe? *The older generation likes to hold a grudge. Good luck with that old battle-axe.* So many things I've heard about June Spencer over the last twenty-four hours suggest that there's a whole lot of small-town drama going on here that I know nothing about. And I haven't even gotten June's side of it yet.

I have to wonder what she'd have to say about all this.

"So . . . why would you think you have a lease when I have a lease, on paper?"

"It's a long-standing situation," he mutters. "At least, it was until now." His gaze slices down my curves, that look saying *until you came along*, and heat floods my body. The way this man ignites me with a look is insane.

It's disorienting. The lust that courses through me. The embarrassment. *Shame* . . . for something I didn't even do. I don't even know what he's accusing me of. But it's clear, I *am* being accused.

"How would I know that, Mason?"

His gaze lingers briefly on my lips, his voice lowering. "I find it very hard to believe you had no idea what you were doing."

There it is again, the accusation.

"Doing . . . when?"

"When you asked June to let you lease this place," he growls. "You want to buy it, I assume? And leasing it first is supposed to make that happen?"

I shake my head, trying to sort this out. "I didn't ask her. I don't want to buy it. She invited me here. I didn't even know Orchard Cove or this building existed before that."

"Uh-huh. So, then you won't mind being *un*invited."

"What?" I can't even believe he just said that. The businesswoman in me is instantly outraged.

And the woman in me . . . the woman who'd started to like this man—very much, in a very short time—is humiliated.

He wants me to leave? Like, leave town?

I hear Sophie move closer to me. Probably ready to tell this man to F the hell off, the way only Sophie can—politely, definitively. She doesn't speak, but Mason gives her and the building behind her a withering once-over.

Then he glares at me again. "You can just pack up and go back to the city, if this building isn't important to you."

I scrape my jaw off the pavement as the businesswoman in me elbows her way to the front. "I just said, I have a lease agreement."

He scowls deeply, brow furling. Full lips in a pissed-off pout. "For how long? Just one month?"

It is truly unfair how attractive this man is, even angry. But at this moment, I'm acutely aware that he's a stranger. And Businesswoman Sierra is, thankfully, here to protect the rest of me, pointing out that he's being downright rude right now.

Just because he spooned me in his childhood bed and he made me laugh and made my panties fucking wet, I don't owe him anything.

I wrap my arms around myself. "I don't feel comfortable answering that."

Mason takes a breath, looks away. And for a split second I glimpse the man I spent the night with. Then that man is gone, and the man I first met in the bar yesterday is back in full force. And he couldn't give a fuck about me.

I'm just some stranger from the city.

An irritation.

The enemy.

He fixes me with his blue eyes, and there's such searing disappointment in that look. Such finality.

"Stay away from my family," he growls.

Like I'm some kind of *danger* to his family.

Then he gets back in his truck and drives away, leaving me standing here, dumbfounded as fuck.

My best friend wraps an arm around me gently. "You were saying . . . ? Something about his inner teddy bear?"

I watch Mason's truck disappear up Cherry Way.

Then it's just me and Sophie . . . and a few random shoppers lingering outside the grocery store and Bev & Bill's General Store, staring.

Maybe they just witnessed that whole scene.

Sophie waves at them, then points at the building behind us. "Best smoothies you ever tasted! Grand opening on Wednesday! Bring your friends!"

"Remember that thing I said to you yesterday?" I ask her in a small voice. "If I ever plan anything more than a week in advance with a man, I want you to kick me in the junk?"

Sophie actually looks surprised, bless her. "Si. You were already planning a future with that man?"

In an even smaller voice, I confess, "When I walked by the orchard on his property, in the back of my mind, I kinda thought it would be a nice place to have a wedding."

"That sounds more like a fantasy than a plan," she says generously.

"It counts."

"Shit. I really can't kick you, though." She turns me by the shoulders and steers me into the building, away from all the looky-loos. "So how about one tiny little 'I told you so,' and a bottle of wine?"

I let out a *fuck my life* sigh. "Make it cider and I'll feel sufficiently punished."

CHAPTER 7

Mason

I should've fucking known June Spencer would betray me.

Grandpa was right. You can't trust that woman.

He's always warned me that June is fickle, disloyal, and self-interested. He's told me, my brother, and our parents over the years, ad nauseum, never to count on her, and I know, in his mind, he's got his reasons. His own history with June.

But I've never seen this side of June before.

And I did not see *her* coming.

Sierra Daniels.

A woman with haunted green eyes, the ability to win over a roomful of strangers while singing into a cider-bottle microphone, and sob-story her way into my bed. Last night, we laughed together. We laughed until we fucking *cried* together.

And I have no idea if one word she said was true.

I liked her so much, we didn't even have sex. She asked me not to kiss her, and later, in bed, when she changed her mind and *begged* me to kiss her, I surprised the hell out of myself when I didn't. When I wanted to be a gentleman about it, take care of her, even more than I wanted to take her clothes off.

I actually found myself entertaining the thought that I might've just met the woman of my dreams, and maybe this would be our messy, funny, sexy origin story.

What a load of shit.

Now I know the truth: that she was just way too good to be true.

That she's actually the enemy.

That I let a stranger into my office at the bar, and into my home. She could've accessed or taken anything she could get her hands on.

A stranger . . . who's working with June.

She probably knew exactly who I was when she walked into my bar and played me.

I can't even decide if I'm more pissed off about that or the fact that she seemed to have so much fun doing it.

I should've charged her for those fucking drinks.

"Man, are you gonna pout all day?" Jace wipes the back of his work glove across his sweaty forehead, scowling at me across the room. "I can hear you moping right over the music."

He turned it way the fuck up a few minutes ago, and The Black Keys' "Please Me (Till I'm Satisfied)" is rolling out the giant open holes in the primary bedroom where the new windows will soon be installed. The music can probably be heard clear across the cove.

"I didn't know you could read my mind," I mutter as he sets down the nail gun he's been using, then lowers the volume on the music.

"What?"

"I said, I didn't know you cared."

"Of course I do. You've barely grunted two words at me all day. I'm getting lonely over here." He eyes me where I'm kneeling on the floor, putting together a shelving unit and generally ignoring him. He sighs, digs in his pockets, lights a joint.

"Can you not?" I grouch. "It's fucking Saturday." Which means Kaylie's not at school and could be around here anywhere. He knows this.

"Right," he says and puts it out. "Forgot."

"And you wonder why Tommy doesn't want you around."

He chuckles. "Your grandpa doesn't want me around because I remind him too much of his misspent youth. In other words, his glory days."

I snort. "Is that how you see it? I realize you're fairly delusional at the best of times, but shit."

He ignores that. "So, what happened? I take it all this sulking is about Miss Behaving, from last night?"

I don't respond to that.

"She turn out to be married? Or just not interested? Was she sadly unaffected by your massive pecs and soulful blue eyes?"

"Soulful?"

"I've heard they're quite captivating. Or, wait. Are we still pretending you're not interested in her? I'm afraid I can't keep up with your alarming and ever-increasing tolerance for self-denial."

"I'm not denying anything. We spent the night together. But to be clear, I'm *not* interested."

Jace seems unconvinced. But the last thing I am is interested. I'm so pissed at myself for being interested in the first place, I'm fuming. I seriously can't believe I slept with the enemy, totally unaware. And now she'll be sleeping right next door, according to her, in June Spencer's "cozy private cottage." For god knows how long.

A month? All summer? Longer?

As soon as I pin down June, which I will, I'll find out how long that lease is. But how the hell do I convince such a stubborn, hateful old mule that it's in her best interest to terminate it in favor of our original agreement?

"You're doing it again," says my annoyingly clairvoyant best friend.

"Yeah? Why can't you read my mind when it's saying *fuck off, Jace?*"

"Oh, I can." He wanders over and sits down on the newly assembled bed, close to me, like we're having an important heart-to-heart.

"You really could've lectured me from the other side of the room," I inform him.

"I get it, okay? You're a fucking grump, you're jaded, you're guarded. And maybe you have reason to be all those things. But what're you gonna do, just renovate your castle tower, build the walls up nice and high, pimp out this bedroom, for what . . . yourself?"

"That was the plan."

"It's a stupid plan, man."

I sigh.

I know I might as well tell him. Jace is a magnet for gossip, worse than all the old ladies in the local knitting circle and the jam and jelly club combined. The only reason he hasn't heard anything yet is that he's been up on the third floor of my house all day installing wainscoting and the new bed frame.

The moment he leaves the house, or maybe checks his texts, he'll get the scoop, I'm sure.

"Alright. Fuck. When I stopped off at Bev and Bill's on my supply run this morning," I tell him, concentrating on my work, "Bev was in, and she asked me if I'd heard about what was going on at Pier Seven. She said she heard a rumor from a farmhand over at June Spencer's that someone from the city was opening up a pop-up shop there."

"Uh-huh. And you think *I* gossip."

I raise an eyebrow at him. "I've heard you and Bev have an ongoing text conversation absolutely loaded with conspiracy theories."

"So?"

"So, she's a fifty-seven-year-old woman who runs the local general store with her husband. You have literally nothing in common except your bloodlust for other people's private business."

"That's an important commonality." He picks up a bottle of water and chugs half of it as I just shake my head.

"Well, Bev said she dropped into Pier Seven this morning to take a look, and there was a woman setting up with red streaks in her hair and tattoos. Definitely not local. You know Bev knows everyone."

"Huh. Sounds potentially hot. Did you see her?"

"You're missing the point. Bev asked her who owned the pop-up shop, and she said a woman named Sierra."

I leave out the part about how, after talking to Bev, I came straight home to confront Sierra, and when I found her gone, I took her suitcase over to Pier Seven intending to leave it there for her—but found her and her employee out front and made a giant scene instead.

I really don't need Jace telling me I overreacted.

I did not overreact. There's no telling what Sierra Daniels is capable of, and Layne already told me that she met Kaylie and my grandpa in my kitchen.

I feel like a fucking fool bringing that woman into my house.

"Okay," Jace says. "And judging by the look on your face, this is not good, because . . . ?"

"Are you kidding me? I've been negotiating with June for *months* to buy that damn building. Which my parents were negotiating for months before that." Jace frowns. I try to ignore it, but my irritation is creeping up. "There was a *plan*. The next step in that plan was that we'd run our pop-up there this month, leading up to Sunshine Fest. It was a fucking given."

Jace cocks an eyebrow. "Was it?"

"And now June leases out the building to someone else, without telling me? It's fucking bullshit."

"So, talk to her about it. Maybe there was a misunderstanding."

"Right. How can I trust a word that woman says now?"

"Who? Sierra or June?"

"Both."

Jace sighs as I ignore him in favor of screwing shelves into place. "Look, I know you're used to things going your way. And you're stubborn as fuck. That's what happens when you're a natural leader and you're usually right about everything, and people respect you, even if they don't like you."

"Uh-huh."

"I'm just saying. You're very comfortable being the big alpha at the table, whether people like it or not. Because you only care what a few people actually think anyway. Including me."

"Now *that's* an unproven rumor," I mutter.

"You keep your inner circle tight, love it that people trust you, but you don't trust *them* easily. And you liked this girl. I mean, you *liked* this girl. I haven't seen you into someone like that since—"

"*Really* don't say it."

"So, now you feel stung because, what? You think her pop-up shop stands in the way of your plans? You think you're in competition with her for June's favor now?"

"We *are* in competition. Whatever deal she's made with June, it's supplanted mine. And in case you didn't get the memo, June hates me and my entire family."

"Whatever. You're local, Sierra's not. June isn't stupid. She knows that building belongs with your family. She probably just forgot about your pop-up."

"We ran the same pop-up there last summer."

"A lot has changed since last summer," he reminds me.

I ignore the way his voice takes on that wary, gentle tone. The tone everyone, even my best friend, has used with me since the accident, every time my parents come up in conversation. Like I'm delicate now. Fragile. Like there's some hidden part of me that's been turned to glass and should be handled with care—or it'll break and puncture something vital, and all my ability to deal will leak right out.

Maybe it will.

"There was a plan, Jace," I reiterate.

"A verbal agreement, maybe. But since the parties that made that agreement aren't here to get specific about it," he says carefully, "maybe you need to revisit that agreement with June. And this time, get that shit in writing."

"It was my parents' *dying wish*, Jace," I growl at him, as if any of this is his fault. I set my tools down and press my fingers into my eyes, taking a breath. "What the fuck am I supposed to do if I can't finish what they started?"

◆ ◆ ◆

When I walk into the bar in the late afternoon, my mood has only worsened.

Did Sierra know who I was, and that I want Pier Seven, when she walked in here? Did she know before I did that we're business rivals?

How would I fucking know?

I don't know *her*.

And starting to think that I somehow did after mere drunken hours in her company was nothing but sheer stupidity. A dumbass bout of temporary insanity brought on by alcohol, her ridiculously beautiful eyes, and her incredibly convincing damsel-in-distress act.

That woman was never in distress.

I shut myself into my office, try to focus on what's important. Work.

Tourism surges in Orchard Cove in early June with the lead-up to Sunshine Fest, which happens over the solstice weekend and kicks off the summer season. We have a uniquely Mediterranean-like climate here in the Cowichan Valley; the area yields a wealth of organic produce and artisanal products, and Sunshine Fest is our town's opportunity to proudly showcase what our home has to offer.

In the coming weeks, daily temperatures will steadily climb, local farm stands will start loading up with goods, and the wineries, craft beverage producers, and restaurants in the region will open up their patios and doors all day long as tourists flow through, winding their way along the Vancouver Island Wine Route and the Cider Trail. In Orchard Cove, other than harvest season, it's the busiest time of year for me and my family.

Which is exactly why I planned to run a pop-up restaurant in Pier Seven—to showcase Sea Haven's artisanal ciders and spirits, pairing them with seasonal foods from the menu at the bar.

I even would've offered June's ciders on the menu, like my parents did when they ran the pop-up at the pier last summer. We don't carry any of June's products at the bar, but during the festival, I would have.

I should be deep in preparations for the pop-up and everything else that comes with festival planning, like the increased volume of business both the bar and the cider house can expect, and the beer and cider garden we set up in the bar parking lot during the festival.

Instead, I find myself searching for Sierra Daniels on the web and every social media app I can think of. I study her website, and all the accounts she runs to promote her pop-up smoothie bar, Cutie Fruitie.

When I search her name on Instagram, I find her personal account, some posts on other accounts about Cutie Fruitie . . . and a strange meme featuring her and a purple dildo. "*I can't believe how BIG it is!*" she cries enthusiastically.

I sit back and watch it play, looping over and over.

Who *is* this woman?

Is she in porn or something?

I almost don't even want to know.

But I can't let June or this seductress from the city interfere with my parents' dream. I've got to be smarter than this.

Since when was I ever such an idiot for a pretty face?

There's a knock on my office door, and Beckett sticks his head in. "Hey, Mason. That Sierra woman is here. You said to tell you if—"

I'm already on my feet and brushing past him.

And there she stands, at my bar. Looking every inch as beautiful, lost, and fucking treacherous as she did last night. And earlier today, when I told her to stay away from my family.

"Hey," she says stiffly. "I just—"

"Not out here," I cut her off. "In my office."

She hesitates but follows me inside.

I close the door behind her and she crosses her arms over her chest. She wears the same T-shirt and sweats I saw her in outside Pier Seven hours ago, and she looks tired. Dark circles under her eyes and, if I'm not mistaken, the remnants of last night's makeup. Like she hasn't showered yet or settled in anywhere. Or had a moment's peace since we met.

That makes two of us.

She still looks hungover, actually.

She tears herself away from the eye-contact vortex that we both just got inexplicably sucked into. "Look, I'm just here to get my phone," she says. "I think I left it here last night."

I study her, trying to suss out the truth from her bullshit.

She didn't have her phone at my place last night? And this morning?

I reorient myself around this fact. She couldn't have used it, then, to take photos of any of the tax documents or other business records I keep at the house.

Of course, this could just be part of her story. She could have another phone.

She could be lying to my face. Again.

"I don't have your phone. But if my staff found it, it's likely behind the bar. We have a lost and found."

"Great. Then I'll go ask them." She turns on her heel, and I wonder, did she choose *right now* to come over here because Jace just took my truck into Duncan? Did she think I wasn't here, because she didn't see it in the parking lot?

How disappointing for her.

I put out an arm, press a hand to the door, keeping it firmly closed. "You sure that's all you want?"

She blinks up at me. "Meaning what?"

"Well, what was the next phase of your little plan? Dupe me into a marriage proposal? Signing over all my property? The orchard? Did June give you a list?"

She takes a deep breath. "I don't know what's going on between your family and your neighbor, but trust me, I want nothing to do with it."

"I don't trust you," I say bluntly. "And I'm surprised June trusted you to pull this off. You don't lie well."

She looks nervous as hell. Shaky. But maybe that's just the hangover.

“Well,” she says, “you don’t seem to have the best judgment on that—”

“Clearly.”

“—because I’m not lying.”

“So, you’re telling me that your whole damsel-in-distress act wasn’t designed to manipulate me?”

She huffs out a laugh. “You have a very inflated sense of self-importance. I literally don’t know you from Adam. And there was no *act*.”

“Then everything you said to me was true?”

“I don’t know *what* I said. I was drunk!”

“You said your boyfriend dumped you, just days ago.”

She looks away. “So? He did.”

“So, you were just gonna use me for a rebound lay,” I press. “A casual hookup. Nothing else.”

She looks up into my eyes, hers flooding with resentment and . . . hurt. But that could be a lie, too.

“As you know,” she says coldly, “there was no ‘lay.’ But if I wanted to, yes. It would’ve been a rebound.”

My heart thuds dangerously. Anger and mistrust and something much more thrilling at war in my blood.

I swallow.

If I wasn’t so damn attracted to her, would this be easier? Would I be seeing whatever’s going on here more clearly?

Yes.

“You’d just have sex with a total stranger you met in a bar,” I press. “For no reason.”

“*You* were going to have sex with a total stranger you met in bar,” she snaps back, “when you thought I was with that bachelorette party, which means I’d be leaving town tomorrow. Double standard much?”

“I wasn’t planning to have sex with you.”

She laughs in disbelief. "You would have. If I didn't tell you to keep it in your pants."

"You were the one who tried to take it *out* of my pants." I scan her shocked expression. "Or did you forget that part?"

She did forget, maybe. Until right now, when I said it.

Now, I can feel her soft, warm hand wrapped around my cock, and wonder if she can feel it, too. Because last night, in bed, she put her hand right down my pants.

And now I'm getting fucking hard all over again.

"Get out of my way," she grits out.

I decide I need her gone. All the blood in my head is rushing south, anyway. I'm probably not thinking straight.

I push away from the door, clearing her way.

She grabs the doorknob but pauses, her green eyes spitting cold fire at me. "You know, I thought you were a gentleman. But all I learned from that is that I have a really broken asshole detector. So, thank you for the learning opportunity."

She leaves, and I still don't know what to believe.

It's just past sunset and I'm standing out in the bar parking lot, alone. Staring at Pier Seven across the intersection, lit up in the night. The door is propped open and pop music pulses out, impossibly bright in the evening air.

I'm pretty sure it's K-pop.

Hard to tell for sure with the Sabrina Carpenter singalong going on in the bar behind me. The bachelorette party is back.

Somehow, not nearly as entertaining without their ringleader.

Who I haven't stopped thinking about for a single moment of the damn day.

When Sierra Daniels walked into my bar yesterday, the very last fucking thing I was expecting was to meet, or like, someone new. But it's been a really fucking rough year. And maybe I let my guard down too fast.

Maybe that's what I'm most angry about.

That she made me start to feel something for the first time in fucking *years*.

Ever since my wedding day.

I haven't thought about it in so long because I don't want to. I don't need to.

But not only did Sierra make my heart race, make me *want* again in a way I hadn't thought I could, she made me fucking *remember* . . .

Everything that comes on the heels of that kind of wanting.

The heartbreak.

The days and weeks and fucking months of struggling to get over something that you were so sure about—but turned out to be so dead wrong about.

I will never, ever let myself make that mistake again.

The fact that I could feel so drawn to someone I just met and then be so spun around when she turned out *not* to be what I thought she was—all in less than twenty-four hours—has me shaken to the core.

I don't need this. I really don't need these fucking feelings coming at me faster than I can handle them, out of fucking nowhere.

But at least now I know: June Spencer plays fucking dirty. Grandpa tried to warn me, but now I've learned. The woman is not to be trusted.

Just because my parents trusted her doesn't mean they were right.

All it means is that they were conned.

I make my decision as I'm crossing the street, and I walk into Pier Seven without knocking.

Sierra is inside with her tattooed employee. Just the two of them, dancing their asses off and singing along to the incredibly loud music that is definitely some girly, hip-hop-infused K-pop, in the middle of Sierra's nauseatingly adorable pop-up shop. The walls of my family's former restaurant are now decked out in signage, neon lights, and temporary decals for Cutie Fruitie smoothies. Multicolored cartoon fruits smile at me from every direction.

But I barely notice any of it.

Unfortunately, when my eyes lock onto Sierra, my pulse races. Just like it did earlier, in my office, and every other time I've been near her.

It only gets worse when she looks at me. She notices me standing here and stops dead.

I can *taste* her. Feel her against my body. Last night, outside the bar. And in bed.

I can hear her laughter, feel her heart beating against my skin.

And I just need it to stop.

Her employee turns down the incredibly loud music as Sierra just stares at me.

Then she says, confused, "We're not open until Wednesday," as if I actually might've wandered in here for a smoothie.

I take a few more steps toward her, until we're standing close. Her eyes widen as she holds my gaze.

"You want me to believe," I say, heart pounding, starting to sweat for no reason but *her*, "that you didn't plan this whole scheme with June Spencer to fuck with me?"

She answers, "I really don't care what you believe, Mason." But her cheeks are flushed pink. She's breathing too hard.

"What I believe," I tell her, "is that you walked into my bar and tried to seduce me because June put you up to it."

She laughs softly, green eyes sparking with anger. "Then you are absolutely delusional."

But I can feel her defenses wavering. Either there's some truth to what I've said, or she's wondering if there is.

"You're telling me that June didn't put you up to it?"

"Put me up to *what*? I'm here to run my smoothie bar. That's all."

I take a deep breath, trying to reel in the electric current and the prickling heat and the fucking *want* that pours off me like warm maple syrup. I wonder if she feels it, too.

The way she stares at me like every hair on her body is standing on end suggests that she does.

"*No.*" It comes out of me like a cough, an allergic reaction. This can't be happening.

I can't be this stupid.

I can't *still* want this woman.

Sierra glances at her employee, then studies me, incredulous. "What do you mean, *no*?"

"I need you to leave," I growl.

Her employee steps forward and clears her throat. "Excuse me, but who made *you* the boss of Orchard Cove?"

I ignore her, focused only on Sierra. "How much will it cost me?"

She blinks at me, clearly stunned.

"I'll pay you," I tell her. "To pack up your little shop, immediately, and clear out of my town."

CHAPTER 8

SIERRA

"You're late." This is the first thing June Spencer says to me that evening, when I finally meet her.

After a long day setting up the smoothie bar, I was exhausted—and still reeling from my *three* run-ins with Mason—when Sophie and I arrived at the address June gave Soph this morning. The sign on the driveway said *Twisted Tree Orchard and Cider Co.*

June never mentioned that she owns an orchard and a cider company.

She told me that she owned a local farm, and a waterfront building at the town pier, and my only research into it centered around the pier building itself and Sunshine Fest.

Major oversight.

Pretty obvious now why June and the Grants don't like each other: they're direct competitors. Like, live-next-door-to-each-other-and-run-extremely-similar-businesses direct.

An obnoxiously flirtatious staffer who turned out to be June's nephew and orchard manager, Lee, finally located June for us after much searching, and now Sophie and I are trying to keep up with the older woman's strides as she leads us deeper into the property and around her cider tasting house—a different layout than the one owned by Mason's family but a similar vibe, right down to the abundant use of wood and flora and the "craft farmhouse" feel.

"I invited you here," June goes on crustily, "because you're a female entrepreneur with wonderful potential, kind of like a younger me. I wouldn't have if I knew you'd be late."

Soph and I exchange a look. *Is this me in forty years?*

I am *grouchy* as an old woman.

"Actually, I got here early. You'd mentioned in one of your emails that I could check in as early as this week. I texted you that I was coming yesterday afternoon."

"Well, I wasn't expecting you yesterday afternoon." June mutters something about bathing that I don't quite hear as we pass the guesthouse where that bachelorette party must be staying. It's super cute, and I can only imagine our cottage will be similar.

Final-fucking-ly, things are looking somewhat up.

"Excuse me?" I say. "I'm sorry, I missed that."

"I was forest bathing," she says, louder. "In the forest. No devices." As if this makes perfect sense.

I'm now unfortunately picturing the seventy-six-year-old woman in front of me naked in a wooden bathtub in the forest, and pretty sure I have no idea what "forest bathing" actually is.

Before I can decide whether to ask for clarification or not, she says, "Where did you stay last night? There isn't a vacancy in town."

"Uh, I was fortunate enough to meet the owner of Sea Haven Bar and Grill," I manage to say without making a face. "Mason. He and his friends showed me some hospitality. So, it worked out okay."

June snorts with derision and mutters, "I'm sure they did. Those swinging dicks think they run this town."

So . . . the hostility goes both ways.

"Uh, speaking of which," I venture. "There seems to be some kind of confusion. Mason seems to think that he was going to lease Pier Seven for a pop-up of his own this month. Is that true?"

She frowns deeply. "Of course not. You have exclusive use of the space. It's in your lease agreement."

"Right. That's what I thought. Mason just seems really . . . unhappy that we're here."

She makes a *hmph* sound. "I'm sure he is. But whatever claim on Pier Seven any member of the Grant family might think they have—I can assure you, they do not."

"Okay . . ."

June eyes me sidelong. "You're a smart young woman with a nice little business. And ideas. And *grit*. I saw that as soon as I met you last year."

Really? I thought all she saw was my "curious branding" and "is that the actual menu?" menu. She seemed to think my entire business model was a gimmick. I was stunned when she invited me to run my pop-up in her town. I'd never heard of Sunshine Fest, but once I looked it up, it seemed like a brilliant opportunity to have a summer getaway with Kyle. Go glamping. Take long walks on the beach. Rekindle our love.

Now, it seems like a terrible joke—that this woman might actually be my biggest supporter right now.

"So," she concludes, "take it from an old woman who's learned to *mind* her own business over the years. You ladies would do best to focus on *your* own business while you're in Orchard Cove." She stops abruptly and I almost bump into her. She fixes me with her pale-gray eyes. "And stay away from Tommy Grant, his grandsons, and their assorted associates."

I exchange a look with Sophie. "Yeah. That won't be a problem."

We continue onward, past some farm buildings and work sheds, Sophie and I hauling our luggage along the gravel path that is just a bit too rocky to use the wheels on our suitcases. We circle a rambling, gorgeous, old yellow farmhouse, tall and proud, with intricate gardens wound around it. June's home, I imagine.

Then we come to a stop. The path has led us past the landscaped backyard toward an entanglement of trees, through which I can see a decrepit shack.

"Here we are," June says.

"Here . . . ?"

"Your lodging. That was part of our deal." She eyes me with disappointment, like: *You should really have read that lease agreement.* "I'm providing you with lodging at my cozy cottage."

"Yes, I know," I say.

"So, you ladies just let me, or Lee, know if you need anything." I feel her steely gaze on me, judging. "Are you alright, Sara? You look a bit ill."

"Uh . . . it's Sierra."

Sophie loops an arm through mine. "She enjoyed a little too much of the local cider last night."

I definitely did. But that's not why I look like this right now. "Cozy" my ass. The so-called cottage looks more like a glorified outhouse than that dreamy retreat Mason's brother has next door.

"Well, go get her some water, Sophia," June says pragmatically, pressing a key on a keychain with a wooden apple on it into Sophie's hand.

"Sophie," she corrects her.

I wonder if she flubbed my name *and* Sophie's on purpose. June is already striding away. She's rather spry for a septuagenarian. Wiry and athletic in her gardening smock. I'm still panting from trying to keep up with her.

She turns around just before she's out of earshot, silvery bob blowing in the breeze. "And don't worry about the bucket!" she calls. "We're not expecting any rain." Then she's gone around a bend in the path.

Sophie looks as confused/apprehensive as I feel. "Bucket?"

We approach the cottage warily. The weather-beaten wood, desperately in need of repair. The faded old curtains in the dirty windows. The sadly sagging porch. The unwelcoming piles of farm junk on either side of the door.

An old, hand-carved sign mounted over the door, somewhat crooked, says *Cozy Cottage*.

"Really," I say flatly.

"It might have *once* been cozy," Sophie says optimistically.

"Fifty years ago."

"Come on. Don't we love old things?" She works the key in the lock, which at least seems to have been installed this century.

"Sure. Like, retro-old. Vintage vibes. Not falling apart and moldering."

When we step inside, unfortunately it just gets worse.

The windows, left to gather dirt on the outside glass for years, let in little light. When I find the light switch and turn it on, it doesn't help much. The cottage is gloomy, barely furnished, and tight.

"Well, there's the aforementioned bucket." It's a steel pail, sitting in the middle of the kitchen floor. Above it, obvious water damage stains the ceiling and the drywall has a hole in it.

"At least they're being proactive?" Sophie says.

"Proactive would be burning this place down."

"It did look better in the pictures . . ." she admits.

"Yeah. I think those were as old as the cottage. It looks like it hasn't been touched since the 1970s, and not in a good way."

"It's not that bad. It's just . . . rustic."

"I know," I say in horror. "I don't do rustic, Soph."

"Me neither, but we'll figure it out. Do you think there's internet?"

"Jesus Christ. I didn't even think to ask. I'm now realizing that I may be much less intelligent than I took myself for." I blink at her. "Is this my fault? Is the universe punishing me?"

"Don't be silly."

I follow her to the bedroom area. It's not far. There's no hallway, just a couple of doors off the kitchen/living room. There are two bedrooms, as promised, but they're so tiny, each fits only a twin bed and a wooden chair.

And there's one very small bathroom with a tiny shower cubicle, toilet, and a sink with no space for the amount of hair products Soph uses.

"Shit. I'm so sorry I'm crashing your space," I tell her. June offered me this cottage as lodging for any staff I brought with me, which meant Sophie was supposed to have it all to herself. Kyle and I were going to be staying at the Vance Oceanfront resort, half an hour up the highway—one of the most luxurious resorts on the island, and the lodging of his choosing, which he was paying for. "I'd take us to a hotel, but I really can't afford it, and no way would I let you pay for even a fraction of it."

"It's fine. I'm totally happy here," she says. "I got you." She starts singing the Jack Johnson song.

I groan. "I seriously don't deserve you. I'm taking the smaller room." I haul my bags into the bedroom that is somehow even tinier than the other, leaving her to the one in back with the bigger window.

I can make anywhere home with Sophie, right?

Even this dump.

She pops her head in as I drop my duffel bag and suitcase on the bed.

"You're not actually going to unpack *right now*," she says. "It's Saturday night! Let's have girl talk and do our nails. You need to chill, babe." She perches on the corner of the bed as I unzip my suitcase open and lay it flat.

"I know, but you know I can't sit still when I'm stressed."

"But I think sometimes you need to. You'll burn out."

She watches as I start putting clothes away in the minuscule closet and search the corners for evidence of moths and rodents. Thankfully, I find none.

"You've gotta process what happened," she says.

"How?"

"By feeling all the feelings, sitting with them, building some tolerance for dealing with them." Sophie's into things like therapy and feelings in a way that I can't comprehend. Paying someone to let me emote at them? *No.* "That's how you build resilience. Then you do your best to let them go. If they come back up, you do it again. If you just stuff them away without examining them, you'll get angry."

"I'm already angry."

"See?" She tosses a pair of balled-up socks at me. "So, tell me. What exactly did Kyle say when you talked to him today?"

Yeah. So that happened.

As soon as I got my phone—and my coffee mug—back from Mason's bartender, I had a very tense conversation with Kyle. I wasn't planning to talk to him yet, but he called almost as soon as I turned on the ringer, while I was still in the bar. Mason had retreated into his office and shut the door, I was still reeling from our conversation, and I really wasn't thinking straight when I answered.

"Honestly, he was petty as hell. I think he's still mad but trying to pretend he's not because he's so above it. He said he was calling because he 'wants his vinyl back.'"

"Just like the Gotye song," she says sadly, like, *Can't he even be original?* "Next he'll be changing his number."

"One can only hope. He said he'd have a 'friend' come get his records. Can you imagine if he sent *her*?"

"Even Kyle can't be *that* out of touch."

"Can't he, though?" I give her a look. "I think he was taking my temperature. Like, making sure I wasn't gonna do anything dramatic. You know, show up at his house and make a scene in front of the neighbors. Dump the dirty laundry he left at my place on his lawn. I don't think he even remembered I'm out of town. Which is extra special since the whole reason I came here was to spend time with him. I guess he's already wiped clean any memory of our lives and future plans together."

"Babe, I'm sorry. He's a dick. I don't know what else to say."

"Yeah. It's pretty clear with every condescending word he breathes that he blames me for everything. Including losing the investment because I don't actually deserve it. And ending up single because I just don't have my shit together."

"So, basically the worst things you fear about yourself," my best friend points out.

Which is when all the emotional buildup from this whole terrible week threatens to bust down the floodgates and I *almost* burst into tears. I bury my face in a T-shirt and try to scrape myself together.

"Oh, Si. I didn't mean to almost make you cry. I know you hate crying."

"You didn't. Life did." I take a deep breath, blink away the unshed tears, and hang up the shirt. "*He* did." In the back of my mind, I wonder if I'm really talking about Kyle, or . . . Mason.

A man I just met.

How gross, that I could let him make me feel this shitty about myself.

And also, where did my internal man picker go so fucking wrong over the years?

I need you to leave.

I can still hear his voice, see the look on his face, jaw set and blue eyes burning with determination as he said those words to me.

"You're just . . . in a slump," Sophie says kindly.

Yeah. It feels like that hell-crack I plummeted into has some wicked gravity.

After I got off the call with Kyle and left the bar, I lost the bar's Wi-Fi signal and therefore the ability to make phone calls, but I could still see all the messages and missed calls that had piled up on my phone. I borrowed Sophie's phone (which works just perfectly) to call everyone who deserved a call back, so they don't have to worry about me.

Each call just made me feel progressively worse.

Mom's super worried about me ("I wish you would just find a nice man and settle down, like Kim") and doesn't understand why I would "make a video like that" anyway. I had to explain to her that I didn't make it, but yes, the dildo was real. I'm not sure that made it better.

My stepsister suddenly decided to tell me she "never liked Kyle" but hadn't wanted to tell me while we were together and "make it worse," because she was sympathetic to the fact that "not every woman has a man as wonderful as my husband."

I know Kim really *meant* that as sympathy, but I almost hurled Soph's phone right into the sea after that one.

Kyle's mom, who I probably shouldn't have bothered calling back at all, told me how sorry she was that she could no longer invest in my business, and could I please return the wine glasses she loaned to me?

Of course I'd return her wine glasses. She made it sound like I was trying to steal them.

"Let's call this whole thing what it is," I say. "It's an all-time low. I need *something* to improve here. But it just keeps getting worse." As if on some cosmic cue system, the overhead light in the kitchen flickers out.

Sophie and I blink at each other.

"See?"

"I will talk to June about that tomorrow," she says. "And about the lodging situation, if you're not happy."

"It's fine." I look around, trying to see things through the rose-colored glasses my bestie perpetually wears. "It's clean," I relent. "And safe. The lock seems solid."

"And the orchard is pretty," she says, jumping on the optimism train, her specialty. "That Lee guy is nice. He *really* liked your boobs."

I groan.

"And there's a gift basket in the kitchen." She pulls me from the bedroom to the tiny kitchen/living room and plunks us down on the couch. She starts digging through the basket, unpacking. "I know you don't want to be here. But let's make the best of it?" She holds out a homemade-looking cookie.

I take it with a sigh. "The truth is, I don't really want to go home, either. Orchard Cove is the rock and home is the hard place. And all I know is I feel unwelcome in both right now. Also, if I've learned anything today, it's that seagulls are assholes." One did actually shit on me while Soph and I were on the pier, having lunch we picked up at the little grocery store. Would've loved to have eaten a real, cooked meal at the bar and grill, but fuck that. "So, no, maybe I don't want to be here." I eat the cookie in one go. It's stupidly delicious. "But the things Kyle said today, Soph . . . I can't help thinking he's right. I've made a mess of my business and my life. Objectively, I'm a failure."

"Sierra. My god. There is no objectivity in that man's judgment. Or love. Someone who loves you doesn't use the things that hurt you the most to intentionally hurt you *more*."

I know she's right, because if anyone knows what true love is, it's Sophie. Her husband adores her and treats her like his queen, his best friend, his partner in every way. And she's not low-key boasty about it like my stepsister is. Soph is incredibly qualified to coach me through the aftermath of this breakup.

I take another cookie and stuff my face.

"True facts. If it weren't for you and Pete," I tell her, "I'd have given up on the fantasy of ever having a successful relationship fucking years ago. The two of you give me hope, even when I'd like to drop-kick whatever hope for a happy ending I'm still naively holding onto into the nearest toilet and flush. I'd already be deep into my 'she seems to be collecting an alarming number of cats' phase without you."

"Pfft. You're allergic to cats," Sophie says easily, blowing that off. As if I'm not one hundred percent serious.

"There are days when I truly think suffocating on cat dander would be better than living with a man."

"But you've never actually lived with a man," she points out, which is sadly true. "You can't write off all future men based on a few bad apples from your past. I've told you before, and I'll tell you again: Kyle put his family before you. He put his career before you. He put his precious house before you by refusing to move in together. He even put his *female best friend* before you, on many occasions. A man who loves you won't make you second-choice. And he certainly won't make you tenth. That man put his *car* before you, Si. He put his freaking *hair* before you—"

"I see we've reached the 'I told you so' portion of the evening."

Sophie blinks at me innocently. "Only because you asked for it. And here's that cider you requested. Consider yourself punished." She pops open a giant can of cider from the gift basket and puts it in my hand. "Now, tell me where it really hurts."

I sigh. Leave it to Sophie to see right through all my anger and frustration—and "let's get this shit done" attitude today as we set up the smoothie bar—to the truth.

That I'm fucking hurt.

"It's just . . ." I groan. "You know I don't do well with rejection. Because Mommy picked the perfect, shiny stepsister over me, and Daddy picked an entirely new family over me. This whole thing just pokes a stick into my festering mommy *and* daddy issues."

"What whole thing, exactly?" Soph prods gently. "The breakup?"

I take a look at the cider can in my hand. *Twisted Tree Cider Co.*, it says—*Bramble Berry Cider*, with a twisted-tree logo. June's cider. I take a tentative sip, treating my tongue to a refreshing blend of sweet blackberry and crisp, tart apple. Unfortunately, it's as delicious as Mason's cider.

I wonder how he feels about that.

"What Mason said to me tonight," I admit in a small voice. "Offering to *pay me* to leave town. That hurt. But it shouldn't."

"Why not? You liked him."

"But he's not Kyle. I didn't give him three years of my life. He doesn't know me well enough to know *how* to hurt me purposefully. And he definitely doesn't owe me anything."

"And it still hurts. That's fair. You were into him."

"Yeah. *Ugh.* I forgot to thank you for not even batting an eye at his hotness. His ego clearly doesn't need it."

She shrugs. "All in a day's work." And it is. For her. Not only is she happily married, she and Pete work as merchandise managers for Dirty, the hottest rock band to ever come out of Vancouver, so she's constantly surrounded by beautiful VIPs, both male and female. Which means Mason and all his hot "swinging dick" friends are not going to faze her.

Me, I'm just a regular girl. And sure, I've met some VIPs, in passing, whenever Sophie's dragged me to some party that's filled with them, but that is so not my scene. I'm way too socially awkward for high-level mingling—unless I'm sucking back shooters or something. And I'm too much of a music fanatic to be chill around a rock star.

Mason, I thought I might actually be able to handle. We had a vibe. He even claimed to love music, just like I do. We made each other laugh.

But now that he apparently hates me? *Shit.*

"I am really gonna need your help thinking straight in the face of that fuck-hot bar owner," I warn her. I'm so fucking grateful she was able to come here with me for a few weeks while the band is on a break in their current world tour. What would I do without her now? "Beard *and* dimples? Fuck me."

"I'm here for you, babe," she says solemnly.

"I just don't understand his extreme change in attitude toward me. Even with the Pier Seven thing. Last night felt . . . magical. But maybe it was only me who felt that way."

"You *were* incredibly drunk. Maybe he just isn't as much of a teddy bear as you thought?"

"Yeah. Maybe. Today he sure turned into a raging grizzly. And he seemed to believe, so easily, that I'm in league with the devil."

"Maybe you are," Sophie jokes. "You may be right about June. Though I'm getting more of a 'forest witch' vibe than Lucifer."

"Maybe so. Or maybe she just lives with too many cats. Maybe one too many men screwed her over, and she went crotchety old lady?"

"Interesting theory."

"On the other hand, Mason is, what? Mid-thirties? Hot, presumably wealthy, owns property and businesses, has every reason to be loving life. And he was cold as hell today. Mean, hurtful, downright rude. He made it grossly clear that he wants me gone."

"He wants the smoothie bar gone," Sophie corrects me. "Maybe it wasn't as personal as it felt."

"Maybe. And maybe there's no financial reason to be here if he'll pay me for the lease and lost income, and I call it a day."

Sophie looks worried. "Do you really want to do that, though?"

I groan. "I don't know."

At this point, I don't know if there would be a point in leaving, when I really have nothing to go back to.

◆ ◆ ◆

Whoever actually puts *I love long walks on the beach* on their dating profile is a fucking psycho. Or has never actually walked on a beach. Or has no feeling on the bottoms of their feet.

Or maybe just hasn't walked on a beach on the Canadian West Coast.

Early on Monday morning, after a terrible, restless sleep, I make the mistake of heading down to the beach at the end of Honeymoon Lane with my yoga towel. I actually check my delicate city-person soles several times for cuts as I stagger painfully over the sharp shards of hell dust that I guess we're calling sand.

I brush it off my feet and put my shoes back on, but there's still so much sand on my skin, now it feels like I'm wearing sandpaper socks.

I pick a spot and roll out my yoga towel, kicking off my shoes again. But it feels like I'm doing my morning sun salutations on rough concrete. The seagulls cry in the distance, probably harassing people walking on the pier and dive-bombing them for food, and it's weirdly hard to concentrate.

I finally give up and sit in a simple cross-legged Sukhasana. I pop my earbuds in and listen to "Somebody That I Used to Know" and just breathe. But it's too sad, so I pluck Gotye out of my ears and close my eyes.

Unfortunately, I'm still sad about the breakup. Mostly, I'm sad about the years I wasted with, apparently, a man who was all wrong for me.

I'm angry at Kyle for diving into his best friend's arms so fast. I'm angry at Mason for trying to evict me from Orchard Cove. I'm angry at my stepsister for telling me on our weekly Sunday-night phone call yesterday that I "really could've seen this coming," and for being so right about Kyle, and especially for having all her shit so perfectly together, as always, while mine is perpetually falling apart.

And I'm angry at myself, for putting myself in a position to get dumped by someone I should've broken up with long ago, for struggling in my business, and for generally fucking failing at life, *still.* At thirty years old. When I really thought I'd have some of it figured out by now.

"Fuck," I curse into the wind.

I try to focus on the gentle sound of the waves and the breeze in the trees. But I'm too sad. And angry. And creepily on guard. I've seen this on influencers' travel pics, but is this supposed to be calming? An axe murderer could sneak right up on me. There's, like, no one out here but me.

I knew it.

Nature is overrated.

A tinkling sound startles me. My eyes fly open as a golden retriever trots up to me, collar tinkling and tail wagging. His tongue lolls out the side of a lopsided doggy smile.

"Hey, you." I reach out to greet the friendly dog, letting him sniff my hand, then petting his soft head. I find myself smiling for the first time today, and I look up as the dog's owner approaches.

I yank back from the dog as if it bit me, and it happily turns to sniffing my shoes.

Mason Grant is walking toward me, blue eyes leveled at me, the dog's leash dangling from his hand. He wears a scrap of a shirt that I guess you would call a tank top, his muscular shoulders, tattooed arms, and the outer curves of his pecs on spectacular display in the morning sunshine. I even glimpse an exposed, dark-pinkish nipple as the thin fabric flutters in the breeze.

My entire body flushes hot. I feel like the girls in the *KPop Demon Hunters* movie when the ripped dude in the boy band flashes his abs, and popcorn shoots out of their eyes.

I try to scrape my eyeballs back into their sockets as I get to my feet, angrier than I already was. But his loose shorts cling to his muscular thighs, the aforementioned breeze making the long *and* girthy package in front impossible not to notice. The fabric is practically translucent.

It's obscene.

Of course this man has an incredible cock, because the universe is an unfair place. And yes, I remember vividly how it felt in my hand. Warm. Smooth. Pulsating, and hard as rock.

Haven't been able to stop thinking about it, ever since he so kindly reminded me that I shoved my hand down his pants and grabbed it, somehow awakening the memory with extreme sensory detail.

But come on. Did he put on the thinnest shorts in the world, *without underwear*, because he knew I was here?

Who is actually trying to seduce who here?

I scowl as he comes too close for comfort. As in, where I can see his bare nipple clearly.

Did he see me come down here? Has he been *watching* me?

"Scar," he calls to the dog. "Come here." He stands there, his gaze roaming over my yoga outfit, and I wonder if *my* nipples are showing through my sports bra. The breeze is kind of cool.

I hug myself as my eyes scramble for something unsexy to fixate on. The dog.

"Your adorable golden retriever is named Scar?" I say incredulously.

"My brother's dog," he corrects me with a frown. "It's short for Scaramouche. It's from—"

"'Bohemian Rhapsody,'" I say blandly. "I guess you didn't believe me that I know all the songs." But why would he? I am a liar, according to him.

"You didn't seem to know 'Hotel California,'" he points out, deadpan.

Damn. Didn't I? Grandpa Alex *loved* that album. "I do. I was just drunk." I change the subject. "What are you doing here? Lemme guess. Here to draw a line in the sand? What is it this time? You want me to stay away from your barber, your mechanic, and your kindergarten teacher? Anyone else you wanna add to the list?"

His eyebrows pinch together. "I'm just walking a dog. It's a public beach. And I live . . . right there." He nods toward his family's expansive property above the beach. We're standing right in front of it.

I thought I'd walked straight down from Honeymoon Lane. I didn't realize I'd drifted over this way.

"So? If you don't mind, your dog interrupted my mindfulness practice." What there was of it. The only thing I was really mindful of was that I really *don't* want to be here, but I think I might *need* to be.

If for no other reason than I can't bear to fail at one more fucking thing right now. And I have a specific sales number I need to hit this month, or my business is for sure going belly-up.

"He didn't seem to bother you," he says, but puts the dog on the leash and draws him in to heel. Scar sits patiently at Mason's feet as Mason stares me down. "You're not at the pier," he says accusingly.

Why is this guy always accusing me of shit? And what is he accusing me of now?

"It's early."

"So, you're all set up for your grand opening on Wednesday?"

"Will be."

He looks away, out over the water, and my eyes rake over him from the cords in his manly neck to his attractive toes. The man even has nice feet. His chest rises and falls in a slow, deep breath. He looks tense all over.

Exactly how I feel.

I meet his eyes when he turns to me again. "Have you given some thought to my offer?"

I snort. "Was that what it was? Felt more like an order."

"It was a legitimate offer. Name your price, within reason. And I'll pay it."

Yeah. That's what he said the other night before I basically laughed in his face, and Sophie politely asked him to get out of my shop or she'd call some of her biker friends to come down and remove him. (Yes, sweet, squishy Sophie knows bikers.)

"Oh, I thought about your 'legitimate offer.' Kinda hard to forget."

"And?"

"And I think I'll have to legitimately decline."

"Much easier if you back out now, before the shop opens."

"And why would I want to do that?"

"Because then you won't have to deal with me anymore."

We stare at each other as my hormones flip out at the thought of *dealing with him*. Over and over. Naked. For some reason, my sex parts seem to think he's flirting with me again.

I never realized before that they're so fucking stupid.

"But dealing with you is *so* enjoyable, Mason," I say, hoping to put across with my scathing sarcasm: *You know what? Fuck you for being so hot, affectionate, duplicitous, and completely despicable.*

"You're making a huge mistake, Sierra," he says in a low voice. I can't quite tell if he's pissed or legit trying to warn me, like he thinks he's doing me a favor.

It definitely sounds like a threat. But I don't feel threatened. Just outraged.

"Maybe you're making a mistake," I retort. "I'm feisty."

I could swear a glimmer of surprise, or maybe even amusement, alights in his eyes, but it's quickly snuffed out with a frown. "You're going to regret your stubbornness on this."

"Uh-huh. You too, I'm sure." I'm not sure, but I'm fucking mad.

"You really think coming into town and making enemies is a smart move?"

"You tell me. You seem to have some enemies yourself."

His full lips tighten into a hard line. Oh, he didn't like that. Because now he's wondering if June has said something about him. Or if I know how much she hates him, his entire family, and his "assorted associates."

"I guess this is war, then," he says flatly.

"Yeah. Let the best woman win."

He grunts. He holds my gaze for a long moment, like, *You sure this is what you want?*

I'm not sure. But I'm definitely not going to stop defending myself against his ridiculous accusations or asserting my right to be here.

That, and I'm competitive as hell. And this guy thinking he can just drive me out is lighting a fire under my need to win.

It has been way, way too long since I just had a fucking win.

"Come on, Scar." He turns, giving me a sudden, unneeded view of his broad back and tight, mouthwatering ass as he walks away.

He turns back once, catching me staring. "Good luck staying on June's good side," he says ominously.

"Whatever!" I call out to his back as he leads the dog away. "June likes me!"

He chuckles, but doesn't look back.

CHAPTER 9

Sierra

"What an incredible day!" Sophie turns up the music. "People really showed up for us."

"I know. Where did they all come from, right?"

It's early evening at the smoothie bar and our last customers have just left, happily slurping smoothies. Sophie dance-wipes the equipment down as she does at the end of every shift whenever she joins me at my pop-ups.

I'm feeling effer-fucking-vescent as we tidy up.

Sure, my life back in the city is in ruins. And my new small-town life, temporary as it is, has been made shittier by one particularly maddening local. But I have Cutie Fruitie, a small business I built myself from the ground up, and no one can take that from me.

No one. Not even a rude, entitled, grossly overstepping, and infuriatingly attractive lumberjack-looking bar owner.

Here in my shop, no matter where it pops up, I'm in slay mode. I'm at my best. Doing what makes me happiest. Which is making super-fun, nutrient-dense, *and* delicious smoothies that put a smile on my customers' faces.

And if our grand opening day here has been any indication, we're a hit in Orchard Cove. As it turns out, things here—other than Mason—are truly looking up for me.

"I have to give it to the forest witch," I muse. "She was smart, inviting me here. I know tourism is supposed to really pick up for the summer season this week, but a lot of the customers I served weren't even tourists."

"It didn't hurt that it was pretty warm out today, too," Soph points out. "And maybe opening day, locals are curious? I wonder if it'll be dead now until the weekend."

"I hope not."

"It does seem like there's been a lot of gossip that Mason doesn't want us here, though . . ." she ventures.

"So far, maybe that's been good for us?"

"Which means they're either super supportive of him and just getting eyes on us, super against him, or just plain thirsty and bored out of their fucking trees from living in a small town too long?"

"Let's hope it's the latter and not the 'super supportive of him' thing. I will not let that man interfere with my business. If he shit-talks me around town, we will have words." I saw Mason today, when I popped out on my lunch break, arriving at the bar in his Sea Haven-branded truck. I don't know if he saw me and I did not go talk to him.

But I will, if he gets in my way.

I step out from behind the counter to go flip the *Closed* sign when the door suddenly opens—and in walks Mason's brother, Layne. With his daughter.

I stop in my tracks and backtrack around the counter as Layne says, "Hey, Sierra. Are you closing?"

"No worries," Sophie says, when I just stutter out a hello. "You're just in time. What can we get you?"

Kaylie looks around the shop with delight. "Ice Cream" pumps over our portable sound system as they approach the counter, which is actually a bar. The guts of a former restaurant remain in Pier Seven and my pop-up barely uses a quarter of the space, but Sophie and I have done our best to Cutie-Fruitify it, as we like to call it, with fairy lights and colorful signage and music. Kaylie's eyes zip like pinballs from the *SLAY ALL DAY* neon sign to the stacks of multicolored smoothie cups to the rainbow balloon arch.

"This place is *so* girly-pop!" she cries.

I'm struggling to scrape myself together as thoughts whirl around my head like fruit in a blender. Is Mason about to come storming through the door? Does he even know his family's here? Is this some cruel test?

But when Layne smiles at me, a warm, friendly smile, I remember that he's miles nicer than his brother. And anyway, why would he bring his daughter with him if he was here to do something hideously arrogant like offer me money to leave town?

So, I greet her like I would any ten-year-old VIP whose uncle is not an outrageous d-bag. "Hey, Kaylie! That dress is fire. You win best outfit of the day." I hand her a lollipop.

Her eyes almost pop out of her head. "Really?!"

"By miles," Sophie concurs.

"But maybe save that for tomorrow," I suggest. "After lunch. If you're here for a smoothie. We don't want *too much* sugar all at once."

"Okay." She hands the lollipop to her dad. "We never have anything this fun here!" she declares.

"Then good thing we came to town, huh?" I meet Layne's eyes. "Layne. I think I met your dog the other day. Scaramouche?"

"You met Scar?" Kaylie says.

"Yup." I lean on the counter on my elbows so Kaylie and I are more eye to eye. "You let your dad name your dog after a lyric in a Queen song?"

She rolls her eyes. "I know, right? So old-school. Why were they even called Queen if they were all boys?"

Oh, my. Sidestepping that one quick.

"So, tell me, who's the bigger music fan, your dad or your uncle?" Not that I care about her uncle. Just making conversation here.

"Hmm. They both listen to music a lot, but I'd have to say my dad because he plays guitar."

"Impressive," I say mildly, feeling oddly victorious that Mason lost that little competition.

"But I listen to the *best* music," she asserts.

"I'm sure you do. Who are your top five?"

"Sabrina Carpenter, Olivia Rodrigo, Tate McRae, Taylor Swift," she rattles off immediately. "Girls are slay, obviously. But Benson Boone is cool, too."

"All excellent choices." I look up at her dad, who's checking out the menu on the wall above. "Do you guys know what you want? Or would you like some help deciding?" *And can we please get this over with so you can leave before Mason hears through the local gossip chain that you came in here, and I get blamed for it?*

"What do you recommend?" he asks.

"Hmm. Do you like raspberries, Kaylie? And strawberries, et cetera?"

"Yes."

"Given your appreciation of female pop stars, it's a Britney Spears-inspired Berry Baby One More Time for you." I hear Sophie already making it behind me. "Would you like a poof of cotton candy on top?"

Kaylie bounces on her toes. "Yes!"

"And for you . . ." I give her dad a narrow-eyed appraisal, making her giggle. "You get a Good Day Sunshine."

"Sounds good," he says, amused.

"Is that a song, too?" Kaylie asks, delighted.

"There's a song and a smoothie for everyone," I say sagely as I tap the order into my tablet.

Sophie hands me Kaylie's smoothie, then goes to make Layne's. I place the cotton candy on top with a pair of tongs, then pass it to Kaylie. "Did you see the rainbow? We have a nice little selfie moment, over there."

She immediately asks her dad if she can borrow his phone, and when he hands it over, she zooms over to the Cutie Fruitie-branded selfie wall, the rainbow balloon arch with a purple-grape balloon cloud on one end.

"It's on the house," I tell Layne when he tries to pay. I lean on the counter between us and when I'm sure his daughter isn't hearing this, add, "Consider it a keeping-the-peace offering between us mortal enemies. I wouldn't want anyone to draw blood in front of your lovely tweenager."

I'm not sure which part of what I just said surprises him most, but he's definitely taken aback. "Well, thank you. But are we mortal enemies? I didn't realize."

"I guess your brother didn't inform you."

"Of what?"

"That he ordered me to stay away from his family. You'll excuse me if I don't come out from behind this counter. I wouldn't want him to glimpse us fraternizing and incite a riot."

Layne's lips quirk. Maybe he thinks I'm kidding. "And why does my brother think you're his *enemy*?" He says this like it's as ridiculous as it is.

I hand over his smoothie when Sophie brings it over, and Sophie makes herself scarce, cleaning up. "Oh, he was very clear,"

I say. "I'm not welcome here. I should go back where I came from like a good little city girl. I stole his precious building out from under him, yada yada."

Layne's eyebrow creeps up. "I see. Well, Mason can be . . . a little . . ."

"Pig-headed?" I fill in, as he seems to be grappling for the right adjectives to somehow excuse his brother's deplorable social skills while not totally throwing him under the bus. "Ridiculously objectionable? Outrageously wrong?"

"Sure," he says carefully. "As most of us are from time to time? But if he's reacting so strongly to your . . . presence . . ." His gaze drifts over me thoughtfully and he lowers his voice. "Maybe he's just not used to being so . . . challenged."

I get the feeling from his tone that he thinks the particular "challenge" I present his brother is not simply of the business-rivalry variety.

Is he under the delusion that his brother actually *likes* me? This poor, sweet, misguided man. He's so nice, the sunshine he naturally exudes seems to be blinding him to his brother's unbridled assholery. How unfortunate.

I guess love really is blind.

I open my mouth to point this out as delicately as I can (not very) but am interrupted (perhaps fortunately) by the return of Kaylie. She's already eaten the cotton candy and inhaled half her smoothie, and her eyes are bright with the sugar high.

"When are you coming over again?" she asks me.

"Oh. Uh. Sometime. Maybe. The shop keeps me pretty busy." *And your uncle might shoot me on sight, so.*

"Oh." She seems disappointed. "Uncle Mason keeps talking about you."

WHAT.

"Ah, she means, only nice things, of course," Layne says awkwardly, draping an arm around his daughter's shoulders and tucking her into his armpit. She whispers something to him, and he shakes his head at her: *No*.

And out of nowhere, I remember it. Again. My hand, reaching down into the heat of Mason's jeans. The delight of finding his thick cock hard and ready, and wrapping my hand around it, squeezing, feeling him throb in response.

I knew I was being a tease. I told him *no*.

No kissing. No sex.

And now I remember his words, raspy with pleasure and the pain of holding back. Of resisting me.

You're making this so hard for me.

That's what he said.

I realize as my jaw drops open and my salivary glands engage that I am desperately, aggravatingly thirsty for Mason Grant's secrets.

And what he's been saying about me in front of his niece.

However, Layne is *right there*, so instead of asking any follow-ups, I smash a couple of strawberry-shaped stamps on a buy-ten-smoothies-and-get-one-free card and thrust it at Kaylie. I force my best customer-service smile and send them off with a bright "Great to see you! Have a wonderful night!"

"Thank you!" Kaylie calls out as her dad takes the hint and guides her out of the shop.

"See you, Sierra," he says, as I busy myself wiping down the counter in front of me.

Sophie flips the sign to *Closed* behind them and locks the door.

"Are you kidding me?" I semi-shout at her. "Did you hear that?"

"Yeah. What a great kid."

"Not *that*. The part about how Mason keeps talking about me."

"But we already knew that, right? He's probably telling everyone he sees to boycott us."

"In front of his niece? That doesn't sound like what she meant." But what *did* she mean? She seemed to think I might come over to their house again.

"You've been polishing that spot on the counter for a very long time," Sophie says a moment later. "Just so you know."

"No, I haven't."

"I think you may be reading into things, hon." She lowers her voice to a whisper. "Because you have a crush on the enemy."

I toss my rag at her. "Stop."

When we lock up for the night and leave, Mason is in the bar parking lot with his friends Jace and . . . Ethan? I can't remember his name. The other hot one, who looks like he should be in the military: muscles, commanding air, tight-cropped hair. Jace straddles a motorcycle, a big, black Harley, and they're gathered around it, talking loudly, laughing.

Mason looks right over at me—and stops smiling.

"Okay, I've seen his brother," Soph mutters to me. "And those are his friends? Shiiit. Is there something in the water around here?"

"I know. I think it's the cider," I mutter back as we climb into my van and get the hell out of there.

"I wouldn't call it a crush, per se." I'm standing on the back porch of the Cozy Cottage, smoking weed with my best friend that she procured from some random farmhand because Sophie Moore is resourceful like that.

She breathes out a plume of smoke and smirks at me. "Then what would you prefer we call it?"

I gaze past the thicket of trees that surround most of the cottage. The back porch is the best thing about the cottage, really. From here, there's a clear view of row upon row of apple trees. June's, and beyond, the ones that belong to the Grant family next door.

And beyond those, the water, where dark humps of land, the Southern Gulf Islands and the Saanich Peninsula, look like sea creatures slumbering in the dusk.

The sun is going down and it's a real bummer inside the dank little cottage after dark. Plus, I saw two spiders in there last night. I need to spring for some new lamps at a yard sale or something. And maybe inspect every inch of the walls, floor, and ceiling for cracks. I can't room with spiders.

I take a drag from what's left of the joint and try to explain my fucked-up feelings toward Mason Grant. "It's more of a lust situation. I would do him, *if* he had the completely same body but an entirely different personality."

Sophie considers this seriously. "Whose personality?"

I think on that long and hard as if it *is* serious business—because *weed*—and finally say, "King Kong."

My best friend cackles. "What the hell, Si?"

I shrug. "He knows what he wants. He literally, like, climbed the Empire State Building for her."

"I'm not sure you've actually seen any of the movies . . ."

"And I don't mind a big, burly grump. As long as he'd move mountains for *me*."

"This is disturbing information. How are you even gonna fuck with a giant—"

"Good evening, ladies."

I startle, fumbling and dropping the last of our joint, burning myself in the process. I yelp and Sophie stomps the embers out, waving a hand in the air to disperse the weed smell. "Oh, hey, June. Mosquitos," she bullshits.

June looks skeptical. Of course, she was, what, a teenager in the 1960s? She probably smells what's up. It's not even illegal anymore. And she's not my grandma. Why do I care?

Because I'm high and she's still eyeing us. She doesn't even stop, just seems to take *forever* walking by on the path. And just when she's almost out of view, she pauses. "Oh, Sierra? Didn't you want to talk to me?"

I blink at her maybe eight times before I realize she's waiting for a response *from me*, and that she's referring to the email I sent her this morning because I literally don't know how else to get a hold of the woman.

"Oh. Right. Yes!" I hop down from the porch, tell Soph, "Be back in a bit!" and jog after June, who's suddenly motoring along the path again at her usual improbably high speed. She's carrying a broad but not deep square basket on one arm, loaded with small, leafy plants, like it's weightless. "I wanted to talk to you about our lease agreement."

"Yes?"

"Well, as you know, Sunshine Fest is in just over two weeks. And my lease extends just nine days after the festival, to the end of the month."

"I'm aware."

"So, uh, is there a possibility, if things go well, that I might extend the lease and stay longer?" I've been considering what that would look like. Advantages, disadvantages. And despite my ongoing lack of cell service and my general distaste for nature *and* Mason Grant, the advantages of staying in Orchard Cove, at least for a while, seem to be winning out.

I've decided that I'd probably hang out almost anywhere on earth right now in favor of delaying the return to my disaster of a life in the city. Thanks to losing my investment, I no longer have a venue for the rest of the year, and Cutie Fruitie is already set up here, so . . .

"For how long?" June asks me. Which isn't a no.

"I don't know yet. Maybe the rest of summer?" *Or forever.* "You're a wiser, older woman, June," I venture, because I'm high. "Maybe you could tell me. How long does it take to get over your ex making love to his gorgeous best friend on the Egyptian cotton sheets you bought him for his birthday?"

June stops walking. She's reached the opening in the low stone wall that surrounds her personal yard, and I'd already stopped a few steps back. My ability to walk properly is getting wonky. I try not to squint, but my eyes feel very, very squinty as the weed digs its claws in. I do not handle weed particularly well.

"That's what's happening right now?" she inquires. "Back home?"

My eyes squinch tighter. So, *so* high. "Define *home*," I say carefully, exaggerating the word, which suddenly feels foreign to me. Are we talking his home? My home? The city in general?

"Home is the place where you feel most like yourself," she says easily.

I consider that. Am I taking way too long to respond? Yes.

"I'll get back to you on that."

"Hmm," she says, in her June way—difficult to interpret. She could be judging me, concerned for me, utterly giving-no-shits. "Come. Let's plant basil."

With that, she turns on her heel and marches into her backyard.

"Um . . . okay?" I follow her carefully, along the little winding path through her gardens.

She kneels in front of a long, narrow planter box filled with rich, dark soil, and sets her basket down. I crouch down next to her as she lifts a tiny, leafy plant from the basket, and gives it to me. The leaves are lush and a bright green, and she rubs one between her thumb and forefinger, then brings her fingertips to her nose and inhales.

I do the same. The leaves are smooth and I rub for weirdly longer than I probably should, enjoying the silky, cool texture. When I bring my fingers to my nose and sniff, I let out a small, uncomfortably orgasmic sound at the incredible aroma. I greedily inhale more; it's like mint and lemon and sugar with whispers of cinnamon and fresh green magic.

"Sweet basil," June says. "I'll give you some to take home with you when you go back to the city." She picks up another baby plant, the roots in a small clump of soil, and presses it into one of the holes she's already dug in the planter box. "Just press it in gently, and tuck in the soil around it so there are no air pockets. But not too tight. You don't want to damage the roots." She nods toward another planter box nearby, and I shuffle over to it on my knees.

June places the basket between us and we both set to work, planting little baby basil plants in the fading evening light. They look so happy, their bright green leaves so proud and pretty against the dark, soft soil.

"How did you know I needed this?" I say in wonder.

"Focus on something tactile. Keep your mind occupied on a simple, grounding task. That's what I like to do when I'm high as a kite."

I blink at her. Is she for real?

She keeps planting basil, like this is a perfectly normal situation to find oneself in with someone four decades apart from you in age, and whom you barely know. "So," she says, "you just went through a breakup. And now you're running away from your problems."

"I wouldn't say I'm *running*—"

"Is this what you really want? You want to stay in that cottage any longer than necessary?" She raises a silvery eyebrow at me.

"Uh . . ."

"We'll be fixing that roof soon enough."

"Right. Thank you. I appreciate it. And I can promise you, in the time that I live here, no matter how long it is, I will fix it up. If you'll let me. I really love that kind of thing, and it will be my way of showing you that I'm a great tenant." Stoned Sierra is really running her mouth now, and trapped deep inside, sober me is unable to stop her; I just hope she's not writing checks my ass can't cash.

"Fix it up . . . how?"

"Well, it could use some fresh paint inside. Something brighter. Maybe some updates to the furniture? I'm a fantastic thrifter. You must have some cool yard sales and second-hand stores around here somewhere." Why am I sounding so excited about this?

Because I'm excited.

Maybe I'm just looking for more ways to fill up every second of my day so I don't have to think about the meme or the look on Kyle's mom's face on that video call or that time Kyle invited his best friend to my birthday party and kissed her on the forehead right in front of me.

June eyes me, considering. Or maybe trying to decide if this is all just the marijuana talking.

"So, what do you say? I'll make the Cozy Cottage even cozier for your next guest? And maybe you consider keeping me a little longer?"

"I'm not prepared to promise you anything, Sierra," she says. "It may surprise you to learn, since it came so easily to you, but Pier Seven is quite a landmark. It has history in Orchard Cove. You're not the only one who wants that building."

Damn. "You're talking about Mason Grant?" I was kind of hoping he'd realize that he was being unreasonable, and just find some other location to run a pop-up restaurant. And, you know, maybe he could go back to not hating me.

"It's no secret that the Grant family has been wanting to buy that building for decades," June says.

"Wow. *Decades.* If they want it so bad, why haven't they bought it?"

June seems unusually hesitant, like she's selecting her words carefully. "I'm not one to indulge in gossip." She levels me with a steely look, like, *You better not be, either.* "But I'll tell you this because it's fact. Mason's parents died last year. It was a car accident. Very tragic. Maybe they would have bought Pier Seven, if they could. But the thing is, it wasn't always for sale."

I take this in, the weight of the discovery settling uncomfortably in my chest. The knowledge that Mason suffered such loss, and so recently, tweaks my empathy. For his whole family.

But it feels wrong to ask questions of June about something so tragic. I'm not keen to gossip, either. Not about something so painful.

We're both silent for a moment, sitting with it.

"But now, Pier Seven is for sale?" I ask tentatively.

"Why? Would *you* want to buy it?"

"Oh, no. I'm not in the market to buy a building."

"Why not? I heard your smoothie bar was very busy today. I've been seeing those obnoxious Cutie Fruitie cups all over town."

At this point, her criticism of my business just rolls right off. I actually think it might be praise in June's grouchy old way. "Honestly . . . I was going to buy a building. At the end of summer. But it didn't work out."

"Well, maybe it wasn't the right building."

"I guess not."

"Why didn't it work out?"

"Is it the small town in you that makes you so nosy, June?"

This seems to catch her off guard. "I don't know. I never really thought about it before. I've always lived in a small town."

"Food for thought." I am on a roll, planting these little guys. It's so satisfying, pressing them into the soft soil. "What can I say? I put a lot of faith in someone I probably shouldn't have."

"And what happened?"

"Well . . . I loved him. Gave him three years of my life. Thought we'd get married. Thought the sun rose and set with him. Put everything I had, outside of work, into our relationship. Turns out, it wasn't enough."

"Hmm."

Again, I have no idea what that means.

"Okay, so, I did one incredibly stupid, embarrassing, tiny little thing wrong," I admit, "and he dumped me. And his parents pulled out of the investment they'd happily offered me because they saw how hard I worked, how much I'd put into the business to grow it from the ground up, and they 'believed in' me. Or so they said."

"I see. So, you're Cinderella."

"Huh?"

"You put in all that time on your knees, scrubbing those floors, because you believe deep down that since you're a good person and you work hard, eventually, someday, your Prince Charming will see how special you are and put a crown on your head. Your Fairy Godmother will make your dreams come true. All that nonsense. But life doesn't work that way."

"It doesn't?" I mean, I don't disagree. But this woman's insight into *me* is fascinating, even if I'm not sure how accurate it is yet.

"It didn't even work that way for Cinderella. What happened to her in the end?"

"Uh, the prince married her?"

"And why did he do that?"

"Because she was the fairest maiden in all the land or something? And nicer than her evil stepsisters?"

"Wrong. She went to the ball, even though she wasn't supposed to. She manifested that happy ending for herself. She didn't just sit around accepting what she was given. She saw her opportunity and she seized it."

"Right. She stepped up and claimed her glass slipper."

"So, forget about that fool who abandoned you after you dropped so many glass slippers in his path, he was blind not to see them. You deserve better. Even if you don't totally believe that yet."

"Wow, June. I feel seen."

I catch the hint of a smile that she's quick to hide with a brusque nod. "Well. We've all been fools for love at one time or another."

My eyebrows almost fly off my head. "We have?"

It's hard to imagine this no-nonsense, fiercely independent woman a fool for anything.

But she eyes me like I must be dense. She shakes her head. "Some people are primarily selfish. It's sadly obvious that you are not one of those."

I almost laugh. "Sadly?"

"Learn to put yourself first," she says firmly. "Then you'll know when to fight for what you really want. Instead of just accepting what the world offers you."

CHAPTER 10

MASON

I step out of the woods onto the stretch of dried grass and wind-matted weeds at the tip of a sharp curve in the road.

The guard rail along the road is still broken.

The makeshift section of metal fence that Jace and I put up is still there, bridging the gap. It's been eleven months, and still, no one else has been out to fix it.

Everything on the cliff is the same as always, including the heavy sense of dread I carry with me all the way here through the woods. The only thing out of place is the gray-haired woman sitting on her knees facing the water. She looks out at the Salish Sea, back straight and hands resting on her thighs. Maybe she's meditating.

Maybe she's plotting my death.

I sigh and look up at the sky, willing myself the strength and the patience to deal with this. She hasn't turned around, so I speak softly, trying not to scare the shit out of her. "June. It's Mason."

She doesn't even flinch. "I'm aware that you're standing there," she says dryly. "You're a large one, Mason Grant. For a moment I thought I was being stalked by a buffalo."

Then she makes a show of moving some twigs and leaves around, like she's just tidying up the landscape. She gets to her feet, and I notice the fresh flowers she's left on the ground.

I study her as she avoids my eyes. "Are you . . . visiting their graves?"

She *tsk*s irritably. "Of course I am. You're not the only one who cared for them."

I realize that, of course. Just never would've occurred to me that I'd run into *her* here. This isolated cliff is at the edge of a public park, but I rarely run into anyone here.

"And it's not really a grave, is it," she says brusquely as the wind off the ocean whips her hair around her face. "I just come by on my rounds sometimes."

This woman and her rounds. She's always walking the woods and the beaches and every path that meanders around Orchard Cove. There have been times when I've had to pull my truck over to talk to her on the side of a road when I see her out walking, because it's the only way to pin her down.

And just like that, she brushes her hands off and starts walking briskly, back into the woods.

I consider letting her go and focusing on what I came here for.

The wildflowers dangle from my hand, petals fluttering in the ocean breeze. My parents' actual gravesite is in a graveyard over in Vancouver, in a plot with my mom's family. That was their wish. Maybe it was a concession they agreed to: life in Orchard Cove, for his family; eternal rest in Vancouver, for hers.

But this is the place where I come to visit them most often, and I do think of it as their grave.

A sort of final resting place. The place where their lives ended.

I lay my wildflowers next to the small bundle of pale-yellow peonies June left, and go after her. "I've been trying to reach you for days, June."

"Have you?" she says flatly. "Why?"

Does she really not know why?

This is the thing about June—I never know when she's being straight with me, or what her true intentions are. I don't know if the gaping holes in our ability to communicate are a product of treachery, ignorance, or actual incompetence on her part.

June Spencer is not an incompetent person. Not in business. But the rest of her life? Who knows. I've never known a thing about this woman that someone else didn't tell me, and so my understanding of her is a maddening patchwork of gossip, speculation, hearsay, possible outright lies, and guesswork.

"I'd like to talk to you about Pier Seven," I tell her, because I have literally no idea if she knows this or not. Maybe she missed or just plain deleted/destroyed every voicemail, email, and actual registered letter that my realtor and I sent her over the past few months, or the urgent texts I've sent over the last nine days, since I found out she leased out the building to Sierra. "I was pretty disappointed that you leased the building to a stranger for Sunshine Fest rather than leasing it to me."

"And what does your disappointment have to do with me?" she asks bluntly, like a woman who has no time to waste. She reminds me of my grandpa that way; Tommy Grant has grown more impatient in the last decade or so, as if there's an hourglass in his head constantly ticking down the sands of his time on earth.

"My family leased the space last summer during Sunshine Fest," I remind her. "My parents were making plans to buy the building from you, before . . ." For some reason, I don't finish the sentence. Maybe it's the weight of it, always much heavier the closer I am to that damn cliff.

"Your parents, yes." June stops in her tracks. I stop, and she fixes me with her pale-gray eyes. "Not *you*. I had a lot of respect for your parents. And yes, we talked a great deal about what could be. They had grand plans."

"It was more than plans," I press. "You had a verbal agreement."

"According to whom?"

"According to my parents. And it's one I would hope you'd consider honoring, given the circumstances."

"The circumstance, while tragic, is that your parents died," she says. "Rest their souls. I would think such an experience might teach you not to waste time on what could be and focus on what is."

"That building belongs with my family," I press. "We have the means to get it back up and running. Investing in that building means investing in the town. Now that your family, other than Lee, is long gone from Orchard Cove, you can't possibly have the means to do that." She frowns, but you don't pussyfoot around with someone like June. "And if you'd ever had any interest in restoring the restaurant, you would've done it by now."

"That's a presumptuous position to take for someone who really doesn't know me."

"Come on, June. I've grown up with you. You're the grouchy, stubborn, impossibly difficult lady on the other side of the fence." Her frown deepens. "Or so I've been told. But we don't have to be enemies forever. If we do this deal, maybe it's a long-overdue first step in our families learning to work together instead of always butting heads."

She snorts. "Were you always this tragically naive?"

It's as close to a compliment as I'm sure I'll ever get from her. There's almost a hint of fondness in her tone.

"Probably. I've been told I'm optimistic to a fault."

One person told me that, actually. Long ago. When I was so rampantly optimistic I didn't see the end that was coming until I was standing in it, alone, dressed in a suit and learning a hard life lesson.

June shakes her head at me and looks away, into the forest, like she's considering my words. Optimism stirs in some dusty corner of my soul where I abandoned it, almost convincing me that I'm getting somewhere with her.

Then she nails me with her gray eyes and says, "How is Thomas?"

It's like she's launched a grenade into what could've been a perfectly reasonable chat.

She always calls my grandpa Thomas, which no one else does. I'm pretty sure it's intentional, meant to remind me that the two of them have a history. A history that I'm not a part of and don't understand.

"The same as always," I tell her neutrally, same as every time she asks, which is every time I speak with her, which is rarely.

"And that being the case," she responds, "I have no interest in doing business of any sort with that man."

"You were willing to do business with my parents," I point out.

"And I still would be, if they were here."

"I'll buy Pier Seven myself," I tell her. "For *my* family." I've never made this offer to her before. But I've been thinking it over. I know I can make it work. It would mean selling off the bar, but it would be worth it to get into the larger space, the landmark waterfront building that really *should* belong to my family. We built it, after all.

"You don't *have* a family," she retorts.

"One day I will," my optimism says. But the rest of me adds, "Layne will. And this will be part of their legacy. Tommy wouldn't have to be a part of it."

"No." She turns on her heel and starts up the path again.

"That's it?" I say to her back. "No?"

"As of right now, the answer is no. You haven't even made me an offer."

"I'll put in an offer," I call after her. "I was going to, after the festival. No more taking for granted that it's mine." I know that's probably what irks her. That I *assumed* it would be.

Or maybe, at the end of the day, this is all about money. She just needs to see my offer.

"You can," she calls back. "But you may not be the only one who makes one."

"What?" I hurry to catch up to her and fall into stride. "June. You can't be serious. You're not considering selling to Sierra Daniels."

"Why not?"

"Because she's not local. She sells smoothies. It makes no sense. No one's going to buy smoothies in Orchard Cove in the middle of winter. And the space is far too large for that."

"So maybe she'll expand her business model. Add other items to her menu."

I've never seen June Spencer amused, but I think I'm looking at it right now.

"That would be a very bad idea for Orchard Cove," I say.

I really don't know if it would be a bad idea. I just can't have it.

"Why?" she demands. "You only want a restaurant in that space and think it would be good for the town if *you* run it?"

"I know this town and already run the only restaurant here. Who better than me?"

"I guess we'll see." She glances at me sidelong. "She's already asked to extend her one-month lease."

I stop dead.

"So, I guess you've got yourself some healthy competition," she says, and disappears around a bend in the path.

◆ ◆ ◆

"So, what's going on with Pier Seven?" Evan asks me. "Thought you were supposed to be in there this month."

"Yeah. Turns out that's not the case," I say neutrally.

Everything in town shuts down on Mondays and Tuesdays—not enough out-of-towners coming through on those days to support the local businesses—and we're deep into our third poker hand of the night. The bar is closed. The cider house is closed. And even though there's always work to do when you run a family business, nearly every Monday night for the past few years has been poker night for me and my brother and our best friends.

Sometimes we don't even get around to playing poker. But we all take turns hosting and cooking dinner, and tonight, it's Evan's turn.

He lives across town, meaning on the other side of Cherry Way—past the pier, his house overlooking the water. We've set up at a table on his back porch to play cards and enjoy the view, and the chill, country-leaning rock that is Evan's thing. And even though Evan isn't much of a cook and kind of cheats by bringing in takeout sides he picks up in Cobble Hill to go with the steaks he grills, I'm glad he's hosting this week.

If we met up at my place, there's too good a chance someone would overhear something I don't want them to.

Like my grandpa, who's already given me grief several times about "falling for June Spencer's trickery" ever since he found out about the smoothie bar opening up at the pier. He'd definitely have words for me if he knew I'd seen June today and that she was considering letting some woman from the city have Pier Seven—possibly long-term.

I'm not planning to mention anything related to June Spencer or Sierra Daniels or Pier Seven, but someone—inevitably—brings it up.

"What's Tommy think of that?" Evan asks.

"Exactly what you'd think," I say. "He'd probably rather burn Pier Seven down at this point than let June keep it. He's entirely irrational when it comes to that woman."

"Well, don't look at me for any help with that," Jace says. "I'm on thin ice with Tommy already. I say one word about June Spencer in his presence, he'd probably ban me from the Grant family's illustrious properties for life."

"Thought you were already banned," Evan pokes.

Layne grins. "Yet he keeps coming back."

"The fact that you think I'd come to you for help about anything is stunning," I say to Jace.

"At least I'll admit that I like the old bastard, even if he doesn't like me." He looks pointedly at me. "Some of us are having a little trouble naming our feelings lately."

I flip a middle finger at him.

"Meaning what?" Layne asks.

Evan looks from me to Jace and back. "Yeah, am I missing something?"

"Just that Mason's deep in self-denial mode," Jace announces. "That shit kicked in hard when that fuck-hot brunette came to town. He's been worked up about her ever since. Terrible company. Grouchier than ever."

"What brunette?" Evan asks. I guess Jace hasn't blabbed to him yet.

Shocking.

But I am so not getting baited into this.

"Self-denial?" Layne raises an eyebrow at me in question.

"You know. That thing he does where he won't go after what he really wants," Jace explains, "because he's so busy holding the entire town together, taking care of what everyone else wants."

"I do not do that," I say flatly. What the hell is he even talking about? "I do not do shit because other people tell me to. What the fuck."

"No," Jace says, "you do stuff *for* other people, before they even ask you. You've always put other people's wants and needs before your own."

"Not true."

"Very true," Jace counters. "At this point, you probably don't even know what you want. Which is why I'm here to help you see the light. And for the record, it is shining out of that woman's pussy."

I scowl, but glance at the others, just wondering if they're actually listening to this shit.

"What brunette are we talking about?" Evan repeats, still clueless.

"Sierra Daniels," Jace blabs. "She runs the smoothie bar at the pier. Miss Behaving, from the bachelorette party."

"Oh," Evan says, totally getting it now. "*Her.*"

Jace cocks an eyebrow at me. "Care to deny?"

"Sorry, man," Evan says to me. "I don't know anything about this woman, but I definitely saw you with her. And the rest of it's true. Not that there's anything wrong with being selfless like you are. Some might even call it heroic." He gives Jace a look. "We can't all be unrelentingly self-interested like Jace."

"I mean, it's not hard," Jace drawls. "You just take what you want."

"Noble," Evan says.

"You just haven't been yourself since Sierra came to town," Jace informs me. "So maybe you should give that some thought."

What he doesn't know is that I've given that—her—way too much thought already.

It's sickening how often that woman is in my head.

I'm fucking *busy*.

After my morning workout, and sometimes a walk with my brother's dog, I have breakfast with my family, then I have plenty of work to do as general manager of the cidery. Most days I head over to the bar to work in the office sometime in the afternoon, because I manage that, too. I usually leave when the evening bartender comes in just before the dinner rush, to eat with my family. Some nights I go back to the cidery or the bar to work some more.

And right now, I'm also juggling the renovations on the house and helping out Layne with the final fixes on his cottage so he and Kaylie can move in.

I have more than enough going on to occupy my time and my mind, and yet there she is, taking up too much fucking space.

Definitely doesn't help that I know she's sleeping on June's property, right next door. And her smoothie bar is right across from my bar, which means I see her going in and out all the time. And everyone in town is talking about Cutie Fruitie—and its beautiful owner from the city.

I'm annoyed as hell that both Layne and Jace have been in there. Layne on opening night, last week, and Jace yesterday. And both of them felt the need to report back to me, in detail, about how "hot" Sierra looked and how "adorable" the smoothie bar is.

"I already told you," I grit out. "I have no interest in her. She's just standing in my way."

In truth, I've been feeling weirdly conflicted ever since I declared war against her on the beach. I need June to deny her the extension on her lease. But deep down, I'm fucking disturbed that I don't love the idea of her leaving town like I should.

I can't fall for Sierra Daniels. I can't even like her in any amount. What would be the point? I'd just get hurt. She doesn't live here; not permanently. Anyone can see she doesn't belong here. We have nothing important in common. And I'm way too old to let my hormones make decisions for me.

I don't even approach one-night stands that way. I'm incredibly pragmatic about who I sleep with. Have to be, so they don't get attached, and I don't have to feel guilty about it. Sex is just sex.

And Sierra Daniels is a walking thorn in my side.

I can't risk fucking her and growing feelings, but I can't seem to forget her.

I've even tried to pretend that the owner of that smoothie bar is some faceless corporation so I don't have to feel anything about fighting over Pier Seven with a live human, or the fact that that human is *her*.

Impossible.

For nine nights straight I've been plagued by memories of that night we shared. And they've only gotten worse the more I revisit them.

More vivid. More intense. More real, like they're happening right here and now.

I've zoned out countless times at the bar, remembering how we clung to each other outside, in the dark.

And remembering how we clung to each other after we tumbled into that narrow bed together. How she kissed my neck. Flickered her tongue along my throat, tasting me.

Skimmed my earlobe with her teeth, making my balls throb.

I wasn't nearly drunk enough that night to have mercifully forgotten the details.

I wonder if she remembers them, too.

If they replay in her head all damn night and day, like they do to me.

I've zoned out at the house while working with tools, remembering the sound of her voice and the feeling of her breath on my skin. Her little moans. Her whispered words. I smashed my fingernail with a hammer yesterday and have a bruised nail bed to show for it, but luckily no broken bones.

I've zoned out fucking *driving*.

You'd think after what happened to my parents, I'd be smart enough never to let that happen. I had to pull over yesterday at the side of the road to get my shit together because I got lost in a memory of our hips sliding together, clothed bodies grinding . . . . her thighs wrapping around me as she sought friction, rubbing herself against my erection . . .

You taste like sex, Mason.

You feel like bliss . . .

The lust-drunk, euphoric sound of her sweet laughter.

That woman is a danger to my health.

And my sanity.

I can't remember wanting a woman so much in a long damn time. Or . . . ever?

I wanted *more*. More of her, that night.

And if I'm being honest, every night since.

I lie in bed at night fucking throbbing with the want.

"Mason. Yo. Where the hell did you just go?"

I blink at Jace. "What? Nowhere."

"Really? It's been your turn for like a decade."

I glance around the table. They're all waiting on me.

I finish my turn and take an irritable swig of beer.

"I'm telling you. You're trying to control what you can't. At least be honest with yourself. If you're feeling her, so be it. No matter how inconvenient it might seem."

"We're still on this?" I growl.

"He's right," Layne says. "You haven't been yourself lately. I was trying to stay out of it, but when I went into the smoothie bar the other day with Kaylie, Sierra said something about you telling her she's not welcome here. That we're enemies? What's up with that?"

"She's not welcome," I mutter. "As far as I'm concerned."

"Why? Because of that old building? We don't need it."

It's got nothing to do with need.

Honestly, Layne doesn't have a clue what we need as a business. It's not his job to manage these things. His concerns, as our cider master, are the unique flavor profiles of our products, cider production, and quality control. And, of course, Kaylie.

This is about history and tradition and what's right. It's about our parents and what they wanted.

But how can I tell Layne that? My brother's been through enough. He doesn't need to worry about this.

"I've got it under control. Don't worry about it."

Layne gives me a doubtful look. "Well, you can't really control if you like her. You can choose what to do about it, sure. But it kinda seems like you want to do *something* about it."

"If I wanted to do something," I growl, "I'd do it."

My friends exchange a look with my brother at my expense, like I'm not even fucking sitting right here.

"I can see you guys when you do that, you know."

"Years ago, you would've done what you wanted," Jace says. "But you've changed. Ever since what happened with Jenn. You got really jaded about women when you came back to town after the breakup. But it's been fourteen years, man. Isn't it time to let it go? You've been a one-and-done man with every woman you've met since."

"Not true. I slept with that woman from up island at least three times." I mutter, "What was her name . . . ?"

"Yeah. Congrats." Jace makes a wanking-off gesture, unimpressed. "Sounds like an epic romance."

"Said the man who hasn't had a woman spend one complete night in his bed, ever."

"We're not talking about me. We're talking about you."

"And why is that, again?"

"Because you're the one who needs our help right now."

"He's right," Layne says. "This is tough love, brother."

"So, what is this, group therapy?"

"Think of it as more of a casual intervention," Jace says.

I glance at Evan across the table, wondering if they planned this, or if Jace's big mouth is just getting away from him. Evan's been quiet, focused on his cards, but not suspiciously so. The man doesn't tend to interfere in other people's business. Sometimes I wonder how he and Jace are even friends.

"Hate to say it," Evan drawls without looking up, "but they're right."

"Fuck off."

Jace slaps Evan on the back as Evan says, "You're too good a man not to share what you've got with some amazing woman, Mason. You're good-looking, built like Hercules, smart, loyal, and decently funny. You're inheriting a whole fucking empire, and you deserve a queen. Did I mention you're hot?"

"Wow, Evan." I'm actually a little speechless. That's more compliments than I think I've ever heard out of his mouth, directed at anyone. Women included. "I didn't know you'd noticed."

"I'd be jealous," Layne quips, "but that was beautiful."

Evan gives me a solemn nod. He lies his cards face down, curves his hands together into a heart shape, and holds it to his chest. It's something a ten-year-old girl would do. He probably learned it from Kaylie.

"And that's my cue to call it a night," I announce. "Before one of you starts braiding my hair. By the way, I've got a full house. Queens high."

I lay out my hand, and the rest of them toss their cards onto the table with a round of curses.

I grin. "See? I've got all the queens I need." I scoop up my winnings and stand, shoving their cash into my jeans.

Layne downs his beer and gets up with me. "I'm out, too."

Evan gets up to see us out, but Jace sits back in his chair, studying me.

No, challenging me.

"So that's it? You're just gonna live in denial?"

What the hell is up his ass tonight?

"You know what, Jace?" I level him with a look. "Sometimes you need to know when to just shut the fuck up."

"And sometimes you need to take a fucking risk," he fires back. "The truth is, you won't make a move on her because it's not safe enough for your liking. You never take risks anymore, man. And that is exactly why you should."

"Whatever," I mutter, irritable. "You'd understand not taking risks if you ever worried about anyone other than yourself."

But he doesn't let me bait him, either. "I'm worried about you."

"Don't."

But my best friend ignores that. "And here's why," he says. "Sierra fucking scares you."

I grunt a laugh and shake my head. "That is so off base," I tell him, "I'm not even gonna bother."

But his words stay with me, long after Layne and I head out into the night.

CHAPTER 11

Sierra

"I realize you're an absolute sucker for a fixer-upper, uncomfortably competitive, *and* socially awkward," Sophie says, "but this is extreme, even for you."

I'm not really listening, I'm so deep into my new "Who Needs a Man Anyway?" playlist, but I toss her a dirty look as she turns down the volume on Miley Cyrus buying herself flowers. I was singing along, of course.

Soph leans on the tiny peninsula in the cottage's kitchen, flipping casually through a paperback as I roll a nice, thick coating of Simply White kitchen paint onto the small piece of bare wall that runs next to the cupboards and behind the kitchen table. I managed to get this whole wall taped off today and prepped for its fresh new facelift. This is now the only wall that isn't dank and dreary; light bounces off it, and already the cottage feels brighter.

"This is not extreme," I inform her. "It's *satisfying*."

"You need to back away from the overachieving and get ready. We leave in half an hour."

"I'm not overachieving. I'm actually behind schedule." I start rolling faster, covering the last corner of the sad old wall with its rotten-oyster-colored paint and making it disappear. "I wanted to get this coat done and finish a light sanding on the bathroom cupboards today."

"Of course you're behind," she says sarcastically. "You could teach a masterclass in avoidance—"

"Thank you."

"Which is why you've been fixing up this cottage, which you don't own, in addition to running the smoothie bar, *and* you read a whole mystery novel in the last three days. To avoid Mason Grant and getting on with your uncertain future."

"Didn't *you* read it?" I avoid that last (very accurate) bit she said and place the roller in the pan, wiping off my sweaty face with a rag. "It was your idea to go to this book club."

"Yeah, to meet the local gossips and have girl talk. Drink wine and eat too much cheese. I don't think they actually expected us to read *Murder in the Barnyard.* We only got invited like four days ago."

"It's not exactly *Anna Karenina.* It's a quick read."

Sophie shrugs as she flips, scanning random pages, which I guess is her version of reading the book. "I'll just read your notes."

"How do you know I made notes?" I say airily.

My best friend laughs.

I sigh. I pluck my copy of *Murder in the Barnyard* from my purse, stuffed with Post-its that are scrawled with my thoughts, and toss it to her. "Are we really doing this?"

"Of course we are. What else is there to do in this town if you won't let us go to the bar?"

"Hey, *he* won't let us go to the bar."

"No, he told you to stay away from his family. How do you know if his family's at the bar? And why do you even care? He might not even be there. And if he is, as long as you don't get up and start singing karaoke, he might not even notice you're there."

I snort. "Thanks."

She frowns. "I meant, if it's crowded."

I start cleaning up my painting supplies. "Look. We've both seen Mason and his friends going in and out of that bar all week long, and according to the many rumors you've already gathered and delivered to my ears, Mason and his brother and their buddies are all single. Bachelors. *Playboys.* Even if I wanted to go to his stupid bar, I don't need a reminder of how painfully single *I* am by watching everyone else hook up with the town hotties at the local watering hole."

"Great. Then come with me to this book club meeting."

I mutter something about social butterflies that she definitely hears.

"And don't think you can fake sudden food poisoning or something," she says, unbothered. "*You're going.*"

"Okay, okay. Just let me get ready."

"Yay! Let the awkward forced socializing begin!"

She's way too happy about this.

"I'd rather eat sushi from a dumpster than do this," I inform her grumpily.

"I know, sweetie. That's why you *need* to do this."

"*Why* do I need to do this again?" I inquire as Soph and I walk along a quiet country road, carrying our copies of *Murder in the Barnyard.* I'm clutching three big bottles of cider—Saskatoon Berry, Rhubarb, and something called Farmhouse Scrumpy—from a cider company over on Salt Spring Island, which I hope is a respectful nod to the craft cider industry in these parts and not sacrilege among the locals.

I've got one eye peeled for any sign of Mason, since I keep *almost* running into him all over town.

Sophie has the gargantuan wood platter we found in the Cozy Cottage kitchen, piled high with finger sandwiches. "Because you need to make *friends*," she insists, "given that Kyle took all your so-called friends except two in the breakup."

I'm afraid he did. Though to be fair, other than Sophie and Pete, they were his friends first.

"And since you might stay here a while," she adds, "the sooner you make friends, the better."

"I am so regretting telling you that I'm considering staying in this one-horse town," I say distractedly as I hold up my phone, trying to catch a cell signal.

No luck.

"For the record, I haven't seen even one horse."

"And how do you know for sure that he took them *all*?"

"Honey. Name me one person who checked in on you after that meme went out to *everyone* in Kyle's contact list, because they were actually concerned about *you* and not just hungry for the drama of it all."

I open my mouth to answer, but she cuts me off with "Other than your mom. And your sister."

I shut my mouth.

"And now name me one person from his contact list, or yours, who didn't reach out, that you actually *care* to hear from again."

I think about it for a moment. "Fuck. I really don't."

"Then why are you dreading this book club thing so much?"

"Because I'm terrible at making friends. As evidenced by the fact that I have none."

"We've been friends for years."

"Only because you started it."

She rolls her eyes. "So, I'll help you get started with some new ones."

She will, if I let her. The woman knows no shyness. I actually met her at a Dirty concert when she was working. I was standing in the lineup to buy a T-shirt, and when I got to the front she said, *No, you get a hoodie*, then tossed one at me, charging me only for the much less expensive T-shirt.

When I got home, I discovered that she'd scrawled her phone number on the tag with a sharpie. I actually thought she was trying to pick me up, but I called anyway because she seemed cool. We had a laugh about it and we've been thick as thieves ever since.

She maintains to this day that in all the years of traveling to many continents on tour, that is the only time she's ever done that. I choose to believe her because it makes me feel special, but come on.

Either way, if anyone knows how to meet people, it's Soph.

"Do it for me?" she says. "You've always, always been there for me. No matter where I go or how long I'm gone or what crazy chaos I bring back when I come whirling in and out of your life, you have been the most unfailingly loyal and fun best friend. And I need to know you're okay when I won't be here to have your back."

Shit. *Don't remind me.*

The fact that Sophie has to leave Orchard Cove as planned, right after Sunshine Fest, is even more depressing now that I've got this war with the hottest guy in town to deal with. But just because *I* might want to extend my stay here a little longer doesn't change the fact that Sophie has a big, beautiful life beyond occasionally helping me out with my pop-up shops.

"Two more weeks and then you're gone," I lament, laying it on thick. "My heart is breaking already. Who's going to leave long raspberry hairs all over my stuff now?"

Classic me: trying to pretend it doesn't matter when someone leaves me, when really, it does. A lot.

Sophie knows it, though, and lobs my bullshit right back at me. "I know. Who's going to sing 'Shake It Off' off-key in the shower while I have my morning matcha?"

"Who's going to snore so loud it shakes the walls and wakes me up at night?"

"Who's going to make up lies about how I snore because she can't think of more than one annoying thing about living with me?"

Damn it. It's true.

"You make weird yummy noises when you eat deep-dish pizza," I inform her.

"My unbridled passion for cheese is annoying?"

"It's not. Just go on the road with your amazing husband and the amazing rock band. I'll be fine."

She eyes me as I hold up my phone, trying to catch a signal again. "See, this is why we're going out tonight. In the city, you're way too caught up in your phone, your social media, what people think of you. Even here, without cell service, you're somehow still plugged into all that toxic drama with Kyle."

"Totally your fault for letting me use your phone today. Otherwise, I wouldn't have found out that Kyle's little douche-dick of a cousin made that meme. A *thirteen-year-old* trolled me, for fuck's sake. Just because he has an iPad and thought it was funny. And let's face it, totally gleaned that his older cousin dumped me for the hot blonde upgrade because I own a purple rubber penis."

"Yeah . . . I'm gonna stop letting you borrow my phone."

"It's probably for the best," I mutter. "I don't know how people live in small towns by choice. The inconveniences are innumerable."

I finally give up and shove my phone away. Annoyingly, my cellular service provider doesn't have a nearby tower—unlike Sophie's; her phone continues to work perfectly—so I have to hang out on certain roads in town in order to get (spotty) service. We're so close to Washington State here, my phone keeps trying to connect to a US network on roaming. To fix this, I'd have to drive down to Victoria, the nearest city, during business hours, to sign up with a new provider and switch my phone over.

Who has that kind of time?

"Maybe I should just forget there *is* an outside world."

"I'd die without my phone," Sophie muses. "Petey and I have phone sex every night when we're apart."

"Sophie. Dear god. Have some compassion for those of us who have no sex *at all*, phone sex or otherwise. You cruel, heartless wench."

"Sorry. Sometimes I forget."

"That we haven't all met our soulmate and rock 'n' rolled off into the sunset with him?"

"Well . . . yes?"

"Sadly, I'm coming to think that's the worst part of losing Kyle. Goodbye, regular sex. And by regular, I do mean *regular*, as in nothing special, as you know."

"Hearing about how that man left you unsatisfied keeps me up at night. It's a travesty."

"It wasn't all bad. Sometimes it was . . . adequate."

Sophie scrunches her nose. "We need to talk about your standards, babe. You are kind and beautiful and fucking funny, and that ass won't quit. Fuck adequate. No more settling for less than he-made-me-see-stars. That's your new baseline. Deal?"

"No worries. No boys for the rest of the year, right?"

Sophie frowns. I know she still doesn't believe I mean that.

Then her whole face lights up. "There's the house! It's *cute*."

At the quiet two-way intersection up ahead, beyond the waist-high grass along the ditches and the thickets of trees that go ever on, stands a picture-perfect classic farmhouse. A golden light already glows over the front porch to welcome us, even though it's not quite dusk.

It is cute. If you're into picturesquely updated rural farmhouses painted pale olive green with cream trim, storybook red shutters, and casually idyllic flowerbeds.

I'm just way too grumpy to admit it.

"This is beyond stupid," I mutter as we tromp toward the house; this armful of cider is getting heavy. "I don't even want to be here, and yet I'm trying to convince a woman who also doesn't seem to particularly want me here to let me pay her more money so I can stay. Is this the definition of insanity?"

"Then why are you doing it? All week long, all you do is moan about the lack of shopping and sushi restaurants and yoga studios."

"And coffee bars."

"Right. How could I forget?"

"I know it probably sounds like I'm just running away. But I'm not *exactly*. I was just thinking, since Kyle dumped me and all my plans abruptly fell apart, it kinda blasted a giant hole in my schedule for the rest of the summer. I don't have another location locked down after this. So, maybe extending my lease and staying for a couple more months in Orchard Cove makes sense. The smoothie bar has been doing well."

"It does make sense when you put it that way."

"But it's not a given. I don't even know if I can convince June."

"Well, what exactly did she say when you had that chat the other night?"

"I dunno. She called me Cinderella . . . something about throwing too many glass slippers at Kyle? It was weird. Plus, I was high, so there was that."

"Then our job is to convince her," Sophie says. We've reached the driveway, and we make our way toward the porch. "And what better chance are you gonna get to win over some of the local women?"

Of course, to sociable Sophie, it makes perfect sense to crowdsource support for my cause.

"Uh, they know Mason, though. He lives here. His family is entrenched in the community. And maybe they all like him. Maybe they *love* him. How do I compete with the gorgeous lumberjack bartender?"

"Like *this*," Soph says firmly as we climb the front steps. "Mason can't come to ladies' night, right?"

The words are barely out of her mouth when the door opens from inside and Bev—of Bev & Bill's General Store—appears.

Sophie tells me this woman is a wellspring of town gossip, and while I haven't spoken with her directly yet, I have seen her and her husband going in and out of the store. She's always wearing a plaid shirt and jeans, very similar to her husband's, with a couple of bobby pins tucking her salt-and-pepper bangs to one side.

Tonight is no different.

I feel way overdressed in my body-con Aritzia dress and cropped blazer.

"Ladies! I'm so glad you could join us!" She welcomes us in with unbridled delight.

"Us, too!" Sophie says. "Thank you for having us."

"Come in, come in." Bev waves us in and Soph hugs the woman like they're old friends. I follow them inside, hugging my cider like a life preserver.

"This is Trish," Bev says, introducing us to the petite, curly-haired blonde about our age who hops to her feet in the living room. "Trish lives on Honeymoon Lane, too! Right across from the Grants."

"I grew up with Layne and Mason," Trish says. "Layne and I went to school together. But don't come to me for gossip," she adds in a very gossipy tone. I almost expect her to wink.

"Oh. Okay?" I say.

"The moms are here," Bev announces.

She heads to the door as a couple of women pile in with wine and food. After a round of hellos, the fortyish mom wearing a ball cap and cargo pants with a definite "I coach all the kids sports teams" vibe literally gives me a list of the local committees she's on. The dark-haired, drop-dead gorgeous mom, thirtyish, gives me and my cider bottles a hug.

Then the two of them hurry into the living room, where the food and drink await.

"I'm on a timeline, ladies," Power Mom announces as she peruses the food offerings. I'm told her name is Pamela. "I've got four boys under twelve at home with Daddy, and something's getting burned down or broke if I'm not back in three hours."

Hot Mom is already dumping wine into a large tumbler. Her name is Maria. "Well, I just finished breastfeeding and I haven't been out in ages. Someone please tell me something good. I'm dying to live vicariously."

Then everyone in the room, by some strange coincidence, looks at me.

I almost demand, *What?* Is there a spider in my hair?

"How are you liking Orchard Cove, Sierra?" Trish asks me eagerly.

"And Pier Seven?" Power Mom asks.

"And Mason Grant?" Bev inquires, totally straight-faced.

Hot Mom elbows her in the ribs.

Why do I feel like I'm onstage and they're all waiting for the show to begin?

I manage to stammer out something like "Good. Fine. Yeah. Are those pickles?"

Those are not, in fact, pickles on the plate in Power Mom's hands, but cookies that look nothing like pickles. My awkwardness is showing and I can't even blame it on alcohol yet.

"I should go open this cider," I say self-consciously, still hugging all three bottles, which Bev did offer to take from me but I held onto.

"I'll help you," Sophie says, nudging me toward the kitchen. "Kitchen, Bev?"

"Help yourself," Bev says. "June should be along soon, too. Then we can begin."

I follow Sophie into the kitchen, where she immediately puts her tray down and whirls on me. "Just relax, Si. It's not an interrogation."

I put the bottles down awkwardly on the counter. "It feels like one."

"They literally just asked you how you like it here."

I chew my lip absently. "Do you think they know about me and Mason?"

"There is no you and Mason. Bev's just fishing." She picks up a bottle opener, cracks the top off the Rhubarb cider, and pours me a glass. She puts it in my hand. "You're here to make friends, remember? Win over the local ladies?"

"How? I have nothing in common with these people. Power Mom is way too Type A, even for me, and Hot Mom is wearing hemp."

"So?"

"I've been meeting these small-town people at the smoothie bar all week. They're outdoorsy. And crafty. And they read cozy mysteries set on farms. They're actually *into* camping and DIY and they spend time in nature *on purpose*. Like, for fun." I take a big swig of cider, trying to calm my nerves.

"Since when are you so judgmental?" Sophie says.

"I'm not. I'm realistic. I hate camping and hiking and I've never even been fishing. I like modern conveniences like uninterrupted Wi-Fi and an organized calendar that syncs with all my apps and parking meters where I can prepay for my parking with my phone." I'm truly panicking now, and making zero sense. I know that.

"No one likes parking meters, Si," Soph says calmly.

She's right. And it's slowly dawning on me why I'm so nervous about this night.

Not because I'm worried people in town might be gossiping about me, or whispering about me and Mason.

Because I've somehow gotten myself into a position where I'm vulnerable to a man, *caring* what he thinks of me. And I'm scared as shit that since he wants me gone, everyone in town will take his side.

It feels all too familiar.

"Also," Soph says, "who the hell are Power Mom and Hot Mom?"

"It's obvious."

"What's obvious is you're doing that thing you do where you put labels on people to tuck them into neat little boxes and keep them at a distance. Instead of actually getting to know them. You do it all the time. You did it with me when we met. Remember Retro Rosie?"

"That was a compliment." I turn and peel the plastic wrap off the sandwich tray and start needlessly rearranging the sandwiches. "You were cool and strong, yet stylish, like Rosie the Riveter."

"Remember Hottest Bartender in the Universe, who you met recently?"

"It's just shorthand. In case I forget people's names."

"You pretty little liar."

"Thank you. I think my hair turned out pretty good tonight." When I glance at her, she's frowning at me. "Oh. That wasn't a compliment. I see."

"You're looking for reasons to push people away right now." Sophie cocks her head at me and frowns. "Maybe you're afraid of getting attached."

"To *Bev*?"

"There is literally not one thing wrong with Bev."

I open my mouth to give her a list, but she pokes me in the ribs. "Ow!"

"You're standing in her house," Soph hiss-whispers, "and about to eat her food. Now, act like a grownup!" Then she stuffs a finger sandwich *into my mouth* and turns, just in time to smile at Bev, who's come to see if we need any help.

"No help required!" Soph says. "Just saying what a lovely home you have."

When Sophie and Bev leave me alone in the kitchen, I take a breath, and it hits me, hard. That I have no real friendships anymore except Soph. And this was true long before Kyle came along.

Because the last ten years of my life, I've been working my butt off to support myself in the city, then to make a go of my business *and* support myself . . . and maybe to prove something to myself. That I'm not the failure my mom worried I'd be when I moved to the city alone. That I'm so much more than just the less-successful, less-talented, less-adored of her two daughters.

And so, I've made myself unavailable.

It's a protection mechanism.

And it's bullshit.

I am *ripe* for a new group of friends.

Or at least some sense of community. A family who won't choose my stepsister over me, who won't abandon me at the first sign of conflict—or the first rubber dick they glimpse in my vicinity.

I down the rest of my Rhubarb cider, pick up the tray, and carry it out into the living room, where I hear Trish telling Sophie, "Oh, he's been like that ever since his nasty, horrible breakup."

"I thought you weren't gossiping, Trish," Hot Mom says.

"Who are we talking about, ladies?" I ask, setting the tray of sandwiches down on the table, determined to make an effort here. I take a finger sandwich and sink onto the couch next to Sophie, who promptly hands me a tall, cold can of Twisted Tree Ginger Spritz cider.

She gives me a look, like, *Prepare yourself for this.*

Trish says, "Mason Grant." Her voice drops dramatically. "He was left at the altar."

"And this is why we come to ladies' night," Sophie murmurs in my ear.

CHAPTER 12

Sierra

"It's so similar to his brother's situation," Trish is saying. "Layne just needs the right woman to come along and fix him right up, help him learn to love again, you know? Imagine raising a little girl all alone! That man just needs someone to take care of him."

From the look on her face, I'm getting the sense that the "right woman" to do this for Layne Grant, in Trish's estimation, would be her.

But what's really got me reeling is: *Left at the altar.*

Mason was left at the altar?

When?

And by who?

This nugget of gossip definitely gives me some context for his perpetually crappy mood. I would love to get more info out of Trish, but she's clearly more interested in talking about Layne to anyone who will listen, and I'm not about to ask.

My mind drifts to that first night we met. When Mason took me home and took care of me. When he was in a much better mood . . .

How careful he was with me, never crossing the lines I drew. His hands roaming over my body, seeking out my soft, sensitive places, but never quite venturing between my legs.

The base of my spine.

The backs of my thighs.

The nape of my neck.

Skimming the sides of my breasts or drifting underneath, but never touching my aching nipples.

His big hand cupping the back of my head as he rasped in my ear: *Promise me this isn't all.*

Promise me that I get to see you again.

"So, what can Sierra do to get involved around here?" Sophie asks, startling me back to reality, what must be several conversation topics later. The finger sandwich in my hand is drying out. "You mentioned something about a festival committee, Pam?"

"Oh, we're all on the Sunshine Fest planning committee," Power Mom says.

"That would be a great way to get involved," Hot Mom agrees.

"That sounds *so* interesting," Sophie says, then cocks an eyebrow at me.

I shove the sandwich in my mouth. How many times do I have to tell this woman that I am *not* a joiner?

"We can always use more help with the festival," Bev says. "There's still so much left to do and less than two weeks to do it. You'd be a natural fit for helping out with the food and drink area, Sierra! Wouldn't she, Pam?"

"Oh, yeah." Power Mom looks up from where she's hovering at the dining room table over a charcuterie platter. She still hasn't sat down. "Totally. You can meet up with us tomorrow morning. Eight a.m., right by the pier."

"Well . . . okay. Sure. I'll be there."

How bad could it be, right? Helping organize a festival and getting to know more of the locals . . . I'm good with organizing stuff.

"As long as there's no nature involved," I quip, "I'm in." I pop a breaded shrimp into my mouth.

"Wonderful," she says. "Mason and I can really use the help."

◆ ◆ ◆

It takes a few minutes for me to completely finish coughing after I choke on the shrimp—which I failed to realize I'd dipped in hot chili—when Power Mom says "Mason." As in, she and *Mason*, and now me, are in charge of the food and drink area at the festival, *together*.

I attempt to douse the fire with ginger cider, which only makes it much, much worse.

"Oh, dear," Hot Mom says, jumping to her feet. "That's a spicy sawsawan."

"What?" I cough.

"Siling labuyo. Filipino chili sauce." She utters something in Filipino—swearing, I think—as she rushes into the kitchen. She brings me back a glass of milk.

"It's not that spicy," Sophie says, patting me on the back. "As long as you don't choke on it."

"You and Mason, huh?" Bev muses as once again, everyone stares at me. "I can see it."

I shake my head as best I can while chugging milk, my eyes watering.

After that, June arrives, and we get to discussing *Murder in the Barnyard*, which no one but me and June actually seemed to enjoy, and I suspect half the women in attendance never actually read.

Maybe they think I didn't read it, either, considering how totally distracted I am and how little I add to the conversation.

Once again, I hand over my note-ridden book to Sophie, who has at it.

The highlight of the night is an impassioned debate between the moms and June, who can't seem to agree on whether the hot detective deserved to die. Interestingly, it's June who thinks he should've lived and had a happily-ever-after with the widower, while the moms are out for his blood.

"I would never have guessed you're such a romantic, June," Sophie teases.

To which Bev says, "Oh, June always picks the books with a tragic love story." And June, drifting into the kitchen for a white wine refill, pretends not to hear.

When we eventually get low on alcohol, we say our goodbyes, Bev stuffs our handbags with leftovers, and we head out into the night. She insisted only June stay behind to help her clean up. "Bev wants to gossip about us," Trish tells Sophie and me.

By now, I'm starting to make peace with it. Frankly, all the local cider and wine really took the edge off caring one way or another if the entire town decides to hate me because they're Team Mason.

We say goodbye to Hot Mom at her car—Power Mom left long ago—and the three of us walk together, making our way back to Honeymoon Lane. As Trish peppers Sophie with random questions about the work she does for Dirty, I mentally spitball excuses to back out of this planning-committee thing.

Mornings are me time? Dick move.

Against my religion? Don't have one.

Struck with a sudden illness? Not a good look for Cutie Fruitie.

As we approach the stop sign where Honeymoon Lane begins, a couple of men appear on the road to our left, also approaching the intersection on foot. Tall, attractive men who're built kind of similar. One blond; one with brown hair and a beard.

Oh, no.

Trish gasps ever so quietly. I think she's drunk. And definitely some part in love with Layne Grant.

"Layne!" she calls out. "Mason. What perfect timing!"

Yeah. *So* perfect.

I haven't come face-to-face with Mason since a week ago on the beach when he wore those very thin clothes on a windy day and I drooled all over him while he declared war on me.

I didn't know how weird/uncomfortable/panic-inducing it would be to run into him unexpectedly with other humans as witnesses and *so much booze* in my system.

And he looks *freaking good.*

Stupidly, unfairly good, in a sleeveless black T-shirt and jeans, his haphazardly sexy hair ruffled by the breeze.

Sophie meets my eyes as I edge behind her and mouth, *Help me, I'm drunk!*

"Hey, ladies," Layne says easily as the gap closes between us. "Nice night for a wander, huh?"

"Oh, we're not wandering," Drunk Sophie says, positioning herself smoothly between me and the brothers as we all naturally form a loose group to continue walking together. "Just coming from a serious book club meeting."

"Cool," Layne says. "Just coming from a serious meeting ourselves. Poker night."

Trish giggles, inserting herself between the two men. "Who won?"

"This guy." Layne waves a thumb at his brother. "Always."

Mason hasn't said a word or looked at me. I think. I guess I really wouldn't know since I'm not looking at him, either. But I'm sure he's as hyperaware of my presence as I am of his when Sophie, Trish, and Layne fall into easy conversation and the two of us remain silent.

A mental battle ensues in my head: ignore him, or rip off the bandage?

Ignore him is *almost* winning when I realize he's falling back from the group a bit.

Like me.

Sophie glances over her shoulder to see how I'm dealing with this. This time I mouth at her, *Never mind,* and she kind of rolls her eyes.

Then she pokes out her cheek with her tongue—in a definite reference to a woman having a dick stuffed in her mouth. Because she knows when I'm crushing on a man against my better judgment.

I respond by rubbing my nose with my middle finger.

I can't help it if my body finds him attractive. It's just physical. Biological.

He smells like cedar and cinnamon and sex god, for Christ's sake.

As Mason falls into stride with me, I slow my pace a bit, putting more space between us and the rest of the group so that if he's about to say something outrageous, our friends don't have to be subjected to it.

And maybe just to test if he's actually trying to walk with me.

The others keep chatting as we fall farther behind.

We glance at each other like we're waiting for the other to hurl the first insult.

"How's business?" he says neutrally.

"Much better than you'd like it to be, I'm sure."

"It may surprise you to know, Sierra Daniels, but I wish you no ill."

I make a gagging, choking sound into my fist. "Excuse me. That was the sound of me throwing up in my mouth a bit. Egregious insincerity makes me nauseous."

Shit. And now I remember what I've learned about him in the last few days, and why I maybe shouldn't be such a jerk.

Left at the altar.

Parents died in a car accident.

Damn it. Compassion is kicking in *hard.*

When I sneak a look at him again, he looks down at me over his manly, gleaming beard. I know from experience that it's silky. I bet he takes really good care of it.

He strikes me as a man who keeps himself nicely groomed and smelling delicious at all times just in case a hot babe wanders by and swoons into his arms. I bet he's had a *lot* of pussy. And not in a gross way. Just . . . nicely seasoned.

I bet he knows what he's doing in bed.

I bet he's really good with his hands . . .

You know he is. You felt them all over you.

"So, I hear you want to extend your lease," he says. "Stay in Orchard Cove a while."

"Yeah. That's what I hear, too."

"Then it's true?"

"That I want to stay in Orchard Cove? Not exactly. That I want to extend my lease at Pier Seven? Yes."

"Why would you want to do that if you don't even want to be here?"

"For opportunities like these?" I say sarcastically. Then add with pathetic honesty, "Where else could I wander down a moonlit road and run into you?"

Our eyes meet, and I inwardly shiver at the memory: his hot breath on my neck, his rough voice in my ear . . .

Promise me this isn't all.

When he doesn't say anything and I can no longer take the pressure, I mutter, "If this is about me talking to your family, I swear Layne and Kaylie just came into the smoothie bar—"

"I heard. And I'm not a monster. I'm not going to tell a little girl she can't have a smoothie just because I don't like the proprietor of the shop."

"Right. Thanks," I say neutrally, trying to just draw breath and ignore the tiny, unexpected arrow that pierces my lungs when he says he doesn't like me.

It's fucking deflating, and I hate that he has this effect on me. I know he doesn't like me. But to hear it out of his mouth hits different.

"Especially not when she tells me your shop is 'total slay.'" The tiniest hint of amusement seems to flicker at the corner of his mouth. "I think that means cool."

"I can assure you it does, Grandpa."

He gives me a look, one eyebrow cocked. "You know I'm her uncle, right?"

I do, of course, but giving him even a moment to question whether I actually think Kaylie might be his granddaughter has me snorting inside.

However, I'm trying to convince myself that antagonizing him won't help my cause.

I let him off the hook. "Yes, I know you're her uncle."

"She's ten. And I'm thirty-four," he says defensively.

Which is curious. Why would he care what I think of his age, or anything else?

His left arm is toward me, and a streetlight catches on his bicep. I see the name scripted through his tattoo, which clearly matches the *Samantha* one on his right arm.

This one says *Christopher*.

I'd love to not say anything about it, but it feels wrong. Too cold. And that's just not me.

I clear my throat. It's still kind of sore from the chili shrimp incident. "So . . . Samantha and Christopher . . . Those were your parents, right?"

I know I'm right. He doesn't have to say a thing. I can feel it; the sudden shift in the night air around him. The tension in his body.

I take a deep breath and rip off the bandage. "I just heard from some of the locals about what happened to them. I'm so sorry that your family has suffered such a loss. I know you wanted me to stay away from them, but I really like Layne and Kaylie."

Mason slows his pace as I speak, and I slow along with him. I don't even look at him. I can't.

I don't think I want to see his pain, if it's there, or his discomfort. And I'm not in the mood to handle his anger, so I hope he's not mad. I really don't know if I just upset him or not, but I do know he doesn't trust me.

So, I offer up something that I think will prove I'm sincere. That this isn't some trick or a cruelty.

"I lost my father when I was young," I say quietly, looking off into the night, "like I told you. He left me when I was three. I know it's totally not the same thing as the loss you experienced, but I'm just saying, I know how it feels to lose a parent too soon. To no longer have them in your life when they should be."

I can hear Mason breathing next to me, but I still don't look.

He doesn't say anything.

The others are really getting ahead of us as we approach Twisted Tree Orchard, and we just keep walking, slowly, side by side.

"It's not something anyone can really understand," I go on, "unless you experience it first-hand. And you definitely can't prepare yourself for it. There was no way I could prepare myself for my own father choosing his next family over me."

We both come to a stop. We've reached the entrance to June's property, the *Twisted Tree Orchard* sign wrapped in fairy lights.

Small lanterns light the way up the drive, toward the cider house and beyond.

Sophie stands next to one of the lanterns, waiting for me.

Layne and Trish are farther up the road, maybe oblivious that they've lost us. Trish's laughter floats to us on the breeze and skitters away into the trees.

A shiver runs up my back.

I can feel Mason watching me.

When I turn to him, our eyes lock. "This isn't about our 'war,'" I tell him. "I promise." I feel disarmed. My weapons, for the moment, tucked away. My armor laid down.

If he wants to take a jab, now would be the time to hit me with whatever he's got.

But I can feel his weapons withdrawing, too.

"That's . . ." He seems to search for the right word to respond to what I just told him about my own loss. Then he admits, "Terrible."

A bubble of laughter floats out of me. If he only knew; "terrible" is the absolutely correct descriptor for the way my biological father treated me that one time I got to speak to him in the last twenty-seven years.

"I'm sorry," he adds softly.

I don't know what he's sorry for. His loss of words? The fact that my own father crushed my self-esteem into a snarl of shame and uncertainty and self-doubt that I'm still trying to untangle?

I kind of laugh again, and there is absolutely no reason for it.

Mason stares, like he's trying to make sense of me. His gaze weighted and dark, his hands crammed in his pockets. And neither of us moves.

I feel rooted to the road, to this moment where neither of us says another thing as the night air between us charges with potential energy. A lock of hair dances across my face, and I swear he's about to reach out and smooth it aside for me. Or move closer. Or say something else, good or bad, that I will *not* be able to handle.

An impulse throbs deep in my chest, overwhelming and dangerous.

It's the urge to touch him.

Followed quickly by the urge to push him away.

I take a step back before I can do either.

He waged war on you.

He told you to leave town.

You have to be tougher than this, Sierra.

"Anyway," I blurt. "We're in charge of the food and drink area at the festival. You and me. You know, together."

His eyebrows pinch together. "What?"

"So, I guess we have a meeting with Power Mom in the morning?" I bite my lip. "Shit, I mean Pamela. I've been calling her Power Mom all night in my head," I explain, though I know that's not the part he's confused about. "So. See you tomorrow, I guess!"

Then I turn and run. Up June's driveway, where I know he won't follow.

CHAPTER 13

Mason

Pam and Sierra are already waiting at the pier when I show up in the morning, five minutes early. When I see that each of them has a large Cutie Fruitie cup in hand, I drop one of the two takeout cups of coffee that I brought from the bar into a trash can before Pam can see it.

Yeah, so maybe I brought her a coffee to kiss up.

I see Sierra has already beaten me at that game.

But I need Pam to see that me and Sierra, working together—it ain't gonna work.

Unfortunately, Sierra sees me dump the coffee and smirks at me as I approach. "Something wrong with that coffee, Mason?" She wears a short white tennis skirt that flutters around her creamy thighs in the breeze.

"Just finished it," I mutter. I take a sip of my coffee as my gaze skims her perky cleavage in the skimpy, strappy yoga top she chose to wear for this meeting.

Savage. The woman is savage.

I guess whatever kindness she showed last night was a one-time thing.

Maybe she was just drunk again.

"Good morning, Mason," Pam says briskly. She's holding a loaded clipboard, and her three-year-old son is driving a toy dump truck up and down her leg, so she gets right to it. "I was just bringing Sierra up to speed about the festival, explaining how visitors will walk in under the big banner where Cherry Way meets Water Street. They'll smell the barbecue, hear music from the stage, see kids making chalk art along the sidewalks. The vibe is community spirit and family fun, but we all know the real draw to Sunshine Fest is the food."

"And the drink, of course." Sierra slurps her smoothie.

"Right," Pam says. "And our key concern is maintaining flow between the various entertainment zones and the food service areas. Main stage. Farmers' market. Family fun zone. Food trucks. Barbecue pit. And both of your places."

"About that," I say. "Considering that we're essentially in competition, professionally, right now, I'm not sure that Sierra and I can ethically work together, so—"

"Oh, I have no problem working with Mason," Sierra says, not even looking at me.

Pam looks from her to me.

I grind my molars, then grit out, "Great. Just checking. I have no problem with it, either." Because no way am I letting her win *this* power struggle. I am not letting her make me look like the bad guy here.

"Okay . . . Now that that's settled," Pam says, "here's the issue we still need to resolve. We need to rethink our food service layout, now that Sea Haven isn't running the pop-up at the pier like we thought it would be. Instead, we have a smoothie bar."

"Oh. How does that change things?" Sierra asks.

"Well," I fill her in, "maybe because where we were expecting to offer people actual food, now they only get liquid fruit."

Sierra's light-green eyes fix on me, ridiculously beautiful in the morning sun. "I don't see a problem. My smoothies are packed with nutrients. They're way more nutritious than pub grub."

"Excuse me, 'pub grub'? Is that what you're calling the food in my establishment?"

The unflinching look in her eyes says, *You waged war on me, buddy. Take it like a man.*

"I'm adapting my menu to highlight local ingredients during the festival," she says pleasantly, kissing up to Pam. "And I'm happy to share my patio area with vendors who can provide 'actual food.'"

"Great," I say. "Because you have the most visible spot. So, you won't mind if my bar serves food on your patio."

She snorts. "I don't think so."

"Look," Pam interrupts. "I already have four kids of my own and fires to put out elsewhere. So, I'm gonna let you two kids work this out." And with that, she shoves the clipboard at me, answers her buzzing phone, and she's gone, three-year-old in tow.

"Way to go. You pissed off Pam." Sierra sips her smoothie and gazes at me innocently. "She's a busy mom, you know."

"You need to be flexible here. This isn't even your town."

She rolls her eyes. "We are not serving food from *your* bar on *my* patio. It makes no sense. I'm happy to partner with one of the food trucks. Or the community barbecue pit that Pam mentioned. You have your whole parking lot for the beer and cider garden. Don't be greedy, Mason."

"*I'm* being greedy?"

"Why don't you keep to your own establishment, I'll keep to mine, and we'll just see what people prefer," she says coolly.

"What are you proposing? Some childish contest?"

"Doesn't have to be childish. We just see which business is more popular during the festival."

"Sounds childish."

"It's market research."

She has no idea. "You want to pit alcohol against smoothies? The beer and cider garden will *crush* you."

"Bring it on. And let's be real. Alcohol is *not* included in this challenge. While I'd love to offer June's cider for sale and go head-to-head with yours, my smoothie bar is unlicensed. So, we're talking my smoothies versus your 'actual food.'" Her eyes glitter at me in a way that can't be misconstrued.

This woman is competitive. She's *living* for this shit. She'd fight me and even lose trying, rather than sit back and share with the likes of me.

"If that's what you want," I tell her.

"Great. Whoever sells more, we take that to June. It's proof of what people want, and therefore which business should get to lease Pier Seven for the rest of the summer. Unless, of course, you're too scared of losing to a woman and a bunch of 'liquid fruit.'"

We stare each other down. And Jace's words come back to haunt me.

Sierra fucking scares you.

"Fine," I say. "Agreed. When you lose, you can pack up and move out."

I turn on my heel and head over to my bar just to get the sight of her out of my eyes. My heart is racing. Every fucking word the woman says gets under my skin.

"Cool!" she calls after me. "When you lose, you can throw yourself a pity party at your bar! I'll send over smoothies!"

CHAPTER 14

Mason

I lie sprawled on my back in my new bed, staring at the fan that loops lazily on the ceiling, around and around. I smell freshly brewed coffee. Hear birds singing in the trees outside the new windows, the purr of farm equipment in the distance, and the soft *shoosh* of the sea beyond.

But I can't seem to muster a fuck to give about getting up and getting started with my day.

Now that this is my bedroom, it feels entirely new. New paint, new floor, new furniture. Not one hint remains of the years my parents spent in here, or my dad's parents before that. My grandpa said this was right, that I needed to make it mine. But I needed it, too: the change.

How could I rest, sleep, fuck in a bedroom with my parents' ghosts?

This was the last room to finish in the extensive renovations that my dad began and I finally just completed. But somehow, the family house still doesn't feel like mine.

I want it to.

I don't know if it ever will.

Maybe because it wasn't supposed to be mine nearly so soon.

I lived in this house for the first eighteen years of my life. But nothing has quite felt like home since the accident.

Or maybe it was long before they died that this problem began.

Maybe it started when I came back to Orchard Cove, all those years ago, a different man than the one who left.

Maybe I thought there would be a change once the primary bedroom was mine and I moved into it. A shift inside me.

I'm still waiting for that shift to happen.

But every morning this week, since I finally moved up here, it's been the same sense of dread when I open my eyes and smell the coffee my brother's brewing downstairs. The house is done, but it's not *home* yet. That's the feeling.

I'm not at home.

Something is missing. Out of place. And I don't know what it is.

I keep telling myself it's because I'm not used to living with people. It will be better soon, when Layne and Kaylie and Scar move into their cottage, and everyone is finally settled in their own home. Just a few more days, and we'll get there.

But what if they move out, and the shift never comes?

I need to get up, get on with my day, get to work. Get busy. That's the only way to escape the dread. I've learned that over the past year.

But my daily routine, my work, no longer provides the escape that it used to.

Because Sierra Daniels is now all up in it.

Now, I need to first work up the will to face another day battling with that woman. Over the most stupid shit. Fighting her, because I can't fuck her.

That's what it comes down to, doesn't it?

Yes, I want Pier Seven.

My body wants *her* more.

I've tried to fight my attraction to her. Tried like hell not to get caught up in whatever she's doing and where and with who. But all week long as we've prepared the town center for the festival, I've only become more preoccupied with her.

Just laying eyes on her, even knowing she's around, fucks with my head.

And she's always around.

In the corner of my eye, coming and going from Pier Seven, stopping to talk to someone outside of Bev & Bill's. Getting to know the locals. Winning them over. Popping into my bar to ask one of my staff some inane question or bringing them smoothies to "taste test," like she's just putting herself in my face to irritate me.

All while ignoring *me*.

I have no idea if she notices my fixation. But my growing obsession with her hasn't gone unnoticed by my friends, who continue to bombard me with unsolicited advice. *Maybe you should just fuck her and get it over with.* (Jace.) *Maybe you should just stay away from her and save your sanity.* (Evan.)

And my personal favorite: *What the fuck is wrong with you, bro? She's gorgeous.* (Layne.)

My brother doesn't even bother with advice, just makes it clear he thinks I'm being a dumbass. He doesn't understand my fixation on Pier Seven, or why I wouldn't be all over Sierra by now. But Layne has already carried on our family's legacy. He has Kaylie.

What the hell do I really have?

Selfishly, I could flirt with Sierra, try to get her into bed.

But what good would that do for my family?

Layne has no idea of the responsibility I feel as the older brother, the pressure of one day stepping into our grandpa's shoes. And the shit that I would be willing to give up, sacrifice for him and Kaylie and their future.

I'd give up anything. The woman in my dreams included.

I'm still haunted by memories of the night we spent together, especially at night. Instead of fading in intensity, they're only getting worse. In my dreams, I'm running my hands over her body all over again, seeking out every sensitive place she'll let me touch, and savoring her shivers when I find each one.

I wake each morning to the sound of her soft, hungry little moans.

And in the hazy moments between sleeping and fully awake, I'm acutely aware of how much I want her. When I'm alone and hard as hell, and she's in my head . . .

No filter. No stopping the direction of my thoughts before I've got my hands wrapped around my cock and I'm stroking, pulling, aching for release. Fantasizing about things we've never even done.

Her mouth, teasing and biting my nipple.

My fingers, slipping between her legs and finding her hot, wet, slippery insides as she moans.

My cock, pushing into the back of her throat as my balls—

"UNCLE MASON!"

My hands fly off my cock like I've been struck by lightning. I shove a pillow over my crotch as my niece's footsteps pound up the stairs toward my bedroom, and my thoughts scatter like marbles. *Jesus.* Did I lock the door?

Yes.

Maybe?

Fuck. I yank the covers over myself.

"MASON! I CAN'T FIND MY LABUBU HAVE YOU SEEN IT?!"

"Kaylie!" Layne shouts up the stairs, and the footsteps abruptly stop. "It's down here."

"You found it?"

"Yes. Stay out of Mason's room."

The footsteps pound back down the stairs.

I blow out a breath and sink back into the bed, heart thudding.

Three seconds later, I tense when Kaylie screams, "MASON!!" and my nervous system fires up again. "BREAKFAST IS READYYY!!!"

"OKAY!" I call back.

It's like she truly believes no one can hear her unless she screams the place down.

I groan, shove off the covers, and get up, still half hard. Trudge to the shower. Consider jerking off as I get the water running.

Instead, I make it cold and quick.

Try to be grateful that my brother just made me breakfast.

But fuck me. I need to get the renos finished on that damn cottage. Get Layne and Kaylie and the dog moved out of here.

I just need some fucking space.

Some alone time. One fucking moment of sanity in my goddamn day, to jerk off or do whatever the hell I want to, in fucking peace.

Just a few more days.

◆ ◆ ◆

The sun has just gone down and the smoothie bar has closed for the night when I find Sierra on the pier.

The set of steps down the side of the pier to the sand, right outside Pier Seven, is the only public access to the beach in Orchard Cove's town center, and it's the one that's used by most tourists. Which is one of the main reasons this is such a prime location for a restaurant.

But there's no one else on the beach that I can see in the fading light right now, or on the pier.

Just her.

As I approach, she's holding out her phone and posing with a refillable Cutie Fruitie cup under one of the pier's lamp posts, fiddling with the angles. Unzipped hoodie, hot-pink sports bra, yoga pants, platform sneakers. Hair smoothed back into a ponytail and braided.

Lips glossed. Nails done. Pierced navel showing.

She looks like a woman who could sell millions of anything without trying so hard, but has no idea.

"Taking selfies?" I inquire. "Hashtag: *suck it, Mason Grant*?"

She lowers the phone. "Just some social media," she mutters irritably. "For Cutie Fruitie."

"You got your phone working?"

"I'll upload it later" is her non-answer. She stashes the phone and the cup, which turns out to be empty, in her bag. "What's up?" She zips up her hoodie, blocking my view of her cleavage.

Doesn't matter. She's sexy as hell either way.

But less distracting, at least.

I turn to look back at the pier building, slide my hands into my pockets. "It's beautiful from this angle, isn't it? All lit up in the evening, with that backdrop. The dusk sky in the west shifting colors."

"Yes, it is," she says warily.

"There used to be tables out on this side, and dancing on summer nights."

"Really?"

I look at her. Decide to take a chance. Because I haven't *really* tried to talk to her.

To reason with her.

"Maybe this is what bothers me the most. That you don't know anything about the history of this building. Or understand why it's important to Orchard Cove."

Or why it's important to me.

She crosses her arms over her chest. "I'm just selling smoothies for the summer, Mason. Maybe I don't need to understand."

I consider that. And this disturbing feeling under my skin, the strange, conflicting tension that stirs in me whenever I think of her staying . . . or leaving.

"Do you even know why it's called Pier Seven?"

"Because there are at least six other piers?" she guesses.

"No. There's no official numbered pier system around here. My great-great-grandfather built the original pier here in Orchard Cove. His wife, my great-great-grandmother, was the seventh in a family of seven children. He would call her his lucky number seven. He named the pier after her."

"Oh. That's . . . nice," she admits.

"That original pier burned down, but my great-grandfather, my grandpa Tommy's dad, and June's dad were friends and they rebuilt it. They also added the building. It started out as a fish and chips stand, then was expanded into a larger restaurant and meeting place. It served as a social hub for the growing community at the time."

"So, how did June Spencer come to own it?"

I'm glad she's asked, because it shows that she actually has an interest. I want her to know why this place is important to my family. Though this is definitely my least favorite part of the story.

"Well, the government owns the actual pier now. But the building we call Pier Seven . . ." I rub my hand over my face. "Now that I think of it, you might not even believe me if I tell you. It's so ridiculous."

Her eyebrow lifts. "Now I really need to know."

I sigh quietly. "Tommy's dad and June's dad were friends, like I said, but they became rivals. Stopped talking to one another. Except for one fated night when they sat down to 'settle' their dispute, probably after a few too many drinks. With a poker game."

Sierra gapes at me. "Are you telling me that your great-grandfather *lost* this building to June's father in a poker game?"

"That is exactly what I'm telling you."

"Wow. How embarrassing for you."

I hold back a laugh. "You could say that. June's father didn't care to run a restaurant here, but he also didn't care to give, gamble, or sell it back to Tommy's father, so it sat empty for a long while. One of June's sisters and her husband ran the last active restaurant here for many years, but they struggled with it. I don't think they ever fell in love with it. They moved away from Orchard Cove eight years ago. It's been empty since then, except when June rents it out to the community or local businesses for events, exhibits, pop-up shops . . ."

"Okay. I can see why you'd want it back to run a restaurant. But you have to understand, I didn't know any of this when I came here. I didn't come here to compete with you."

"But you're so good at it," I say dryly.

She actually smiles. Genuinely smiles at me.

It makes my pulse pick up—and my defenses rise.

"Why do you want to extend your lease here, Sierra?" I press.

Her smile dies. "That's really my business. Not yours. What kind of warrior would I be if I just handed my enemy more ammunition for his gun?"

That's perfectly sensible, of course. But I'm not looking to shoot to kill. I just want the damn building. Butting heads hasn't gotten us anywhere so far, and maybe my unfortunate crush on her has given me the idea that if I offer her a chance to understand my position, she'll back off this fight.

I take a deep breath and tell her, "Buying back this building for my family isn't just something I want. It was my parents' dying wish. The last thing they were working on before they died. I've come to realize, especially in recent days . . . that I feel an extreme responsibility to carry out that wish."

I fully expect her to put up some argument, to tell me that none of this is her problem.

It's not.

But instead, she says, "That sounds like a really heavy responsibility to bear." She gazes at me with sympathy.

I look away, over the water.

"What were they like?" she asks, her voice gentle. "Samantha and Christopher."

Fuck.

Do I really want to stand here and talk about them? With her?

Yes. How can I not talk about them? With anyone who asks?

How else do I keep them alive?

"They were . . ." I rub the back of my head, an old nervous habit. Scrape my fingers through my hair. "Great parents. They were always . . ." How do I even put it? "So excited about the idea of us as a family. But it wasn't just an idea. We *lived* it. Matching pajamas and yearly photos by the Christmas tree and marking our heights on the wall every birthday. We ate every breakfast and every dinner together around the table. And if we fought, they told us we had to have each other's backs, me and Layne and Haven, no matter what—"

"Wait. Who's Haven?"

"My sister."

"You have a sister?"

"Yeah. A little sister. She lives in Seattle."

"Hold up." Sierra blinks at me. "Your sister . . . is a city girl?"

I chuckle, caught off guard. "You could say that."

She stares at me. "Who the fuck even are you, Mason Grant? Just when I thought I had you figured out, you throw me a curveball. I thought you *hated* city people."

I don't even know what to say.

As usual when I find myself talking to her, I've hit a point where I don't even know what the hell is happening. I have so many conflicting thoughts and emotions fighting to get to the surface, I don't know which one to respond to first.

"Who the hell are *you*, Sierra?" I growl, letting some of my frustration slip to the top.

She laughs shortly. "What do you mean? I'm no mystery. What you see is what you get."

I swipe my hand over my mouth, considering whether to go there.

Yup. I'm going there.

"Well, what I saw is a meme. With you in it. You . . . and a purple dick?"

Her eyes widen comically. "Oh, Jesus. Did someone send it to you?" She looks panicked, and I'm overcome by the urge to reassure her.

"No. When I found out you'd leased Pier Seven, I looked you up. It was in a comment on one of your social posts."

"Oh, dear god."

"It disappeared later," I say. Though in telling her so, I'm revealing that I looked her up more than once. "I have to admit . . . I didn't know what to think."

"Ugh." She walks over to the edge of the pier and drops her bag. She sits down, legs dangling over the side.

I hesitate only briefly.

Then I go sit down next to her. We watch the water lap and froth against the rocks in the shadows below the pier. I wait for her to explain, or to tell me to fuck off, or to do anything.

I don't care if I have to wait here all night, I need to know. I need to know *her*. Just a little fucking something so I can stop fucking wondering and driving myself crazy.

She *is* a mystery.

Beautiful and kind of sweetly awkward, sassy and sharp and a fucking mystery.

I have no idea what really makes her tick, and at this point, I would kill to know one fucking thing.

One thing she tells me herself, and not when she's drunk.

"Look, I did not make that meme," she says softly. "I told you my boyfriend broke up with me days before I arrived in Orchard Cove. The whole story is, his family was investing in my business. I was going to buy a small brick and mortar store in Vancouver to open a permanent Cutie Fruitie location. And they were providing the down payment, connections, experience. I really couldn't have done it without them."

She kicks her feet slowly in the air, and I wait for her to spill the rest of her secrets to me and the sea. As many as she'll give us.

"We were on a video call, to celebrate, because they'd found me the perfect location," she goes on. "Kyle, me, his parents, and several other relatives involved with their family-run investment business were on the call. And I made the incredibly stupid mistake of not realizing that there was a large, anatomically detailed dildo on my bedside table in the background. Everyone noticed it before I did. Kyle was at his place and like, yelled at me over the video call. His family hung up. But not before I guess his sneaky, pimply little cousin recorded the whole mess so he could immortalize me in a purple dick meme. Which he then blasted out to Kyle's entire contact list for shits and giggles."

Silence stretches, marred only by the rhythm of the water hissing over the rocks below.

"Fuck me" is all I can say.

"Yeah. Technology in the hands of the children. Terrifying."

"So . . . that comment about how 'big' it was . . . ?"

"I was talking about the location Kyle's dad found for me, for the smoothie shop. It was way beyond my expectations and I was fucking thrilled."

I swallow the urge to laugh and clear my throat instead. "I mean, I could see that. You seemed very excited about the size of it."

Our gazes connect and she bites her lip. Is she trying not to laugh?

"I suppose it wouldn't salvage some small part of your opinion of me," she ventures, "if I were to explain that the dildo was just a gag birthday gift from my best friend, and not, like, my faithful bedtime ritual or anything. Kyle sure didn't believe it."

"Hey, no judgment here. My opinion of you is already as low as it gets, based entirely on our business rivalry."

A hint of amusement flickers over her pretty lips. "Well, thank you. I appreciate the professional courtesy."

We sit in silence for a moment, warmth in the air between us. A tension effervescent with humor that *almost* bubbles to the surface and breaks. I'm still not totally sure if she's struggling not to laugh, but I sure as fuck am.

"So . . ." I test the waters. "Never used it, huh?"

"Oh, I did," she says sharply. "Once. After Kyle dumped me and refused to even hear that it was brand new and had never been sullied, because he was so offended I'd subjected his parents' eyeballs to a sex toy that had intimate knowledge of my vagina . . . there was a definite hate-fuck situation."

I study the side of her face as she gazes into the water, and heat spreads through my body. "You . . . hate-fucked the dildo to get back at your ex-boyfriend?"

"Oh, yeah." She glances at me, eyes sparkling, but covers her mouth with her hand. "It made a *lot* of sense at the time."

I swallow. "Very sensible."

"Therapeutic," she agrees.

Then she laughs, snorting into her hand.

I laugh. I laugh so fucking hard, my eyes tear up.

She drops her hand and laughs out loud, her pretty voice floating away over the water.

"Anyway," she says as she calms down, wiping the tears from her eyes, "I had to get *some* pleasure out of it. That stupid blunder cost me everything."

My smile fades. "What?"

She sighs. "It's not about the stupid meme. That was just a prank from a thirteen-year-old. Embarrassing, but I'll get over it. The worst part was Kyle dumped me like yesterday's trash after that call. And his parents snatched back their investment. They all dumped me. And life as I knew it fell apart overnight. That clumsy mistake put my business in serious jeopardy."

I digest this. "Sierra. Christ. That is so not okay."

"I know," she says, so lightly I have to wonder. *Does* she know? "But what am I gonna do about it? The relationship is over, and with each day that passes I understand better what a good thing that is."

"Okay. But what about your business?"

She eyes me. "Oh, I'm sure you'd love it if I still had some wealthy investor to help me set up shop far, far away from here . . ."

"That's not what I meant."

"It's fine. I'll figure it out. And this whole thing . . . The dildo, the meme, my boyfriend breaking up with me and diving into bed with his beautiful best friend—"

"Wait. What the hell?"

"—it's all just *so* stupid compared to what you've been through."

But it's not.

"No, I get it," I tell her. "Your whole life plan fell apart overnight. That's no joke." No way am I telling her about Jenn abandoning me at the altar. But I do get it in more ways than she could possibly know.

Unfortunately, I also understand *her* position better now.

Even respect her more as a rival.

One who maybe deserves to be here and have a fighting chance to keep this building, almost as much as I do?

I also feel some of my will to fight her slipping away, which is fucking bad.

So why am I doing this?

I don't know. It just feels right as the words come out of my mouth. "Quite frankly, Sierra Daniels, I'm fucking shocked you'd let some asshole who doesn't even respect you interfere with your life."

She cocks her head. "But you're so good at interfering with my life."

"I meant your ex," I growl.

She smiles. "I know, Mason."

I'm not letting her brush this off as a joke. This part is for real.

"And I do respect you," I tell her. "I respected you enough as a stranger to take care of you when you were drunk. And I respect you enough now to tell you that you should've stood up for yourself. Your ex should've stood up for you, too. If you gave that situation half the pushback you've given me over this building, your doubters would cower and scurry back into the shadows. And maybe your ex's parents still would've invested."

Her smile is gone. "You don't know them, Mason. And really, it's a blessing. I couldn't have gone into business with people like that."

"You're right."

We stare at each other, and my desire for her thrums through my veins, a constant tension that's only growing stronger.

I still don't know if I can trust her. How much of *this* I can trust. Her words. This feeling coursing between us.

Is she just telling me all these things, presenting this vulnerable front, to manipulate me into letting my guard down? Feeling sorry for her? Letting her have the building?

I don't know.

All I fucking know for sure right now is how badly I want to kiss those soft, sweet lips.

So instead, I tell her, "You're a formidable opponent, Sierra Daniels."

"You know, I'm just gonna go ahead and take that as a compliment."

"You should." I get to my feet before I can say anything really fucked-up. This whole conversation has been risky enough. "I need to get back to the bar."

She looks up at me. "Yeah. I need to lock up the shop."

I hesitate, transfixed by the way the pier's few lights skim the curves of her face. "Goodnight, then."

As I start to walk away, she says, "So . . . what does this all mean, Mason? Are we friends now?"

I pause to look back at her. So fucking gorgeous, sitting at the edge of the pier with one knee pulled up under her chin, gazing at me.

"Fuck, no," I say softly.

She smiles, just a little. And it is not good, how warm it makes me feel.

"You want me to let you have Pier Seven?" she says.

"Yes."

"Fuck, no. You want to call a truce?" She cocks a sharp eyebrow at me. "Scared I'm gonna outsell you at the festival?"

"No chance, beautiful," I tell her.

Then I walk away, before I can say anything I'll really regret.

CHAPTER 15

Sierra

The night before the festival begins, after a long final day of setup, most of the planning committee goes out for drinks—at Sea Haven Bar & Grill, where apparently the owner is buying.

It wouldn't be my first choice of venue, considering that no matter how well said bar owner and I occasionally, unexpectedly, get along or how thoroughly he eye-fucks me or how smolderingly he calls me "beautiful," he still insists we're not friends, he doesn't want to call a truce, and he *still* hasn't taken back his ridiculous demand that I stay away from his family.

But hey, there's really nowhere else to go out drinking in this town after dark. And since he's buying . . .

When I walk in, Mason is behind the bar, helping Oscar, his Brazilian bartender with the big smile and many earrings, get all the drink orders out. I now know all Mason's staff by name, because I've popped in often enough to get to know them a little. The room is filling up with locals as the committee volunteers flood in, but there are tourists, too.

Like the four women sitting along the bar, drooling over Mason in his fitted T-shirt.

Kind of like I did the first time I came in here.

They look like city types, and it weirds me out that I notice. As if they're outsiders and I'm now one of the locals. When in fact I'm not even sure if I'm allowed to be in here.

I've come in here many times, sure. Mainly to fuck with Mason. But I mostly just speak to his staff, ignore him, and leave. I've never actually had the audacity to stroll onto enemy turf like any other customer and expect service.

Maybe I should've. Sounds kind of fun, actually.

None of Mason's family is here, and miracle of miracles, he doesn't kick me out the minute he sees my ass taking a seat. Instead, his gaze clings to me as I settle in at a table by the jukebox with Sophie and Trish and Hot Mom/Maria.

I meet his gaze across the distance, and there he goes, eye-fucking me all over again.

All day, I've felt his eyes on me.

I've managed to hire some extra staff at the smoothie bar to get us through the festival, and to help me out when Sophie leaves town afterwards—including Bev and Bill's twenty-year-old niece, Chloe, who's come home on summer break from college and has been an absolute godsend. Which means I was able to step away from Cutie Fruitie today, and spend hours outside instead—me, Mason, and many of the other volunteers, setting up the market tables and shade structures and festival signage. And every time Mason came near me, I felt the tension radiating between us. This hot, bothersome push and pull.

Not the tension of two people who can't stand each other, but the tension of two people who can't help noticing when the other one is near.

Who can't stop *looking*.

And who want to do much, much more than look.

Or maybe that's just me.

When he comes over, the women at my table fall suspiciously silent as he serves me first. It's a coincidence, I'm almost sure. Until he sets a bubbly cocktail in front of me, tinged with Sea Haven's violet gin. "You seem to like purple," he says, his voice low in my ear, and heat explodes through me. A spark of embarrassment followed by an intense surge of lust.

Is he flirting with me?

A very large part of me can't fucking believe I told him about the purple dildo incident. But another, much hornier part is fucking thrilled that *I think he's flirting with me.*

I take a sip and meet his gaze as he serves up the other ladies' drinks. We didn't even put in an order, he just brought these over, and they all get cider. Mine is the only one that's different, and it gives me all the wrong ideas.

God help me, I kind of love it when he pays attention to me.

Maybe I should've told him *why* Sophie bought me that dildo—because I'd confessed to her how shitty my sex life with Kyle was. He didn't know what he was doing; he had terrible aim; worst of all, he didn't even seem to *try* anymore.

Soph had labelled this state of affairs "the trifecta of disappointment" and gave me the dildo for my thirtieth birthday along with a bottle of lube.

Maybe if Mason knew how sexually deprived I've been, he'd take pity on me and just do me already.

"Wow, that was blatant," Maria says, delighted, as Mason walks away from our table and I stare at his muscular ass. "Swear on my children, I have never seen Mason look at someone like *that*."

When I find every eyeball at the table locked onto me, I take a *just chilling over here* sip of my drink even as I feel my cheeks turning pink. "Look at who? What?"

"She's in deep denial," Sophie explains to the others. "But it's not her fault. She doesn't have eyes in the back of her head. So, she doesn't actually see him taking a mental bite out of her ass every time he's behind her. You know, same as she does to him."

"Ahh," Trish says, like some confounding mystery has finally been solved.

"What?" I say innocently. "Who's biting whose ass?"

"Mason Grant," Maria enunciates, like maybe I am actually this dense, "is completely obsessed with you, Sierra."

I blink. "He is not."

"Say more," Sophie says, shushing me with a flap of her hand.

"Oh, Mason's a total playboy," Maria says. "If you haven't heard. *So many* women around here have tried to lock him down, fix him up, make him their man. All for naught. But I've never seen anyone turn his head like this baddie does." She flips her thumb toward me, like *I'm* the baddie she speaks of.

"Who . . . me?"

"You are a baddie," Maria informs me. "Own your own business. Won't put up with his shit. Hot as fuck in yoga-wear. Check, check, check. If that man has a wish list, I'm sure you're it."

"More," Sophie demands. "This is gold."

"He's very hard to get," Trish concurs, happy to jump onboard. "He's always been, like, the hottest guy in town, you know? It was like that in school, too. Girls *love* him."

"And not just the locals," Maria adds, nodding her head toward the bar, where those four women are perched in a line. "They come and go every year, especially in summer, and he just takes his pick. Never seems to care when they leave. Never gets attached."

"It's like that with Layne, too," Trish gushes. "It's like he just hasn't found the right woman for him yet . . ." She turns the conversation to Layne, while my attention remains riveted on the show at the bar.

Not Mason, exactly, but those women. Their backs are to me, but I don't need to see their faces to know they're watching his every move. It's in their posture. The way their heads angle toward him. Their hands—touching themselves while they speak to him, playing with their hair.

And before I even notice she's left the table, Sophie is getting up to something.

Suddenly, she's up at the bar, leaning over to talk to Mason. He nods, then turns up the volume on the music at her request. Led Zeppelin plays loudly over the sound system as she strolls over to the jukebox—where she switches up the song, putting on "Into You" by Ariana Grande instead.

Which could not be more fucking fitting.

Maria and Trish are chatting and don't seem to notice what Sophie is up to as she comes to sit down next to me again. I lean into her. "Tell him you think I want to fuck him without telling him you think I want to fuck him," I say dryly.

She sips her cider like a lady, eyes dancing. "You're welcome."

I know, I really brought this on myself. By telling my best friend, last night, about my conversation with Mason on the pier. I told her everything. How he makes me laugh. How he makes me *long*.

How he makes me wonder . . .

I told her how totally thrown off I was by his reaction to my confession about the meme and the stupid purple dildo—which was completely opposite to the way Kyle reacted—and the resulting loss of my investment.

I hadn't planned to tell Mason about any of it, but when he told me he'd seen the meme, I *had* to tell him. Because maybe I didn't want him to judge me for it as badly as he might if I didn't at least try to explain.

I never would've anticipated that my "enemy" would be so understanding. So supportive. That he'd show more respect for me than my boyfriend had.

Can I trust Mason's reaction? I don't know. I have no way of knowing if it was genuine, or if he was just trying to manipulate me into feeling better about the whole thing so I'll go back to the city, find somewhere else to run my business.

And it's driving me crazy, the wondering.

I even told Sophie in frustration that I should've brought that dildo with me to Orchard Cove. Never would've thought I'd want to fuck myself with a sex toy while my best friend is trying to sleep right in the next room—because I'm so hard up for a guy who doesn't even like me that I'm hornier than I've ever been in my life—but it's the sad fucking truth.

I want the man, badly. And any way I look at it, my days in Orchard Cove are numbered. And last night, when Sophie realized how much I want him, she told me the same thing that my hormones keep trying to tell me.

Maybe you should just tell him you're into him.

Maybe you should just sleep with him.

Maybe it can just be about sex. Just for fun. Just putting yourself, and what you want, first for once.

But since I'm clearly *not* going to tell him I'm into him, I guess my best friend decided to let a song say it for me.

Unfortunately, the song totally misses its mark. Mason is either oblivious to the vibe or pretends to be.

Meanwhile, my least favorite local responds like a salivating dog offered a whiff of raw meat. Lee Weston, June's fortysomething nephew and orchard manager, a man who gives overt horny-womanizer vibes every time I run into him, pulls up a chair next to me and sits down. "Hey, Sierra. How's your night going?"

Unfortunately, I think he has a thing for me. Between his legs.

"Hey, Lee. It's good . . ."

I can't help looking for Mason across the room.

He's still behind the bar, with those women fawning over him. He glances over at me, notices Lee sitting next to me, and . . .

Does absolutely nothing about it.

In fact, not five minutes later, when Lee is still chatting me up, Mason leaves the bar.

Maybe an hour later, Sophie and I walk back to Honeymoon Lane along the beach walk. We're talking about anything other than Mason, because I asked her, shortly after he left the bar, not to mention him again.

I didn't want to spend another night thinking about a man who isn't thinking about me.

Who cares if Maria and Trish and even Sophie think he wants me? They don't *know*. They're not Mason, and Mason left.

Mason, who could probably have me with just one touch, one *word*, business rivalry or no, hasn't made a move and clearly isn't going to.

But when the path spits us out onto Honeymoon Lane, I find myself gazing up the Grant family's driveway, because I am thinking about him.

Of course I am. The man is impossible not to think about.

Have I ever been this attracted to anyone else on earth?

Sadly, no.

I can't see his house from here. I can't see the cidery or anything at all but trees. But I know he's probably in there, somewhere.

It's disturbing how well I know his routine by now. How I mentally track him all day, filling in the gaps between my glimpses of him. And since he's not at the bar, and I know the cider house is closed for the night, I can guess where he'll probably be.

At home.

Showering, maybe. Cleaning up. Going to bed.

Doing laundry or watching TV or jerking off?

And not thinking about me.

I stop in my tracks at the entrance of his driveway, by the *Sea Haven Orchard* sign.

"I'm going to pop in," I tell Sophie before I can change my mind. "To see Mason."

She considers me thoughtfully. "How drunk are you, and should I veto this?"

"Not very. I had two drinks. And no, I'm okay."

"Hmm. Do you want me to wait here? Or come with you?"

"No. No, you go home. I'll catch up with you soon."

"Okay . . ." She gives me a quick hug. "But if you don't come home, I'll just assume . . . ?"

"You can assume that some member of the Grant family shot me for trespassing."

"Not funny."

"Humor is all I have left." I give her a kiss on the cheek. "Go have phone sex with your amazing husband."

"He is amazing," she says dreamily. "Good luck! And if you want to yell at him or screw him, just know that I support you one hundred percent."

"Love you," I call after her as she fades away into the dark between the far-flung streetlights.

I walk up the quiet drive and climb right over the low traffic gate that says the cider house is closed. I pass the cidery building, the distillery, and take the fork in the path that leads me to another, smaller gate. It has a *Private Property* sign on it, meant to keep customers from wandering up to the house.

I go right through, and up the path to where it splits off again. I take the way that leads me to the front porch of the Grant family home.

The house is large and white, a modern farmhouse, probably updated from its original form, with a charcoal-gray roof and black window frames, and a dark-blue front door. There's a wide white porch along the front, and a faint glow coming through the windows.

I climb the steps in the dark, my heart thumping. After I ring the bell, it takes a minute before the porch light flips on and the door opens from inside.

Mason.

Wearing nothing but a pair of dark sweats.

Dear god.

My gaze ravages his naked torso as he stands there, staring at me. I think I've shocked him.

He's shocked me more.

Juicy pecs. Abs for days. Leanly muscled V disappearing into the low-slung sweats . . .

"Sierra. Is everything okay?"

I blink up at his eyes, struggling not to gawk.

How can he even ask me that? Has anything ever been "okay" between us?

When I don't answer fast enough, he glances past me, trying to figure out what exact disaster is at play. Like if I'm standing here, at *his* door, the town must be on fire.

"You left," I finally manage to say. Because that sums up the disaster, doesn't it?

I was there. You left.

"Left?"

"The bar."

"Yeah. Uh, I always leave the bar around that time."

"But I was there."

He takes that in. Nods. "You were there," he agrees softly.

So, at least he's admitting that he knew I was still sitting there when he left.

"You could've come over and had a drink."

"I could've."

The acknowledgment reinforces the rejection. *I know I could've. I know you would've let me. I didn't want to.*

I swallow. "So, you just want to be enemies? Is that it?"

His bottomless gaze slides over me. "No. I don't want us to be enemies. But that's just how it is, right?"

Maybe.

Or maybe we could be something else. Something more?

Like enemies, plus . . . I don't know.

Lovers?

Yes. Fuck yes, we could.

We both know we could.

He's single. I'm single. And I can't stop undressing him with my eyes wherever he goes, no matter how much of an ill-mannered jerk he's being. He must notice it.

How I fucking thirst for him.

Yet he's making no move.

"This is a bad idea."

I turn to leave, but as I reach the bottom of the porch steps, he says, "Wait."

I stop, heart lurching into my throat, and look up at him.

His jaw has hardened, and he wears that guarded look that I know so well. The one that tells me he thinks I'm trouble. "If you're thinking of hooking up with Lee Weston," he says in a low voice. Hesitates. "I should warn you, he's bad news."

I laugh humorlessly. "Let me guess. He's a playboy? Uses women for a quick fix, then tosses them aside? Doesn't get attached?"

He frowns, like he's surprised that I already know. And bothered, maybe, that I seem unbothered by it. "Something like that."

"Do you know that's the same thing people say about you?"

He takes a step toward me, his brow furling. "What? I don't use women. I don't toss them aside."

"No? So, telling them to stay the hell away from you after you've spent the night with them isn't your usual move?"

He's silent for a moment. Then: "I never told you to stay away from me."

"Oh, that's right. You just ordered me to stay away from your family. Are they here right now? Should I leave before I poison them with my toxic presence?"

His chest rises and falls in a small sigh. "They're not here. Layne and Kaylie moved into their cottage out back."

I'm not sure why he's telling me this.

I wrap my arms around myself, even though it's not cold. "What about Tommy? Doesn't he live here, too?"

"My grandpa lives in a fully contained suite on the back side of the house. Technically it's attached, but he'd never wander in here uninvited. This is my house now, and he respects that."

We stare at each other.

I don't know what to think of this information, except that he seems to be telling me that we're alone.

"Great," I say lightly. "We wouldn't want him to stumble upon you fraternizing with the enemy like this."

"Sierra . . ." He sighs again. But he says nothing more. Just my name, hanging in the air between us.

It feels like when he called me "beautiful" last night, then walked away. And when he stared at me tonight, across the bar, then went home.

It's so, so frustrating.

I think I liked it better when I thought he actually hated me. At least that was clear.

"Are you trying to fuck with my head on purpose?" I ask him. "I know we're rivals and all, but this is cruel."

He looks confused now. "How am I being cruel?"

"You flirted with me at the bar. With that purple drink."

He rubs his hands over his face.

But I don't care if he's uncomfortable. Or frustrated. Or all fucked-up over me.

He *did* flirt.

And I'm definitely all fucked-up over him.

"You want me to keep thinking about you," I press. "To *want* you."

"Why wouldn't I?" he growls, frustration slipping through.

Good. Emotions are sexual lubricant, and with him standing there with his shirt off and telling me we're alone right now, my head is firmly in the gutter. If he's trying to be a tease, to get me back for that drunken night when I wouldn't let him hit it, it's working.

"Do you think about me?" I demand.

"Of course I do. How can I not? You're every-fucking-where I turn."

Nice try.

"No. It's more than that." I climb the porch steps and stand in front of him. "That first night, in your bed . . ." My voice drops to a whisper. "You wanted me."

"Yes." His voice is gravelly. "I did."

"But that's changed now?"

"It never changed," he says gruffly.

Then he grabs me, his hands sliding into my hair as he pulls me to him, and he *almost* kisses me.

I suck in a breath.

His mouth hovers over mine for one breath, two. Testing. *Do I want this?*

Will I tell him to stop?

"Don't stop," I breathe.

His mouth slams down on mine. Hot. Hungry.

No, ravenous.

His lips are soft, his beard is silky-rough, his tongue is greedy for mine, and I love it all.

I kiss him back with all the pent-up hunger I feel.

He pulls me into the house, slams the door behind us, and presses me up against it.

"This is . . . just sex," I gasp between kisses, panic spiking at the back of my mind. Vulnerability. His kisses feel way too good. "Right?"

He pauses, breathing heavily and studying my face. Maybe wondering if I meant it, when I accused him of using women for sex. "If that's what you want."

But of course that's what I want.

"I'm leaving," I pant. "At the end of the month or in a few months. I don't belong here. This isn't my home."

He isn't my home.

He's just a hot, delicious man I don't want to deny myself the pleasure of getting naked with for one more second.

"I know," he says.

"Great."

"Okay."

"Yeah."

We stare at each other, my heart beating wildly against his chest, his knee pressed up between my legs, his hands buried in my hair.

I know this is a risk.

But he wants me, too.

It's in his eyes and his hammering pulse, his rock-hard cock against my hip. And somehow, just knowing this is enough.

All my worries are silenced in the crashing waves of want as we slam together, making out against his door, and then on his floor.

He peels off my clothes, piece by piece, as his mouth moves over my skin. Kissing. Sucking. Softly biting. Testing with his teeth and tongue as he explores every curve.

And I let him, fucking basking in it.

When he strips off my bra, he cups my breasts and suckles my nipples into hard peaks, making both of us moan. He kisses his way down my belly with a fervor.

He strokes his beard on the insides of my thighs as he moves between them, nuzzling my pussy through my panties, inhaling my scent.

I shiver, feeling dizzy with lust, my heart pounding with excitement. His desire is palpable and it's making me feel high.

As soon as he rips my panties down and gets them off, he buries his face between my legs, groaning in pleasure. He wraps his lips around my clit. His mouth is warm and insistent, and he goes after it as hungrily as he did my mouth.

Fuck. I knew he'd be good at this.

He sucks on my pulsing clit and I gasp.

So, *so* good . . .

He eats me out like he's been craving it for days, weeks, ever since we met. Lapping and kissing and suckling as I pant and dig my fingers into his hair. His tongue delves inside me, making me groan.

Then he flickers it over my clit, teasing. And when I shiver, gasp "*yes*," he rewards me with more ravenous sucking.

"Mmm, Sierra," he moans as he makes out with my pussy, and heat shudders through me.

He slides a thick finger inside me, fucking me with it as he sucks. The flood of sensations is almost too much to handle and I cry out, bucking against him.

"Shh," he soothes me. "I've got you." But he sounds thrilled. Like he's just discovered his new favorite game. Then he slides a second finger up my pussy.

I whimper, swear, and he groans.

"This what you needed, baby?" he murmurs against my thigh.

It's like we've both been reduced to this singular act, stripped down in mere frantic moments to our aching bodies as he pours all his focus into guiding my pleasure, and I just try to hold on.

I want to come.

I don't want to come so fast.

I bite my lip. Struggle not to grind against his hand, his face.

I can't even respond to his question, and he doesn't need a verbal answer.

My body says it all. My moans and helpless gasps as he strokes his fingers in and out. I spread my thighs wider, wanting more, more, more.

"Good," he murmurs drunkenly. Sucking on me. Teasing with his hot mouth. "That's good, Sierra. You feel so good, don't you?"

In his voice, the pain of his aching resistance, his own struggle to hold back.

I don't know if I've ever felt more beautiful, more magical, more fucking desired.

The floor is hard and kind of cold, but I don't care. There's something fantastically raw and dirty and fucking perfect about sprawling naked on Mason Grant's hardwood floor while he urges me toward orgasm.

"You're gonna come," he mutters. "Aren't you. *Fuck* . . . you're gorgeous."

The words this man utters in between the things he's doing to me . . .

And all the while he watches me. Every shudder and twitch of my body, every roll of my hips as he fucks me with three fingers now. I think. It's all rolling into a blur of bliss and mounting need. My core tightening, bearing down . . .

"Please," I gasp. "Oh, god." I grab at his hair, just trying to anchor myself in the pleasure as he controls me completely.

He picks up the pace a bit, making me cry out.

"That's it. You need to come, don't you, baby?" He urges me on between licks, his carnal kisses. "Come for me . . ."

Oh, fuck. His words undo me. His rough, sexy voice, strained with his arousal.

The way he calls me "baby" before he lavishes my throbbing clit with his tongue.

His eyes, pupils blown wide as they lock on mine . . .

When he closes his hot, wet mouth on my clit again and hungrily sucks, eyes on me, I come in a rush, screaming. Clenching on his fingers as my core spasms. Clawing at his hair as the pulses rack my body and my eyes roll back in my head.

"Mason," I sob as he keeps sucking, keeps stroking . . . patiently lavishing my body with wave upon wave of pleasure.

For a few stunning moments of pure euphoria, I'm no longer in Orchard Cove. I'm not naked on the floor in my enemy's house.

I'm rolling in the ecstasy where Mason put me, totally forgetting that this could hurt me tomorrow.

CHAPTER 16

Mason

The second time Sierra comes for me is in my bed.

I carry her there, up two flights of stairs, after I peel her off the floor. Her legs wrapped around my waist, her arms around my neck, and her perfect ass in my hands. Her chest against mine. Her hands in my hair and her kisses on my lips.

Her lips are soft, swollen now, like the rest of her.

The flesh between her legs that I kiss as I lay her down on my bed. Her nipples, flushed and taut, that I suckle into hard, aching points.

All the while, the music of her sweet moans urges me on.

I pause only to shuck off my sweats. Fumbling, I'm so worked up. My heart beats a frantic rhythm, my breaths coming hard and fast, those goddamn doves in a frenzy every time I look at her face . . . like my chest might burst right open and all my insides might come flying out.

She's so fucking beautiful, sprawled in the moonlight that spills through the windows, waiting for me. Naked and panting, and for the moment, all mine.

I shift myself over her body, settling my hips between her legs, and she opens for me.

Hip to hip, chest to chest, and mouth to mouth, we move against each other. Sliding together until I almost slide right in. She's so wet. Her thighs are coated in her climax, her juices mixed with my spit.

I pull back to take a breath.

Her light-green eyes are aglow with pleasure in the moonlight. I nudge my cockhead into her opening, whisper, "Tell me you want it."

"Yes," she breathes. "More."

A shudder of arousal sweeps through me as her hands run down my back. My cock flexes. I fist my hand in her long, soft hair.

I hold her gaze as I fill her in one thrust.

She cries out—that soft, sexy, broken sound that means she's in pleasure.

I'm a connoisseur of it by now.

My head spins as she squeezes me inside. "*Fuck*, baby. You're so tight. So fucking wet for me . . ."

"Yes," she sobs. "Fuck me . . ." She spreads her thighs, grabs my ass, and digs in her nails as I thrust.

Slow, luxuriating in the feel of her as we kiss. Deeper. More passionate now. Tumbling into each other.

Then faster and faster as we lose our breath.

"You want to come again?" I whisper against her lips.

"*Yes.* Fuck, Mason . . ."

My balls tighten when she says my name. And this wicked euphoria is gathering in my chest, at the base of my spine, in the base of my cock . . . fucking *all over*. Tingles are spreading all over my skin.

"Good, baby," I pant. "Come for me."

She whimpers as we strain together, deeper and harder, and I feel it when she reaches the edge. She bears down on me, squeezing. Her breath catches. She gasps for air.

"Yeah. Good girl," I coax her, kissing her neck. "Come all over my dick."

She moans.

Good thing she likes my dirty talk, because I can't stop.

"*Fuck*, I can feel you coming," I groan as she spasms around me. This time as she comes, she moans helplessly, a sound that sends shivers down my back. "Your pussy, squeezing me . . ." Her hips snap up to meet my thrusts, and I close my eyes, reveling in her pleasure.

I keep fucking her, deep and slow, and she trembles with aftershocks even as she starts to go limp.

"*Mason*," she gasps. "Come. I want you to come."

Fuck, the *rush*. When she gasps my name.

When she asks for my orgasm.

"You want it?" God. I can't stop. I mean, I can. I will.

If she wants me to.

"Yes," she breathes. "It's okay. I'm on birth control."

Harder, I slam into her. Still slow, but deep, my own arousal ramping up to the brink. "Are you sure?"

"*Ungh*," she groans in pleasure as I pound her. "Yes."

"You want me inside?"

"Yes." She grabs at my ass, clutching, pulling me closer. "Gimme . . ."

And that does it.

My resistance is gone.

A few more thrusts—and my cock stiffens. Pulses. Pleasure surges through me as I unload inside her with a groan.

I'm lost in it for a long, breathless moment, in *her*, as I empty myself out. Wrapped in her arms, our damp bodies entwined as my heart slams.

Afterwards, as my other senses gradually seep back in, I struggle to catch my breath. Sierra has taken it away. I'm aware of the sound of wind in the trees outside, and hope we weren't too loud.

I have no idea if we were.

Fuck.

That was nothing like I imagined it would be.

And I've imagined it a lot. Taking her, in every imaginable position, fast—and fucking angry. Frustration fucking.

None of my fantasies came close to reality.

Her eagerness.

Her softness.

The smell of her, the naked curves of her body, the sound of her voice while I'm inside her. The parts of her she let me have this time, no holding back.

The way she makes me feel . . .

I'm still inside her when I become aware of her heavy breathing. I lift some of my weight off her. I shift my hips, and pull out carefully.

"Don't go," she whispers, so quietly I barely make out the words. Her arms are still around me, and I relax against her.

It feels way too good.

I bury my face in her hair and inhale her soft scent, again.

Her fingers curl into the hair at the nape of my neck and a warm shiver runs through me.

My pulse throbs against her body, almost in time with hers.

It throbs in the back of my mind, like a clock, ticking down the days, hours, minutes. Like a bomb . . . it warns me not to get too close. Not to get attached, or it'll blow up in my face.

Because she's leaving Orchard Cove.

Sooner or later . . .

She's leaving me.

◆ ◆ ◆

When I wake up in the morning, the ceiling fan loops lazily overhead.

I hear birds singing in the trees through the open windows, the purr of farm equipment, and the soft *shoosh* of the sea.

I smell freshly brewed coffee. Because when Layne and Kaylie moved out, my niece got upset, and I promised her we'd still have breakfast together, every morning.

I smell Sierra's soft scent all over me, and I stretch my arms out, between the cool sheets, seeking.

Wanting.

But I already know.

She's gone.

CHAPTER 17

Sierra

The first day of Sunshine Fest rushes by, most of it in a blur of music, food, sunlight, and happy faces.

Following the opening ceremony at noon is a pet parade for the kids down Water Street. Then the farmers' and artisans' market stalls open all along Water Street, along with the food trucks, Cutie Fruitie, and Sea Haven Bar & Grill.

The beer and cider garden opens at four, and by five o'clock, Mason's bar is *packed*, along with his parking lot, now lined with tables and chairs. I send Chloe over there—an annoying (to her, I'm sure) many, many times—to scope out the crowd and report back to me. How many heads does she count, and are they eating?

Lots, and they are.

Although the smoothie bar has a steady flow of customers and even a lineup out the door for most of the day, by six p.m. it's clear that Mason is slaughtering me in sales.

And just before seven, I realize that my ice machine is broken.

Then we run out of the ice we have left. Which means we can't make any of the popular slushy drinks on the menu. And it's still hot out.

I can't afford this.

I call June from Sophie's phone but get no answer.

So, I sanitize a couple of large tote bins and haul them across the street, weaving through the crowd at the main stage, which is set up in the street in front of the bar, a local country band playing a pretty hot cover of that classic Fleetwood Mac breakup song "Go Your Own Way."

I push into the bar, where I'm greeted with a wall of noise and heat, and a totally different vibe.

The room is fuller than I've ever seen it, and Warrant's "Cherry Pie" blasts over the sound system, giving that retro-raunchy vibe you don't know you need until you're packed into a bar with hundreds of other sweaty bodies and a drink in your hand. Behind the bar, Oscar is spinning cocktail shakers and glasses like a juggler at Cirque du Soleil, and I'd be impressed if I had that kind of time.

I spot Mason behind the bar—beyond a throng of women, *huge* surprise—and hurry to the end of the bar, leaning over.

"Mason!" I have to shout to get his attention.

We haven't seen each other since the middle of the night, not even twenty-four hours ago—before he fell asleep after all the sex, then I slipped out of his bed, gathered my clothes off his floor, and left, to avoid another awkward morning-after scene in his kitchen—but I don't have time to overthink the frown he gives me.

He comes right over, but something about that frown annoys me. So, I point up into the ether, in other words, the music. "*Please* tell me you teased your hair in the nineties."

"I was born the year after this song came out," he says dryly.

"If you say so, Grandpa."

"What's wrong? And why am I old every time you're annoyed with me?"

"I'm not annoyed with you." I skip past the rest of the jabs I was probably about to spew because I'm nervous about all that naked stuff I let him—no, practically begged him to do to me. No time for that, either. "I'm freaking out because my ice machine died. And I realize this is great news for you because we're rivals and all, but this is very bad news for me, so could I pretty, pretty please use some of your ice?" I hold up the bins I brought.

He raises his eyebrows, taking this in. And very possibly loving it that I need him right now.

Evil.

And way too much like that first day we met.

"Seriously, Mason. Come on. It's *ice*. You are outselling the shit out of me right now. I see food on every table, and yes, I've been watching, and yes, I know I've already lost our stupid competition. Just please, don't make me beg."

"Sounds like you just did."

I groan. "Aren't you too busy for this? I see *many* thirsty women leaning on your bar, just waiting for you to hydrate them."

He narrows his gorgeous eyes at me.

Yes, that sounded jealous. I don't care right now. "You don't even need ice, technically. You can serve beer and cider and wine all night. The ladies won't complain, and neither will the men, so long as the ladies are happy and the beer keeps flowing."

He looks unconvinced, but probably just because it's *me*.

I sigh impatiently. "Google review: *The bartender was hot and the drinks were good, but damn, we had to wait forever to get them. Not recommended if you're thirsty*."

He rolls his eyes and takes a tote bin from my hands. "For the record, I like it when you beg."

"Cute." I pretend that statement didn't go right between my legs, and follow him behind the bar. His ice machine is twice the size of the one at Cutie Fruitie. He flips open the lid, revealing a cache of ice. He takes a plastic beer jug from a shelf, hands me another, and starts scooping ice into the tote bin.

I join him, reaching into the machine for ice at the same time, and we bump heads. "Sorry," I mutter. "Didn't see you there." I try to pass it off like it didn't even hurt, but fucking *ow*.

"Do you mind?" he drawls. "You have a very hard head. How can I hydrate the thirsty masses if I'm knocked out cold?"

"*I* have a hard head? God, you're really imperious when you're helping me out."

"It does seem to happen remarkably often. You, needing my help. Me, helping . . ."

"One might even think we're more than enemies."

I don't even know why that slips out. Our eyes meet, but at that moment, my phone rings. It's jammed into the tiny, stretchy pocket in the waist of my yoga skirt. And yes, the fact that I'm still carrying it around when it rarely works speaks to my absolute addiction to it.

It's Kyle, and I'm so frazzled, I answer, because why is he calling me unless something is seriously wrong? I haven't even spoken to anyone outside Orchard Cove in days.

"Hey. What's up?" I shove the phone between my shoulder and ear and keep scooping ice.

Mason frowns at me, but we find a rhythm, taking turns.

"Hey . . . Sierra . . . glad . . . finally caught you."

Finally? What, has he been calling me a lot? He's cutting in and out, so maybe I've misheard him.

"I can barely hear you," I shout. "Speak up."

"Where are you? Is that 'Cherry Pie'?"

"In a bar," I shout. "I can't talk right now."

"Okay," he shouts back. "I just wanted you to know that I talked to Dawson. You know, my cousin?"

Oh, I know Dawson. The little fucker. "Uh-huh. What did he do now? Release a deepfake of me blowing the purple dildo?"

I realize I'm still shouting when I find Mason staring at me.

"I just wanted you to know," Kyle shouts, "that he apologized to me."

I have no idea what he expects me to do with this information. Slow-clap?

"What do you want me to say, Kyle? Congrats on your apology. I have to go."

"Wait! Sierra—"

I hang up and keep scooping, avoiding Mason's eyes until the tote bins are full. I pick one up. "Sorry. Shit. I should've brought the lids so I could stack them. I'll take this one over, then come back for that."

Mason picks up the second tote. "That's a waste of time." He calls over to Oscar, "I'll be back in a few." Then he leads me through the bar.

We carry our bins through the crowd outside as my head reels with Kyle's words.

I just wanted you to know that he apologized to me.

Fuck. Way too little, too late, Kyle.

And way off the fucking mark.

Why the hell did he think I'd want to hear that his cousin apologized to *him*? As if he's the only one who deserves an apology?

It's not the kid's fault. He's a kid.

But Kyle . . . he's so fucking clueless.

"You okay?"

I look up into Mason's endless blue eyes. His eyebrows are drawn together in concern.

"Yeah."

We've arrived at Pier Seven and he one-arms his tote to open the door for me, then follows me behind the counter. My staff are working hard and I feel guilty for leaving. And pissed that I picked up that call.

Every time I start to let that shit fade into the background, Kyle just has to stir it back up again.

We set the ice down and I take a breath, squeezing back hot, angry tears. But I haven't cried over it yet, and I'm not going to. Ever.

"You're upset," Mason says, without even seeing my face.

I put on a smile and turn to him. "Much better now that I have ice! This will go a long way. Thank you. But I might have to come back for more later, if your machine can keep up."

"No worries. Come over if you need more." He lowers his voice. "You sure you're okay? That was your ex on the phone, right?"

"I'm fine. Just busy. Congrats on kicking my ass, by the way."

His frown deepens.

"I really have to get back to work."

He eyes the lineup at the counter, and my employees hurrying about. "Yeah. Me, too."

I dive back into work, and he leaves.

An hour later, he comes back to fix my ice machine.

It's just past ten p.m. when I lock up Cutie Fruitie for the night. I've already lost Sophie somewhere around the popcorn stand, so I make my way along the beach walk, headed for the Cozy Cottage.

Families and couples are tucked in all along the sand in chairs and blankets, deep into watching *The Princess Bride* on a movie screen that's been set up on the beach.

Sophie made plans to catch the end of the movie with Trish, then the last live music performance of the night at the main stage. But I have other plans involving my bed. I was up at five this morning after a restless sleep and went straight to work on festival business by six. I'm planning to turn in early so I can do it all again tomorrow.

But first, a quick stop along the way.

I head up the driveway at Sea Haven Orchard, smoothie in hand. The traffic gate is still open, but I know the cider house just shut down for the night. The hours are extended during the festival, same as at June's cider house.

This is the first time I've ever walked into the Grant family's cider house. The door is propped open to the night, and inside the front entrance is a small gift shop lined with shelves displaying products for sale. Dried apple chips and creamy apple butter and blackberry jam; bottles of jewel-toned berry liqueurs; crystal-clear and violet gin.

Beyond that, there's a lounge area furnished with a mixture of cozy chairs, cushy loveseats, and high-top bar tables. The bar is along a side wall, facing the lounge, and along the other side several sets of bifold doors stand open to the night.

Unlike June's cider house, which looks out over her orchard, the Grants' looks out over the water. We're up a small hill here, and the view is epic.

And Mason is right where I'd expect to find him. Behind the bar, holding court with the last customers of the night. Two fortysomething women stand at the bar, purses slung on their shoulders, like they're on their way out, but they're definitely lingering. Enjoying his attention.

I know that feeling. At this point, I openly thirst for it.

Not good.

I know this, and yet I can't help myself.

I stand back, waiting for his eyes to find me. And when they do, an absolute thrill runs down my spine—and right through my core. I swear my ovaries throb.

Mason bids the women a good night, then says something to the staffer behind the bar; she sees the customers out as Mason strolls over to me. I lean on one of the high-top tables and place the Cutie Fruitie cup on top.

"For you," I say ceremoniously.

"Wow. My first Cutie Fruitie smoothie."

"Say that five times fast."

His dimples flicker under his beard and my panties instantly flood.

Christ. Does he have any idea what he does to me?

Yeah. Maybe he got some idea, last night.

"I would've come over to try one sooner," he says, "but I didn't think the proprietor would want me there."

"You mean, the proprietor you don't like?" I say casually, recalling what he told me about not depriving Kaylie of a smoothie *just because I don't like the proprietor*.

He cocks his head a bit, like he doesn't understand.

Maybe he forgot he said that. But I definitely haven't. It stung. It still stings.

I change the subject. "I was just heading back to the cottage and popped into the bar, but you weren't there. Figured you'd be here. I had to say thank you. For the ice. And for coming over to fix my ice machine like a hero, despite our little competition. That was cool of you."

"No big deal. I've fixed those machines before."

"Well, I appreciate that you were willing to sheath your sword long enough to help me out."

My cheeks heat as his gaze darkens and drifts down to my lips. And I realize that "willing to sheath your sword" has an entirely different connotation. One I didn't intend.

Because I am *not* hitting on him. Or inviting him to fuck me again.

Last night, I came to his house and basically challenged him to fuck me.

Brave, maybe.

And the result was excellent.

But I am never, ever doing it again.

If he doesn't come back for seconds, I am over it.

I hope.

"I brought you an extra-large." I fill the silence when he doesn't take the smoothie. "In the expensive cup. You can keep it. It's double-walled to keep it cold. Dishwasher-safe. Enjoy. I promise, it's not poisoned."

The corner of his mouth flickers with amusement. Finally, he picks it up and takes a sip. I wait while he savors.

His eyes lock with mine.

"Good?" I prompt, weirdly nervous about his reaction. Is this how he felt when I first tasted his cider, at his bar?

"I may have been wrong," he says mildly. His gaze slides over my face. "About smoothies. Maybe you're onto something with this liquid-fruit thing."

I cock my head. "I mean, aren't you also in the business of liquid fruit?"

His eyes sparkle. "Good point." He takes another sip, then says seriously, "It's really good, Sierra."

"I know. I just whipped that up tonight, for you. I'm thinking of adding it to the menu. It's called Cherry Pie."

A small laugh bursts out of him, and warmth shivers across my skin. "Layne mentioned you name them after songs."

"Yeah. People identify with the songs so much that they'll try a flavor they wouldn't have otherwise." I shrug. "It's fun."

"It's more than fun. It works, so, it's brilliant marketing."

"Do what you gotta do to make those sales."

"Speaking of which . . ."

I sigh. "It's fine. You won, fair and square. It was my stupid idea. I'll tell June the results."

"You really don't have to tell her about our little contest."

"She's not dumb, Mason. It's pretty clear who was busier. Alcohol or no, your bar outsold me by miles."

"We have a way broader menu."

"Don't start making excuses for me."

He's silent for a moment. "I'm sorry. I know you really wanted to win."

"Oh my god, do not feel sorry for me. Major ick. I'm leaving before this gets embarrassing for both of us."

I hear his warm chuckle behind me as I head for the door.

"Hey," he says. "You wanna take the shortcut?"

Mason walks me down the grass behind the cider house and along the edge of the orchard. We walk in silence with only the moonlight to show us the way. The night air is warm and fresh on my skin, and butterflies flit happily in my stomach.

Mason is quiet, in his thoughts, and so am I.

I almost don't care where he's taking me.

I'd probably go anywhere with him.

Sad.

After passing many rows of trees, light spills across the grass from the back of Layne's cottage. And a definite path is revealed. A very old path, the gravel now embedded in the dirt, grass overgrowing much of it. It leads down from Layne's cottage and skirts along the edge of the orchard . . . then disappears into it.

I follow Mason's lead as we take this path, moving away from the cottage, and definitely in the direction of June's property.

"What is this?" For some reason, I whisper it.

"This, Sierra Daniels," he whispers back, "is the secret passage between the Grant family's property and the Spencers'."

I let out a gasp, which is half fake-dramatic and half real. "Secret passage? This is scandalous. How many people know about this?"

"Not many. Besides the families, just the few employees that need to access this area."

We pass through the rows of apple trees.

"Where does it go, exactly?"

"It leads all the way from Layne's cottage to the cottage where you're staying."

"No."

"Yup."

"Interesting. How the hell did I not know this path is here?"

"I guess you never asked." I give him an unimpressed look and he shrugs. "It wouldn't be much of a secret if I told everyone."

"Who uses it?"

"We are. Right now."

"Seriously, though. What's the deal? You have dueling orchards, right next to one another, and you both have a cider business. And you hardly speak to one another. How does that even happen?"

"Well, the answer to that is both complicated and simple. Kind of depends how you look at it. Our families have been fighting over this orchard for decades, and at some point in history, they split it into two, literally, by putting a fence down the middle. That's the complicated part. It started way back, with my grandpa Tommy's father. He and June's father were friends, as I mentioned, but became enemies. Legend tells it that they fought over a girl." Mason glances at me. "Maybe that's the simple part."

"A *girl*? You're telling me . . . there was a freaking love triangle? And now there's a fence down the middle of the orchard?"

"So the story goes."

"Okay, I really, really need this story."

"Wish I could tell you, but that's all I know. Kind of hard to get the story when no one who was there is alive anymore to talk about it."

I consider that. "Oh."

"It just becomes a rumor. An anecdote."

"Bummer."

"What's really interesting," he says alluringly, "is how history has a way of repeating itself. Rumor has it . . . that my grandpa and June were once an item, too."

"No!"

"Again, just a rumor. But Tommy was friends with June's former husband, originally, and I guess they fought over her or something. I'm not exactly sure how it went down. Because again, no one talks about it."

"And what happened?"

"Well, I guess my grandpa lost."

"And then . . . he married your grandma?"

"Guess so."

"And she . . ."

"Passed away about fifteen years ago."

"I'm sorry. What happened to June's husband?"

"They divorced, years ago. Never seemed like the best match anyway."

"Why?"

"Well, she runs her family's alcohol company and he had a real drinking problem. Pretty easy math on that. I hear he moved to the mainland, somewhere way up north."

"And they never had children?"

"Nope. Her sisters had kids, some of them grew up here, even had kids here. I imagine she's still in touch with them, even though they've all moved away now. Lee is the only one who stayed. He's managed the orchard for June for years, but they've had to hire on every other position, including cider master."

"Huh. You'd think that June, and Lee, would be even more interested in knowing their neighbors, getting along and maybe even supporting each other, since their whole family is gone."

"You'd think."

"That's a hell of a grudge. Like, imagine how much energy it takes to maintain it."

"Yup. Kinda seems like . . . a waste."

Our eyes meet, entangle for a moment in the moonlight.

I look away. "Do you think the grudge is more on June's side or Tommy's?"

"Hard to say. It's just always been there, long as I can remember."

"Do you think there's something more going on between them *now*? Like . . . old feelings, still there?"

"Fuck, no." We glance at each other. "You think we're enemies?" he says. "You should see those two when they cross paths."

"I haven't seen it."

"There's a reason."

I consider all this, and how fucking weird it must be to live so close to your enemy. To be at war with your neighbor for so many years.

A neighbor you once maybe cared for?

"Do you think she's lonely?" I ask, though I don't know why I'd expect him to have an answer.

Mason is silent for a moment. Then says, "I think . . . some people live alone so long, they just get used to it."

God. I hope that's not me one day.

We've reached the end of the apple trees. The orchard stops, or rather, is cut in half, by a simple, raw-wood farm fence. "The infamous fence, I presume?"

"Correct," he says as we come to a halt.

It's chest-high, with three vertical slats of wood. Some of it is ensnarled with weeds and bush. It appears unattended, forgotten.

Even more interesting and decidedly picturesque than the modest fence are the several large trees that stand along it on June's side. The most impressive of which is the very first one, right in front of me. It's immense, easily over twenty feet high and just as broad, dark and twisted, with long, thick arms covered in dark purplish leaves. It looks majestic and timeless in the moonlight.

I wonder how long it's been here.

The path leads right to it.

I realize that I've seen this tree, at least the top of it, from the back porch of the Cozy Cottage; it stretches above the thicket of trees and bushes that surround the cottage.

"Did I mention you have to climb a tree?"

I gape at Mason, then at the long arm of the tree that swoops down over the fence and past our heads.

"It's a plum tree," he says, "so try not to knock off the blossoms as you go."

"Uh . . ."

"Just kidding. There's a gate." He brushes aside some weeds to reveal the latch.

"And why is there a gate in this incredibly symbolic fence?"

"So you don't have to climb the tree?"

"Wait. Is this *the* tree? Like, the twisted tree of Twisted Tree Cider Co.?"

"This is it."

I gaze up at it in awe.

Mason opens the gate for me and I step through. When I turn to face him, he hasn't closed the gate, but he hasn't followed me through, either.

We stare at each other as an unspoken question passes between us.

"We used to sneak over there," he says casually. "When we were kids."

"Of course you did," I say lightly. "Sneaking around can be fun."

There's a moment of silence in which my heart pounds and I wait to see what he'll do.

Then he steps through the gate and closes it behind him. He comes close to me. Closer. "June wouldn't want me here, on her property."

"June doesn't have to know."

I turn on my heel and follow the path that leads up to the bushes behind the Cozy Cottage. We only have to shove a few branches out of the way to get through.

The motion-activated light on the back porch turns on as I climb the steps, heart thudding.

As I unlock the door, Mason is right behind me. He follows me inside, shuts the door, peels my bag off my arm, and places it gently on the floor.

Then we smash together. Making out, groping, stumbling through the near-dark. I steer him toward my bedroom.

"Sorry the bed is so small," I say.

"I seem to remember," he mutters between kisses, "that we fit into a small bed . . . very nicely." He drives me over to the bed, kissing his way down my neck. He yanks my shirt up and off, over my head, and we go at it again.

But then I get distracted, wondering. Did he say that because he's thinking about *staying* in the small bed with me, all night?

"We're still enemies, right?" I pant. "Just checking."

"Of course." He undoes my bra. "With incredible benefits . . ." He whips my bra off.

"Good. 'Cause I'm not yielding."

"Wouldn't expect you to." He peels down my skirt. My panties go with it.

I step out of them and he tosses them across the room. Then we keep making out.

"I don't want you to think . . ." I say between kisses, "that just 'cause you creamed me . . . in sales today . . . that anything has changed. I still want Pier Seven."

"Cool. How about I make you cream right now?"

Before I can react, he pushes me back on the bed and drops to his knees on the floor. He spreads my thighs and goes down on me immediately, his hot, wonderful mouth making me melt.

"Oh god" slips out of my mouth. "Don't I need to shower first . . . ? It's been a long day . . ."

"Mmm. No shower." He laps at my clit, savoring me like I'm his favorite meal. "You just need me, making you moan." He wraps his lips around my pussy and sucks.

"Ahh. *Fuck.* This doesn't mean I like you," I moan.

"Mm-hmm. Be a good girl and keep still."

He focuses all his attention and that amazing mouth of his—warm, soft lips; silken beard—between my legs, and I go limp. I forget how to argue. He is so, so good at this. Kyle didn't even like going down.

How did I live like that for so damn long?

I was blinded by love.

Maybe all I need is hot, hot sex with my enemy.

Fuck love.

I watch Mason, feasting between my thighs. He runs a hand up my thigh and shoves a thick finger inside me, making me squeal and convulse. We lock eyes, right before mine roll closed.

"Sierra," he murmurs, and I shiver. "Look at me."

I look. I watch him eating me out, and I know it thrills him; that I'm submitting to him. Because this is the only way I do.

He pulls away abruptly, stands up, impatient to get his zipper down. His erection presses at his jeans. "Spread your legs," he orders.

I spread, like the good girl he says I am, as he peels off his shirt, and an ecstatic thrill runs through me. My pulse beats in my core, the driving need to be possessed by him.

His chest rises and falls, fast, as he takes out his fantastic cock and palms it, thick, hard, and ready.

I take a deep breath. My heart is beating way too fast.

His eyes haze with lust as he runs his hand up and down his length, and he looks between my legs.

I know this is just sex for him. I insisted on it.

But . . . it's *not* just sex for me.

As his eyes roam over my body and he settles over me, I wrap my legs around his waist.

As he pushes into me, filling me with his heat, he kisses me . . . and I'm afraid that I like him, way too much. And that he just doesn't see me that way.

Enemies.

With hot-as-fuck benefits.

It's all I've ever asked him for.

It's all he's ever offered me.

CHAPTER 18

Sierra

On the second day of Sunshine Fest, Sophie and I help out at the community pancake breakfast alongside Layne and some other volunteers. Cutie Fruitie is busy all day, and thanks to Mason fixing the ice machine we never run out of ice.

On my lunch break, I grab food at the chili cook-off. I swing by the games area in the field at the north end of Water Street, just past the grocery store and the food truck area, to hit up some of the community fundraising events.

I manage to drop Mason's friend Evan in the dunk tank (fun), win the ladies' sack race (more fun), then stop to watch Mason, Layne, and some other guys slaughter a group of RCMP officers in the men's tug-of-war (hot).

Then, somehow, I get roped into participating in the three-legged race—while bound to Mason.

Maria's bright idea.

She ties us together, we wrap our arms around one another's waists, then stumble our way down the field, totally unable to find a rhythm. Maybe because my pulse is flying and I'm way too aware of the man next to me to even remember how competitive I am—or that there's a finish line I'm supposed to be focusing on.

I end up tumbling into the grass with Mason on top of me, and the man I had sex with last night murmurs in my ear, "You have much better rhythm when you're naked."

"Maybe if I wasn't bound to a giant, sweaty anchor." *Who smells like fresh grass and cedar and what dreams are made of.* I shove him off. "You're totally ruining my winning streak." Truth. I've already got gold ribbons from the sack race and the cornhole tournament this morning with a *#1* on them, pinned proudly to my chest.

He just laughs.

"You're a curse, Mason Grant," I tell him as we receive our last-place consolation ribbon, which he pins to my shirt.

I'm already back at the smoothie bar before I realize that the ribbon says, with a big smiley face: *Nice guys finish last.*

I leave it on, just because Mason gave it to me.

Pathetic.

Cutie Fruitie is one of the locations on the kids' scavenger hunt today, and we give out hundreds of Cutie Fruitie coupons, which bring a steady stream of families through the door. By closing time, I'm pooped.

Sophie and I stagger over to the beer and cider garden, and I don't know if I'm just exhausted and deliriously sleep-deprived, but I'm flooded with this incredible warmth when I see Trish, Maria, and Pamela saving seats for us.

My new friends.

Not friends by association—people who go through the motions of allowing me into their lives because they're actually friends with my boyfriend.

Real friends, who smile when they see me, wave at me from across a crowd, and save me a seat, hoping I'll show up.

Such a simple pleasure, but one I've been missing in my life.

They're already drinking, so Soph and I order from the waitress. The Sea Haven Honeyed Perry "patio-style pear cider" she recommends is just the crisp, tart-but-sweet refreshment I need on this perfect, warm summer night. The sky is a clear, dark blue shifting to black, and the stars are out. And Layne is playing guitar on the main stage with his band: a group of friends who've jammed together for fun ever since high school, according to Trish.

The music, too, is warm. They're playing a cover of "One of These Nights" by the Eagles, and they're *good.* After a long day listening to neon-bright music like BLACKPINK and Wham!, my favorite kind to play at the smoothie bar, it's a welcome change.

I check out the crowd, wondering if I'll run into Mason, if he's here or inside the bar.

I wonder how much June's been around.

I know Cutie Fruitie has not been as popular as Mason's business. I know he's outselling me by *a lot.* And he told me that I don't need to point this out to June.

Maybe I don't. But maybe I should make a proactive move, before she decides Pier Seven would be better off without Cutie Fruitie. I've managed to bring on some solid employees, and I know I can make it work for the rest of the summer.

I just need to find out if she sees any future here for me.

The festival is over tomorrow, and reality is going to set in. I need to know that my business has a temporary home here, and if not . . . I need to start looking elsewhere, like now.

Soph leans in. "Do you need to call Kyle back? You can use my phone."

"Uh . . . no." He called her today, trying to reach me. Again.

"Well, what did he want? You look stressed."

"It's not that." Weirdly, I haven't told her that I've screwed Mason, twice. I don't even know why. Maybe I'm just not ready for the truth bombs I know she'll drop on me when she intuits that

I'm developing serious feels. How can I remain in denial if my best friend smacks me in the face with reality? "Kyle just said he's been watching my socials, that he's seen how I'm 'killing it' in Orchard Cove." I roll my eyes and wash down my resentment with pear-and-honey cider.

"Do you think he misses you? Regrets what he did? Because he fucking should."

"I don't know." Honestly, the call confused me. *Does* he miss me? "Or maybe he just wants to be able to convince himself that he's not the bad guy? I have no idea." I had to hang up on him again because I was busy working. I said I'd call him back, but . . .

I find myself scanning the crowd for Mason, again, who I'd much rather talk to. I don't see him, but I do spot June. Standing on the sidewalk across the street, just beyond the concert crowd, talking to Bev.

"Shit." I take a big gulp of cider then tell Soph, "I'll be back. I need to talk to June about the lease."

"Good luck!" she calls after me.

I dash through the crowd, but by the time I get across the street, June's not with Bev anymore. I glimpse her silvery hair; she's walking toward the pier, but when I get there, she's already heading down the steps to the beach.

"Hey, June." I catch up with her at the bottom of the steps and we walk together onto the sand. "Where are you headed?"

"To help set up the bonfire area. Are you coming down?"

"Yeah, I'll probably come later. After the band is finished. I was wondering, can we discuss the lease?" I stop walking and she stops with me. "I'd be happy to show you my sales numbers, so you can see how well we've been doing—"

"I'm aware of how well you've been doing." She eyes me. "You still want to extend the lease?"

Did she think I might change my mind?

"Of course I do."

She frowns, which doesn't seem like a good sign. "Why do you want to stay in Orchard Cove, Sierra?"

"Well, the smoothie bar is doing well. I've surpassed my sales goals for the month already. And the location is perfect for summer. It makes sense right now, and honestly . . . the next few months I have nothing lined up, because the place where I thought I'd be landing . . . well, that's not an option anymore. Because of that investment I lost. But . . ." I hesitate.

I look out across the water briefly, at the humps of land in the distance. Vancouver is out there, farther north, though maybe it's become a comfort that I can't even see it from here.

"Maybe you were right. Maybe I am running away from my life in the city. But is that so bad?"

She nods. "It takes guts to admit it. The question is, why? What are you really running from? And don't tell me it's that ex of yours."

I take that in, really try to digest it, and dig deeper. "Jeez, June. You really get into it, don't you?"

"I don't have time for dancing around the point," she says bluntly.

Yeah. Maybe I don't, either. "I guess . . . I do have this fear, of always being second-best. It's kinda haunted me all my life. Rejection is . . . hard."

"Rejection is hard for everyone. Why is it hard for *you*?"

"Wow. Okay." I rub my neck. Am I saying this? To someone I barely know? "Uh, I really hesitate to tell you this because you already called me Cinderella, but I do actually have a stepsister. Unfortunately, she's not evil."

"No?" June says, a note of amusement in her voice.

"No. Kim . . . that's my stepsister . . . is eight years older than me. She's an esteemed neurosurgeon. She has two perfect kids and a perfect husband. She keeps bees and makes honey to gift to her friends. She has a *lot* of friends. And somehow she still finds the time to be perfect at golf, tennis, baking, canning. And origami. That's her latest thing. I know this because of her flawlessly curated Instagram page."

June raises an eyebrow.

"Ugh. I know, I just made it sound like I hate her. I love her, truly. What's not to love?"

"You tell me."

I sigh. "She lives in Ontario. And she calls me every Sunday to keep in touch."

"And that's bad?"

No, it's not bad. But I've been avoiding her calls. I've been avoiding almost everyone outside of Orchard Cove since I came here.

"It's just . . . hard," I admit. "When someone is so big, they can make you feel small without meaning to. That's my fault, not hers, I know. I'm working on it."

June considers that, nodding again, slowly. "You're self-aware. That's a good thing."

"I'm becoming more so," I say hopefully. "My smoothie business has been successful, overall. Profitable. And I know I can grow it. I have big plans for it." None of which include a solid location for the rest of the year, unfortunately. "I just need a place to land for a while. And get my bearings, I think."

"I've given it a lot of thought, Sierra," she says. "It's obvious that Orchard Cove has enjoyed having you and your smoothies here . . ." Her gaze dips over the ribbons that flutter on my chest.

"That's kind, thank you."

"But I'm not looking to lease out Pier Seven for any extended length of time," she concludes.

"Oh. Okay . . . Does this mean you're going to sell it?"

She purses her lips briefly, then says, "I've received an offer to buy the property. A generous offer. So, unless you'd like to also make an offer to purchase, our business with one another is finished as of the end of this month."

Shit. *Ten days.*

That's all I have left in Orchard Cove? Officially.

That's all I have left . . . with Mason.

I swallow as I grapple for something meaningful to say. And in the back of my mind clings the fear: that he only slept with me to try to win this battle.

That he's the one who made this generous offer to buy Pier Seven from June.

But of course he's the one.

Maybe he's enjoyed sleeping with me, for whatever that's worth. But ultimately . . . whatever he wants with me comes a distant second to how much he wants that building.

It's like my greatest fear has been shoved right in my face.

But June is right in front of me, and this is not her problem.

"Okay," I tell her. "I understand. Thank you for being honest. I'm not prepared to make an offer to buy. So . . . I guess that's it."

June frowns at me again. "This is not a rejection, Sierra."

"Right."

She sighs a little. "You can try," she tells me, "but you can't run away from your life. You've heard of 'wherever you go, there you are'? So, live your life, and live the hell out of it. You're the only one who gets to. Not your sister, not anyone else. See it as the privilege it is and stop waiting to be chosen by some man. Or some place. Or some perfect business opportunity. *You* be the one to choose. That's my advice to you, unsolicited as it may be."

Once again, I feel so seen by this woman . . . I want to be annoyed with her, but I'm really not.

"You know what, June? I appreciate you."

I give her a hug, and she stiffens.

But then she pats me on the back. "I . . . appreciate you, too." She pulls away. "Now, go have fun."

I watch her walk away up the beach, alone, silver hair blowing in the breeze.

And I wonder if one day I'll end up as self-possessed and fiercely independent as her.

Or as alone.

◆ ◆ ◆

I'm sitting at the bonfire when Mason sits down next to me. It's just past midnight and Sophie vacated her spot on the log beside me a while ago to walk home with June.

There are about thirty of us still lingering around the fire, making s'mores and drinking. Layne is playing "Harvest Moon" on his acoustic guitar, a few people are singing along, and Bev and Bill are slow-dancing down at the shoreline.

Me, I'm staring into the flames and avoiding tomorrow.

"How was your day?" Mason asks me, as if we're friends like that.

Or maybe he just wants to know how badly he demolished me in sales today.

I look at him, and when the slight smile falls from his face, I realize tears are shining in my eyes.

"Shit. That bad?"

I wipe my eyes. "It's just the fire. My eyes are sensitive."

"Okay . . ."

"And the alcohol." I point at the big cooler Layne brought, filled with ice and cans of Elderberry cider. "I may be slightly drunk. I blame your brother. How was your day?"

"Decent," he says carefully. "Didn't get much sleep last night."

I don't know what to make of that. After we had sex at the cottage, I told him it would be best if he didn't stay over, and he went home.

"Me neither," I say. "I did have a realization. Wanna hear it?"

"Do I?"

"Yes. Maybe. I realize that you really meant it when you said I'm a formidable opponent. And you really think that the meme and what Kyle's family did to me is a crock of shit. You were nicer to me than he was, about all of it." I'm staring into the fire, and I blink back the water in my eyes that insists on returning. "And even if he's trying to make up for it now by trying to be nicer to me so he can uphold his opinion of himself, you fixed my ice machine and you didn't have to do that. It was very cool."

I don't want to lay too much gratitude on him all at once, so I add, "I even forgive you for ruining that three-legged race for me."

He doesn't laugh like I think he might.

"You are a formidable opponent," he says seriously.

I take a breath. "June turned me down for the lease. She won't be extending it. I won't be staying."

Mason doesn't say anything for a moment, and my words hang heavily in the air between us.

When I look at the side of his face, his eyes are downcast. Maybe I want to ask him about the offer he made June, and when that happened, and why he didn't tell me. But maybe I don't.

He doesn't bring it up.

So, I don't, either.

"I'm sorry you didn't get what you want." He looks in my eyes. "You deserved to win."

I laugh. "It would be nice. Just to win at *something*."

He glances at the ribbons still pinned to my chest. "I think you win a lot more than you give yourself credit for."

I look away. "Not at the things that matter."

Silence falls between us again.

Layne starts playing U2's "All I Want Is You" on his guitar, and it's so hauntingly bittersweet, I push to my feet. "I think I need to go to bed. Sleep off the cider."

I don't even say goodbye.

I just turn and make my way up the sand toward the beach walk. And I know Mason is with me. I hear him. I *feel* him.

"You don't have to walk me home," I tell him, but he does anyway.

Together, we walk along the path, where paper lanterns made in the kids' craft tent today now dangle from every possible tree and bush.

"Maybe you could help me out here," he says after a moment. "So I know whether to offer a shoulder to cry on or just tell you to forget him." Our eyes meet briefly. "How serious was it? Your relationship with your ex."

I guess he thinks that's what I'm really upset about?

But I don't correct him.

"That is a great question, Mason Grant. I thought it was serious. We were together for three years, but we didn't even live together. He had his place, I had mine."

"What's your place in the city like?"

I think about it and all that comes out is: "Cold. I actually don't spend a lot of time there."

The concept of "home" hovers in the back of my mind. Where the hell is mine?

"June said home is the place where you feel most like yourself," I say. "How fucked-up is it that I don't know where that is anymore?"

Mason says nothing for a long moment, then offers, "You will. Sometimes . . . it takes time."

I raise an eyebrow at him. "And how would you know? You've probably always known where home is."

"No." He pushes his hands into his pockets. "I thought I did. But there were times that I questioned it. I almost left. I did leave, actually, for a short while."

"But you came back."

"Yeah, I came back."

"Well, all I fucking know for sure is that Kyle is not my home."

"Maybe, for now," he says, "that's all you need to know."

I glance at him as the moonlight and the glowing lantern light shifts over the curves of his face. It plays in his eyes, making me see something in their depths that's not really there.

I know it's just a trick of the light.

He didn't tell me about the offer he made to June, the one that may have cost me the ability to keep leasing the building; if June didn't have a solid buyer, maybe she would've leased it to me for the rest of summer.

It was a solid play on his part, making that offer. I can't blame him.

He's a formidable opponent, too.

But his silence tells me the truth, clearer than any words or any misconstrued spark of desire in his eyes.

To Mason Grant, I'm still the enemy.

I feel the emotions swelling up in my chest even as I try to push them down. To hold them back.

Because I'm starting to understand that I have a deeper longing to stay in Orchard Cove than I thought. And maybe it only has a little to do with the smoothie bar.

But is it just my confused feelings for Mason making me feel this way?

Is it just that I want more of *him*?

I'm really not a complicated person. Sometimes, I'm disturbingly predictable.

Ever since my biological father rejected me for his other family—his other kids—I know I've been hesitant to get close to anyone. To trust. To attach. To believe I'm good enough to be anyone's first choice.

My busy, high-pressure work life—running my own business, trying to grow it, and never knowing for sure if I'm going to have enough money to keep going, to make rent, to support my life in the city—has provided me with such convenient means to avoid true intimacy.

This has never been more obvious to me than when Mason walks me all the way through his property in the moonlight without a word, down the secret path, through the secret gate, and right to my door, and he kisses me goodnight, on the forehead . . . and I don't say what I mean.

When he says "Goodnight" like it's a question and hesitates on the step, I just let him go.

I say, "Goodnight."

I don't say, *I want you to stay.*

CHAPTER 19

Mason

The final day of Sunshine Fest begins early, with a sunrise yoga session on the beach led by Sierra.

I hear about it from Abby when she comes into work. I'm tied up most of the morning helping out at the community brunch, and the bar and the cider house are both busy again from opening until close.

I don't even see Sierra all day.

At this point, I'm fucking gutted about her leaving. I want to see her, badly. I feel like shit about making an offer on Pier Seven and not telling her.

I wonder if June turning her down is my fault.

There's so much that's been left unsaid, undone, between us.

But what am I supposed to do—turn around and ask June to lease the building to Sierra instead of selling it to me?

I can't give up that building.

But I'm fucking deeply conflicted.

Because I don't want to give her up, either.

Not my choice.

I keep trying to remind myself that it's her choice to leave Orchard Cove. That she has a life back in the city. That our relationship hasn't evolved beyond sex anyway.

But I know I'm fucking lying to myself.

I like her more than I ever thought I would.

And that's nothing but a mistake.

She left after we had sex in my bed, while I was sleeping, without a word.

And after we had sex in her cottage, she asked me to leave.

Last night, when I walked her home, she didn't even kiss me or invite me in.

She's asked me, more than once, to reassure her that we're still enemies. Making a game of it, maybe, but definitely trying to keep me at a distance.

She's told me, loud and clear, the way she wants it.

This is just sex.

I'm leaving.

This isn't my home.

I don't know why it's so fucking hard for me to accept it.

When I leave the bar just before closing, the beer and cider garden is still fairly full. Layne's band, the Imposters, are closing out the festival with a finale show on the main stage.

The warm but bittersweet romance of Blue Rodeo's "Try" drifts through town as I make my way through the festival crowd.

I'm planning to drop by the cider house for closing. But when I walk by Pier Seven on my way to the beach walk, I hesitate. There are still a few customers inside, lights twinkling in the windows, and I glimpse Sierra behind the counter. She's laughing at whatever her friend Sophie is saying to her.

And I feel happy for her, even as my heart fucking breaks.

Jesus Christ. I've got it *bad.*

The lights along the pier are on, and past a group of teens hanging out halfway down, I glimpse the lone figure standing at the end, just beyond the last light, silver hair floating in the night.

I walk out there and join her. "Giving some thought to my offer?"

June glances up at me. "Actually, yes."

I lean on the railing next to her. Water laps at the wood beams below. Along the beach, people are gathering to get a good spot for the upcoming fireworks show.

"Really? I didn't even tell you my sales figures yet. Did Sierra tell you about our . . . little wager?"

June raises an eyebrow. "She didn't."

"She bet me that she could outsell the bar during the festival. Food only."

She laughs dryly. "Well, that was bold of her. And foolish."

"She deserves a real chance at this, June," I say seriously. "Maybe we could work something out. You let Sierra lease Pier Seven for the rest of summer, and I buy it from you in October or November. I can have it up and running with a pop-up for the holidays, then get started on renovations, have the new restaurant open by the spring."

"I'm not leasing Pier Seven out, Mason," she says. "And I'm not selling it, either."

"What?"

"Look." She turns toward me. "I was going to have my realtor let you know once the festival is done, just let us all enjoy the weekend."

"But . . . ?"

"But I can't accept your offer. If this year's festival has proved anything to me, it's that I don't want to let the building go. I seriously considered it, yes, when your parents were part of the equation. But they're not. And that's reality."

I can't fucking believe what I'm hearing. "So, you'd rather have it sit empty than belong to my family, so we can run a restaurant in it to benefit the community?"

"No, Mason. I'd rather hold onto it because it is a special place in this community. And I've always wanted to utilize it. But it hasn't been possible when I've had to make so many adjustments over the years as my family has gradually left Twisted Tree. The cidery is profitable. But now the guesthouse is also profitable. And I can leverage some of those resources to bring Pier Seven back to life."

I shake my head. "You're making a mistake—"

"Maybe I am. And maybe I thought there would be more time to figure it all out. But with your parents gone, and Sierra Daniels coming to town and breathing new life into this place . . . Who knows? I'm feeling inspired."

"June, you can't be serious."

"Can't I? You young people can be quite inspiring. You remind an old lady that some things are worth fighting for."

Shit. Is that the message Sierra and I have sent her?

Our competing interests in the building just made June want it more?

Fuck me.

"But didn't you invite Sierra here to compete with me? To drive up the price? I thought that was the whole point. To squeeze me, or maybe her, out of as much as you could get for the building."

June actually looks offended at the thought. "I invited her here because I saw some of my younger self in her. Or . . ." She sighs. "Maybe I saw the young woman I really wish I'd been. If I'd had half the ingenuity she has at her age, I might've made better choices, instead of coasting on the efforts my parents put in before me. And quite frankly, I resented your presumption that Pier Seven would be yours, just because of the work your parents put in before you."

"Your grandfather won Pier Seven on a gamble," I say, frustrated, "and for generations, your family has mismanaged it, neglected it, and hoarded it. And now you're taking a gamble on some vague idea that you might one day figure out how to run a restaurant? Instead of taking a legitimate, above-market-value offer? From someone who knows what it takes and is more than willing to do the work?"

"Don't be condescending, Mason. I'll be consulting with other local businesses, suppliers, and producers in the coming months, and I will figure it out."

"And that's it? You won't even negotiate?"

Her steely eyes sharpen at me as the sea breeze whips her hair around her face. "Let me be crystal clear with you, Mason Grant. I will never negotiate with you or your brother or your grandfather, unless he apologizes to me first."

For a moment, I'm speechless.

"For . . . what?"

"Why don't you ask him."

June starts to walk away.

"Can I at least be one of these local business owners you consult with?" I ask her, fucking desperate.

She pauses, considering that.

"Of course you can. Your family has deep roots in this community. Maybe I'll even sell your products at my new restaurant. It's more than you've ever done for me." And with that, she leaves me on the pier.

◆ ◆ ◆

I find my grandpa sitting in a lawn chair in the middle of Water Street, way at the back of the crowd, alone. People-watching, as he likes to do, and enjoying the music. Layne's band is now playing a Dirty classic, "Road Back Home."

I crouch down next to him. "How's the show?"

Grandpa nods toward the band. "He looks so much like your dad when he plays guitar."

"I thought I was the one who looked like Dad."

Grandpa chuckles. "Careful, that sounded like jealousy."

I watch the band for a minute in silence. "June rejected my offer to buy Pier Seven."

After a moment, Grandpa says, "Did you expect anything different?"

"Yes. A part of me did."

He sips his beer. Grunts. "Juniper Spencer isn't gonna do a single thing you want her to. Not as long as I'm alive."

"She said she'll consider carrying our products at the restaurant she's going to open."

He snorts. "Believe it when you see it. Until then . . . don't believe a word that woman says."

How many times have I heard him say that over the years?

Innumerable.

"Grandpa. Is there any way you would ever consider apologizing to her?"

He scowls at me. "For what?"

"I don't know." I sigh. "Whatever you did that hurt her so bad."

He fixes his gaze on the band again. "Yeah. *I* hurt *her*. That's a good one."

◆ ◆ ◆

After I lock up at the cider house, I feel ancient. This day felt like it was never going to end. And at the same time, I feel impossibly young. Naive and jaded all at once.

Fucking stubborn old people.

Dealing with Tommy and June is like trying to push a boulder up a steep hill with my bare hands and flip-flops on my feet.

When I walk back over to Water Street, the band is done, the stage empty. The market stalls have closed and packed up, the crowds have thinned out, and the only music comes from Pier Seven.

Sierra set up speakers outside the smoothie bar for the festival, and lights in the windows that twinkle in time to the music. "No Scrubs" drifts down Water Street, making me think of her, in my bar, singing the same song into a cider bottle that first night we met.

I see Sierra, alone, behind the counter at Cutie Fruitie as I approach and nudge the door open.

She looks up as I walk in, and I'm really not sure how to read that expression on her face.

"Closing up?"

"Yeah. I was just about to lock the doors."

"You watching the fireworks?"

She blinks. "Um. Yeah. I think Sophie was getting a spot for us on the beach."

"Cool." I rub the back of my head. "Any chance you want to take a drive?"

I wait, heart thrumming, as she absorbs my offer.

Then I'm rewarded when she smiles.

CHAPTER 20

Mason

We drive along the water to one of the highest points along the cliffs at the northern end of the cove. I park along the grass, backing the truck up to the edge. Then I tell Sierra, "Wait there."

I climb out and come around to her door. I open it for her, offer her my hand, and when she steps down, I walk her around to the tailgate.

From here, we have a sweeping view over the entire cove, and the glittering lights of the small town in the middle of the shoreline. Lights flicker on the beach below Orchard Cove, where people are waiting for the fireworks: cell phones, lanterns.

"Wow," Sierra breathes. "It's beautiful."

"The fireworks should start soon." I open the tailgate. "Just give me a sec." I hop into the back of the truck and unroll the two sleeping bags I brought to create a nice, padded surface on the hard bed of the truck, then drape the cozy wool blankets overtop in case we get cold. I brought pillows, too, several of them.

And a couple of tall cans of Sea Haven Orchard Blush, a rosé cider with blackcurrant and wild cherry, which I pull out of a backpack.

When I offer Sierra a hand, her smile is like a beam of sunshine. She takes it, and I pull her up, catching her by the hips. I tug her to me and we stand there, pressed together, already breathing too heavily.

"This is cozy," she says.

"Have to show you a good time," I tell her, gazing down at her from hooded eyes. "So maybe you remember me when all those city slickers let you down."

She laughs abruptly.

Then she pulls away.

We sit down, and her smile fades. She slips off her shoes to get comfy, so I do the same. The silence is heavy, almost uncomfortable between us, and not at all what I wanted.

But some things need to be said.

"June isn't selling to me, Sierra. She rejected my offer. Said she's keeping Pier Seven. She wants to open her own restaurant there."

"Really?"

"Yeah. So, I didn't win after all."

She takes this in.

Then she slides her hand onto my knee. "I'm sorry. I really am." She sighs. Wraps her arms around herself.

The breeze coming off the sea is cool, and I drape one of the blankets around her shoulders. As usual, she's not wearing much. A little tank top with inviting cleavage and denim shorts.

She glances at me. "I know how much you wanted it. And what it meant to you."

"Yeah, well. Can't always get what you want."

With that, I fish the portable speaker out of the backpack and put on the Rolling Stones song. And she laughs again: that sound, the most beautiful music I've ever heard.

"Where did your love of music come from?" she asks me as I crack open an Orchard Blush and hand it to her.

"I guess . . . when I grew up, there was just always music on." I open my own cider and tap her can in a cheers. We both take a sip and I get comfy on the pillows. "My dad would always be working in the cider house and the bar, and there was music on. My mom would be at the house or in the orchard with my little brother and then my little sister, and I'd be with her, or with different people who came to work at the orchard, or their kids, and there was always music. On the cider house patio, in the cidery where my grandpa was working, and in our house. My dad played guitar, too."

I pause, clear my throat of the sudden lump that forms.

"It's so quiet now that they're gone."

"Yeah," she says, kind of sadly. "I can imagine. That must be hard."

I swallow again, try not to get too emotional about it. "As soon as they died, I moved back home. I'd been living in a house that I still own next to the bar, where Jace lives now, but I threw myself into continuing the renovations my dad had started on the family home, and I took over his position as general manager of the cidery and the bar. Layne had been renovating the old cider master's cottage out back for a couple of years as a hobby project, planning to move in there one day. He was renting a place, but he got rid of it and he and Kaylie moved back into the house, too, temporarily. There was no discussion about it. It was just what had to be done. Grandpa was there alone, and I think we all knew we needed each other."

"Of course you did," she says gently.

Then a silence falls. Not uncomfortable. Just kind of depressing.

At least there's music now.

"I think the silence is one of the hardest things," I say after a moment. "There's this whole piece of the family, a whole generation, just . . . missing. And one day when my grandpa passes away, it'll just be me and Layne to carry on the family and the business."

"What about your sister?"

"Yeah. Haven, too. If she ever comes back to live here again."

"Do you think she will?"

"I hope so. I understand that she wanted to go to university and try to make it on her own in the big city. She was always driven like that. But I hope there's a piece of her heart that will always feel at home here."

"I'm sure that's true."

"Thank god I've never really had to worry about her. She's the good kid of the family. Never had a rebellious streak like I did, and Layne did, too. She was a straight-A student, never gets in trouble. But maybe since she's been gone . . . it's been harder. 'Cause there's another piece of the family missing, you know?"

"How old is she?"

"Twenty-five."

"Then she's young," Sierra says. "Plenty of time to come back home, get knocked up, make you some little nieces and nephews. And maybe by then, Kaylie will be all grown up and she'll make some babies, too. You'll have little grand-nieces and -nephews . . ." She laughs at the look on my face. "Oh my god, your face."

"I was not ready for that."

"I'm sorry." She snort-laughs. "I know she's only ten. Too much?"

"Way too much. Christ. I feel like my baby sister just went off to the big city and that was hard enough. And that was seven fucking years ago. Shit. Am I getting old?"

"You're only as old as you feel, Mason," she says brightly, teasing me.

She sips her pink-hued cider, licks her lip, and fuck, she's beautiful. I could stare at her all night.

If I'm lucky, maybe the fireworks will take a while.

"Where did your love of music come from?" I ask her.

And she says easily, "My grandpa. My mom's dad. Grandpa Alex."

"The coolest human on the planet?"

She smiles, maybe delighted that I remember how she described her grandpa the first day we met.

"That's him. He was like my safe place, you know? My happy place. All of that." Her smile fades a little. "I guess I really needed one. I grew up in Carlton, this really small town that you do not need to feel bad that you've never heard of. It's in the Okanagan Valley, and I don't want you getting any foolish ideas that I lived in some gorgeous corner of wine country. This place is trash. But it's where my mom grew up."

"I see. And all this time, I thought you were a city girl, born and bred."

"Nope. My dad was, though. My biological father, I mean. Mom met him while she was in high school. He was older, just out of school, and was just passing through her town with some friends. And she decided to put off her plans to go to Vancouver for university to go backpacking in Europe with him. And like I told you, that's where she got pregnant with me. They came back to Carlton and had me, but I guess he never liked it there, and he left when I was three. I have no solid memories of him from those early years."

She pauses, takes a sip of cider, and I wait for more.

"My mom was a very unhappy single mom who resented being stuck in Carlton because of me. Or at least, that's how it felt to me. She leaned a lot on her parents to take care of us, but my grandma died when I was seven, and it was hard. When I was nine, Mom got married to my stepdad. He was a divorced, older man who already had a seventeen-year-old daughter, Kimberly. Kim was nice as an older sister, but we weren't super close. And she went away to university within a year of the marriage. She was the driven one in my family. By the time I was twenty, she was a doctor, settled in Ontario and married, and my mom and stepdad moved out there to be closer to her when she had kids. I think my mom has lived vicariously through Kim's successes over the years, and sometimes that's made it easy to forget about mediocre me. Kim is definitely her favorite daughter."

"You don't know that," I offer.

"Oh, I know. I've made my peace with it, more or less." She bites her lip a little. "I guess they thought I'd just stay in Carlton. I kinda shocked them all and became a source of perpetual stress and gossip, I'm sure, when I picked up and moved to Vancouver by myself. And I guess the rest is history."

When she goes silent, I prod gently, "And why did Grandpa Alex become such a happy place for you?"

She sighs. "Because I truly hated growing up in that town. I was bullied. I didn't have a lot of friends. There wasn't a lot to do in Carlton, but there was a drug problem, and the last thing I wanted to do was hang out with most of the kids at my school. So, my grandpa was the best part of my day. He was a refrigerator repair man, and we had appliance parts strewn all over our yard. That was one of the reasons I was bullied. But I didn't care. While so many kids were experimenting with shit like meth and overdosing on fentanyl, I was with my grandpa in the garage. Safe. Loved. Listening to music while he worked."

She goes silent again for a moment, like she's lost in a memory.

"He didn't play any instruments, and neither did I, but he loved music and he taught me how to really listen. It opened up a whole other world that I couldn't have accessed any other way. And it helped me to process my emotions, even when he died." She blinks at me, like she's coming back to reality now. "I guess you could say music saved me," she sums up simply. "*He* saved me."

But it's not simple at all.

The first pop of fireworks goes off, and her face lights up. She gasps and looks out at the sky over the water, where bursts of white and blue fire sparkle, then fizzle out. Then burst after burst lights up her face, and I can't look away.

I would've thought June turning down my offer to buy Pier Seven would be the worst thing that could happen. But when I look at Sierra, I know that's no longer true.

I know that in so many ways, we're different. Her life is in the city, mine will always be here, and maybe we're not supposed to work. But we both know what it is to be abandoned. I want her to feel wanted, right now, more than anything else.

I touch her shoulder, draw the blanket down her arms. She looks over her shoulder at me and smiles.

I reach for her face, her breast, her waist. We meet in a tentative kiss.

Then it deepens.

I pull her into my arms.

She starts undoing my jeans, then tears my shirt off over my head.

I help her out of her little denim shorts, out of her panties. We meet again in a clumsy kiss, and she laughs against my mouth as she pulls my jeans down my hips.

Then the song changes, and an old April Wine ballad comes on. As the opening bars of "I'm On Fire for You Baby" starts, Sierra draws back a bit.

"Did you make this playlist for me?" she says breathlessly. "For this?"

"I might have."

She grins at me.

Then I kiss her again, and she melts against me. I peel off her shirt and bra.

I pull her with me as I lie back on the pillows, drawing her on top. I hold myself back and submit to her as she takes over. Guiding me to her. Sliding me inside her.

Working her hips up and down, slow . . .

Then hungrily and fast, riding me with a desire that makes me lose my breath. My moans are broken and desperate as I try to hang on, long enough to let her explode first . . .

I shove my thumb between her legs, work her clit in quick little circles as she takes me, hard and hurried. Her moans mingle with the music. Her bare breasts bounce, nipples peaked in the evening air. Her soft hair glows all around her face, backlit in red and gold and violet glitter.

When she comes, she cries out. Then she whimpers my name.

She keeps fucking me until I come, filling her in a molten burst as the fireworks explode all around her.

I don't close my eyes. I want to etch this into my memory.

Trails of glitter and sparkling stars, and the most beautiful, haunting eyes.

Sierra.

Afterwards, as we lie entangled in the back of my truck, half-clothed, I don't feel any better.

How could I?

I've lost on every front.

I'm feeling all kinds of things for the woman in my arms that I'm not ready for. Have never been ready for, not from the moment she walked into my bar.

My parents died, suddenly and tragically, less than a year before that moment, and I'm only starting to realize now how deep I still was—still am—in the ugly process of grieving for them. Finishing the renovations on our family home; getting my arms lavishly tattooed with apple blossoms and their names; burying myself in work—none of it has really helped me deal.

While I've plowed onward with my life, taking on more responsibilities and making my family and our business my top priorities, I've tried to keep everything under control, including my grief.

But just below the surface, I'm devastated.

The hole they left in my life is still so raw. I'm wounded, and some days, I'm a fucking mess of nameless emotions that seem to be pulling the strings even as I try to ignore them.

And maybe I haven't been able to see things clearly.

When June invited a stranger to lease Pier Seven, denying me that right, deep down, it felt like a much worse betrayal than it was. I had no real claim on the building, but it felt like my parents did, and June's refusal to negotiate with me felt like a betrayal of *them*. That's what really pissed me off.

And Sierra . . . I was so wrong about her, it hurts.

I'm just starting to recognize—to admit to myself—how deeply fucking wrong I was about her, her intentions, her reasons for coming here. Her reasons for every little thing she's said and done in Orchard Cove.

Including the things she's said to me.

The things she's done with me, and every moment we've shared.

Even the most beautiful moments have been tainted by my lingering distrust. My unwillingness to admit that maybe I've been wrong the whole time.

I haven't even manned up enough to tell her so. To apologize. To try to make it right—all the things I said and did to her that were just so damn *wrong*.

And now she's *leaving*.

"I feel like I've fucked up," I say to the night sky, breaking the silence. The fireworks have ended, and we're lying on our backs, faces tipped up to the stars.

"Don't blame yourself, Mason. Losing Pier Seven is not your fault. It was June's decision to make." Then she adds dryly, "And we've both met June. You are not going to change that woman's mind if she's decided."

Maybe she's right.

But that's not the only thing I fucked up. Badly.

"I should've prioritized it more," I say.

I should've prioritized you *more.*

"You did what you could. There's a lot on your plate."

I sigh, so fucking exhausted. "It feels like everywhere I am, I should be somewhere else. There's always something more I should be doing. Someone who needs me, who I could be failing. Even if I don't want to."

There's a long, fraught silence as maybe she considers that.

And how fucking exhausted I sound.

I hear it myself: the weariness in my own voice. The weight of the responsibilities I've been carrying.

I want to seize this moment, to tell her how sorry I am for all the mistakes I've made, but the truth is I'm scared.

And maybe I don't want to ruin this.

This perfect moment with Sierra in my arms, *not* reminding her what an asshole I've been.

She pushes herself up on an elbow and looks down at my face.

"Have you ever, in the year since your parents died, just sat alone for a moment," she asks me softly, "and asked yourself in the silence what it is that *you* want?"

I swallow, hard.

The truth is, I haven't. Not really.

But I think I know the answer to that question now.

I look into those haunting green eyes.

Then I have to look away.

What I want is closure. They died so suddenly. So unexpectedly. And I know I'm having trouble letting go.

Because I don't *want* to let go.

Just like I'm having trouble letting her go.

Even though I know I have to.

This wanting—which is just wishing that things could be different—is futile.

June was right. I need to face reality.

No matter what I say to Sierra, or don't say, she's still leaving.

She has a life to get back to in the city.

"I think I want to feel like their work isn't done," I say, my voice rough with emotion. "Because maybe that way, their lives aren't really over." I laugh without any humor in it. "Stupid, I know. I mean, I know they're gone. And I know I can't change that."

Sierra lays her head on my chest. "Then why are you still trying to?"

CHAPTER 21

Sierra

We spend the next day tearing down what's left of the festival, me and Sophie and the whole committee, and anyone else who's able to volunteer.

Then I spend the evening with Soph at the cottage while she starts packing her things; mostly, we just talk and listen to music and laugh.

I confess to her that I've been sleeping with Mason. I tell her how good he's been to me when we're together, and she offers me the most priceless advice that a best friend can. "As long as it makes you feel good, enjoy it for all it's worth. You deserve to be happy."

The next day, we all come together again to clean up Water Street. And afterwards, the committee gathers in the bar for a celebratory round and a "thank you" dinner, courtesy of the Grant family.

Sophie and I skip out early so that I can help her finish packing up at the cottage. She's leaving first thing in the morning to catch an early ferry from Nanaimo to Vancouver. Pete and Dirty need her back.

Which means that tonight I've organized a little goodbye party in my best friend's honor with the help of some of our new friends, over at Bev and Bill's house. I put on my sexiest little body-con dress, sage green, because Sophie tells me it makes my eyes look like "sex on fire," and my favorite Kiss & Tell lipstick, a dreamy, soft coral shade called Make Him Remember, because Mason is going to be at the party.

Sophie is killing it in a dramatic fit-and-flare, black with white polka dots, her hair in a retro updo, when we arrive at the party to much fanfare.

It's just after eight, and everyone else is already here, except June. She walks in just after we do, with flowers for Bev and a bottle of Twisted Tree cider for Soph.

I'm just amazed that I managed to get June and Mason to come to the same party.

"Is Tommy coming?" I ask Mason and Layne when I find them in the kitchen with Bill.

"Uh, Grandpa had some things to do," Layne says. "He sends his regards."

Mason gives me a look, which I'm pretty sure I can interpret. And when Layne turns away to chat with Bill, I venture, "Tommy didn't want to come because June was invited?"

"You'd think it would be difficult to avoid your neighbor at every single social event in a small town," he says dryly. "However, neither one of them is very social, so it kind of works out. June must really like you to show up for this."

"She likes Sophie," I say.

For the next hour or so, I basically pay watery-eyed tribute to my best friend with as many toasts as I can think of. I say a dramatic goodbye to her even though she's still coming back to the cottage with me tonight, and I give her a million sloppy hugs.

I'm not even drunk, just emotional.

Not only is she going back to Vancouver tomorrow, she's leaving on tour later this week. Which often means I won't see her for weeks at a time, even months.

And Mason is really cool about it, bringing me a glass of cider, checking in to see how I'm holding up when it's clear I'm slightly falling apart.

"Yum, this may be my favorite one," I tell him after taking a sip. It's Citrus Zest, the first one he poured me at the bar on the day we met. "Tastes like memories." I meet his eyes and my cheeks heat, because maybe that was TMI.

He smiles.

After my second glass, I work up the nerve to pull Mason out to the back porch—where June is already waiting, alone, because I told her I wanted to talk to her about something important.

"Oh. I see," she says as soon as she sees me with Mason. Her back straightens.

Before she can bolt into the house, I block the way to the door, put up my hands, and implore them both, "Wait wait wait. Please. Can you both just hear out what I have to say? I have an idea."

Mason glances at June.

June sighs irritably. "Well, get on with it. We don't have all night."

"Okay, look." I take a breath, gathering my thoughts. "I've been thinking about this a lot. And since I can't lease out Pier Seven for my smoothie bar, my next wish would be to see one of you reviving the space and opening up a super-cool restaurant in it that the amazing people of Orchard Cove, and all the tourists who come here, can enjoy. I totally get why you'd want that, and I can see it. Diverse menu featuring fresh, seasonal offerings. Partnering with local producers, farmers, wineries. A place to showcase your own products." I eye them both sharply. "*Both* of yours."

June continues to appear put-out. If she had a watch on, she'd probably be looking at it.

"It can be a wonderful gathering place for the community," I press on. "It'll bring more people to the beach at Orchard Cove. It'll bring more people out to your cideries. And it will encourage them to stick around for a meal rather than just having a quick cider tasting and leaving town. So, it's win-win. And it can be more family-friendly than the bar. It can be whatever you want or need it to be. But you know what the downside is?"

Mason cocks an eyebrow, like, *Where do I start?*

"There's no guarantee that if *you* open a restaurant across the street from Mason's bar and grill," I say to June, "and *you* keep running your bar and grill across from June's restaurant," I say to Mason, "that you'll both be able to make it work. Especially in the winter. If you remain in direct competition with each other, right across the street, you might actually kill each other's business. The town might not be able to support more than one restaurant year-round. And if I figured this out as an outsider, you are both smart enough to know this already."

"This is the choice she's making," Mason says evenly. "Sea Haven Bar and Grill has been there for years. If June wants to open up a restaurant to compete with me, so be it."

"But don't you see that this stubbornness, this unwillingness to work together as neighbors, may be what shoots you in the foot?"

"What is it you're suggesting, Sierra?" June says with impatience.

"What I'm proposing is that the Grants and the Spencers join forces, to open up a new restaurant at the pier *together*."

When neither one of them jumps for joy at this idea, I feel the need to keep selling it.

"I mean, I think it's brilliant. You both leverage your strengths and experience, and you offset the risk by sharing in the investment. Together, you'd be exactly what this town needs. Which is an end to this generations-old rivalry. Lay all your disputes to rest and start seeing each other as what you should've been all along: allies."

Silence.

Inside the house, The Guess Who provides a warm, light-rock backdrop to the neighborly chatter and the clink of ice in drinks.

But outside, it's stone-cold silence.

June's arms are still crossed. Mason's hands are on his hips. His jaw is locked; her mouth is compressed into a tight line.

"Look, Sierra. I hear what you're saying," Mason says gently. "But—"

"Just think about it? Why don't you both just think about it, and then maybe actually talk about it?"

"There's nothing to talk about," June says. "Mason knows where I stand. I've made it very clear." She moves toward the door, and I step out of her way. But she pauses. "Thank you for all your efforts, Sierra. Your energy is . . . admirable. It's truly inspiring how you've come to care about this town." She puts her hand on my shoulder, squeezes.

Then she goes back into the house.

My shoulders drop. "Well, that went well."

Mason sighs. "I'll talk to her."

Hope surges through me. "I really think it's the best thing for the town. And I think, deep down, you do, too." I take a step toward him. Look up into his gorgeous eyes. "Imagine, you could be running a restaurant at the pier, like you wanted to. You just have to open your mind to the idea that June could be involved, that you could do it together. Your businesses are so similar, it makes sense."

I feel kind of desperate to convince him. To convince them.

I tell myself that it really is what's best for the town. And what's best for Mason. What's best for June, too.

But honestly . . . maybe it's also a selfish proposal.

Because wouldn't it be amazing if they asked me to be involved somehow, too?

"I can't promise anything," he says. "You know June."

"Yeah. I know. Just . . . think about it?"

"I will." He comes closer, slings an arm around me. "You're a real sweetheart, Sierra Daniels." Then he kisses me on the forehead.

It's the last thing he says to me for five long days.

◆ ◆ ◆

My hope that Mason and June might consider the brilliance in my proposal fades day by day as the week progresses, and I get closer to the end of the month and the day I'll be leaving Orchard Cove. I don't hear a word about it from either of them.

I only see June a couple of times, speed-walking about her property, though we barely exchange words. She's busy. I'm busier than I've been since coming to town.

I'm still working on the cottage, replacing some of the decor with cute thrift-store finds from Duncan and Ladysmith and Nanaimo. It's busier at the smoothie bar without Sophie there, even with the part-time help I've brought on.

And yet I still can't seem to find enough work to do to take my mind off Mason.

Mason, who hasn't gotten back to me about my proposal.

Mason, who I've only seen in passing around town because, at this point, I'm steadily avoiding him.

It's now Sunday, and the smoothie bar is busy all day. Since we're always closed on Monday and Tuesday, and Tuesday is the end of the month, today is Cutie Fruitie's final day operating in Orchard Cove. Layne and Kaylie, Trish, Pam and Maria, Jace, Evan, and so many others drop in to thank me for coming to town, to buy a final smoothie, and wish me well.

Mason does not.

I spend the evening dismantling the shop and packing everything into my van. Mason comes over to help, along with Bill and Chloe. So at least the work goes fairly fast. Chloe helps me clean up, then I go back to the cottage to shower and start packing up my things.

While we were tearing down the shop, Mason brushed against me, asked me if we'd see each other tonight. I told him I wasn't sure. That I had packing to do.

I know I've been avoiding him because I'm fearing the rejection. Fearing the end. Fearing goodbye.

All the worst things in life, really.

Things haven't been the same without Sophie here, and it's a painful reminder of the life I'm going back to. No Sophie. No solid future plans for my business. I haven't even been able to secure my next location yet. Places I've leased in the past are all booked a year out. I'll have to do some serious searching and financial gymnastics when I get back to the city to make things work. Maybe find some farmers' markets or festivals I can crash.

Meanwhile, it feels like summer is just kicking off in Orchard Cove. It feels wrong to be leaving.

Especially when I have so little to go back to.

Kyle calls while I'm walking back to the Cozy Cottage from the beach, where I just took a few minutes to sit and listen to music and think. I'm in one of those random, rare spots where I get cell service, right on Honeymoon Lane, between the Grants' property and the Spencers'.

I stop in the road to talk to him. I don't even know why.

What more is there to say?

"You said you'd call me back," he says, "but you never did."

"Yeah. Sorry. It's been so busy here."

I don't know why I'm apologizing to him for anything. I owe him nothing. And yet in some way, I feel like I still do.

"How has it been there? It always looks like you're having fun."

"It's social media, Kyle. For the business. It's supposed to look that way."

"I really wish you'd called me back," he says, putting pressure on me in that way he does. Passive-aggressive. Implying that I should've done better.

Pressuring me for communication, when he didn't put enough effort into communicating when we were together. As if we still have something to work out.

Do we?

"Let's talk when you get back. Okay? When are you coming?"

I gaze along Honeymoon Lane toward the sea, where the water ripples, darkening in the fading dusk light. How many more times will I get to look out at that view I've come to love? To crave, even.

"I don't know, Kyle. The end of the month. Tuesday. I haven't booked the ferry yet."

"Let me know which one you'll be on? I'll meet you. I think we should talk, face-to-face."

"Yeah," I say, but mostly just to get off the phone. "I'm about to lose the signal."

I go back to the cottage and finish packing up my bags, for the most part. I leave out a few clothes and toiletries. Then I sit on the bed in Sophie's room, wondering if it would be best if I just left tonight. I might be able to catch the last ferry, if I left right now.

What's the point in dragging this out for two more days? Cutie Fruitie is closed. June made it clear I'm welcome to stay until the thirtieth. And I thought I might.

But why?

Goodbyes are hard enough.

Maybe I should just leave.

But I find myself stepping out onto the back porch of the cottage. Wandering beneath the twisted tree, and pushing through the secret gate.

I follow the path through the Grant family's orchard. Then I make my way up the lawn to the house, tap on Mason's back door.

When he doesn't answer, I go around to the front and ring the bell.

Finally, Mason comes to the door. Skin damp, hair wet, towel slung around his waist.

I think he looks happy to see me. But I don't really know. The little pinch between his eyebrows, the weariness in the slight circles beneath his eyes, like he's become chronically under-slept lately.

"Sierra. I was just getting cleaned up. Then I was gonna come see you."

"Oh. I was . . ." I glance away, then say it right to his face. That's why I came, right? "Thinking about leaving."

He stares at me.

Then he takes my hand and draws me into the house, shutting the door.

"Leaving. Now?"

"Yeah. Tonight. Cutie Fruitie is done, so . . ."

"I thought we had two more days." He searches my eyes. "You aren't leaving until Tuesday . . ."

"Yeah. That's what I thought."

"What's wrong? What happened?"

I wrap my arms around myself. "Why haven't you come to talk to me?"

He runs a hand through his wet hair. "I tried. I barely saw you all week. Every time I get a glimpse of you, you're running in the other direction. Kind of feels like you've been avoiding me."

"Kind of feels like you don't want to tell me the truth."

"What truth?"

"I'm not in business with you, I know. But I did make a proposal that I thought you might actually take seriously. If nothing else, you could've given me a response after giving it some thought."

"I was going to. *Shit.*" He struggles, like maybe he's trying to find the gentlest way of letting me down. "It's not going to work, Sierra. I gave it some thought. I really did. And you're right, I never really looked at it quite that way before. Working with June never seemed like an option. And maybe it would be, if she'd actually consider it."

"She won't?"

"I spoke to her yesterday. There's no way. She won't work with Tommy, no matter how I present it to her. And working with me means working with him. My grandpa and I own all our businesses together, with Layne. And even if the restaurant is a separate venture, even if I sell off the bar to invest in Pier Seven, the money still comes from the same place. The way June sees it, that money is tainted."

"Because of your grandpa?" I consider this. "And you're sure there's no old feelings still brewing between them or something? Because it sure sounds like it. Who holds a grudge that long over nothing?"

"It's definitely not nothing." He sighs, looking weary as hell. "But I don't think it's what you think it is. Land, property, money . . . it makes people do crazy shit. Wage wars that last . . . well, generations."

"Yeah." My gaze drifts down his naked chest. "So . . . you were just gonna wait until the last possible moment to tell me this? Shout it at me as I drove away down the highway?"

He groans.

I allow a small smile to play at my lips.

"Maybe," he admits. "Probably, yeah. Fuck." He rubs his face. "I'm sorry. I'm shit at this." His eyes lock on mine, blue, endless. "I don't really know how to do this."

"Do what?"

We stare at each other for a long moment.

"How to say goodbye," he says, then swallows.

"Me, neither," I say softly.

Then I reach for him. His solid shoulders, his neck, the thick, silken hair at his nape. I don't have to pull him to me. He's here, his mouth claiming mine, his tongue delving inside, his hands in my hair.

I kiss him like it might be the last time, and I don't want him to forget.

He picks me up and carries me up to his bedroom. There, he strips off my clothes. His touch is reverent, his eyes relishing every glimpse in the near-dark.

I peel off his towel, and we fall together on the bed.

When he fills me, the high I feel is like nothing else.

The way he rocks into me with hunger and need. The way his hands move over my body. The way he inhales my scent and tastes my skin.

The way he fucks me like he can't get enough . . . so attuned to my every response, like there's nothing else that matters.

I've never had pleasure like this.

Never been so taken care of . . . so savored, and so desired.

And as we move together, he murmurs in my ear, "Promise me. Promise me this isn't all. Promise me that I'll get to see you again . . ."

I meet his eyes. "I promise," I whisper.

When we climax, we cling together, kissing, clutching, desperate to hold on.

I have no idea how I'll keep that promise.

I just know that he needs to hear it. And I do, too.

Deep in the night, I wake up in Mason's bed. He lies on his back, his head tipped away on the pillow, his chest rising and falling in sleep. The sheet is draped over our hips as the ceiling fan loops above.

His hand rests on my thigh.

I lie there for a long while, listening to him breathe, memories of all the moments we've shared playing in my head on a torturous loop.

Then I slide out from under his hand, gather my clothes, and slip out.

I walk the secret path back to my cottage, trying to savor every moment. Drawing the fresh night air into my lungs. Memorizing the curves of the trees, the flutter of the leaves, the pretty, haunting shapes they make against the night sky.

I collect my bags from the cottage, get into my van, and leave Orchard Cove.

I can barely breathe, my chest is so tight. I'm aching to spill all my feelings to Mason. But I know it's way too little, too late.

Because that old fear of mine has come back to haunt me.

He didn't choose me.

He didn't put me first.

Mason never once asked me to stay, to be his.

He never even wanted to try.

He was a bachelor when I met him, a playboy, and nothing has changed.

I hear Sophie telling me, *You deserve to be happy.*

And a lot of things June said are loud in my head.

So, I'm making my own choice. To not repeat the mistake I've made in the past by chasing him, trying to fix him. And contorting myself to try to fit somewhere I'm not even wanted. Not really.

Promise me that I get to see you again just isn't enough.

So I've made my choice.

It's a choice I never would've made in the past.

But this is long overdue.

It's time I put myself first.

CHAPTER 22

MASON

I wake up in the morning, weirdly cold. Birds singing, ceiling fan looping, sea *shooshi*ng.

Heart pounding.

I reach for her, but somehow, I already know it, again—Sierra's gone.

Her clothes are no longer on my floor.

I pull on some sweats and a T-shirt, race downstairs, don't even put on shoes. I run out the back door, down the grass, through the orchard. Don't stop running, all the way along the path to the gate, under the plum tree, and up to her cottage.

I knock on the back door, tap on a window, but by the time I get around to the front of the cottage, it's clear.

She's *gone*.

I can see the driveway that curves around the side of June's house, and Sierra's van is not there. I head over there anyway, frantic.

June is on her knees in her garden, and when she sees me, she frowns deeply. "Mason . . ."

"Don't worry, I'm leaving." I don't think she's ever actually seen me on her property before. I haven't been many times. "Have you seen Sierra?"

"Not today. She left already."

"When?"

"I don't know. Early this morning . . ."

I'm already disappearing around the house. I follow the driveway around to the front, then all the way out to the road, just in case. But Sierra's van is nowhere to be seen.

How long ago did she leave?

It doesn't matter.

She made her choice.

I walk all the way back up Honeymoon Lane to my driveway, swearing to myself. Telling myself that this is how it has to be. That I knew this was coming. All that shit.

It doesn't help.

I take the fork in the driveway where it splits, the private driveway that leads up to my house. The front door is locked, and I didn't even bring keys.

I'm a fucking disaster.

I think I cut my foot.

I go around to the back, limping a bit, and find Layne in my kitchen. Coffee brewing, making breakfast.

"Where's Kaylie?" I ask him. "And Grandpa?"

"Good morning to you, too. They're outside somewhere, with Scar." He gives me a curious look. "Out for a jog? With no shoes?"

I'm breathing heavily and prop myself up against the island. "*Fuck*" is all I manage to say.

"You want eggs?" he asks, cracking some into a pan on the stove. "And maybe some coffee? Your shirt is inside out."

The idea of eating right now just hurts my stomach. "*Shit.* I fucked up, Layne."

My brother takes a long look at me, and says, "Sierra?"

I just nod.

"You hooked up with her, didn't you?"

I pinch the bridge of my nose, trying to get a hold of myself. My head is scrambled. "I did more than hook up with her, Layne." I take a deep breath. "And now she's gone. She went back to the city, early."

"Well, shit." Now he looks sorry for me. "How did you fuck it up? What did you do?"

"I don't know if it's what I did or what I didn't do." I drop onto a stool. "She wanted me to find a way to work with June. To go into business together. Open a restaurant at the pier, together." I swear again, press my fingers into my eyes. "I think . . . maybe she hoped we'd ask her to stay. You know, be a part of it."

"That's not a bad idea," my brother says.

And hearing him say that . . . Jesus.

"I know. But June . . . she wouldn't go for it."

Why didn't I come talk to him sooner? Layne would've told me to just ask Sierra to stay. We could've let her sell smoothies at the bar or set up a smoothie truck in the lot or something.

Fucking *anything*.

If I wasn't so fucking afraid.

"Did June give you a reason why?" he asks.

"The only reason she ever gives is Grandpa. She refuses to do business with Tommy."

Layne kind of snorts. "I'm not surprised. Imagine it. You've lived next door to Sierra for your entire seventy-plus years of life. All that time, you've loved her, and you've had to watch her marry someone else, live a whole life without you, right in front of your eyes. Sounds like a goddamn nightmare."

I watch him scrambling eggs as if he didn't just blow my world right open.

"What? What are you talking about?"

"I'm talking about Grandpa. And June."

"You think he *loves* her?"

"I think he'll never admit it if he does. He married someone else, too. Who knows where the heartbreak started. But I guarantee you, those two have wounds. Of the amorous variety."

Jesus Christ.

Mind blown.

"How do you know this?"

My brother, who is admittedly more sensitive than I am, just shrugs. "I don't know. It's not that hard to see that *something's* going on. Usually you hate someone because deep down you fear something about them, right? So, ask yourself. What would make Grandpa afraid of June Spencer?"

Fuck me.

Sierra fucking scares you.

That's what Jace said to me, and he wasn't wrong.

"*Fuck*, Grandpa." I lean on my elbows, rub my hands over my face. "You're telling me that his unrequited crush on our next-door neighbor is why I can't buy that goddamn building?"

"Hey, I didn't say it was unrequited."

I consider that. "June said she wanted Grandpa to apologize to her. That she'd never consider negotiating with us until he did. Do you really think that's all it would take? 'Sorry I hurt you'?"

"Hey, it couldn't hurt. A lot can be mended with the right words." He glances at me as he plates eggs. "If they're sincere."

Yeah. Maybe. "What the hell do you think is stopping him? What's he so afraid of?"

"Well . . . imagine he tells her after all these years that he's sorry. And she won't hear it. What do you think *he* thinks will happen? They just go back to the way they were? Or do you think his heart breaks all over again?"

I swallow. Trying to imagine that scenario: decades of life with Sierra as my neighbor, just out of my reach. Finally, pushing aside all the years of calcified resentment and guilt and fear to apologize, only to be rejected.

"Maybe he's right to stay silent."

Layne makes a disgruntled noise. "If that's what you think . . . *shit*, brother." He puts a mug of steaming coffee in front of me. "All I'm gonna say is if you wanna sit there looking like a sad sack of shit, regretting that you let Sierra go, and not do anything about it . . . you are more like Grandpa than I ever took you for."

It's not a compliment in this context, at all, I know.

"Do I look that bad?" I say dryly.

"Bro." He levels me with a look. "Get a mirror." Then he goes to stick his head out the back door and shouts, "BREAKFAST!"

While I sit there, trying to look normal.

Distractedly, I sip my coffee, rub Scar on the head when he nudges against my leg. Watch my niece and my grandpa and my brother gather around the table, Kaylie chirping on about something. Layne scooping eggs and bacon onto plates. Pouring apple juice, bumping into each other, looking for the butter.

Suddenly, I see my life fast-forwarding in this place.

It's not hard to do.

I can see myself at my dad's age, when he died . . . only I don't have a loving wife and children.

I can see myself at my grandpa's age, as a widower . . . only I never had a wife at all.

Because that's the way I'm headed right now, isn't it?

I used to tell myself that it wasn't my fault. That I tried.

Jenn left *me* at the altar. Her choice.

I was ready and willing to be a husband, start a family. I wanted a family of my own, more than anything.

Maybe I still do.

But maybe after she left me like that, I got angry.

I got angry . . . because I was fucking scared.

And after my parents died . . . maybe I convinced myself that it's just not safe to love. Because people leave you, and that's beyond your control.

And if I keep believing that . . . maybe I will end up alone. Wishing things had been different, regretting things I never said.

Risks I never took.

Just like Tommy and June.

Maybe all it would take to turn things around would be to tell Sierra how I feel. To tell her I'm sorry if I hurt her.

To take a risk, because she's worth it.

But maybe I'm already too late.

Maybe I've already lost her.

Hurt her too badly by hitting her right where she's wounded, letting her believe that she was never what I wanted most.

CHAPTER 23

Sierra

"So, you know how you told me that Kyle chose his family and his career and everything else in his life over me? And you were totally right?"

"Uh, yeah," Sophie says through the speakers in my van. I'm driving back into Vancouver after landing on the ferry in Horseshoe Bay when I call her to tell her that I came home early.

"Well, I think I've hit an all-time low. Mason chose a *building* over me. A building that's not even his."

"You don't know that's true. Did you actually talk to him about it? Did you *ask* him?"

"I can't," I tell her, getting choked up. "It hurts too much."

I'm afraid.

Sophie does her best to reason with me, of course. Talk me down off the ledge. And I thank her and tell her I love her, and that I'll call her later this week to let her know how I'm doing. I tell her I'll be okay.

But I'm not so sure how I'll hold to that.

The decision I made to leave Orchard Cove, which seemed like such a healthy decision at the time—putting myself first and all—now feels like an act of extreme cowardice.

The truth is, I was running scared.

I moved to Vancouver in my early twenties and went searching for my biological father, and I know that I was deeply and maybe irreversibly wounded when I found him, called him up, and he told me in no uncertain terms never to call him again because he had a family and he didn't want me to "ruin things."

And I know that there's been a part of me that must fear I'm not good enough to be anyone's first choice.

Otherwise, why would I keep repeating this pattern? Letting the wrong people into my life, and shutting the right ones out.

Trying so hard to fix things as they fall apart around me—not knowing when they're really unfixable, not knowing when to leave before it's too late.

And not being brave enough to stay, to take a chance on something that might actually be good for me.

As I drive home in thick traffic across the sprawling Lions Gate Bridge, through Stanley Park, and into downtown Vancouver along West Georgia, lined with its gleaming glass towers, then pull into the secure parkade under my building, everything looks the same. But I can feel it—that nothing is the same as it was when I left the city a month ago.

Because *I've* changed.

I've grown, so much, into someone more like myself, that maybe I don't fit into this life anymore.

Maybe it's more than that, though.

I can feel it when I go out for lunch, walk into a sushi place by myself, and sit up at the bar alone to eat, listening to music in my earbuds. While I run errands and go pick up groceries, alone.

How painstakingly I've isolated myself.

How maybe I never really fit in here like I hoped I would. Because when I came to Vancouver, I was running away, and maybe I've never actually stopped running.

And maybe these last few years, as I got my business off the ground, I was also trying too hard to fit into the life Kyle wanted for me.

A life that was bigger and busier and more expensive than anything I could reasonably carry, and yet he refused to help me carry it.

I realize as I ride the elevator back up to my apartment that it really wasn't living in a small town that I hated growing up. It was the people I was surrounded by, the ones who made Carlton into a place that I didn't fit into. And I never really had people there who saw *me*, who liked me for me, except my grandpa.

Here in Vancouver, I've never really had people of my own, either. I had Sophie and Pete and some of their friends, and some of my employees who came and went. And later, I had Kyle. But I've never really had a friend group here, because I've never really tried.

I expected to hate Orchard Cove because I thought it would remind me of the place where I grew up. I was wrong.

What I found was a beautiful, welcoming town filled with people who liked me for me.

Maybe I'll just have to find some way to go back. So I can see Mason again, somehow. Like I promised him I would.

It's not that far.

Though with the ferry, it's at least a four-hour trip—on a good traffic day—from my apartment to his front door. I don't know how often I could feasibly make it work when I'm hustling all over the GVRD from one pop-up to another.

And meanwhile . . . plenty of eager, horny tourists will be lining up at his bar.

I work the key in my lock on that depressing mental image. When I throw open my apartment door, arms loaded down with grocery bags, there's a man sitting in my living room. I startle, dropping a couple of my bags.

"*Jesus Christ.* What the hell."

"Hey. Sorry. Did I scare you?" He gets to his feet. Five-foot-eleven, broad shoulders, wavy, honey-brown hair. Wearing a suit on a Monday afternoon; he probably dipped out of work.

"Uh, yeah, Kyle. What are you doing here?"

"You said we could talk." He picks up the bags I dropped, takes them to the fridge. Starts unpacking and putting all the cold stuff away.

Honestly, he was never this considerate when we were dating.

I hand him the rest of the bags, sigh, and shut the door.

"Right now? I just got back."

"I know." He gives me an almost sheepish look. "When you said you were on the early ferry, I just figured I'd come by today. And when I texted, you said you were at the grocery store. So I let myself in with my key."

Right. His key. The one I really need to get back from him.

"Well, while you're here, you can collect your records." I take one of the now-empty grocery bags, head into the living room, and start packing them up. When I told him I was getting groceries, I thought I made it clear I'm busy today.

Guess not.

He follows me. "I kind of took the key as a sign."

I look at him blankly.

"That maybe the door wasn't totally closed between us . . ."

What the hell?

"I forgot you had a key. I was in Orchard Cove. I've been busy."

"Yeah. I know." He takes a step closer. "And I want you to know . . . I'm proud of you, for the way you picked yourself up after what happened and kept going."

I laugh bitterly. "What did you expect me to do? Curl up in a ball on my couch and cry into my ice cream for the rest of the summer? Hide away, so I wouldn't have to run into you and Estella groping each other at the bar?"

He swallows, actually looking regretful. "I wish you didn't have to see that."

I laugh shortly. "I'm glad I saw it. That night taught me a lot about you that I might've refused to see otherwise." I finish sorting out his albums from mine and get to my feet.

I grab another grocery bag from the kitchen and go into the bedroom, start stuffing it with the clothes he left here. Once again, he follows me, and it grates.

How I would've loved to have his attention back then, even just another hour or two of his time, to talk things out face-to-face without arguing in circles. But he wouldn't even give me that.

"I didn't want you to find out like that, Sierra," he says lamely.

"Then why were you in public?" I shoot back. "I may not have as many friends as you, but at least I have damn good ones." I refuse to look at him. Or get upset about it all over again.

But I can remember that night so clearly, sitting right here, alone on my couch just three days after he broke up with me, still hurting, still hoping we were salvageable, still trying. Calling him and getting no answer. Texting him and getting no reply. Instead, I got a text from Pete. He'd just walked into a bar and happened to see Kyle and Estella there—all over each other.

When I was dating Kyle, seeing him wrapped around his gorgeous best friend would've been my worst nightmare. I'd always been uncomfortable with their relationship; he'd always convinced me to trust him anyway. But that night, when Sophie's husband sent me that text, I went straight down there to see it for myself. And I'm glad I did, so there could be no misunderstanding here.

I will always be grateful to Pete for having my back like that. For saving me from making the mistake of seeing potential with Kyle, holding on, when there was no reason to. The way Kyle treated me when he broke up with me and ricocheted into the arms of the nearest hottie made it clear that he didn't really care.

While I was hurting, he was getting laid. And when I confronted him about it at the bar that night, all I got was more arguing.

I didn't get an apology that night, or any day since.

"I'll pack up your mom's wine glasses, too," I tell him coolly. "She wanted them back."

He follows me into the kitchen, where I start wrapping the wine glasses in paper towels to protect them, and tucking them into the bag with the records.

"Sierra. Jesus." He scrapes a hand through his hair. "You're not making this easy for me."

In my head, I hear Mason's tortured voice that first night in bed, and a shiver runs down my spine. *You're making this so hard for me.*

"I don't need to make this, or anything else, easy for you, Kyle."

"But I'm trying to tell you . . . Estella and I split up. It didn't work out. We're not together."

I take a deep breath. *This* is what he wanted to talk about so badly? Not us, but *her*?

I realize he wants some reaction from me, but I literally have none to give.

"I'm sorry," I say flatly. "You guys made a good couple."

"Come on, Sierra. It doesn't have to be like this. I never cheated on you with her."

"I'm not going to argue the finer points with you, Kyle. Let's just agree to disagree about how loyalty works."

"I just think . . . it's a shame to toss away three years."

"Yeah. It is a shame." *It's a shame that I wasted them on you.* I bite my tongue on that, because there's no reason for us to be enemies. We have a history, but that's all it is. "But it's over now. And I need to move on. Because I deserve better." I turn to face him. "Honestly, we both do. We weren't good together."

"How can you say that?"

"Because that's how I feel. And maybe it's not your fault that I never told you so. But I'm telling you now. With you, I always felt like I was trying to do some overly complicated yoga pose that I could never quite get into, you know? Or trying to squeeze myself into a dress that didn't quite zip up, only because it was expensive and *you* liked it, and that meant I was supposed to like it, too. But the whole time, the real me kept trying to fall out, and I just wouldn't let her."

"What are you talking about, Si?"

"I'm talking about *me*. Because that dress never fit, and no matter how much I try to fix it, it never will. Because it was never supposed to. So, it's time to unzip that dress and see what's underneath."

His gaze flickers down my dress.

Oh my god. He doesn't get it.

"I'm not talking about getting naked, Kyle." I sigh, frustrated. "I mean, I kind of am, but not the way you think. What I mean is . . . it's time for me to get on with my life. The life *I* choose. And it's time for us to say goodbye."

He blinks at me. "You really mean that."

"Yes, Kyle. I really mean it." I hold out my hand. "Can I please have my key back?"

He frowns.

Then he digs in his pocket. He works the key off his keychain and holds it over my hand, but hesitates there. When his eyes meet mine, there's anger in them. Contempt. Resentment, disbelief, and disapproval.

But it doesn't bother me like it would have in the past.

"You're going to regret this," he informs me. He presses the key into my hand, then seems to be waiting for me to cave or something.

I don't.

He grunts. "Don't expect me to be waiting around when you change your mind."

"You should go."

He stares at me for a moment longer. But when it's clear that I have nothing else to say to him, he leaves with a final huff of incredulous laughter.

As soon as the door closes behind him, I exhale with relief.

Then I look around my apartment.

It's never felt so small, so cold, so fucking empty.

My gaze locks on the two stuffed grocery bags on the counter. The ones with Kyle's stuff in them. *Shit.*

I grab my keys and the bags, and fly out the door. Jab the elevator button. All the way down, I pray that I can catch him. So this is truly the last time I ever have to deal with him.

The little traffic loop in front of my building is lined with parked cars, and when I step outside, I see Kyle. A couple of cars down, door open, just about to get in.

"Kyle!"

He looks up and I jog over, bags held out.

"You forgot your things."

He scowls. Takes the bags and stuffs them in his trunk. Then he skewers me with an expectant look. "That's all you have to say?"

"Uh. Have a good life?"

He stares at me for a moment, apparently in total disbelief that I would actually let him go without some dramatic scene, begging him not to leave.

But I already did that once, which was more than enough.

He shakes his head and gets into his car. “Goodbye, Sierra.” He shuts the door and pulls out, taking off in his beloved Audi.

I watch it go, up the short drive to the stop sign. The tires squeal a little on the pavement as he disappears into traffic, and out of my life.

I take a deep breath. Let it out.

And my heart stops.

My gaze has locked on another man, standing across the street. In front of a parked black pickup truck with a golden apple on it, staring at me.

I blink, hesitant to trust my own eyes. He looks like a total vision in his dark-blue fitted T-shirt and jeans, with his sexy hair all a mess.

His gaze moves over me with hunger and regret.

I want to run to him, throw my arms around him.

But he also looks so out of place in front of my high-rise in downtown Vancouver, I don’t know whether to laugh or pinch myself.

I wander forward a couple of steps until I’m standing in the middle of the street.

“Mason,” I breathe. “Are you really here?”

He takes a few steps toward me, too.

“You’re here,” he says. “Where else would I be?”

CHAPTER 24

Sierra

Mason starts to reach for me, I think. To move toward me again, but he stops himself. He rubs the back of his head, digs his fingers into his hair, looking nervous as hell.

"Is this okay? That I'm here?"

"Of course it's okay." I hug myself, unsure what to do or what's happening. My pulse is flying. "How did you know where I live?"

"Uh, I may have begged June to pull your home address from your lease agreement." He buries his hands in the pockets of his jeans. He looks worried, like I might be upset about this. "Unethical and wrong, I know. But I told her I had to talk to you. Face-to-face."

"June did that for you?"

He takes a small step toward me. "I guess she could tell I really meant it."

I hesitate, too, but quickly realize the only reason I'm hesitating is that Kyle hated public displays of affection. But I'm not trying to fit into his idea of the perfect girlfriend anymore, am I?

So, I do what I really want to do and run to Mason, throwing myself into his open arms. As I hug him, I can feel his tension easing away.

"I'm sorry, baby," he says into my ear, holding me tight. "I'm sorry I let you go."

I bury my face in his neck, squeezing back the relief and happiness that threaten to explode from me in a torrent of tears.

His voice is scratchy with emotion when he says, "Am I too late?"

"For what?"

"Everything."

I take a deep, shuddering breath and look up into his worried eyes. "No, Mason. You're not too late for anything."

I see the relief all over his face.

And when he kisses me, I kiss him back, deep and passionate, right there in the street.

When we step into my apartment, Mason and I, we're holding hands. He took hold of mine on the way up in the elevator, and I feel giddy, effervescent, like my heart is filled with soda pop.

"So this is where the magic happens." His low, warm voice feels out of place in the modern, sharp-edged apartment.

I snicker. "What magic? Are we talking about the physics-defying manner in which I've managed to IKEA this shoebox into a marginally livable space?"

He lets my hand go to do a slow walk around the small apartment, which takes seconds. It's newish and clean, but it's definitely a home meant for one person. The mere five hundred square feet means we're standing in the tiny kitchen the moment we walk in the door.

In three more steps, we're in the living room/office/dining room, where I've wrangled every available inch into somehow fitting a small L-shaped couch, a coffee table, and a decent-sized desk/entertainment unit/vanity table where I work, eat, watch TV, and put on my makeup.

In the small bedroom, I've managed to fit a queen-sized bed with a bedside table, but there's not enough room for a dresser.

Because of the limited space, I've always kept it as clean and sparse as possible so I feel like I can breathe. But that also means it lacks personality.

I'm actually proud of how I've made the space work, but I realize I'm self-conscious about it because Kyle always seemed embarrassed by the way I live. As if I should've been able to do better. But Kyle wasn't paying my rent, was he.

He wasn't even paying his own rent. He has a mortgage, or rather his parents do, which they pay for him.

"Don't take this the wrong way," Mason says thoughtfully, "but I can't really see you living here."

At this point, I can't really, either. But I ask him, "Why?"

"It doesn't feel like you. Except for this." He points at the one piece of art on the living room wall. It's a portrait of Sophie by local artist Katie Mayes in a pop-surrealism style that totally suits Soph's eclectic-retro vibes and vibrant, playful personality.

I move to stand next to him. "I bought that at a music industry charity event that Sophie dragged me to, for way less than it's worth but more than I could really afford. I just had to have it."

Unfortunately, I also thought it might impress Kyle. *See, I have art. I'm cultured.*

Kyle called it "lowbrow art," as if that was an insult.

"It's awesome," Mason says. "It's so . . . her."

"I know, right?" I find myself smiling, thrilled that he gets it.

But of course he does.

I gaze at him, that handsome face I've come to adore. But when he looks at me, I look away.

"Come on, I'll show you the best part."

I grab his hand and pull him with me to the sliding door that opens onto the small but useable balcony. We're way up on the nineteenth floor, with a sweeping view over the Georgia Viaduct, the stadium, False Creek, and across the water, Olympic Village.

Directly below, traffic flows and, admittedly, it's noisy.

Right across the street is the enormous arena where a large digital sign shows a billboard for MGK's Lost Americana Tour.

Mason chuckles. "You live right above the arena?"

"Yep. Totally sold me on this place. I go to as many concerts as I can, and I don't have to worry about parking or fighting traffic, I just walk right down. Do you wanna know what the *best* best part is?"

He gazes at me, affection in his eyes, and warmth floods my veins. "I do."

"I don't even have to *go* to a concert to hear it loud and clear."

He laughs again.

"Swear to god, when I'm broke, I just open the windows. Sometimes I don't even need to open the windows. When Korn played last October, I thought it was gonna cause an earthquake."

He's laughing, so I laugh, too, happy tears pricking my eyes.

"You do realize that some people would consider that a reason *not* to rent this apartment."

"Oh, I know. But I'm not one of those people. In the last two years alone I've seen Justin Timberlake, Pearl Jam, Olivia Rodrigo, Bruce Springsteen, Katy Perry, Nine Inch Nails, and Cardi B, and eavesdropped on so many others from this balcony. I do actually have to open the windows if I really want to hear what's going on over at the stadium, because it's farther away. Unless it's Guns N' Roses, U2, or AC/DC. Then, no window opening needed."

"Wow. I'm shocked you weren't actually at those stadium shows."

"Hey, I already saw GNR at the stadium once, and a girl's gotta set *some* budget. I already spend too much on music."

Mason leans on his forearms on the balcony railing. "Sounds like this balcony is a melomaniac's dream."

I grin. "A polyjamorist's, too."

He grins back, dimples and all.

"Wait. MGK is playing tonight . . ."

"I see that. And are you going, or just eavesdropping?" he teases.

"Well, I sold my tickets for a pretty penny, because I thought I'd be in Orchard Cove . . ." I bite my lip a little, then just say it. "Wanna hang out on the balcony and listen with me?"

"Hell, yes."

"Great." I try to play it cool, but inside I'm fucking dancing. Does this mean he's sleeping over? "I think we can wrangle a couple of chairs out here and a couple of ciders. There's a liquor store down the block. I wonder if they carry Sea Haven? Or Twisted Tree?" I raise an eyebrow, teasing him back.

"If they're independent, they may. If it's a government liquor store, no chance."

"What?! That's a travesty! They don't support you?"

"It's not a support issue. It's a supply issue. We can't possibly supply enough product to get into those stores. But that's fine. We're a craft brand and will always be a craft brand. Small batches, high quality, no compromise."

"Aw. It's sweet the way you turn into anime when you talk about your products."

He laughs again. "What?"

"You get these cartoony little stars in your eyes."

"Oh, yeah? Kind of how you look when you talk about music. And smoothies, actually."

I snicker. "Yeah. My two great loves."

He smiles softly and I glance away.

Then I take a breath and plunge.

"Doja Cat's coming in October," I say casually. "I've already got my tickets. I always get two." I try to keep the smile on my face. But my heart is pounding and those good old persistent self-doubts rear their heads, making me almost chicken out. "Maybe you'll come back?"

My bones feel like they're vibrating with the force of my pulse, and I squeeze the handrail to steady myself as Mason takes a long, long time to respond. I focus on the way the lowering sun, behind us, reflects off the glass of the other towers, molten-pink and crimson and gold.

It's beautiful, though not Orchard Cove beautiful, and I wonder what he thinks of it.

"Sierra." His voice is low, hesitant. "I think you misunderstand."

I swallow the jagged lump that's suddenly lodged in my throat.

"Look at me, please."

I take another deep breath, then meet his eyes.

"I'll go to any concert you want," he says softly. "But I really don't want to go back to Orchard Cove for any length of time without you."

"What?" I whisper.

He hesitates, seems to be choosing his words with care. "I know how it feels to be abandoned by someone you love. To be discarded. And I know you don't deserve that any more than I did." He edges closer to me. "I should never have made you worry that I wasn't going to choose you. I know that's what your father did to you. And I know it's what Kyle did. And I'm so pissed at myself for not just telling you how I feel, *all* the things that I feel when I'm with you. It all just poured down on me like an avalanche when you left. When I *let* you leave."

I'm breathing so fast now and my heart is pounding so hard I can barely get the words out. "Well, to be fair, you were asleep. I didn't really give you a chance to—"

"No. I should've made it clear to you. I should've told you I wanted you to stay, and given you a chance to choose. To choose me, if that's what you wanted. The only reason I didn't say it was because I was scared that if I did, if I gave you that choice, you *wouldn't* choose me."

I laugh abruptly, I'm so shocked. "I think I chose you as soon as we met, Mason Grant. When you locked onto me that day in your bar, pouring me cider . . . the rest of the world didn't even stand a chance."

He studies my face for a moment, then takes hold of my hand. For some reason, he doesn't look elated to hear it. He looks worried.

Which just makes me worry. I'm practically vibrating, and I wonder if he can feel it.

"If you need time or space to think about things," he says gently, "to think about what you want, I understand. I don't want to pressure you into anything you don't want. I just really want you to know, no matter what happens between us, that I know I was wrong. The way I picked a fight with you as soon as I found out you'd leased Pier Seven . . . I made you feel unwelcome. I pressured you to leave town. I accused you of conspiring with June, trying to manipulate me, and so many shitty things."

He rubs his forehead, peers up at me.

I lift an eyebrow, like, *Go on.*

"I'm sorry," he says seriously. "You deserve an apology. Because you didn't deserve any of that. Not only were you not guilty of anything I accused you of, you're kind. And hard-working. And sweet and lovely and amazing, and you deserved the building and the lease, and all the support you got from June and the community. You should've had mine, too."

I take a deep breath, my heart lifting with a rush of pure joy as this new sensation fills me with warmth. *Acceptance.*

"Honestly," I tell him, "that was all I ever wanted from you in the beginning, Mason. To be welcome in your town. It was hard enough for me to even be there at first."

"I know," he says, and I can see the deep remorse in his eyes. "I know that now. I just made it worse. And I'm so fucking sorry. I wish I could go back and kick my own ass."

I laugh a little. "Why didn't you tell me you were sorry before I left town? It would've been nice to hear."

"Because I didn't think it would change anything." He sighs. "Maybe I tried to convince myself it didn't matter. But that was cowardly and fucking selfish. I think . . . *Fuck.* I think I've just been afraid of people leaving me, ever since I was left at the altar. And it's made it harder for me to take risks. Like telling you how I really feel."

I *feel* his fear when he says those words, and I know this can't be easy to admit.

"I'm so sorry that happened to you." Tentatively, I ask, "Tell me about it?" Because I want to know everything there is to know about him, and it's obvious that event shaped him somehow.

He takes a deep breath and kind of sighs.

"Okay. If you want to know . . . I met Jennifer in high school. After we graduated, I moved to Victoria with her because she was going to university there. I did some business college, worked in restaurants, all with the plan to return to Orchard Cove and work at the bar. Eventually, I'd take over managing it so my dad could focus on the cidery. I'd always planned to join the family business, and Jenn knew that from the day we met. That plan never changed. Not for me."

He looks out toward the water. "We got engaged the second year we were in Victoria, and we even planned to have the wedding there because that's what she wanted. All her family and mine came down for it." He looks down at our joined hands, and I rub my thumb gently over his skin. "I could see her trembling as she walked up the aisle in her white dress, and I think I just knew. But I didn't want to know, you know?"

He meets my eyes. "Obviously, she walked away. And afterwards we had a long talk, and she told me she didn't want to come home. She didn't want to live in Orchard Cove forever. But I still did."

He pauses, rubbing his forehead. Then he looks at me, and I can see all the fear piling up behind his eyes.

The pain—that the one place he wants to live could mean that he has to live his life alone.

"I think in some ways that felt like the biggest betrayal of all. Because all those years, she let me believe that she wanted the same life I did, when she didn't."

"Maybe she did," I say gently. "For a while."

"Yeah. But at some point she decided she wanted something else, and she didn't tell me. But hey, at least she didn't fake it and marry me and then tell me later, right?"

I draw closer to him, until we're almost pressed together. "Mason . . . that's heartbreaking. But maybe it's better that she stopped the wedding from happening."

"Yeah. Way better, for sure. But it really fucked with my sense of trust. I returned to Orchard Cove with my family to live the life I always wanted, but things had changed for me. I became this staunch bachelor with these rigid beliefs about dating and relationships. I didn't even want to date anymore. I just preferred to stay single and have casual, no-strings-attached flings, mostly with tourists who came and went."

I don't say a word. Because even though it hurts to hear this, to think that I could have been one of those flings, I appreciate that he's being honest with me.

"I let that breakup turn me into this resentful, jaded, self-protective person. And last year, when my parents died . . ." He gets choked up a bit. "I think it made me close right up and just say *fuck it*. The idea of getting attached to anyone new just felt . . . too risky." He stops there, and I instinctively loop my arms around his waist.

He wraps his arms around me, too.

"But then you came along." He looks down into my eyes. "And you, Sierra, are exactly what I needed."

"I am?" I say in wonder.

He chuckles softly. "Yes. Hell, yes. You're fun when I'm serious. You're light when I'm heavy. And I think you are extremely, unfairly beautiful. And sexy. And fascinating. You stood up to me, and you held your ground. You weren't afraid to be who you are, no matter what anyone in Orchard Cove thought. I admire that."

"Oh, but I am afraid."

He smiles a little and brushes a lock of my hair off my face, studying me with affection. "In some ways, you are my total opposite. And in some ways, we are weirdly alike. And any way you want to look at it, you knocked me on my ass when I least expected it. When I honestly wouldn't have thought it would be possible for any woman to do that. You lit a fire under me, and you made me *want* to fight for something again."

"I know," I say shakily, so many emotions cascading through me as he says all these lovely things about me. "Pier Seven."

"I'm not talking about that damn building, Sierra."

I sniffle, dangerously close to crying, barely daring to believe that he's saying what I think he's saying. "You're not?"

Mason shakes his head slowly. "I should've told you sooner. I should've told you that I wanted you to be mine."

"You did?"

"Fuck, yes. I *do*. I should've told you that if we're together, I'll never abandon you. I know that has to be a sore spot for you, because it is for me, too."

"Oh my god. And I left while you were sleeping." I drop my forehead to his chest. "How could I do that to you?"

He slips a finger under my chin and lifts my face to look into my eyes. His lips quirk with amusement. "I forgive you. But don't do it again."

"Okay." My cheeks warm as I blush a little. "The brutal truth is . . . I wasn't really thinking about you when I did it. I was just protecting myself. Getting the hell out of there before I could get hurt. But it already hurt. Leaving you was the hardest thing I've ever had to do."

"Then come back with me." He takes a deep breath, his chest rising and falling against me. "We could have a life there, together. I know we can, because I keep fantasizing about it. Picturing us together, in my family home, listening to music and making each other laugh."

I blink away the pesky tears that keep quivering in my eyes. "What a beautiful picture."

"It is. And I don't expect you to just drop everything, give up your whole life for me. I understand you have a life here, in the city." He looks out at the view. "I can't compete with this, if this is what you want." Then he looks deep into my eyes again. He cups my face in his hands. "But I can give you a place to call home. And a place to run your business."

"What do you mean?"

"I've been talking to Layne about it. And there's no reason we can't find a permanent home for Cutie Fruitie in Orchard Cove.

But best-case scenario . . . I really think you can help me fix things with June. She likes you. And I understand now that she'll never go into business with me the way things are. But she might with my grandpa, under the right circumstances."

"Really?" A spark of hope and curiosity ignites in my chest.

"I think we can convince her to open a restaurant with us, because you were right. Layne thinks that June and our grandpa have more going on between them than either one of them wants to admit. And if anyone can convince those two cranky old cynics to take a chance, I think it's two young fools in love."

I blink at him, my heart thrumming. "In love?"

"Yeah," he says softly. "In love."

I'm kind of speechless.

Is it actually possible that he really feels about me the way I feel about him?

What does it feel like when your dreams come true?

I don't know. I've never been here before.

Mason's brow crinkles. "Are you okay?"

"I'm having a moment."

He looks concerned.

"I'll be okay. I think."

"Look, I want to show you something." He pulls a sheet of paper from his back pocket and unfolds it. "This is a plan my parents drew up for their proposed renovations of Pier Seven, back when they were in talks with June about buying it from her. I modified it, a few days ago, to include your smoothie bar."

I stare at the technical drawing, absolutely stunned, but elated. I recognize the floor plan of Pier Seven. The main differences from the way it looks now are the little circles that indicate patio tables outside, on the water side, and the words *Cutie Fruitie* running along the second, smaller bar at the side of the main room.

"I thought it would be perfect on the south side," he explains, "where everyone walks by to access the pier and the beach. We can put in a big window so you can offer walk-up service, and we'll have stools along the bar inside, for your customers to sit."

When I meet his eyes, the tears in mine are so thick I have to wipe them away to see. He still looks worried. "Are you upset?" He folds the paper and stuffs it back in his pocket. "If you don't like it, we can do it another way. This is just an idea. To show you I've been thinking about this. And how much I want you to be a part of—"

"Mason," I sob. "It's perfect. This is the most beautiful, meaningful, thoughtful, fucking amazing thing anyone has ever done for me. Or proposed to do for me."

His face softens. "Yeah. *Shit.*" He rubs the back of his head. "I didn't really think this through, how I was going to do this. Not entirely. But really . . ." He looks out at the view again, then back to me. "This is as good a place as any. A place that makes you happy. Your home."

I don't understand what he's talking about—until he gets down on one knee.

Then I swear I almost pass right out.

I grab the railing with one hand. Bite my tongue and cover my mouth with my free hand as I blink back tears.

Mason looks up into my eyes, and I can see that whatever he's about to say, he means it. Deeply.

"A moment like this," he says, "is probably the thing I've feared the most since I was abandoned on my wedding day. I thought I would never do this again. But then I never could've imagined I'd meet someone like you, Sierra Daniels."

He reaches into his other back pocket, and pulls out a little velvet satchel. He opens it and pours the contents into his hand. It's a ring.

A diamond ring.

"Oh my god, Mason." I'm laughing and almost crying at once. "What else have you got stuffed in those pockets?!"

He smiles up at me through his tears. "Nothing much. It's just my mom's engagement ring. I couldn't even find the box, so I hope this is okay."

And that's it. Now I'm crying, for real. The tears pour down my face, and I haven't cried in so damn long, it feels like a relief. Ecstasy and agony all at once, because all I want to do is throw my arms around him.

But I do my best to stay on my feet, and just listen to what he's saying as blood thrums through my ears.

"I love you, Sierra. And I'm so sorry that I didn't tell you before. But I'm telling you now. I want you to be my wife."

I'm crying so hard I can't answer for a long moment, struggling just to catch my breath.

"Are you all right?" He takes my hand and gives it a squeeze.

"I think . . . I just needed you to say you love me," I sob. "I needed to know."

"I love you," he says devoutly. "Will you marry me? And open your eyes? Please?"

I've squeezed them shut to try to hold back the flood, but it's unstoppable. I open them to see his gorgeous face tensed with worry, tears and hope glistening in his eyes.

I wipe the wetness from my face and offer him my tear-streaked left hand. "Yes! Yes, I'll marry you." My hand shakes as he slides the ring on my finger. I laugh a little through my tears and so does he. It's a little loose, but I know we can get it sized to make it fit.

Then he gets to his feet, takes me in his arms, and kisses me, deep and slow.

When we finally come up for air, he says, "Do you like the ring?"

I don't have to look at it to know I like it. But I look.

It's simple, elegant. Gold, with a sparkling, round diamond. *Perfect.* "I love it."

"And I just want you to know, I didn't propose to my ex with this ring. My mom still had it at that time. But she took it off a lot when she was working in the orchard. She wasn't wearing it when she . . . when she died." He swallows. "So it's not a bad omen or anything, putting it on your finger."

I blink back tears. "Of course it's not. It's a symbol of a great love. And a symbol of ours, too." I cup his bearded jaw in my hands. "It's a *good* omen."

I can see what this means to him, that I want to wear his mom's ring.

He takes my face in his hands and kisses me softly.

"We can have the wedding whenever you want," he murmurs against my lips. "We can take our time moving you over to Orchard Cove, keep your apartment in the city, whatever you need. We have the rest of our lives, and there's no rush. But . . . promise me?" His eyes gleam with emotion. "Promise me forever, Sierra."

Tears stream down my face at his words, the vulnerability in his voice.

"I'm not a crier, Mason," I protest, trying to blink the tears away, but they just keep coming.

He swipes them gently away with his thumbs. "Then, this means . . . ?"

"It means *yes*," I tell him. "Forever."

CHAPTER 25

Mason

We spend the evening in Sierra's apartment, just the two of us. I bring in the overnight bag from my truck. We walk hand in hand to the liquor store and pick up takeout pizza, and hang out on the balcony while the concert crowd gathers below.

I laugh when the concert starts and I hear the wall of muffled noise that greets us. Music, maybe. Power, definitely. And yes, you can tell what song it is, but it's hardly front-row seats.

Still, we hang out for several songs.

Then we go inside, lie on Sierra's couch, entwined, with the windows open, and just listen for a while.

We spend the rest of the night in her bed, fucking with a kind of wild abandon there's never been between us before. The freedom of knowing that this isn't the end.

It's only the beginning.

I wake in the early morning to Sierra sliding over me, naked. I flip us over and we press together, skin to skin, hurried, wanting more.

Then slowing down once we're joined, making love as the sun comes up, washing the sky in violet and gold outside the windows.

"I was so scared I'd lost you," she whispers against my skin.

"I promise," I whisper back, "I'm not going anywhere. Not without you."

◆ ◆ ◆

That day, we pack a few bags for Sierra, so we can drive back to Orchard Cove as an engaged couple. Layne knows why I'm here in Vancouver and what my plans were, and so does my grandpa, but I can't wait to bring Sierra back, tell them in person that she said yes, and settle into the house with her.

But before we leave Vancouver, we have a video call with Sophie and her husband, Pete, to tell them the news. Sierra insists this is mandatory.

Sophie is ecstatic, and Sierra cries again.

Sophie tells me, "She never cries. You better make her smile, or I'll have words for you."

I promise Sierra's best friend, "Always."

She's crying, too.

Then we go by my parents' graves with flowers. Sierra lingers longer than I do; it's still hard for me to see their names etched in stone and the years etched beneath.

But I hear her say, "Thank you for making such an amazing human. I promise, I'll take care of him."

After that, she has to drive us to the Horseshoe Bay ferry terminal up in West Vancouver because my eyes are a little blurry.

When we get off the ferry on Vancouver Island, I take over at the wheel, and we hold hands on and off as I drive. We listen to music and talk the whole way, laughing and not really arguing but kind of breathlessly recounting so many of the moments we shared, or avoided, or passed each other by . . . just fucking dying to touch. Or talk. Or grab each other and blurt out, *I fucking want you.*

"I knew it," she keeps saying. "I knew you liked me."

"I thought you hated me," I admit.

"There's a very fine line between love and hate, Mason Grant," she teases.

I clear my throat. "Do you realize that you haven't actually told me you love me yet?"

"I haven't?" She frowns.

"No, you haven't. *I* told *you*. Which, for the record, is not the same thing."

"Hmm. It's not?"

Oh, I see. She's playing innocent.

"No. And I know how competitive you are. So I definitely think we should keep score," I tease back.

When I glance over, a small smile plays at her lips.

I know she loves me. She's wearing my mom's ring. She promised my parents, at their graves, that she'll take care of me.

"But I should warn you," I tell her, "if you don't say the L-word between now and the time I undress you in my—*our*—bedroom and make passionate love to you again, I might have to do something drastic like point it out. There may even be pouting."

"I'll take that under advisement."

I glance at her again and she bites her lip.

"Tease," I mutter.

She laughs. "It's not that I *mean* to deprive you of that word. It just hasn't flowed out yet."

"Uh-huh. And now you're holding it in just to drive me crazy."

"I *love* . . . the way you get worked up when you don't get your way," she says in a sultry voice.

I say nothing, just focus on the road ahead as my pulse beats in my cock. It's crazy, how vulnerable I still feel. How much I want—no, *need*, viscerally, completely—to be loved by this woman.

My fiancée.

Those damn doves take flight in my chest as she laughs again, a soft, happy sound.

We're nearing the turnoff to Orchard Cove when she says, "Hey, Mason. Did you make this playlist . . . for any particular reason?" Finally, she seems to clue in that every song that's been playing has been for *her*.

"What? I can't listen to an eclectic variety of totally random music?"

"Yeah, it's just a total coincidence that you're now listening to girly pop all the time. And romantic ballads. And a random mix of classics like 'Harvest Moon,' that just happen to factor into our story."

"Do we have a story?"

"God, yes. We're writing it now. In fact, we're just getting to the best part. And I have a feeling . . . the best part's going to last a while."

I like that. I squeeze her hand.

"Almost home," I murmur as we turn off the highway and wind our way toward Orchard Cove—but there's a question in it, for sure.

I hope this place feels like home to her now, or will. Soon.

I hope she never wants to leave. The town or me.

When I look over at her, she's smiling, gazing out the window at the passing farmlands as her hair blows in the wind.

So fucking beautiful.

And like some kind of melomaniac magic, "Sweet City Woman" starts playing.

Sierra laughs. "You *did* make this playlist for me," she accuses.

"It's just songs that make me think of you," I admit.

She gazes at me like she did that first night we met, when she was nicely drunk, let her guard down, and seemed to like what she saw. A lot.

I could get totally lost in that look, but train my eyes on the road.

"That's a sweet gift, Mason. I can't imagine a sweeter gift than a playlist, made by you."

"How about a diamond ring?" I say dryly.

She laughs. "It's pretty sweet, too."

"Oh, shit. I almost forgot. This is for you." I reach into the console and pull out the new phone, handing it to her.

"What's this?" Her delight makes my heart lift.

"Your new phone. It even works."

"What?! Fancy." She reaches over and squeezes my thigh. "Seriously? This is awesome!"

"Anywhere you want in Orchard Cove, you, Sierra Daniels, can now connect to the outside world."

"Revolutionary," she quips. Then: "You did this for me?"

I give her a look. "Woman." Does she not know by now?

I'd do anything for you.

No. Maybe she doesn't.

Good thing we have the rest of our lives for me to show her.

"I got it a few days ago," I confess. "You know, when I was deep in the *how do I convince her to stay without actually asking her to stay because I'm too chicken* phase."

"Well, this is amazing," she says dreamily. "Although . . . it was actually kinda nice being disconnected so much. And just having some space. To take a break from worrying what other people think, and just *live*."

"Good."

"But thank you, so much, for the phone. This is so thoughtful."

She slides it into her purse and undoes her seat belt, just as we turn onto Honeymoon Lane. She leans over to me. "Thank you," she murmurs, nuzzling the hair behind my ear and inhaling my scent. Then she kisses my neck, sending warmth down my spine.

"You're welcome. And if you miss the city . . ." I glance at her, worried that she will. "I'll take you back to visit, any time. And we can go to Seattle, see my sister. We'll get overpriced coffee and do that hot-yoga torture thing and go shopping at a mall."

She snickers. "Can't wait."

We turn into Sea Haven Orchard, then take the fork in the drive. I pull up to the private gate and stop to get out, so I can open it and we can drive through. But Sierra follows me out.

"Wait," she says. She jumps up into my arms and wraps her legs around my waist, and I catch her, pressing her back against the truck.

The truck is still running. "Sweet City Woman" is still playing. Somewhere, I hear my brother's dog barking happily. Sierra kisses me with passion and hunger and a promise that takes my breath away.

And I couldn't really ask for anything more.

Then she looks up into my eyes.

"I just wanted to tell you. The memories I have with Grandpa Alex, in the garage, listening to music . . . that was the best, warmest, truest feeling of *home* I've ever known. Until now."

Her words hit me right in the heart.

I rest my forehead against hers and take a breath, overcome with emotion. I don't even know if she understands . . .

"Did you know," I say, my voice rough, "that is probably the most beautiful thing you could ever say to me?"

"Yeah? How about this . . ." she says softly. "I love you, Mason Grant."

CHAPTER 26

SIERRA

Summer swirls by in a wonderful blur of moving and organizing, settling into my new life in Orchard Cove, and wedding preparations.

The wedding will be simple, the way Mason and I both want it, but even the simplest weddings, as I learn, aren't simple to plan.

It's kind of become a full-time job in itself.

But I'm loving every minute of it.

I've already given up my apartment in Vancouver, because I don't need it anymore. That chapter of my life is now closed, and I'm eager to write so many new ones with Mason.

We went back there a couple of times in July, so he could help me clear out the rest of my stuff and bring it over to Orchard Cove. We also visited his parents' graves, and each time, he lingered just a little bit longer, speaking to them.

When I heard him tell his mom that he gave me her ring, and that he knew she'd love me, if she could, I cried like a baby.

When July turned to August, Mason told me to "brace myself" for the upcoming apple harvest season. He warned me that it would be busy. It's the reason we planned to have the wedding so fast; before the end of August, when it's time to start harvesting.

It was either that or get married after, and neither of us really wants to wait.

I don't even know how I've found the time to train Mason's staff to make smoothies. When he suggested we move some of my equipment into the bar so we could offer them on the menu, I was thrilled. The way Mason has welcomed me into his life, in every way, has been entirely gracious.

There are moments when I feel like I've been floating above the earth, too excited to quite come down. I even named a new smoothie on the menu "Walking on Sunshine."

As the long summer days grow slightly shorter, I now live for the evenings when Mason comes home from the bar or the cider house as the sun goes down, to find me agonizing over flowers or fabric samples at the kitchen table. He rubs my shoulders, pours me a drink, and we sit out on the back porch overlooking the orchard and the sea beyond, listening to music.

Sometimes we dance together, slow. Sometimes we talk about our day, and we make each other laugh so hard we cry. Sometimes Kaylie joins us in her pajamas, sneaking out of the cottage and trying to delay her bedtime, or Scar curls up at our feet.

Those are my favorite moments.

With *him*, just living.

Our happy nights, together, just before we go up to bed . . . and then we do.

Getting undressed in our room together.

Having the kind of deliciously carnal yet soul-deep sex that, before Mason, I'd only ever fantasized about.

But tonight isn't one of those nights.

Because tonight, my best friend is throwing me a bachelorette party at the bar.

I've been drinking Sea Haven Raspberry Rosé sparkling cider interspersed with water, and I'm pleasantly buzzed, but no way am I getting too drunk to remember *this*.

The jukebox glows. The music is pumping. All my new lady friends have come out to celebrate with me. Mason's sister couldn't make it here for this, but she's promised to be here for the wedding. And most importantly, Sophie has flown in for five whole days.

So have my parents—my mom and stepdad.

My sister is also here from Ontario. When Kim and her family piled out of their rented minivan after flying across the country for this—for *me*—I gave her the biggest hug ever, surprising her, I think. And for the first time in my life, I truly believed her when she told me how happy she is for me. Maybe because I'm truly happy for her, too, without bitterness or resentment or jealousy tainting it.

"My wild, beautiful sister," she said to me, with admiration and tears in her eyes. "I'm so glad you've finally found your home, Si. Mason and Orchard Cove are lucky to have you."

After that, I was a mess and needed to redo my makeup, which Kim helped me with.

Now, my adorable but rowdy nephews are at the orchard with Tommy, Kaylie, and my parents, while my sister gets cider-drunk with me. Her husband is with Mason and the boys at the bachelor party. They're playing poker over at Evan's place.

Or at least they were—until they walk right into the bar, just as Sophie and I are singing our hearts out to a high-energy Wham! duet, on the actual karaoke system that Mason put in—in honor of his bride-to-be. And, as he put it: *Your undying love for singing along to songs you have no business singing.*

Sophie has a way better voice than I do, so at least there's that.

But music, for me, has never been about perfection. It's about *feeling* it.

And I am definitely feeling the second verse of "The Edge of Heaven" as the men pile into the room. I meet Mason's eyes across the bar, and my whole body lights up. I laugh and flub the lyrics, but recover. Sophie throws her arm around my shoulders as we sing, and it's just like that night . . .

That very awkward, emotional, special night when Mason and I first met.

Only it's so much better.

The guys all clap at our exuberant performance. Jace whistles.

And Mason just gazes at me, giving me that look he so often does. The one that says, *I'm a fool. I can't believe I almost lost you. I'll never make that mistake again.*

I grin and hand off my microphone to Trish.

Then I toss myself into my fiancé's arms. "I can't believe you're crashing my bachelorette," I say with a giant smile.

"I can't believe you didn't invite me."

"I'm sorry," I say with glee, "but there are no penises allowed at this party."

"Really?" He kisses my neck and murmurs in my ear, "I thought this was a celebration. Same penis forever, right?"

I roll my eyes, but grin like a fool in love.

We kiss so passionately that our friends cheer, then start to groan.

"Get a room," Layne calls out.

So, Mason winds his fingers through mine and tugs me toward the office.

"Uh, we'll be right back!" I tell our guests as I hurry along behind him, my heart soaring.

He pulls me into the office, which I'm proud to say I've managed to tidy up and redecorate quite nicely for him. Kind of had to. More room for all the office sex.

He shuts the door and pushes me up against it, where we go at it.

"Mmm. This will never get old," I pant. How many times has he pulled me in here to have his way with me now?

Many.

"I know. God. When can I get rid of all the dudes and get you naked?"

"Soon." I giggle as he paws at my clothes. "I promise. But . . . guests. We should really behave ourselves . . ."

He groans and rearranges his cock in his jeans. "Fuck." He runs his hands through his hair and draws back, trying to be good. "Sorry. I won't keep you from the party too long." He gives me a smile, and I melt.

I give him a hot, sweet kiss on the lips. "Worth it."

"Mmm. I just wanted a moment alone, to tell you the good news."

I gasp. "Tell me!"

He smiles, deep dimples flickering under his beard. "June has accepted our offer. Tommy convinced her to go into business with us."

"Yes!" I throw myself at him again and he hugs me tight, burying his face in my neck. "Oh my god," I gush, fighting back tears. "I'm so happy, Mason."

"Me too, sweetheart."

I draw back to look up into his face. "Mostly, I swear, I'm happy for you. This is all you ever wanted."

He gazes into my eyes with so much love, it takes my breath away. "Not even close," he murmurs. "But yes, Pier Seven is a part of everything I want. And now, it's ours."

"Ours and June's," I correct him.

He chuckles. "Yes. That's what I meant."

"Uh-huh. What the heck did Tommy say to her?"

Over the past few weeks, Mason and I have met with June, several times. She definitely seems impressed that I came back to

Orchard Cove. That I'm putting down roots here with Mason, that we're planning our wedding and even invited her to come. And that we're so damn set on wanting to partner with her, to contribute to the future of Orchard Cove together.

But there's still that missing piece, and no matter how much ground we seem to gain with June, grumpy old Tommy, unfortunately, seems to hold that piece.

"I don't know," Mason says, and I deflate. "He wouldn't tell me."

"Ugh! That is so not what I wanted to hear. I want gossip!"

His eyebrow lifts. "You *are* from a small town."

I smack his chest lightly.

"I did go by June's to thank her, after my grandpa gave me the news," he offers. "And she did say, 'You and Sara will have nice kids together.'"

"Aww, June! She's such a romantic," I joke. "I love the way she pretends to forget my name when she's irritated. Do you think he told her that he loves her, and now *they'll* get married?"

"Uh, no."

"Oh. Bummer."

"But I guess whatever he said must've been enough? Maybe he finally apologized like she wanted him to."

"A good apology can go a long way." I smile, so he knows I mean the way he followed me to the city and apologized for letting me go.

"Whatever he said, though . . . I think it was about this." Mason pulls out his phone and shows me a photo onscreen.

It's in black and white. A young woman stretched out on the long, swooping bough of a twisted tree.

A tree that looks very much like the one on the secret path.

I touch the screen, spreading my fingers to enlarge the photo, zooming in on the woman's face. She has long, straight, light-colored hair, and a sort of Mona Lisa smile.

"Is that . . . June?"

"Yup. Juniper Spencer, circa 1970-something, if I had to guess. I think what we're looking at is the original twisted tree."

"Really? No!" I don't know why I'm so excited right now. But it feels like we're peeking into a secret from the past.

"I just assumed Twisted Tree was named after that big plum tree by the gate that's been there all my life. But those plum trees only live thirty years or so, max. Maybe forty. There must've been older trees there that died before the current ones grew."

"Wow. Where did you get this photo?"

"That, Sierra, is the best part. I took a snapshot of this photo when I was in my grandpa's living room today." He tucks his phone away, a mischievous glint in his eyes. "It was in a *frame*. On his *wall*."

"*No.*"

"Oh, yes. You and Layne were right that there's something going on there. When I asked Grandpa about the photo, he grumbled at me and stomped out."

"Oooh. Interesting . . ."

"All I know is that it wasn't hanging there before. Like, two days ago when I was in there. I think whatever he said to June last night, if he apologized or whatever . . . she gave him that photo in response."

"Oh, god. Can I *please* meddle? Pretty please?" I bounce on my toes, leaning on his chest. "I don't really consider myself a meddler, but I *need* to meddle in this. How beautiful would it be if those two old grumps got over themselves and professed their undying love for one another?"

Mason groans. He wraps his arms around me and tucks me under his chin, kisses the top of my head.

"Maybe, for now, we leave well enough alone? They just started mending the fence. And we just got our agreement from June, in writing."

I sigh. "Sensible." I peer up at my man. "But it would be so fun, though. I just want everyone to be as happy as we are."

Mason's eyes sparkle and a beautiful warmth overtakes his face. "I know, babe. For now, let's be happy for ourselves. We're getting married in two days. We've got the rest of our lives to deal with family drama."

"You know what?" I gush. "I kind of can't wait."

He laughs.

Then he presses me up against the desk. He hooks a finger under my chin and gazes at me like I'm the most beautiful thing he's ever seen.

He kisses me, deep and slow, and when I moan in response, he starts sliding his hands up my skirt.

"You know what, Sierra?" he murmurs in my ear. "I can't wait, either."

EPILOGUE

Haven

The wedding is in my family's orchard. It's beautiful and intimate, just family and friends. The whole town is invited to the party afterwards, but I'm glad there aren't too many people here to see this, because as I walk up the aisle between the apple trees with my brother, Layne, I can't stop crying.

Seeing Mason getting married kind of unglues me, mostly because I know how much Mom and Dad would've wanted to be here for this. I was only eleven when it happened, but I remember my brother's first wedding, the one where his bride ran out.

Mason was so distraught that day, Mom and Dad cried; it was the only time I ever remember my dad crying in front of me.

Today, they would've been so happy. To see how happy Mason is as he and Sierra say their vows, exchange rings, and become husband and wife. Because this is obviously how it was meant to be for Mason. The way he looks at Sierra says it all. Their love is palpable.

Even Grandpa has a tear in his eye.

It feels good, like the family is growing again, instead of falling apart.

The last time we were all together like this was for Mom and Dad's funeral. I barely remember it, I was so deep in grief.

After the ceremony, when I give Mason a hug, he tells me how glad he is that I'm here. "Feels more like home" is how he puts it.

"This is always home," I say, because as much as I might try to deny it to myself, it's the truth. Nothing will ever feel like home the way Orchard Cove does.

But my brother surprises me. He gets this serious look on his face and says, "It hasn't felt like it in a long time. But with Sierra here, it feels more like home than ever." He gives me a meaningful look. "And your room's always ready for you, Haven."

I know he wants me to come home for good. Move back. Settle down. Play my part in the family business.

He even kept my childhood bedroom intact in the renovations, just like our parents did.

But I'm not ready for that. Not yet.

I don't know if I'll ever be ready for that. But how can I tell my big brother on his wedding day that I might never come back to Orchard Cove? Worst wedding gift ever.

"You guys did a great job with the house," I deflect. I know Sierra helped him with decorating after the renos, and they did a gorgeous job together. "Mom would love it."

Then we get mercifully interrupted as the whole wedding party is herded deeper into the orchard for photos. I pose dutifully with my bouquet and a smile alongside the other bridesmaids. And the moment we're done, I beeline back to the other guests while the bride and groom are photographed alone.

I need to check in on my plus-one. My boyfriend, Bryce, is a lot to manage, and he doesn't do well in situations like this. Situations where he's not in control.

However, he seems to be okay at the moment. Grandpa has him cornered, cider in hand, and while my first impulse is to rescue him so he's not pissed about it later—at me—I'm kind of emotionally tapped out right now.

I thought bringing Bryce here would make it better—like having a security blanket, a buffer between me and my old life. Instead, it's just made the whole thing even more stressful.

Caterers circle, offering champagne and cider, but I could really use something stronger. Some of the guests have already started to make their way down to the beach walk, which has been decorated with flowers all the way to the pier. Dinner and dancing will be at Pier Seven tonight, but I'm not ready for more mingling just yet.

When no one's looking, I sneak away to the cider house, seeking a moment alone and a stiff drink.

But when I slip inside, I'm not alone.

There's a man behind the bar, plucking a bottle of Sea Haven's award-winning violet gin from a shelf.

A man I've known forever, but have tried so hard to forget.

Jace Crofton.

My brother's best friend.

He's dressed in a fine navy-blue suit and sage-green tie instead of his usual motorcycle jacket and jeans, his normally shadowed jawline shaved clean, and his thick dark hair is neatly tamed into place. He looks different, but the same.

It's always the same, every time I see him, the way my heart pounds and my insides generally freak out.

I consider backing right out of there.

But too late.

He sees me, and a charming smile transforms his features, taking them from handsome to *Dear god, please help me.*

"Haven," he says in that rough, sexy voice I hear sometimes in my dreams. I mean, my nightmares. "Get your ass in here, girl."

Ugh. *Shivers.* I get full-body shivers when he says my name.

This was not supposed to happen. Ending up alone with Jace is never a good idea.

Running into Jace in public is uncomfortable enough. I said a quick hello to him yesterday at the rehearsal dinner to get it over with and managed to painstakingly avoid him for the rest of the night, and again all day today, even though we're both in the wedding party.

I wasn't supposed to have to talk to him again, if at all, until maybe tonight, *if* I run into him at the reception and have to make nice in front of others. Maybe then I'll at least be drunk.

What the hell am I supposed to say to him sober?

"Caught stealing, huh?" I let the door close behind me. "I guess some things never change."

He kind of snorts, surprised. "Pretty sure Mason won't have me locked up. Tommy, maybe."

I let a small smile slip. "Oh, if Grandpa finds you in here, you're dead."

"Then let's not tell him."

The conspiratorial look he gives me makes my toes curl.

He sets the bottle of gin on the bar. "How about you?"

"I won't call the cops. Too much effort."

"I meant, do you want a drink." He says it like it's a given, placing two shot glasses next to the gin.

I sigh. "Yeah. Guilty."

He smiles like I've just made his day.

Please don't do that. It makes me weak.

His dark eyes roam over me as I approach the bar in my sage-green bridesmaid's dress, and I wonder what he sees. I thought I'd be so different by the time I saw him again. But every time we run into each other, no matter how much time has passed, I still feel like the same teenage girl who left this place all those years ago.

Yeah. Some things never fucking change.

He pours out two violet-hued shots. "How's life in Seattle?"

"Oh, it's amazing."

Yeah. *Totally happy.*

"Must be. Haven't seen you around here in years."

And there it is. The guilt that hits whenever someone back home reminds me that I've been missed. They all do it.

But when Jace does it, it both aches and pisses me off the most.

"Yeah, well. I've been busy."

Mostly, I've been busy keeping away from Orchard Cove. It's kind of exhausting as far as lifestyles go.

Other than attending my parents' funeral last year in Vancouver, I haven't been back to the West Coast of Canada much at all in the last seven years. I didn't know when I left that I'd be gone permanently, but it just kind of became a thing.

I also didn't know that I'd long for this place like I do.

Or . . . for certain people.

It's just made me avoid them all the harder.

He picks up a shot, and I do the same.

"To Mason and Sierra," I say, before he can say anything. We clink our shots together, then drink.

"Who's that boy you're with?"

I cough slightly on my gin. "Uh, you mean that man?"

He just raises an eyebrow.

"That's Bryce."

"Your boyfriend?"

"No. He's a rent-a-date. I have to return him by midnight or his rate doubles."

Jace laughs. That throaty, full-body laugh that scorches my insides. God, the *rush* of it. I probably couldn't be more turned on if he stroked my clit with his tongue.

"And why would you need to show up to your brother's wedding with an escort?" he inquires, playing along.

"Crowd control. A hot man on a lady's arm really keeps the wolves away."

"You really could've gotten better for your money," he says.

My face feels warm, and so does my belly as he pours us another shot.

"You think?" I can't help playing along myself.

He raises his shot glass, his eyes flashing at me. This close, they're a molten brown, like liquid fire. "To you, Haven." We clink our glasses. "I'd protect you from the wolves for free."

Oh, shit. He did not just say that. And I did not like it. A lot.

We toss our shots back, and he casually licks his lip. My core contracts, way too hyperaware of his every move.

Okay, nope. Not going there.

Not getting carried away with what this isn't.

I focus on his hands, which doesn't help. He's already pouring us more shots, and this is getting out of hand. *Me.* I'm getting out of hand.

My body.

My imagination . . .

"Uh, I should really go. Bryce may need rescuing. You know how my grandpa can be."

"Oh, I know." His expression grows serious. "But if your date can't handle Tommy, he's not getting far around here."

I clear my throat. "Yeah. I realize that."

"Then why did you bring him?"

"Well, I'm not from around here. So it hardly matters."

He stares me down for an uncomfortably long moment. But this is my family's property, not his. He doesn't get to make me squirm here.

But damn, I am squirming.

My insides writhe with discomfort. Anxious. Fucking *eager*.

Hungry for his attention.

"You, Haven Grant, will always be from around here. Incidentally . . ." He slides a shot in front of me, the tattoos on his hand sexy, distracting. "When are you moving back?"

"Does 'never' sound too soon?" Still trying to play it cool. *You can handle this*, the alcohol tells me. *You can handle him.*

He holds my gaze. "Not soon enough."

"Way too soon, if you ask me."

Something falters in his playful, calculated veneer of charm. His eyes soften, and it sucks the breath out of me. "Mason will be disappointed to hear that."

That's putting it mildly, and we both know it.

"Which is why you won't tell him."

His eyes spark, a kind of devious delight he can't even hide. The man is a born flirt, a player, a mischief-maker. "More secrets, huh? How many do you expect me to keep for you?"

"If you're referring to that time you caught me sneaking home late—"

"Ha. Which time?"

"All of them. And yes, you better keep them all."

He lifts his shot of gin. "To keeping secrets, then."

After a moment's hesitation, I pick up my shot. We clink our glasses. The gleam in his eyes is wicked.

I know this is a mistake.

But where Jace Crofton is concerned, I've already made so many.

"To keeping secrets," I agree, and together, we drink.

Don't miss Jace & Haven's book, *Juicy Little Secrets*!

NOTE TO READERS & ACKNOWLEDGMENTS

A huge and grateful thank you to Sammia Hamer and Hannah Shaw at Amazon Publishing UK for exuding so much passion and excitement about my writing, from our very first conversation. I could feel your support from across the globe.

It was dazzling. (Who *are* these ladies who are *so excited* about *my writing*?)

Book angels.

This book might never have actually happened, and certainly not this soon, without you ladies popping into my life when you did and making me think: What *do* I want to write next, *really*?

As I pondered that question, it was summer here on the West Coast of Canada. I was eager to visit the local cideries, one of my favorite things to do in summer, and one of the many book ideas (there are always so many!) floating in my brain and fighting for attention leapt to the front.

A small-town romance.

But not about just any small town. A small town built around a cidery. Actually, two cideries. *Dueling cideries.* I was so tickled by the idea of an orchard, split right down the middle, by feuding families, and a love story (within a love story) at the heart of it all.

Orchard Cove was born.

If this is your first Jaine Diamond book, lovely reader, welcome. And whether you're a new or long-time reader, I hope you loved this visit to Orchard Cove.

I like to think of Orchard Cove as existing in a sunlit corner of my book world, loosely connected through the supporting character of Sophie (who also appeared briefly as a side character in one of my earlier books). My readers and I affectionately call this book world the Dirtyverse, because it all kicked off with the Dirty series. If you've been with me all along, or have recently binged all the books in this world, you may have noticed some Easter eggs I tucked into this book to make you feel right at home. Did you find them all?

Before you go looking for Orchard Cove on your map app, though, there is no real Orchard Cove on Vancouver Island, British Columbia, Canada (unfortunately). There is no Pier Seven, no Sea Haven Orchard, no Twisted Tree Orchard, or even a Honeymoon Lane. (If there is, somewhere on the island, unknown to me, it is merely a coincidence.) The entire town and its immediate surroundings were created by my overactive imagination.

However, the fictional town of Orchard Cove is located in the (real) area of Cobble Hill, in the (real) Cowichan Valley wine region. The Cowichan Valley is unique for its Mediterranean-like climate, and is known for its organic growers, wine route, and craft beverage producers. It's a truly beautiful area, and especially if you're a foodie, wine lover, or cider lover, I highly recommend you add it to your travel bucket list. I hope that while you've read this book, you've been able to picture it, taste it . . . and perhaps it's even made you thirsty. ;)

Thank you to my family and friends, who have let me drag them around to the local craft cideries so many times. It never gets old if you're a cider lover like me. I also need to thank my favorite cideries in this area: Merridale Cidery & Distillery in the Cowichan Valley, Sea Cider Farm & Ciderhouse on the Saanich Peninsula, and Salt Spring Wild Cider on Salt Spring Island. If it weren't for these local cideries making amazing artisanal cider, this book would not exist. These cideries would be my recommendations to any readers who ask, "Which cidery should I visit?" (If you don't drink alcohol, many craft cideries make delicious non-alcoholic ciders, too.)

Thank you to editor Lindsey Faber, who has also been so enthusiastic and supportive, and to copy-editor Gemma Wain and proofreader Sarah Day for the exceptional attention to detail—I truly feel like I've worked with a dream team on this book. And to every person at Amazon Publishing and Montlake who has worked to get this book out into the world and into the hands of readers—I truly appreciate you.

Thank you to Valentine, Sarah, Ratula, and the whole team at Valentine PR, to Alyssa, and to Jackie, for passionately getting my books in front of readers while I'm being antisocial, at work in my author cave.

Thank you to Brent, who lives in a tower overlooking the arena in Vancouver and was able to inform me which bands are actually loud enough to hear in concert at the stadium when he's in his apartment—with his windows closed. (These details, to me, are important. Like Sierra, music saved me. Like Mason, I'm a polyjamorist. You will find music throughout my books; maybe this is my way of paying it forward.)

Thank you to my sweet, smart, and totally slay daughter, who was exactly ten and a half when I was writing this book and certainly inspired some of Kaylie's dialogue and preferences. You're not old enough to read Mommy's books yet, but one day when you are, I know you'll be thrilled to know you inspired me already.

As always, thank you to my love, Mr. Diamond, for all the things. Literally. I would not have this life without you. I would not even write what I write without you. You influence and inspire and support me in so many ways—they are innumerable and often immeasurable, but they are definitely here, between the pages. You are my home.

Finally, lovely readers, THANK YOU for reading this book. I could not do what I do, what I *love*, without you. If you've enjoyed Mason and Sierra's story, please consider posting a review and telling your friends about this book; your ongoing support means the world to me.

With love and gratitude from the West Coast of Canada,

Jaine

PREVIEW OF *DIRTY LIKE ME*

Not ready to leave the Canadian West Coast just yet? Curious about that hot rock band Sophie works for? Don't miss the Dirty series! It all starts with rock star Jesse Mayes and sweet Katie Bloom in *Dirty Like Me*!

Dirty Like Me is a steamy, fake-to-real romance, featuring a charming, famous heartbreaker, a sweet "regular" girl, a salacious job offer, a ridiculous bet, and way too many shared hotel beds.

CHAPTER ONE

Katie

I didn't mean to crash the meeting.

I fully intended to knock before entering, like a civilized person. Max had other plans. For one thing he was a dog, and for another he knew we were dropping in on my best friend, Devi. Devi was a total babe, and Max totally dug hot babes. One glimpse of the door to her office, which was ajar, and he streaked past the front desk, big wet tail wagging, startling a couple of Devi's coworkers.

"On it!" I blurted, diving after him, but he'd already hip-checked the door open. By the time I caught up, my wayward black lab was shaking off his rain-wet fur in a flurry of excitement, spraying Devi and the three other people standing in her office. I made a mad grab for his collar.

I missed.

Hovering awkwardly on the threshold, I clutched the tin of miniature pies I'd been unpacking in the lobby and mouthed a *Sorry!* at my BFF.

"Hey, Katie!" Devi smiled brightly, tussling Max's ears with a friendly pat. "Max! Aren't you wet." She shot me a look that said something like, *Nice to see you, but what the hell?*

"Um . . . hi," I said. Devi was a talent agent; her agency repped models and actors, so I was used to running into beautiful people in her office. Though I didn't usually crash her meetings with my dog, wet and disheveled in my paint-stained jeans. "Sorry about my dog. Come on, Max." I gave Max the *get-your-furry-butt-over-here* look, a look he knew well but completely ignored, since Devi and her pretty female guest were now loving him up.

"No problem. We were just finishing up." Devi gestured for me to stay put, though I really just wanted to grab my delinquent dog and get the hell out of there. I felt ridiculously conspicuous in my white tank top, which I'd regretted wearing about two seconds after it started raining. As Devi wrapped things up with her guests, I took stock. Yep. Purple bra totally showing through my now-transparent tank.

Great.

Devi was shaking hands with the built dude in the short-sleeve button-down, and I noticed some tattoos on his muscular arm, but that was about it. My attention had already snapped to the other guy as some unconscious, primal part of me registered his hotness before the rest of me could catch up.

Plus, he was staring at me.

Or at least, my see-through shirt.

Devi strode to the door to see her guests out and I stepped aside, holding my tin of pies, trying to disappear into the wall. He was coming at me. Tall and broad-shouldered, his thick, dark hair in unkempt waves that gave him a decidedly just-fucked look, like some lucky bitch had just clawed through it. Totally worked on him. He wore a fitted black T-shirt, which I swore I could see his well-defined abs through, and ripped, dark jeans molded to his long, hard thighs . . .

My brain must have short-circuited, because my gaze got stuck on the package in the front of those jeans. When I looked up, his molasses-dark eyes were locked on mine. He stopped a foot in front of me and stared.

Fair enough, since he'd just caught me checking him out like a horny perv.

I cleared my throat, which was suddenly tight. "Pie?" I fumbled with the tin, lifting it between us, blocking his view of my bra. "They're cherry."

He glanced in the tin, where two dozen hand-crafted miniature pies were neatly arranged, my signature cherry filling peeking out through the crisscrossed pastry tops. Then his gaze lifted to mine again. He had the longest, darkest eyelashes I'd ever seen on a man. High cheekbones. Luscious, kissable lips. Strong jaw shadowed with dark stubble, like he hadn't shaved in days. And those beautiful dark eyes, smoldering at me and making me blush, big time.

"Maybe another time," he said, the deep, sexy rumble of his voice stirring parts of my anatomy that hadn't been stirred in a crazy long time. I noticed something tick against his teeth as he gave me a faint yet heart-stopping smile. A piercing?

No. Candy.

Cinnamon. His breath smelled like cinnamon.

I glanced over at Devi. She and the others were standing in the doorway, staring at us.

Max, ever the opportunist, snuffled into the hand of the hottest guy in the world as I stood there, dazed. I noticed the big, silver rings on his fingers as he stroked Max's velvety ears, and the tattoo on his wrist, a pair of dark wings wrapped around his strong forearm.

“Come on, Max.” I pulled Max back so he could get by. “Sorry. He, um, likes you.” Normally Max preferred the ladies, but I could hardly fault his taste.

The hottest guy on the planet said nothing. He didn’t really get a chance before the ever-charming Devi intervened and herded all three of them out the door.

I set my tin of mini pies on Devi’s desk, feeling kind of wind-blown, like I’d just stepped in out of a storm rather than a light Vancouver mist. Really, a girl should be warned before a guy that hot gave her the most thorough eye-fucking of her life.

Did I really offer him pie?

Cherry pie?

Ugh. So fucking smooth.

I tidied Max into an obedient ball on the rug beneath the desk and willed him to stay put as Devi returned, shutting the door behind herself.

“I know,” she gushed. “So fucking hot, right?”

Um, yeah. But I knew better than to answer that honestly. The last time I casually inquired about a hot guy I glimpsed at my best friend’s office, she took it upon herself to hook the two of us up on a blind date. And when a hot male model gets set up with someone he assumes will be some equally hot female model, but turns out to be just some regular girl, things do not go well. For the regular girl.

Luckily, Devi didn’t even wait for my response. “Jesus, Katie.” She strode over, a takeout coffee cup in each hand. “What the hell?”

“I know. Max just bolted for your office—”

“Not that.” She gave me a no-contact air hug, then glanced down at my chest. “You look like a sexy drowned rat. Heard of an umbrella?”

“My hands were full.”

Devi scowled. “Do not tell me you rode your skateboard in the rain. I hate it when you do that.”

I rolled my eyes a little. My glamorous best friend had never understood my love affair with my skateboard. Of course, she drove a luxury SUV her parents bought for her and lived in her own suite in their giant house, so she didn't exactly relate to my thriftiness. In the case of my preferred mode of transportation, she just saw it as risky behavior. Unfortunately, my big sister agreed with her. "Becca already gave me the lecture when I stopped to pick up the coffees."

Devi set my cherry-vanilla latte on the desk with a little *harrumph* and eyed the mini pies with suspicion. "You've been baking."

"Just some pies." I flopped into one of the chairs facing the desk, which still had hot guy pheromones all over it. I sucked back a deep breath, savoring the lingering scents of cinnamon, leather, and the faint, intoxicating musk of a warm, clean male.

"Katie."

"What?" I glanced up; Devi was studying me accusingly.

"*Just* pie?"

"And some scones."

She raised a slender eyebrow.

"And a few cookies," I added.

"What flavor?"

"Chocolate chip."

"Uh-huh."

"And pecan butter ripple."

"I knew it. What's wrong?"

"Nothing."

"Bullshit. You look . . ." Devi looked at me sideways. "Horny."

"I am not horny," I lied. Who wouldn't be after getting eye-fucked like that? My head was still dangerously deprived of blood.

Devi sat down behind her desk. She looked gorgeous, as always, her dark hair smoothed out, flawless cappuccino skin set off with velvety red lipstick, sleeveless black top tricked out with a chunky necklace and leopard-print leggings, all of which she'd probably worn specifically for the meeting she'd just had. Fashion was just one of the many ways Devi built a rapport with people.

I, on the other hand, considered myself coordinated if I managed to pull on matching shoes.

"Spill." She gathered up the slew of model photos that littered the surface of her desk, stuffing them into a file folder. "I've got like ten minutes before my next meeting. What's up?"

"Nothing. We just miss you." It was true; my best friend had been pulling a lot of overtime, which was great for her career but not so great for me.

"I miss you guys too." She reached beneath the desk and pet Max. "But that's not the reason you busted in here."

"Again, sorry. Just wanted to talk to you. I figured this may be my only chance to do it face-to-face."

"Talk about . . . ?"

I took a breath and sighed. "I think . . . I may be ready."

Devi lit up, then caught herself and cooled her reaction. "Oh?" She was trying really hard not to jump for joy. It was kind of cute.

"I know you've been telling me this for a long time. I just had to get there myself."

"For sure."

"For so long I just wasn't ready, you know? And then maybe I was, sort of, but I was scared. And then it just got easy to keep avoiding it. But now . . ."

"Now?" Devi fluttered her dark eyelashes hopefully.

I sipped my latte. "Are you sure you have time for this?"

"Hell, yes."

"Okay. I think I need to go on a date."

"Halle-fucking-lujah!"

"Alright. Ugh. I'm so bad at this." Just saying it out loud to Devi made me nervous. Especially when she got all sparkly about it.

"What? Dating?" Devi sipped her coffee, waving a manicured hand in the air. "You always say that, but you never date. How do you get good at anything unless you practice?" She waggled her eyebrows, making me grin.

When it came to dating, Devi was a total pro. I, on the other hand, was pretty much a born-again virgin, more or less by default.

"You're going to meet someone who blows your lid off, babe. You just have to put yourself out there." Devi's cell phone buzzed and she glanced at the screen. "Oh! I should take this." She picked up. "Hey, Maggie!"

I wandered over to the stack of magazines on the coffee table. These days, I was getting used to sharing Devi with her other life. Just one more hint from the universe that I needed to get a life of my own.

I sank onto the couch and flipped through a French *Vogue*. Max came to lie at my feet and I toed his soft fur with my sneaker. Devi was such a natural with people. She'd forgotten more hot men than I'd ever dreamed of meeting. The concept of *not* putting herself out there wouldn't even cross her mind. But for me, the whole idea of exposing myself to rejection and failure made my stomach churn.

Still, she was right. I wasn't about to meet guys sitting at home with my dog.

Not like I hadn't tried.

"Okay? Oh. Okay . . ."

I glanced up at the odd tone in Devi's voice. Bad news? Her eyes met mine, but I couldn't quite read the look in them.

"Mm-hmm. Right. Okay . . . no, no problem. I totally understand." I went back to my magazine while she finished up the conversation, which was brief and consisted of a lot of "Totally," and "No problem," and "Of course."

I looked up again when Devi hung up. She was staring at her phone, like it might somehow explain to her what just happened. "Well. That was interesting."

"A client?"

"No. Maggie Omura. You just met her. Kind of."

"Oh." Right. The pretty dark-haired waif with the hot guy and the even hotter guy. "Max liked her. Didn't you, Max?" At the sound of his name, Max woofed contentedly.

Devi leaned back in her chair, assessing me. "You also just met Jesse Mayes, which you're playing it awfully cool about."

"Who?" I slurped whipped cream from the top of my coffee.

Devi sighed. "Honestly, Katie. Are you kidding me? Jesse Mayes?"

"What? That guy who just left?" I pretended to be enraptured with a deodorant ad in my magazine. "One of your models?"

"I wish. Jesse Mayes is only one of the hottest rock stars in the world, and as an incredibly cool young person you should really know what I'm talking about."

I assumed she added the "incredibly cool young person" comment since last week we got into an argument when she said my apartment looked like an old lady lived in it. And after I'd rigidly defended my music collection (on vinyl), my home phone (on a cord), and my TV (which didn't exist), I realized she had a point, and maybe she was just scared of losing her best friend to spinsterhood at the age of twenty-four, which was probably a realistic fear.

I gave her my best stink eye anyway. "So?" Then I went back to my magazine, because in truth I had no idea who Jesse Mayes was. Other than the hottest guy in the known universe.

"So," she said, "I thought you liked Dirty."

"Dirty what?"

"The band. Dirty."

"Oh. Who doesn't?" I looked up again. "You mean, he's in that band?" I knew music. Kind of prided myself on it. But people? People were Devi's domain.

"He's their lead guitarist. And he sings like a sexy beast."

That, I could believe.

"He just put out a solo album and they're shooting a music video in town. The woman they cast to star in it with him as his music video girlfriend bailed." Devi tipped her pretty nose in the air. "Not from our agency, of course."

"Of course," I said, but she'd lost me somewhere around "sexy beast." I was now trying to recall every Dirty song I knew, and imagining how Jesse Mayes would look playing guitar, and singing under a spotlight all covered in sweat.

"Anyway." Devi sipped her coffee, eyeing me over the rim. "Long story short. I met Maggie at a party a while back. She works with Dirty as the assistant to their manager, you know, the dude with all the tattoos."

Uh-huh. Hottie number two.

"She's involved in a lot of their publicity and whatnot and naturally we've been in touch."

"Naturally."

"She called me up last night. They're looking to recast, but they're having some issues getting Mr. Rock Star to commit to what he wants. Maggie knew they'd be in the neighborhood today, so she took the opportunity to haul his ass in here and have him choose one of our girls."

"That'll be some lucky girl." I kept flipping through the magazine, but I didn't really see the pages. I was too busy trying to picture Jesse Mayes with his shirt off.

"Exactly. They just hired one of our models."

"Well that's good for you, right?"

"It's great for me. Katie, pay attention." Devi stood, came around her desk and took the *Vogue* from my hands. "They changed their minds. They just called to drop her."

"Oh. Well, that's shitty." Why was Devi all up in my face about it?

She dropped the *Vogue* on the coffee table with a resounding splat. "They dropped her because they want *you*."

Get *Dirty Like Me*: https://geni.us/DirtyLikeMe

ABOUT THE AUTHOR

Jaine Diamond is a Top 50 Amazon US and a Top 5 international bestselling author. She writes contemporary romance featuring badass, swoon-worthy heroes endowed with massive hearts, strong heroines armed with sweetness and sass, and explosive, page-turning chemistry.

She lives on the beautiful West Coast of Canada with her real-life romantic hero and her daughter, where she writes, reads, and makes extensive playlists for her books while drinking chai (and sometimes cider).

Get the Diamond Club Newsletter at https://jainediamond.com for new release info, insider updates, giveaways, and bonus content.

Join the private readers' group to connect with Jaine and other readers: https://www.facebook.com/groups/jainediamondsVIPs.

Facebook: https://www.facebook.com/JaineDiamond/
Goodreads: https://www.goodreads.com/jainediamond
BookBub: https://www.bookbub.com/authors/jaine-diamond
Instagram: https://www.instagram.com/jainediamond/
TikTok: https://www.tiktok.com/@jainediamond

Follow the Author on Amazon

If you enjoyed this book, follow Jaine Diamond on Amazon to be notified when the author releases a new book!
To do this, please follow these instructions:

Desktop:

1) Search for the author's name on Amazon or in the Amazon App.
2) Click on the author's name to arrive on their Amazon page.
3) Click the "Follow" button.

Mobile and Tablet:

1) Search for the author's name on Amazon or in the Amazon App.
2) Click on one of the author's books.
3) Click on the author's name to arrive on their Amazon page.
4) Click the "Follow" button.

Kindle eReader and Kindle App:

If you enjoyed this book on a Kindle eReader or in the Kindle App, you will find the author "Follow" button after the last page.